PAPER HEARTS
& SUMMER KISSES

Christie Chapman is a single mum who spends her days commuting to her secretarial job in London and looking after her teenage son, Finn. It's not an easy life but Christie finds comfort in her love of crafting, and spends her spare time working on her beautiful creations. She makes intricately designed cards and personalised gifts and it's not long before opportunity comes knocking. Christie can see a future full of hope for her and Finn – and if the handsome Max is to be believed, one full of love too. It's all there for the taking. And then, all of a sudden, her world is turned upside down...

PAPER HEARTS
& SUMMER KISSES

PAPER HEARTS & SUMMER KISSES

by

Carole Matthews

Magna Large Print Books
Long Preston, North Yorkshire,
BD23 4ND, England.

British Library Cataloguing in Publication Data.

A catalogue record of this book is
available from the British Library

ISBN   978-0-7505-4535-8

First published in Great Britain in 2017 by Sphere

Copyright © Carole Matthews 2017

Cover illustration © Hennie Haworth by arrangement with
Little, Brown Book Group Ltd.

The moral right of the author has been asserted

Published in Large Print 2018 by arrangement with
Little, Brown Book Group Limited

Magna Large Print is an imprint of Library Magna Books Ltd.

Printed and bound in Great Britain by
T.J. (International) Ltd., Cornwall, PL28 8RW

Hi there

Thanks so much for choosing to spend some time with me in Paper Hearts and Summer Kisses. *I hope that you find it to your liking!*

People often ask me how I find ideas for books. Mostly, I have to scratch around a bit and pull a few threads together – something I've heard or seen – until I have the semblance of a plot which I can then mould and shape. But, occasionally, a story is handed right to me on a silver platter.

This lovely story came from the gift of a die-cutting machine which sparked an obsession with paper crafting, a weekend away and, quite probably, a bottle of wine. I owe a debt of gratitude to my friend Christine and her son Elliott for allowing me to tell this amazing tale. It's full of tears, laughter and the incredible determination to overcome obstacles. I'm full of admiration for them both.

So settle back in one of the comfy chairs, enjoy the view and, maybe, it might persuade you to try your hand at some paper crafting.

With love from

Carole ☺ xx

To my dear friend Christine and Elliott

Who knew what it would lead to when we first met all these years ago? From short stories and cars to paper crafting and major house renovations. And now a novel! Many thanks to you and Elliott for being kind enough to share your story and letting me dip into your lives. I have nothing but admiration for you and wish you both health and happiness for the future. I really hope you like the bits I made up! I look forward to lots more gossipy, giggly, glittery days with you and the crazy crafting ladies.

Chapter One

'No. No. No.' Much groaning. It's five o'clock in the morning and my wake-up alarm is ringing its head off. My dear son, Finn, has set it to play an altogether too cheerful 'How D'Ya Like Your Eggs in the Morning?'. Right now, I'd opt for served on a silver salver by a butler at an infinitely more civilised hour of the day. This getting up at the crack of dawn every day is too cruel. I put out a hand and fumble to turn it off, knocking my phone to the floor and out of reach. Which is just as well as the temptation to smash it is overwhelming. I flop back and pull my pillow over my head. I hate five o'clock in the morning. Hate it. With a passion. Yet it comes round far too quickly every day.

I'd really love to stay here and have a much-needed duvet day, but I catch my commuter coach into London in less than an hour and any thought of dilly-dallying in bed is out of the question. Though I might be a reluctant getter-upper, I'm actually quite a loyal employee. To my eternal credit, I've rarely had a day off sick in the eighteen years I've worked for the same company. Impressive, eh? Well, I think so.

Another reason I can't delay any longer is that Dean Martin is still crooning into the carpet and the dog is starting to whine along too. The only way I can shut them both up is to get out of bed. I am resigning myself to my fate, but I still do it with much groaning.

'Come on, Christie Chapman,' I mutter to no one but myself. 'Let's be having you.'

I move my bedfellows as kindly as I can – two cats and the aforementioned dog. Eric wags his tail, does a full circle of the bed and settles down again. How I envy him. The cats – Lily and Pixel – reluctantly rouse themselves from sleep and both eye me with a depth of loathing that only our feline friends can convey. It's the same every day. They hate the alarm too but, like me, you think they'd be used to it by now.

Quietening the chirpy Dean en route, I stagger towards the bathroom. If they ever need any extras on *The Walking Dead*, I could do it. Without the need for a costume. Or make-up.

I didn't really get enough sleep last night as I went to bed way too late. I wasn't out partying or anything. I don't want to give you the impression that I actually have a life. Oh no. Sad single that I am, I spend my sad single evenings paper crafting while watching rubbish on telly. To pass the hours, I make cards, gift tags, scrapbooks, that kind of thing. I'm currently in the throes of making a birthday card for a friend. My lovely mate, Sarah Plimmer, is about to turn forty and she's really special to me, so I want to do something totally fab for her. The perfect design is eluding me. Consequently, I spent aeons on Pinterest – as you do – and fell into bed at midnight when I really like to be tucked up at half past ten. Latest.

The sight of my morning self in the mirror is truly scary. My forty-odd-year-old face takes quite a lot of time to reassemble itself into the right symmetry after being reshaped by the pillow all night. Seriously, it's a good half-hour these days before the creases go. I keep thinking I should get some decent eye cream to slather onto the puffy bags that greet me pre-dawn, but I never quite manage that level of beauty routine. I'm a sort of soap and water kinda gal. But I'm getting to the age where I need considerably more help than that.

In my sleepy state, I get on the scales. That always scares me as well. I don't know why I do it. I like to think that a daily weigh-in will help me to keep my middle-aged spread in check. In reality, it just depresses me and has me reaching for a comforting chocolate bar instead. If I had any sense, I should just throw them in the bin.

I rely on the power of hot water to bring me back to life and prepare me for the long day ahead. I put on my frog shower cap. I bought it because it's green and yellow and has those big white eyes where the black bits rotate. I thought it would cheer me up at the start of my day. It doesn't.

I'm hoping that I can get away without washing my hair for another day. It's long and brown – as my plug hole can attest to – and I keep meaning to get it cut short so that it will be more manageable, but never quite find the time. I'd like one of those styles that you wash and go in three minutes, even though I think they might be an urban myth. There are a few grey hairs showing too, but I'm trying to put off dyeing as it will not only require even more time, but also additional expense that I can well do without. Currently, I'm just pulling them out as I see them and hoping that they don't start coming through so thick and fast that I go bald.

I keep my eyes closed in the shower so that I can hold onto the pretence of sleep for just a little while longer. I don't mind commuting. Actually, yes I do. It's four precious hours out of my day that I could, surely, utilise in a much better way. It's mind-numbing, expensive and exhausting. On the plus side, I avoid the hideous crush of the train and travel by comfortable coach which picks me up at the end of my road and deposits me right outside my office on the Embankment. There is a train station in Wolverton, where I live, but it's at the other end of the town and the journey would cost twice as much *plus* involve a long walk, a train and a tube. Hideous. On the coach I sit still for two hours each way and they serve me coffee. I think that last bit was the deal clincher.

I'm a PA in a legal firm specialising in civil, criminal and family law. We have an unwritten dress code of dark suit and blouse, which is fine by me. It takes the decision of what to wear every day pretty much out of my hands. I lay my outfit out before I go to bed each night in an effort to shave a few minutes off my routine and give me more pillow time. On autopilot, I pull on my clothes, brush my hair into some sort of top knot – the success of which varies daily – and I'm ready to rock. I never wear make-up. That would involve too much complication at this time of day and I'd probably go out looking like a pantomime dame. I try to convince myself that natural is best and that in years to come I'll be reaping the benefits for not having put all that stuff on my

16

face. That's my theory, anyway.

On my way downstairs, I pass Finn's bedroom and poke my head inside. In the gloom, all I can see is a heap in the middle of the bed. My darling boy has never been a tidy sleeper. He's fifteen now, but I still think of him as my baby. You always do, don't you?

Braving the ripe fug of a teenage boy's bedroom, I tiptoe in, crossing the minefield of discarded clothes, trainers and PlayStation games. Despite my best efforts Finn's bedroom has remained steadfastly untidy since he was about seven. In all other ways, he's been a model child, so I cut him some slack and only insist on a quarterly fumigation. I go to sit beside him on the bed. His mop of dark hair is just visible above the duvet. I plant a kiss on it.

'Muuuuum,' he complains sleepily.

'I'm just leaving, sweetheart. I'll see you tonight.'

'OK.'

'Don't be late for school.'

'I've had a headache all night,' he says, still drowsy. 'Can I stay off today?'

'Come on,' I urge. 'You've had so much time off, Finn. I had a letter from the headmaster about it last week. You need to get yourself up and out. You'll feel better after a shower and I'll leave a couple of paracetamol on the table for you. Pops will come round at eight to do your breakfast.'

'He doesn't need to.'

'I know. But he likes it. And it makes me feel better too. Deal?'

Finn nods and snuggles down again. I stroke his hair. Sometimes I worry about him. He's not a

17

robust child. He's not one of these hulking great teenagers with shoulders like prop forwards that you see at the school gates towering over the teachers. Finn is small, slender and never has much appetite. He seems to be plagued by a constant stream of minor infections and headaches. If he catches a cold, he never seems to shrug it off and it can last up to a month. He seems to live on antibiotics and, surely, that can't be right. Recently, he's had so many days off that the school are getting quite grumpy about it. I've asked him if he's being bullied or if there's another reason why he doesn't want to go in, but he says not.

'I've got to go.'

'Have a good day,' he murmurs.

'You too. You've done all your homework?'

'Sort of.'

'Oh, Finn. I'm hoping you're going to become a brain surgeon or something and keep your old mum in the style she'd like to become accustomed to.'

'I'm not sure some half-completed course work on the Rise of the Roman Empire is going to make any difference to me getting me there.' He looks up at me from beneath the covers and grins.

My heart melts. It's been just me and Finn for a long time now and we're a tight little unit of two. I probably should be more strict as a parent but he knows and I know that I'm a complete pushover when it comes to him.

'Besides, we're just going over old stuff now for the exams. We're not learning anything new.'

'At least try. Don't ever regret not doing your best.'

'OK.'

'I'll feed the fiends before I go. Don't let them do the starving animal routine on you and get two breakfasts.'

'I'll do it. You'll miss your coach.'

I glance at my watch. He's right.

'Thanks, love. You're a star. Be ready for when Pops comes.' And, with a final kiss, I head out to face another day.

Chapter Two

The coach stops at the corner of my road and, as I get there, I see it trundling towards me. It's big, shiny, blue and very comfortable, but I loathe the sight of it nevertheless. My fellow commuters are waiting here too, huddled on the pavement, and I nod hello to them. Despite some of us having commuted together for several years, we don't generally speak to each other. Well, only in times of crisis. If the bus is late or the weather is particularly bad, we all have a good moan then.

At ten to six there aren't many other people about and the usually busy street has a pleasant stillness about it. As it's the tail end of March, it's also about half an hour before sunrise but it's heartening to know that the dark days of winter are behind us and the mornings are getting a little bit lighter with every passing day. Soon I won't be leaving in the dark and coming home in it too.

This is not the best area, but it's not the worst

either. I live in a nice Victorian terraced house. Not one of the ones with original sash windows and a slate roof – no one thought to make this a conservation area – but rather one which has been modernised with UPVC windows from Zenith or someone and has had all the fireplaces taken out. It's not one with huge rooms and high ceilings either, but is a small, modest abode. However, the kitchen is big enough to fit a table in, which is its saving grace and a boon for an addictive crafter like me, as the dining room table is usually swamped with paper, glitter and stuff. At least we have somewhere else to eat our meals rather than on our knees with trays in front of the telly – though I do favour a bit of that sometimes.

The bus pulls up and we all file on. Despite not having allocated seats, we all sit in the same place every day and God help anyone who goes off piste and decides to try another seat. The looks! They say that they can't kill, but I think they can come pretty close. My personal Seat of Choice is left-hand side at the back just in front of the gap for the rear emergency door. That way nobody is sitting directly behind me. No knees in the back. No snoring if someone nods off. There's only one stop before mine, so it's more often than not free but, if someone else tries to make a bid for it and is already sitting there, I am totally screwed for the entire day. Nothing else goes right.

'Morning, Christie,' Toni says as I take my seat. She's been the morning assistant on this coach for nearly as long as I've been travelling. 'Usual for you?'

She hardly needs to ask. I prefer an extra five

minutes in bed to breakfast at home, so I always have two strong cups of coffee on my journey to kick-start my engine. As soon as we set off, she bustles about serving us all our warm drinks with a cheery smile.

'No Susan?' she adds as she pours.

'No.' My new morning run coach companion hasn't turned up today and there's an empty seat beside me. 'She said she had a sore throat yesterday. Maybe she's come down with a cold.'

'Seems like a nice lady.' She hands me my coffee and I tip up my two quid. But that does include a free refill.

'Yes.' Susan has already demonstrated admirably that she understands commuting etiquette and keeps chat to a minimum, respecting the need for peace and quiet. The only time that a buzz of whispers goes round the bus is when Toni checks the tickets and someone is caught on the fiddle. Thankfully, she has the sense to give us all coffee before she checks the tickets. The good ladies and gentlemen of the commuter coach couldn't cope with a scandal with low caffeine levels.

'Ted in the office told me that she's just bought an annual season ticket, so it looks as if we'll be seeing more of her,' Toni confides.

'That's good.'

Toni nods at my cup. 'Give me a shout when you're ready for your top-up.' Then she moves onto the next seat.

The coach is always cosy and warm and sometimes, if I'm lucky or particularly knackered, I manage to catch up on another hour or so of sleep before we hit London. I nurse my cup with

21

its cardboard jacket and pop in my earphones. I'm listening to an audio book. Chick lit. It's the closest I ever get to romance these days.

We swing onto the A5 and head towards Hockliffe, our next passenger pick-up point. I settle down and close my eyes and let the words of the narrator wash over me.

My ex-husband Liam Chapman and I divorced five years ago now. It sounds strange to say this, but there was nothing really wrong with our relationship. Our only crime was to marry too young. There was no big drama, no other person on the sidelines, it was just that I don't believe we'd ever really been in love. Not properly. We liked each other well enough and we'd been together since we were fifteen, so we didn't really know any different. We were so comfortable together that we just assumed that the next step was to get married and so we did. Yet, even on my wedding day, I didn't feel any great rush of love and that's not right, is it?

Liam worked in the hospitality industry – managing a chain hotel in Milton Keynes – and, eventually, was offered a job overseas. A new hotel complex in Dubai needed a general manager. It was at that point we both stopped to question where we were going. He was desperate to take it. The job was a big promotion and came with a nice, fat salary – tax-free – paid-for accommodation and a dozen other perks that I can't even remember now. The very thought made my blood run cold. I was as reluctant as Liam was keen. It just seemed like too much upheaval. Finn would have been starting secondary school within the

22

year. It would have taken me away from my parents who are, and have always been, my lifeline. Liam would have been working long hours and it wasn't guaranteed that I'd get a work permit, so I could have been stuck at home all day. Liam wanted to get out of Wolverton and see more of the world. I liked the fact that I knew everyone in the local shops – still do – and a week in Cornwall every year is enough of the world for me. The more he pleaded, the more I could see it wouldn't work. When it came down to it I realised that, although I really liked him a lot, I didn't love him enough to turn my world upside down for him. I didn't want to go to Dubai. And, more importantly, I didn't really want to go to Dubai with Liam.

We both cried a lot when we reached our final decision. I would stay here and Liam would go. There were lots of promises about him coming home regularly and talk that Finn wouldn't miss out as he'd Skype him every day and we could both fly out to the hotel for regular holidays. And I'm sure we both meant it.

I went to my parents' house and drank tea and talked about the weather while my husband packed up and left our lives. Within a month of him going, he'd met someone else who adored him. Of course he did. Essentially, he's a nice man. We divorced without fuss and Liam re-married. He has a lovely wife called Jodie and, now, five years or so later, they have two small children of their own. He sends us money regularly. Not that much, if I'm honest, but it all helps. I can't fault him for that. However, though they do keep in

23

touch, the daily Skype sessions with Finn never quite materialised and, to date, he's never been there on holiday. Liam has made a few flying visits home, but it's not really enough. He never forgets Finn's birthday or Christmas, so that's some small comfort. It doesn't seem to bother my son – my dear old dad has seamlessly stepped into the parenting role for him – but I do wonder if it plays on his mind.

The coach draws into the coach stop at Hockliffe, just before we turn towards Toddington to hit the motorway and join the endless stream of traffic heading south into the city. I clear a patch in the condensation on the window and scan the people who are waiting without really seeing them. In this day and age, you do think that it would be possible for more people to work from home than join this tedious daily exodus to the big smoke. What's the point of all these advances in technology if it can't even achieve that? Toni comes and lifts her coffee pot and an enquiring eyebrow. I take the lid off my cup and hold it out for a refill.

When she moves off to the next passenger, a man flops down into the seat next me. He throws his bag on the floor. Clearly he doesn't realise that this is now Susan's seat. Although, admittedly, she still has quite a slim claim on it. I haven't seen his face before and I have to admit that it's quite a nice face. Even at this hour in the morning, I register that.

'Phew,' he says. 'That was a bit of a rush. I cut it too fine today. I can see that I'm going to have to get up earlier in the morning. Snatching that last five minutes was a mistake.'

'A man after my own heart,' I quip.

The doors close and we set off again towards the M1.

'I'm Henry,' he says holding out a hand. 'Henry Jackson.'

'Pleased to meet you. Christie Chapman.'

'First day at a new job,' he tells me. 'Bit nervous. First-time commuter too. Is it hideous?'

'Yes.'

He laughs at that, as if I'm joking. People are looking round to see who, other than Toni, has the temerity to be quite so chirpy at this hour.

As I noted, Henry Jackson is not a bad-looking bloke. Not that I'm any kind of judge of these things. He's a bit dishevelled, but then he did say that he got ready in a rush. One side of his shirt collar is turned up and his tie's not quite straight. His hair is dark and wavy and looks as if he hasn't got round to combing it yet. And it needs a cut. But when he turns to smile at me again, I see that he's got nice teeth and rather kind grey eyes. Hmm. It's a long time since I've noticed the colour of anyone's eyes.

'Tea or coffee, love?' Toni asks.

'Tea, please.' His accent is northern. Manchester or somewhere. Flat vowels. 'This is very civilised.'

She pours him a cup and moves on to bring joy in the way of beverages to the new arrivals.

'Have you been doing this for years?' he asks.

It doesn't seem the right time to tell him that the first rule of commuting is minimal conversation.

'It's quite exciting,' he adds without waiting for my reply. He takes in his surroundings. 'Where did you get on?'

Giving up with my audio book, I pull out my earphones and say, 'Wolverton.'

'I'm new to the area,' Henry Jackson tells me. 'Where's that?'

This one's obviously going to be a talker. I hope we're not on the same coach home otherwise I'll never find out if the dappy heroine falls into bed with a man who is quite clearly unsuitable.

Chapter Three

My office is on the Embankment and the firm I work for is ancient – started in the year dot or something. On the other hand, our offices are bright and contemporary and are full of fancy artworks. The old guard has pretty much been pensioned off and are probably now spending their cossetted retirement at the second homes in Spain, so all the partners in the firm are currently younger than me. Such is the way of the world. The new bunch are all kindness itself though. Maybe because they are hotshot lawyers and realise they could get their arses sued off if they were mean to their employees.

I work for five lawyers, all men except for Robyn Reynolds who has been at the firm almost as long as I have. Robyn joined straight from university as an intern, then did her training here and has, over the course of the last eighteen years or so, worked her way up to being a senior partner. Whereas, in the same space of time, I have worked my way up from being a secretary to a PA. Hmm.

For my sins, I organise their travel, conferences and meetings, talk to counsels' clerks, sort out billing and put together trial bundles for hearings. I also have the world's most complex telephone with so many buttons that I still haven't managed to work out what they all do. We have a big television screen in the office too that's always, quite depressingly, set to Sky news.

'Morning, Christie.' Robyn is already lurking by my workstation. 'You're looking frazzled. Traffic bad?'

'No.' I strip off my coat. 'I had a talker on the coach. Missed two hours of beauty sleep.'

'A talker. How rude.'

'He's northern. Doesn't understand that people in the south don't speak to each other on public transport.'

'He'll learn.'

'It felt mean to tell him to shut up. So I now know that he's divorced. Recently. Moved down here from Manchester for a new start.' Go me on spotting the accent. 'He's starting a new job today in publishing.'

'Hot?'

I shrug.

'That's not an absolute no.'

'Quite handsome, I'd say. But I didn't really look that much. I just wanted him to shut up so I could go back to my book.'

'Wild night on the tiles?'

'Yes. Went to a rave, popped a load of e's and got shit-faced. Didn't bother going to bed, just came straight here.'

We both roll our eyes at the ludicrous nature of my answer. I don't even know if those are the right terms these days.

'I was up late, making a nice birthday card for my friend.'

'Ah. Crazy fool.' Robyn is well aware that my life is one long trip to the fun palace. 'Sit. I'll get you a coffee.' She heads off to the machine.

This is no time to remind her that, generally, the PA gets the coffee for the boss. But this is why I love Robyn so much. She's not afraid to get her hands dirty in the coffee department. She's also smart, savvy and is a player. Whereas I am not. I don't have a law degree either, but that's by the by. Some days, I feel as if I do.

Although we're pretty much the same age, we couldn't be more different. She is tall, athletic, blonde. I am not. She has one of those sharp, chippy haircuts that I so desire. Robyn spends hours in the gym working out. I do not. At lunch-time she eats alfalfa sprouts or some such from our posh restaurant on the thirteenth floor. I nip to Tesco and get their three quid meal deal. I have a cheese sandwich, a bag of crisps and a diet Pepsi. She drinks Phresh Greens to keep the pH of her body in balance or some swamp-coloured smoothie she makes herself which she calls Warrior Juice, which – quite frankly – just sounds pervy. I prefer to go down the vodka and Red Bull route. Robyn also has a lesbian lover and I definitely do not. Though she often tries to persuade me that going over to the pink side was the best thing she ever did.

The Robster puts my coffee down and perches

on the corner of my desk. I move papers about and try to remember what I was doing yesterday. 'Have you ever considered green tea?'

'No.'

'I worry about your caffeine intake.'

'So do I,' I say. 'I don't get nearly enough to keep me focused.'

She rolls her eyes. 'Imogen said thank you for the anniversary card, by the way.'

'I can't believe it's a year.'

'Me neither.'

Robyn married her partner, Imogen, in a lovely ceremony in the Westminster register office and then had a reception on a boat on the Thames. I organised most of it for her. When I say organised it, that might be bigging up my part. I was the go-between with her uber efficient and slightly scary wedding planner, Cressida – who we all nick-named Cruella. When she barked orders, I did her bidding. At Robyn and Imogen's request, I did make the invitations, place cards and more than my fair share of decorations – miles of per-sonalised bunting and the like. I was so pleased – and relieved – how well they came out.

It was a glorious day. No expense spared. Imo-gen – now Mrs Reynolds – is also tall and blonde. She's a fêted interior designer and is as rich as Croesus. They live together in the swankiest house I've ever seen in Hampstead and throw an annual star-studded garden party for Imo's clients who are mainly people from the reality soaps and footballers' wives who I never recognise.

I might be small, on the curvy side due to never letting an alfalfa sprout pass my lips, and be somewhat challenged in the climbing the career ladder area, but I do have a fantastic son, a tiny house that would benefit from Imogen's attentions, and a great family. Robyn does not. She's desperate for kids, but it's just not happening for them despite half a dozen different attempts at IVF. One has no eggs left at all, the other is starting an early menopause – which just seems like too much bad luck. I keep trying to get them to consider pets, but they find the thought of pet hair in their minimalist home abhorrent. Quite how they'd cope with kids running around is another matter.

'Imo says that you're wasted here,' Robyn says as she sips her brew. 'You should be doing something artistic.'

'I take that as a compliment.'

'Imogen is A Woman Who Knows.'

She is. There's a long list of eminent and up-coming artists who are among their friends. Even after the success of their wedding decorations, I was slightly terrified when Robyn asked me to make her an anniversary card. It's never just a card for either of them. It took me three nights to get it right. Robyn even took a snip of each of their Alice Temperley wedding dresses – inside the hem – so that I could use it in the design. Despite the angst, I have to say that I was rather pleased with the result.

'She says that you don't charge enough.'

To be honest, if I had to charge by the hour it would be the most expensive anniversary card on the planet. 'It's not about the money,' I say. 'I didn't want to charge you anything at all. You

30

know that.'

'Nonsense,' Robyn says. 'Don't underestimate your talent.'

'It's just hard to make any serious dosh from arts and crafts. Not unless you're Kirsty Allsopp and are all over the telly.'

I spend my entire lunchtime at work online looking at craft bits and bobs – while eating my unhealthy cheese sandwich and bag of crisps and avoiding Robyn's sideways glances. Sometimes she mouths 'NutriBullet' at me and I mouth back 'Sod off.'

Mostly, I make cards for friends and colleagues. It's hardly going to buy me a Learjet or a top-of-the-range Merc, but it brings in a bit of pin money and covers – mostly – the cost of my crafting addiction. Unless I have a particularly mad splurge on eBay, of course. Frankly, you can never have too many crystals or decorative mini-clothes pegs.

I'd always dabbled with crafts, but I guess I started doing it in earnest when Liam first left. What can you do at night on your own when you've got a child upstairs in bed? You can't go out gallivanting. You can't crank the music up. I could only prevail on my dear parents to babysit for Finn every so often while I had a wild night on two glasses of wine at the local pub with my girlfriends. Finn never much cared for me leaving him. My son liked it best when we were snuggled up on the sofa together with the fur babies, even when he hit his teens, and, frankly, I did nothing to discourage it. There was never really the spare money either. We're not exactly on the breadline, but by the time I've paid for all the household

31

bills, Finn's school stuff, my crafting addiction and food for several more animals than is strictly necessary, there's not much left to splash around.

Plus – dare I say it – I quite like being at home on my own sofa. I'm not a natural goer-outer. However, I'm not the sort of person who can sit still just watching soaps. I like to be doing something with my hands. Over the years, I've knitted, crocheted, embroidered and cross-stitched. I get it all from my mum. She's always been keen on home-made crafts. I don't think I had one school uniform which Mum hadn't run up on her Singer sewing machine. She had a few little craft businesses herself over the years too. When Care Bears were all the rage, our dining room was wall-to-wall fur fabric as Mum fashioned Birthday Bear, Bedtime Bear, Funshine Bear *et al.* When I got home from school, I was paid a very poor piece-work rate to stuff them with kapok filling and put their eyes in. If you wanted pocket money in our house, you had to earn it.

I do a bit of a craft blog too. Nothing much. I put up my projects and a bit of blah-blah. I don't do it every day either – just as and when I can. I'm amazed that anyone follows me, but they do. I keep thinking that I could do some videos and maybe become an internet sensation like Pew-DiePie or Zoella or Pointless Alfie. Maybe not. For a start, I'm sort of twenty years too old. I don't think there are that many middle-aged internet sensations. Certainly not in the craft world.

While I'm thinking about all this, Robyn drains her cup. 'Well, we've got work to do, Christie. What shall we start on first? Do you fancy typing up some affidavits or tackling the month end billing?'

'Your call. You're the boss.'

'Oh, yeah,' she says. 'You can do the next coffee run.'

'Now?'

'Why not?' she agrees. 'Let's not be too hasty about these things. We should *ease* ourselves into the day.'

I'm seeing nothing to argue with here.

Chapter Four

I sneak out of the office ten minutes before I'm supposed to so that I can catch the early coach home. The stop is right by Cleopatra's Needle and I have to bounce off the tourists as I walk down the Embankment. Some days I don't mind, but other days – particularly if there's a boisterous group of French students around – I can't bear that they're all wandering about taking photos in a leisurely manner and generally enjoying themselves while I'm on a mission to get home.

Mr Chatty isn't on the bus home and, weirdly, I'm not sure if I'm relieved or disappointed. I put in my earphones and think I must have dozed off as soon we're pulling onto the M1 as a whole chunk of my book doesn't seem to make sense.

The traffic is quite light today and I text my dad as we hit the outskirts of Milton Keynes. Three nights a week – minimum – I have dinner at my parents' house. My dad picks me up from the coach stop and, even though it's right outside my own house, he spirits me to the home of my childhood. With some uncannily eerie timing, my mum is usually dishing up as we walk in the door. Finn goes to them straight from school and, in theory at least, in those few hours he does his homework or, currently, revising for his exams.

'All right, Christie, love?' Dad says as I get into his battered old Skoda. 'Good day?'

'Fine, Dad.' I kiss his cheek.

My dad, Ray Barker, is nearly seventy now and long retired. When he worked he was a security guard on armoured vehicles that delivered money to banks. Mum and I hated him doing it, but he always said that it wasn't dangerous. Then, over the years, the number of attacks on the vans started to increase, the ferocity of them got worse. Dad was badly beaten up a few times, once with a baseball bat which has left him with a damaged shoulder, and he was also sprayed in the eyes with CS gas. Finally, he was threatened with a gun and is only here to tell the tale as it didn't go off when the robber tried to fire it. He lost his nerve after that – not surprisingly – and was retired early on the grounds of ill health. The company gave him a generous payout and a bit of a party as a send-off. I can't tell you how relieved Mum and I were.

Since then, Dad spends his days pottering in his workshop in the garden. He's always got some sort of project on the go. In the past he's made a scale model of the Stephenson's Rocket steam engine and then a two-inch scale Clayton lorry. I can only apologise for knowing so much detail about this.

The lorry was huge and then Dad didn't quite know what to do with it and Mum wouldn't give it house room, so he put it on eBay. A man came to collect it with a trailer and Mum wept tears of joy when she saw the back of it. Perhaps she thought that Dad wouldn't spend hours locked away, humming to himself and buying magazines with 'steam' and 'model' in the title. Some hope. I think she'd probably have even been delighted if the magazines had featured the other kind of 'model' – you know? It wasn't to be. Dad is one of life's tinkerers. Now he's got the love of his life to fuss over. This steam engine has been a longstanding feature in Dad's workshop. He calls her Big Bertha and Mum calls her his fancy piece. If Big Bertha wasn't enough to keep him busy, there's a whole host of antique radios lined up on his bench that he's trying to coax back into life. He's never happier than when he's mooching about in junk shops.

Despite his penchant for fixing and fiddling with broken things, he's always been the kindest of fathers. I have nothing but good memories of my childhood. His disposition is relentlessly cheerful, which sometimes drives my mum to distraction. He never sees the bad in anyone. I look at him with his handsome face now craggy and the head of hair that he's always been so proud of white and thinning and I don't know how I'd manage without him. Unexpected tears fill my eyes and I stare out of the window and, surreptitiously, wipe them away with my sleeve.

'Sausage and mash tonight,' he says, as if he's offering me the finest of champagnes and caviar.

'My stomach's rumbling already.' It obliges by filling the space in our conversation with a heartfelt groan. Just imagine how hungry I'd be on nothing but alfalfa sprouts and naffing Nutri-Bullet. I don't know how Robyn copes. 'Has Finn done any revising?'

'He had a bit of a lie-down when he came in.' Dad shoots me a worried glance. 'He doesn't look all that well.'

'He was complaining of a headache this morning.'

'He's still got it. Mum gave him some more paracetamol when he came home.'

'Perhaps he's getting migraines or something. This is happening too often. I'll make an appointment at the doctor's for him.' Another one. It's so hard to do these things when I'm working in London as our local surgery doesn't open until eight o'clock in the morning and closes very promptly at five – no Saturday or Sunday surgery either, of course. I'll have to have a whole day of holiday for a flipping five-minute appointment or pay extra to take the train in to work for half a day. Either way, it's not great. But if Finn's got to go to the doctor, then he's got to go. And, as his mother, I have to be the one to go with him.

Dad pulls into the drive. My parents' house is in a nice, quiet street in Stony Stratford. They've been there since they first got married nearly fifty years ago. Which is just as well as they'd never be able to afford somewhere like this now. I'm not far away from them – five minutes by car – but I'd really love to live round the corner. However, there's no way that I can afford the silly prices they ask for houses here. They live in a semi-detached on a development of 1960s houses at the top end of the small market town and it was brand new when they bought it. Their long, narrow garden runs right the way down to the River Ouse. My dad always fancied having a little rowing boat moored at the bottom of the garden, but never quite got round to it.

'We're home, Jenny,' Dad shouts as we go into the hall.

Their dog, Trigger, goes crazy, flying out of the kitchen, skittering across the laminate floor. He's a hyperactive and slightly unhinged border collie and tries to round us up by nipping at our heels. We've had a dozen different dogs since I was a child. So many that I struggle now to remember them all. Dad was always a sucker for a rescue sob story and, when I was growing up, there was always a steady parade of moth-eaten rabbits, guinea pigs, hamsters, cats and dogs being nursed to health at our house. Occasionally, when the menagerie got too big, Mum would put her foot down, but Dad always managed to sneak another one in. Peter the pygmy goat was a step too far for my mum, but she did like that he kept the lawn short. Still, it's nice that I've inherited my love of animals from them. It's not a proper home without a pet – or two. Maybe three.

'Quiet, Trig,' Dad says. The dog ignores him.

Eric, our dear little dog – some sort of beagle/collie cross with a permanently anxious expression – trots in behind Trigger. They've become brother dogs and happily spend their days together as Mum and Dad babysit Eric while I'm out at work.

Another small task that my parents selflessly perform for me. Dog walking duties. It's not right to leave a dog shut up all day alone. Well, alone except for the cats, and they just terrorise him. Lily and Pixel, they couldn't care less if you were there or not as long as someone puts food in their bowls. Dogs are different. Eric pines if we go out without him for ten minutes. No such worries here, Mum and Dad fuss him to the nth degree and he gets three good walks a day which means that his waistline just about keeps pace with all the forbidden treats that Dad slips him.

'Just dishing up,' Mum calls back. 'Wash your hands.'

Dad nips into the downstairs loo while I take off my coat and hang it over the newel post of the banister. 'Hi, Mum. Dinner smells lovely.'

'Dad's favourite,' she shouts back. 'By request.'

I go in to the kitchen and give her a kiss. The brown hair that I inherited from her has now turned white and is cropped short as she 'can't bear a lot of fuss'.

'I'm starving.'

'Can't you have something proper to eat in that canteen of yours? It can't be good for you eating lunch at your desk every day.'

'It's too expensive.' The prices are supposed to be reduced for staff, but they're still out of my meagre reach. 'And we don't have desks any more, they're workstations.'

Mum rolls her eyes.

It's been a long time since Mum worked in a proper office. As far back as I remember, she's always had little businesses and has been her own boss. She doesn't do so much work now, but still manages to teach two evening classes a week. One on Tuesday night at the adult education centre – Crocheting for Beginners – and, on Thursday, a Knit and Natter session at a local wool shop which I keep meaning to get to and never quite do. On those days, Finn and I have our dinner at home. Even that's courtesy of my mother though. She takes a casserole across during the day in her slow cooker and switches it on for us. Mum also does my ironing and even hangs it back in the wardrobe for me. Dad cuts my bit of lawn and keeps my garden tidy too. I know, I'm completely spoiled. But, if it wasn't for them looking out for me, I simply couldn't manage to hold down my job. I kid myself that they love doing it for me.

Finn comes into the kitchen. As Dad flagged up, he's not looking too well.

'Hey.' He leans against me and I stroke his fringe away from his face.

'Still not feeling too good?'

My son shakes his head. 'Like shit.'

'Finlay Chapman, mind your language,' my mum snaps.

He looks up at me and grins. I give him my sternest look. 'What Nana said.'

'Can I stay off school tomorrow?'

'We'll see. You've got your exams coming up. You can't afford to miss any more time, Finn. Shall I make a doctor's appointment for you?'

Finn shrugs.

'Dinner's ready.' Mum puts plates of steaming pork sausages, most likely from her favourite butcher, and creamy mash on the table. It's followed by a big bowl of green beans too as Mum likes us to get at least one of our five a day if she can manage it. She is a seriously good cook if you like your food home-made and plentiful.

We all tuck in and, between mouthfuls, I offer, 'This is gorgeous, Mum.'

But I can't help noticing that Finn does nothing but pick at his.

Chapter Five

After he's walked the dogs, Dad drops us off home at about eight-thirty. I get into my PJs and plonk myself in front of the telly with a glass of red wine. I try not to drink wine during the week but, if I'm honest with you, I don't try that hard. My son is snuggled down with me on our sofa that is serviceable rather than sophisticated. The living room is so small that the sofa takes up most of the room, but this is the hub of our life. We have a packet of Percy Pigs between us that are taking a battering. They are the smack of sweeties. Normally, I don't like Finn to have too much sugar, but I make an exception for these.

Finn is playing *Call of the Assassin* on his PS4 while I'm watching the Creative World channel on television. I'd like to watch a film every night but, by this hour, my concentration is poor and I have trouble staying awake. If I ever went on *Mastermind* my specialist subject would be the first half of any film. My son has his legs stretched across mine. Eric is wedged between us and the cats, Lily and Pixel, have taken up residence in the radiator hammocks. They're both moggies – one over-weight ginger, one disdainful tabby – who we adopted from the local rescue centre about five years ago. I thought it would help Finn after his dad went. I don't know what I was thinking. If you want unbridled affection and fun, don't get a cat. Not ones like these, anyway. They are the laziest of animals and will only budge themselves now to move up to the comfort of my bed when the central heating goes off.

This is my favourite part of the day. The fire is roaring away – this room is the only place where a real fire survived, even though it now has an oak surround from B&Q rather than the original Vic-torian one. The curtains are drawn, shutting out the world. It's just Finn and me, plus our furry family. I usually head to bed at ten and often leave Finn still down here watching television or, more often than not, playing some sort of evil shoot 'em up game that all the kids are into.

But I worry sometimes that this is all there will be to our lives. It's cosy, comfortable, but I feel as if we're living in a cocoon. Finn rarely wants to go out with his friends. Me neither, if I'm per-fectly honest. Maybe we are too settled together. I know that some of my friends are having all kinds of trouble with their teenagers – sex, drugs, rock 'n' roll. They stay out late, drink when they shouldn't, smoke dope, look at unsuitable stuff on the internet. Yet Finn never gives me any grief at all. He seems content to be at home with me. Should that give me cause for concern? What

41

happens when he grows up and leaves home? Will I be able to pick up with all the friendships I've so woefully neglected while I've been so wrapped up in my family? Will my life involve me sitting watching the Creative World channel from morning to night under one of those heated slankets with nothing but the cats and Eric for company? God, that's all sounding too possible. Best not to dwell on it.

Instead, I take a picture of Sarah's completed birthday card with my iPhone and upload it to my blog with a few words explaining what I did to create it – which I should do far more regularly. As Sarah is more experienced in the way of cocktails, she is my trusted drinks advisor on our rare nights out. So, for her card, I cut a die in the shape of a cocktail glass in pink glitter paper and decorated it with more self-adhesive Swarovski crystals than is strictly necessary. Sarah likes bling, what can I say? I mounted it on white shimmer card, then die-cut a 'Happy Birthday' sentiment and then found a lovely verse about friendship on the internet which I glued inside. If it hasn't got a decent verse, then it's not a card to me. I embossed the flap of the envelope and then decorated that too with more crystals. Job done.

I'm typing up what products I used, when Finn says, 'You should get yourself a bloke, Mum.'

'What a marvellous idea. I'll put one on my shopping list for the next time I pop down to Aldi.'

'At least aim for Waitrose,' Finn says and we both laugh. But he's not finished yet. 'You should. I mean it. All you do is sit in every night making cards and stuff.'

'It's therapeutic.'

'But a bloke could take you out for dinner or to the cinema.'

'*So* not interested,' I reply.

'You could join a dating agency or something. They must have them for older people.'

I give him the evil eye. 'Thank you, son.'

'You know what I mean.'

'I do. And I'm still not interested. Besides, I like crafting. You can rely on paper hearts much more than love-struck ones.'

Finn snorts.

'It's true. The internet sites are full of psychos and bogus Nigerian gentlemen who want to relieve you of your money.' And sleazy men who want nothing more than a quick shag. I don't share that with Finn.

'Says the woman who knows absolutely nothing about it.'

'I read the newspapers.' I don't actually, they're too depressing. But I read magazines and they're full of gullible women who fall for men on the other side of the world who they've never met and get their hearts broken into tiny little pieces. That's not going to be me. Crafting will never leave me high and dry. 'Besides,' I say to Finn, 'I'm happy as I am. Really.'

But I wonder, even as I say it, whether I actually am. Somewhere in my soul there's a small knot of discontentment. It speaks of things done that I shouldn't have and things that I want to do but probably never will. Finn doesn't need to know that though. Neither does anyone else.

Finn nods at the television. 'Your favourite's on.'

I look up to see the glossiest of all glossy television presenters on the screen. The Diamante Diva is in da house. Sheridan Singleton is all that I would like to be and all that I am not. She's younger than me, shinier than me, more successful than me. She sashays to centre stage and takes her rightful place at the spotlit craft bench. This is a woman who is queen of all she surveys. Her long, auburn hair shines in the studio lights. It's a look that I could achieve if only I spent hours applying conditioner and went regularly for haircuts instead of once a year. Her make-up is immaculate. Her clothes expensive and jewel-coloured. A dozen diamond rings adorn her manicured fingers. Her neck is draped with a heavy gold necklace. She's the walking embodiment of a treasure trove. Her voice is silky smooth. Her diction perfect. You'll never find Sheridan Singleton stumbling over her words. I daren't ever mention it to Robyn, but I *definitely* have a girl crush on her.

She beams out of the television screen. 'Hello, everyone. Today, I'm going to be demonstrating new paper-cutting dies from my own range, Simply Sheridan.'

It sounds as if she's offering a night of illicit and unbridled pleasure.

'She has her own range,' I mutter enviously. Fancy being important enough to create your own range. And have people queuing up to buy it.

Then Sheridan goes about presenting her project with shining smiles and sleek demos and I'm transfixed. Her hands move effortlessly over her work, she smiles as she holds up her wares for sale and gets those phones ringing. Usually, mine included. What this woman doesn't know about crafting – and selling, for that matter – isn't worth knowing.

My son puts down his games' controller. 'She's no better than you, Mum.'

'Oh, she is,' I protest. 'Look at her. She could have wandered in off the set of *Dynasty*.'

'What's *Dynasty?*'

I ignore that comment. 'She's fabulous. I'd give anything to be like that.' I follow this woman's blog. Sheridan jets around the world to crafting conventions and the like, pops up on all the TV shows sharing her crafting genius. She has two children who look as if they've been rented from a modelling agency. Previously, she had a husband who's a dentist or something like that and earned pots of cash, but she's divorced now according to the gossip magazines – which I only read when I go on my annual outing to the hairdresser, so I'm generally behind the news. She's quite often pictured with some hot man or another, so not quite a sad single like me.

'You could be anything you want to, Mum,' Finn says. 'You're the best.'

'Well, thank you for your faith in me. I just need my big break. Maybe I could do that if I got my big, fat bottom off the sofa.'

'Don't say that.' Finn frowns at me. 'You do so much for us. I hate that you have to work so hard.'

'That's life, Finn.' I sigh. 'I don't mind it. Really. I don't like it that I'm not always here for you and that you have to rely on Nana and Pops.'

'They love fussing over me,' Finn says. 'What else would they do with their time if we didn't

45

need them?'

I laugh at that because he's probably right.

'I'll just watch Sheridan finish this project, then I have to go to bed.'

'I'll go too,' Finn says. 'This headache still hasn't gone.'

I set an alarm on my phone to remind me to call the doctor tomorrow. Then I turn my attention back to Sheridan Singleton, who is smiling warmly at me. I sigh inwardly. I bet she's not up at five o'clock every morning to catch a coach to London. I bet she doesn't sleep with a cat's bottom in her face. I bet when her dog farts it smells of lily of the valley.

Chapter Six

It's dark and it's raining. I had to clear up cat sick from the kitchen floor before I left the house. My mood is somewhere down in my boots.

At the Hockliffe stop, Henry Jackson gets on to the coach again. Susan – still with a cold, I assume – hasn't appeared today and the seat beside me is empty. Henry drops down next to me. I take my earphones out. There goes my book. And I'm at a really good bit.

'Morning,' he says cheerily.

'Morning.' I say it quietly, hoping that he might take the lead from me and speak in a more hushed tone. Frankly, if he continues at this volume, there'll be a riot and someone will throw him off

46

the coach on the hard shoulder of the M1. Or, being British, there'll be a lot of annoyed tutting.

'Bit more organised today,' Henry announces.

He still looks as dishevelled to me. And he's wet. His dark fringe is plastered to his forehead and he looks like he needs a good rub down with a towel like Eric does when we've taken him out for a grubby walk.

He holds up a paper bag. 'Muffins. Blueberry. Want one?'

Hmm. I haven't had breakfast but I don't really want to encourage him. But then they are blueberry muffins.

'They've got seeds and stuff on the top too. Healthy.'

He opens the bag so that I can look in. They are very tempting. And don't look all that healthy at all.

Henry winks at me. 'Be a devil.'

That makes me smile. 'Oh, go on then.' I lift a muffin from the proffered bag and take a bite. 'Mmm. They really are very good.'

He nods in agreement and then says, 'Why are we whispering?'

I don't point out that I'm the only one who is whispering. 'Commuting etiquette,' I explain. 'We treat these two hours with respect.'

'Which involves whispering?'

'We don't generally chat to our fellow coach dwellers.'

'Oh.' He looks very disappointed. 'I've committed a terrible faux pas.'

'Well...' Now I'm feeling awful for mentioning it.

'You'd rather that I sat somewhere else?'

'This is usually Susan's seat,' I inform him. 'But she's off work with a cold.'

'I'll move tomorrow. I promise.' He looks crestfallen. 'That's a blow. I was hoping the coach would be quite sociable. I don't really know anyone in the area yet, so I've become a bit of a hermit. From the minute I get home to when I get on the coach, I often don't speak to another living soul.' He grimaces. 'I can't believe I just said that out loud. That's quite depressing really.'

'I'm sorry. I shouldn't have said anything.'

'Life in the south is so much more complicated,' he confides. 'None of the neighbours speak to each other either. They scuttle off when I try to engage them in conversation over the wheelie bins. I never imagined it being so hard.'

'More coffee, Christie?' Toni asks as she does her second round of the coach. I hold out my cup for a refill. She nods to Henry. 'Tea, love?'

'I'll go mad and have coffee. I need the caffeine.'

Toni laughs as if it's the funniest thing she's heard all morning – which, maybe, it is. I think she's taken quite a shine to our new arrival.

We sit and enjoy our drinks, taking occasional bites from our breakfast muffins, and my mood lifts. Actually, this is quite sociable having coffee and muffins together. We grind to a halt in the traffic on the motorway and, for once, I don't tut with irritation.

'I'll have to join some clubs or something,' Henry continues as he brushes the last of the crumbs from his lapels into the empty paper bag. 'But it's tricky when you don't get home until

48

late. Most of them start at seven or half past and I'm only just walking through the door then. If I'm lucky. Plus I'm generally too knackered to turn around and go straight back out.'

'What kind of club would you do?'

'I don't know,' he admits. 'Perhaps I could go to some adult-ed sessions, learn a language or take a wine appreciation course? My current level is a wine box from Tesco.'

'I quite often appreciate wine at that level,' I tell him and he grins.

'I'm a keen cyclist, so I could join the local Lycra louts at the weekend. That would help me to get to know the lay of the land a bit too.'

'Sounds like a plan.' I try to sound encouraging. It must be difficult to have to start over in a new place all by yourself. 'Are the people you work with nice?'

He shrugs. 'Hard to tell. If they go out drinking together after work, I've not been invited yet, but it's early days. There's a lunchtime running club, but that seems to be mostly middle-aged women in pink leggings. Nothing wrong with that,' he adds hastily. 'But possibly not my bag. Plus I'm not sure if a lunch hour is going to feature regularly in my working day. It seems pretty full on.' Then he looks at me. 'I'm rabbiting on too much.'

'It's fine. I find listening much easier than forming sentences at this time of day.'

'I bet I've broken a million different unwritten laws.' I shrug. It seems not to matter much now.

'I don't know if I can do this every day,' he confesses, gesturing out of the window at the congested motorway. 'I'm having my doubts already. I'm only renting, so I could try moving further into London, I suppose. But then the prices are frightening. I did look at a couple of places in north London, which I thought were quite reasonable until I realised that the agent was quoting me figures for a week when I thought they were for a month. Shocking.'

'Everywhere down here is expensive.' I'm glad that I was able – with a little help from the Bank of Mum and Dad – to buy Liam out of our house. It might be a tiny house that desperately needs some money spent on it, but it's *my* tiny house.

'If it was just me, I could manage in a studio,' Henry says. 'But I want my daughter to be able to come and stay in the school holidays. I need two bedrooms. I don't want Kyra to see her dad sleeping on the sofa.'

'How old is she?'

'Eight now.' He flicks his phone and shows me a picture of a dark-haired, solemn-looking little girl with big grey eyes like her dad's. 'She's a good kid.' Reluctantly, he stops gazing at her picture and slips his phone in his pocket. 'Have you got children?'

'Just one. Finn. He's fifteen.'

'You don't look old enough.'

I smile even though the compliment is hackneyed. 'I married my childhood sweetheart.'

'Lucky guy.'

'He lives in Dubai now with his new wife.'

'Ah.'

'Finn and I have a nice life. I'm not complaining.'

'I'm still at the bitter and twisted stage,' Henry admits. 'My ex and I are very much in the throes of divorcing. Horrible business. She's got someone else. Another teacher at the school where she works. It's broken up two families and they just don't seem to care. They're "in love".' He shakes his head, sadly. 'While they trot off for romantic weekends away in boutique hotels, everyone else is having to deal with the fallout.'

'What about your daughter?'

'Kyra's spending too much time with her grandparents. Helen's folks. They're lovely people. This is killing them. I wanted to be around for her but, on top of everything, I was made redundant. I had six months at home and was going stir crazy and our finances were in freefall. Helen is taking me for every penny I've got. I didn't really want to take this job, but it's all that was on offer and there's no doubt it's a good position. It's just at the wrong end of the country.'

At some point the traffic must have got moving again as we're turning off the motorway and onto the North Circular road. I have to say that chatting certainly makes the journey pass more quickly.

'I'd love to have her here with me, but girls need their mums. Don't they?' He waits for my nod in agreement. 'I couldn't disrupt her schooling or take her from her friends. She's gone through enough.'

'It'll work out,' I offer. 'As time passes these things do get easier to handle.'

'I hope you're right,' he says. 'I'm feeling too bruised to be optimistic, at the moment.'

'One day you'll wake up and you'll realise that

you're OK again.'

'It's being separated from Kyra that's the hardest thing.'

'I can imagine.' I don't think I could have coped with any of my emotional traumas without Finn. I'm the parent, but sometimes he seems like the rock that underpins everything.

'I've said enough,' Henry says. 'What about you?'

'Nothing much to tell. I work for a firm of lawyers as a PA. I've been there eighteen years, so it can't be too bad.' As I say that, I wonder if I even notice any more. I've done this for so long that I can't really imagine doing anything else. 'They pay me well for what I do and, apart from the commuting and the long hours, it's not too stressful.'

'Never thought of working nearer to home?'

'Frequently. But I've never got round to doing anything about it. I think I'd take too much of a hit on the money too.'

We pull up on the Embankment. 'My stop.'

'I'll see you tomorrow,' he says. 'Part of me hopes that Susan will still have her cold.'

That makes me laugh. 'Poor Susan.'

'Maybe I'll risk it and bring two muffins anyway.'

Then I remember. 'I might not be in tomorrow. I need to take Finn to the doctor. If I can get an appointment.'

'Nothing serious.'

I shake my head. 'No. A headache that won't go away.' I gather my belongings.

Henry fixes me with a gaze. His eyes might be grey but they're warm and kind. 'It's been nice chatting to you, Christie. Hope I haven't bored you rigid.'

'Not at all. See you soon.'

And, when I get off the coach and start to walk up towards my office, I do believe that there's a tiny bit of a spring in my step.

Chapter Seven

Finn and I sit in front of the doctor. We waited an hour and a quarter after our allotted appointment time but – even though there's no hint of apology forthcoming – I'm just grateful that we could get in at all. It's never a given. Sometimes you have to wait so long for an appointment that you'll either get better or die. Thankfully, it's always been the former so far. As usual, the waiting room was full of people coughing and spluttering and generally looking sick. I flipping hate that. If you didn't come in here with something contagious, you'd probably go out with it.

'Now then,' the doctor says. 'What can I do for you, Mrs Chapman?'

'Ms Chapman,' I correct.

He looks at me over the top of his glasses.

'It's Finn,' I say, indicating my sullen son by my side. He is also unhappy as a result of sitting among the coughers and splutterers for so long. 'He's been getting frequent headaches. He's had one for days now and when he gets anything – a cold or infection – it takes for ever to go.'

'For ever,' the doctor repeats.

'Weeks,' I reiterate. 'Longer. If he catches a cold that can last nearly a month.'

The doctor takes off his glasses. 'The problem with teenage boys is that they spend too long in front of computers and very little time getting fresh air and exercise.'

I feel a bit guilty about that. Finn, I have to admit, is not the world's sportiest kid. Perhaps if his dad was around he'd be more into football and such.

I glance at my son who's hanging his head and looking as if he'd rather be anywhere else than here where we're discussing his health as if he wasn't there.

'Do you still have a headache, Finn?' I ask in an attempt to include him.

'It's always there,' he mutters.

'I'll give you a prescription for some paracetamol,' the doctor says and taps at his computer.

'He's chain-eating painkillers,' I interject. 'He needs more than that. Can't you run some blood tests or something? What if it's glandular fever?'

'Has he had swollen glands?

'Well ... no. I don't think so. Not that I can tell.'

The doctor reluctantly gets up from his desk and comes to feel Finn's neck in a cursory manner. 'That seems to be in order.'

'Is this usual? He's very lethargic.'

The doctor smiles patronisingly. 'He's a teenage boy.' He rips the prescription from the print and pushes it towards me. 'Take these as it says on the label. Get out into the fresh air more. Take up cycling. It's very good for you. Exercise can work wonders.'

It's probably not polite to mention to the GP that, with his jowly face and pot belly, he looks like a stranger to exercise.

'I've been back here several times now.' My voice is rising. 'The school are getting very touchy about the amount of time he's taken off.'

'How are your studies going, Finn?'

My son shrugs. 'OK.'

'No problems at school?'

'Not really.'

I wonder if the doctor thinks he's making this up to get out of going to school. Finn's not the most dedicated pupil ever, but I don't think he's doing this so he can bunk off. 'I know my son and he really is under the weather.'

'I'm sure.' The doctor looks as if he isn't sure at all.

Then that seems to be it. There's no other solution on offer. Perhaps he's right, there's nothing much wrong with Finn that getting away from *Call of the Assassin* wouldn't cure. I pick up the prescription for paracetamol when I know that I can buy them for a fraction of the cost in Morrisons. 'Thank you.'

When we get outside, Finn says, 'That was a complete waste of time.'

I can't help but agree. When we get into the car, I look at my watch and it's just gone twelve o'clock. 'You should go straight to school.'

'I'd rather go to Costa Coffee for hot chocolate.'

'I should head straight to work.'

'But you want hot chocolate too, right?'

My son has hit the nail on the head. At best, it

will be two o'clock before I can get in – hardly worth it. I'll call Robyn and ask if I can take a day's holiday instead.

'We'll go to Costa for lunch, but you have to promise me that we'll go out for a jog together this afternoon after school.'

'You're kidding me,' Finn says flatly.

'Deadly serious. Maybe the doctor's right. You do get hardly any fresh air or exercise. We should do more.'

'I hate sport.'

'I know. Jogging isn't sport, it's ... exercise.'

'Which is quite like sport.'

'We'll head over to the park near Nana's before we go there for dinner. That way no one we know will see us.'

'If I have to run, can't I do it by myself?'

'I want to make sure you do,' I tell him. 'When I was your age, I would have run to the end of the road and then would have nipped off somewhere for a cigarette.'

'I'm not you,' Finn protests. 'I don't smoke, for one thing.'

'Let's run together. It'll be fun.'

'Sweet Baby Cheeses, Mother.'

'Don't swear. Do we have a deal?'

'Do I have a choice?'

'Not really.'

Finn sighs. He knows when he's beaten. 'Running it is.'

'Excellent. Now you can get your hot chocolate bribe.'

'Seriously. That is worth a ham and cheese toastie too.'

'Fair enough.'

'And one of those big marshmallow things.'

'Don't push it, Finlay Chapman.'

Chapter Eight

We go to Costa and have lunch together. There's no one I'd rather spend time with than my own son. He seems a bit brighter now, but I can still see the pain behind his eyes. My poor child.

I clear the debris from our table. Two hot chocolates, two ham and cheese toasties and, of course, two of those big marshmallow things. We're going to need this jogging tonight. 'Right. I'd better get you to school.'

He wrinkles his nose.

'If it were my choice you could stay at home, but the school are being funny about the amount of time you've had off. You've exams coming up and the doctor thinks that there's nothing intrinsically wrong.'

Finn looks unconvinced. And also quite surprised that I used the word 'intrinsically'.

'I'll pick you up from school and we'll go for a run.'

'You keep saying that as if it's a treat.'

'It'll be fun.'

'I would rather stick pins in my eyes.'

And on that note we walk back to the car. Finn now considerably more downcast than his usual sunny self as I drive him to school.

Instead of dropping him at the gate, I escort him to the door. At the reception desk, the school secretary says, 'Ah, Mrs Chapman. The head-master would like a word.'

'Ms Chapman,' I correct.

'Are you free now?'

'Yes.' I turn to Finn. 'See you later, love.'

He holds up a hand in lieu of saying goodbye and no kiss – the cool dude in case anyone's watching – and then heads towards his classroom.

I fall into step behind the secretary and am shown into the headmasters' office. He stands to greet me. 'Mrs Chapman.'

'Ms Chapman.'

'Ah, yes.' He gestures towards a chair which I take and then he folds his arms. 'I wanted a chat about Finn.' He puts on a very sincere and troubled face. 'Your son does seem to be having an awful lot of time off school. His attendance record really is very poor.'

I'd like to think that they were worried about his welfare, but it's probably more that it will adversely affect some statistic or another.

'He's due on the school trip to London this weekend and I did think about not allowing him to go.'

'I'm shocked that you'd even consider that.' My voice is all shaky. He's talking about punishing Finn for being poorly? 'He's not well. I've taken him to the doctor's this morning. That's why I'm here in the middle of the day instead of being at work. He has a constant headache.'

'As you know, Finn didn't have the best results in his mock exams. He could have done so much

58

better with a bit of application.' It's as if I haven't spoken. 'Finn has a lot of potential but he needs to knuckle down to his work as he's running out of time.'

'He does his best. I don't know what else to say to you.'

'He's quite a popular boy, Mrs Chapman, but his teachers tell me that needs to engage more with his studies.'

'I'll tell him.'

'I'm happy to talk to him, if you can't manage.'

'I can manage,' I say through gritted teeth.

'Good. Unfortunately, if he's off sick again, then I will need to see a note from the doctor. I hope you understand.'

'Perfectly.'

'I'm doing this to help,' the headmaster says when, quite frankly, I think he's being anything but helpful.

I stomp out of his office with a black look on my face doing my very best impression of a moody teenager. Why does no one seem to be listening to *my* concerns? I'm glad to be back to the solitude of my car and take satisfaction in slamming the door. For good measure, I punch the steering wheel several times and then have a snotty cry.

Chapter Nine

I pick Finn up from school. He flops into the car with a 'Hey.' I hold up his trainers and grin.

My son groans. 'I was praying you'd forgotten.'

'Not a hope. I have the memory of an ... er...'

'Elephant,' he finishes. 'Why have you brought the dog?'

'I thought Eric would enjoy it too.'

'He'll collapse. You normally rush him up the road for five minutes.'

'He walks with Pops. He's missed out two already today. This will be good for him too.'

'Pops just wanders about with him. They don't stride out. Eric does as little exercise as I do. If he drops down dead, it's your fault.'

'We'll drive up to Sweet Meadow.' It's where Dad usually walks the dogs and is a pretty area of common land near my parents' house with the River Ouse running through it. Occasionally, there are sheep grazing, but we can dodge those. It's cows I'm not keen on. There's a path that goes all the way round. Far enough for it to be good exercise. Not far enough for it to kill or maim us. It will be an excellent place to start. 'No one will know us there.'

'This is hideous,' Finn complains.

'It's mission Get Finn Well,' I say. 'The doctor said you need exercise and fresh air. Fresh air and exercise, you will have.'

'Great.'

'It's for your own good. The headmaster had words with me today, Finn. About the amount of time you've taken off.'

'He's a knob.'

I couldn't agree more. But responsible parents can't say that kind of thing. 'He's concerned that you're missing too much of your studies before your exams.'

'We're not learning anything else,' Finn says. 'All we do is twat about in class.'

'He was threatening not to let you go on the weekend trip to London.'

'Like I could care less.'

'I do! I've paid for it all. I can't afford to waste money like that. Go, you will!'

'All right,' Finn says. 'Calm it, Mother. You're sounding like Yoda.'

I drive to Sweet Meadow, seething. Finn stares straight ahead at the road. At the entrance to the meadow, I park. It annoys me that I go into the space nearest to the gate so that we won't have to walk too far to get to our exercise.

When I climb out of the car, Finn bursts out laughing. 'What *have* you got on?'

I look down at my pink tracksuit bottoms and flowery lemon top. I've got a pink hoodie too which I'm in two minds whether to wear or not. 'Jogging stuff. What's wrong with it?'

'You look like candyfloss on steroids.'

'Thank you, Finn.' I throw a pair of shorts to him. 'I brought these for you.'

'Where am I supposed to get changed?'

'In the back of the car.'

'Seriously? The last time I did that I was five.'

'Hurry up. No one will see.'

'Oh, the humiliation,' he complains. Nevertheless, he gets into the back of our little Fiesta and takes off his jeans. He does it with maximum huffage and puffage. Just like he did when he was five.

Eventually, he emerges. His legs are like two bits of white cotton sticking out at the bottom of his blue shorts. I want to laugh but I *so* daren't. Instead, I hand him a water bottle.

'We're not going to need this.'

'We might.'

'I don't know how far you think we're going, but I'm not planning to run to the point of dehydration.'

'We should warm up or something. Do some stretches.'

'Spare me.'

So while Finn looks on in disdain, I do some lunges and a few squats. I hold my foot to my bottom, which I'm sure I've seen them do on the telly at athletics competitions. Eric runs round barking, eager to be off. He has no idea what's in store. Me neither, to be honest. It's fair to say that the secret world of exercise has passed me by. At the age of forty-two, I've successfully managed to avoid Jazzercise, Step, Zumba, Bokwa (no idea) and hot yoga.

'Hoodie or no hoodie?'

'No hoodie,' Finn advises. 'You'll sweat like a pig.'

Lovely image.

'Right,' I say decisively. 'Let's get going.'

'Kill me,' Finn says, but he sets off jogging which I take as promising. I follow.

'Come on, boy.' I click my fingers for Eric. He trots beside me, clearly quite surprised by the pace. As Finn pointed out, Dad obviously favours the more meandering style of dog walking.

'We'll start off slowly.' I try to ease the speed back a bit, but Finn's having none of it. He's off. 'Nothing too hasty,' I shout.

Oh, this feels horrible. Everything I've got is jiggling. My boobs are flumping about in all directions. I have legs that could kindly be described as sturdy, but they turn to jelly within minutes.

We jog down one side of the meadow, skirting the trees and the bridge, then turn along the path which is on the other side of the river to my parents' house. I haven't told them we'd be out here running, otherwise they'd be in the garden waving. I'll spare Finn that.

Eric is bounding about like a puppy and Finn has kicked into a determined stride. Already I feel that the colour of my face matches the pink of my joggers. I seem to be sweating quite a lot, as my dear son predicted, even though there's a cool breeze along the river. We pass two swans and I'll swear that they stare at us in bewilderment. They hiss at Eric but he's too busy bouncing joyfully to respond.

Finn, it seems, is a lot fitter than me and he's supposed to be the sickly one. Even the dog is outdoing me.

'Come on, Mumsy,' my son teases, running backwards. 'Keep up.' He's clearly enjoying my torture. I huff and puff a bit more. Finn jogs on the spot for a bit while I catch up.'

I grit my teeth. 'This is nice.'

'Yeah,' Finn says. 'Lovin' it.' Then he sets off again while I put my hands on my knees and wonder what happened to my lungs in the last forty-two years. I'm sure I used to have fully functioning ones. They're burning so much I feel as if I've swallowed fire. I gasp for breath. Can you burst a lung by overexerting yourself? I think you probably can.

Finn does comedy running on the spot, knees high in the air, arms pumping. Eric barks encouragingly. I want to lie on the floor and die. I could stay here for ever and let the sheep eat me.

'Why don't I go for a run and you sit on that nice bench until I come back?' Finn says, grinning.

'Yes, very funny.' But not actually a bad idea.

'Seeing as I'm the unfit one,' he adds.

'I'll join you on the next lap.'

'Yeah, right,' Finn says. 'Will you be OK if I leave you?'

'Yes.' I take deep breaths, until I've stopped feeling dizzy, and slowly make my way to the bench. *In memory of Derek Summerfield,* it says. *Gone too soon.* Perhaps poor Derek prematurely croaked it while jogging.

Finn whistles to Eric and they both set off, Finn's oversize teenage feet rhythmically pounding the path.

I let my head fall back and spread my arms along the back of the bench. I stretch out my legs to make a starfish and then I close my eyes. The weak spring sun falls on my face. I'm tired down

64

to my bones and it's times like this when I realise how much commuting takes it out of me.

Half an hour later, Finn is back. He is pink-cheeked and smiling. I notice that he's drunk all his water. Eric is panting heavily, tongue lolling out but, thankfully, hasn't collapsed.

'That was fun,' Finn says. 'Shall we do it again tomorrow?'

'No,' I reply. 'Let's not.' I heave myself up.

'Need a hand?'

'No. I'm fine. Let's go to Nana's and carb-load with cottage pie.'

'Cool.'

'Has your headache gone?'

'No.' Finn is still grinning and jogging. 'I'll race you to the car.'

He and Eric set off again and, reluctantly, I hobble behind.

Chapter Ten

I don't see Henry on the coach the next day, so I listen to a lot more of my book. Frankly, I could kill this woman for how stupidly she's behaving. There's no way I'd let a man play fast and loose with me like this one is doing to her. But then, as you've probably realised, I haven't had the chance to put this into practice for some years.

On Saturday morning, I'm up with the lark to bundle Finn off on his school trip to London. He exudes reluctance, but they should have a nice

65

time. They're going on the London Eye, to the Tate Modern and other stuff. There are all kinds of good things on the itinerary that I can't remember, but that I know have cost me a fortune.

I drop him off at school at eight o'clock, slightly miffed that I'm having to get up early on one of the days that I usually manage a lie-in. If I'd packed for Finn last night, then I could have had an extra half an hour, but I didn't. It's also not helping that I'm aching all over after my brief flirtation with the evil that is jogging. Never again.

I look at Finn's other classmates waiting to get on the coach and they're great hulking things. And that's just the girls. The other boys all seem to tower over him and it does make me worry. Perhaps he's just a late starter. Or maybe I should ask some of the other parents what they feed their kids or whether they make them sleep in Gro-Bags.

'Are you sure that you've got everything?'

'It's too late now if I haven't,' Finn says.

'You've got paracetamol for your headache.'

He nods. My son looks pale this morning with dark shadows under his eyes. He gives a yawn. I'm concerned that he's always so tired. I wonder if his jogging experience was too much for him.

'I'll give you some extra money in case you need to buy anything.'

He pushes the proffered twenty pounds back at me. 'I'm going to London, not Outer Mongolia. I'll be fine. And I'll be back tomorrow.'

'I'll miss you.'

'Have you ever heard the term "helicopter parent"?'

'I know I'm fussing, but I love you. I want you to have a nice time.'

'Get a life, Mum.' Yet he grins.

'The headmaster says that you need to mix more. To engage.'

'Yes, but he's a...'

'Knob,' we say in unison. I smile at Finn. 'Have a great time.'

'I will. Don't spend your entire weekend watching Crappy Craft Channel.'

That's exactly what I planned to do. I've asked Robyn if I can sell some home-made cards one lunchtime in the boardroom next week and she agreed, so I've actually got to make a load and I need some inspiration from the glorious Sheridan Singleton.

'Don't drink any alcohol,' I warn. 'Mummy will know.'

'That's the first thing we plan to do. Ditch the teachers and head to the nearest pub.'

I laugh. He'd never get in, anyway. At fifteen, he still looks so young for his age. My heart squeezes for him.

'Bye-bye, Bezza.' Finn kisses Eric but not me, then jumps out of the car.

I curb my need to stand and wave Finn off at the kerbside and, instead, drive straight up to Mum and Dad's house. I feel like crying and he's only going to be away for one night. What am I going to do when he goes off to university – unlikely in his current academic climate – gets married, moves to Australia? It could happen.

My folks are both in their dressing gowns when I rock up. Dad gives me a hug, then he finds Eric a treat as the dog is sitting right by the cupboard he's come to adore.

'You're early, love,' Mum says.

'I've just seen Finn off on his school trip.' I could blub just saying it.

'Oh, bless him.'

'I resisted the urge to drag him off the coach and take him home. Is it right that I'm so joined at the hip with him?'

'I think it's lovely,' Mum says. 'He's a good kid. You've done a great job.'

'Thanks, Mum.'

'I was about to cook a full English for your dad. We're having a lazy morning. Fancy it?'

'Is the Pope a Catholic gentleman?'

'One egg or two?'

'Just the one, please.'

'You go and settle yourself in the conservatory. I'll bring you some coffee. The latest *Inspiring Papercrafts* magazine should be on the coffee table. I haven't had a chance to look at it yet. Sit and have a flick through.'

'I could do with a big craft session this weekend. Robyn has said I can sell some cards in the office next week, so I need to get busy.'

'I'll help you,' Mum says. 'We can go down to the summerhouse, if you like. It's lovely out there.'

They dipped into Dad's payout and had a conservatory built on about five years ago now. Then they went completely mad, in the world of my parents, and also had a summerhouse put in the garden. It has the prime spot with an uninterrupted view overlooking the beautiful area of grass and wildflowers called Sweet Meadow. Dad built a small decking area, and the gently curving river runs right in front. It's idyllic. A very good place to sit and contemplate or to do crafting. I think they love these buildings more than me – nearly. They're generally in one or the other to the point that I don't think they use the rest of their house any more.

'That'd be nice. We haven't done that for ages.'

'The only project I've got on at the moment is a new cable knit for Eric for the autumn,' Mum says. 'So I can put that to one side and give you a hand.'

Mum likes to knit sweaters for my dog and Eric, tart that he is, loves to wear them. If she knits them for Trigger, he eats his way out of them.

'We can have some girlie time together. No doubt your dad will disappear into the shed with his fancy piece as soon as he can.' She gives him The Look.

'I need to mow Christie's lawn,' Dad says.

'Leave it,' I tell him. 'It looks fine to me. Have a weekend off and tinker to your heart's content.'

'Ray, do a Nespresso as a treat for Christie.'

'Coming up.'

'You do spoil me.' I kiss them both, then go into the conservatory.

Out in the conservatory, there's a sofa and two armchairs. Dad has a DAB radio in here which he adores. I move Mum's knitting bag and sit on the sofa enjoying the emerging morning sunshine. Trigger slopes in to sit by my feet and Eric, who has no shame, jumps on the sofa to settle by my side.

I pick up the magazine and flick through the pages. There are a few bits and bobs in here that will help me later. Nice. There's the usual piece by Sheridan Singleton, of course. She has a feature about card marking, which is her forte. This week she's showing off some of her own range of distressing inks and there's a free sheet of Sheridan-inspired designs to print out. They're all annoyingly nice ideas. I'll probably give a couple of them a go myself. Then I flick aimlessly through the rest of the mag and it's only when I get to the back few pages that something catches my eye. I find myself sitting up a little bit straighter. You don't often see things like this in craft magazines. Yet, here it is. There's a call-out from a new American company – Contemporary Crafts – for a UK-based designer. The brief is broad. All you have to do is send in three projects for assessment – one card, one home décor piece, one gift-wrapping design. In return, you are commissioned to do a weekly design for their website with materials that they supply and they'll also try to get you openings in UK crafting magazines. That sounds all right to me. This could be the break I'm looking for. I could easily do something like that and it's only a year-long contract, so not too much of a commitment. The only snag is that the deadline isn't far away. Still. Makes me think. Might be fun.

Dad brings me a coffee, made with loving care. Everything he does is invested with love and attention. My dad rushes nothing. I think it's where I get my perfectionism from and my creativity is definitely from Mum's side. Her mum was a seamstress in the East End of London when she

70

was a girl and it's nice to think that the baton has been handed down through the generations.

The smell of cooking bacon is distracting me from the craft magazine and, not a moment too soon, Mum calls me to the table.

The breakfast she puts before me is worthy of a five-star hotel. It's the one area I fall down in. Due to lack of time, the only cooking I seem to do these days involves things that go ping or come in plastic wrappers.

We all tuck in and it's delicious. This will set me up for an arduous day of crafting.

'Shall we walk Eric and Trig together?' Dad says. 'We could do a lap around Sweet Meadow.'

'Yes. I'd like that.' As long as I don't have to do jogging. I don't care to be reminded of my trauma there. The less said of that the better.

'You spend a lot of time sitting down, Christie, and it's not good for you,' Mum chides. 'We've got a Wii Fit in the cupboard gathering dust, if you want to give that a go?'

There is a very good reason why there are many, many Wii Fits in cupboards across the land gathering dust. But what have I got to lose? Mum's right. Yesterday's jogging only went to show that Finn isn't the only unfit one in our house. In fact my parents, pushing seventy, are probably more physically active than I am. 'Great,' I say, when I don't really think it's great at all. 'I'll take it.'

'I'll get Dad to lift it out.'

Joy.

'See anything worth doing in the magazine?' Mum asks, getting back onto safe ground.

'Hmm.' I wait until I've finished my mouthful

71

of toast. 'Call-out for designers for an American company. A new one. Haven't heard of them. Contemporary Crafts.'

'Me neither.'

'Maybe I'll Google them.' More toast. 'They're looking for a UK designer. It's a project every week for their website and they're looking to get into UK craft magazines too. I don't suppose there's much money in it.'

'You should go for it,' Mum says. 'Heaven knows you're good enough. It might push you out of your comfort zone.'

'It's called a "comfort zone" because it's very comfortable there.'

'We could do something this afternoon. What do they want?'

'Just three projects. A card, a home décor piece and a gift-wrapping idea. Shall I bring all my stuff over here or will you come to me?'

'Come here then I can keep an eye on what your dad's up to. I'll make us a bit of lunch.'

'I won't want anything until teatime after this lot.'

'Nonsense. You've got to keep your strength up.'

My mum feels as if she's failed in life if you don't eat on the hour, every hour.

'You're looking a bit peaky.'

'Just tired, Mum. After a week of commuting I'm always knackered.' Then I manage to scrape myself off the floor again just in time for Monday.

Mum insists that I can't help to clear up and, instead, makes Dad go upstairs to get dressed then chivvies us both out of the door to walk the dogs.

72

Chapter Eleven

After our leisurely walk, I leave Eric at my parents' house and go home to fetch all my crafting stuff. You would not believe how much I have. It started off innocently enough with a few bits of this and that. Then somehow it's blossomed, burgeoned, bloomed. Every time Mum has a clear-out, I inherit that too. Now I can't walk past a pound shop without nipping in. From a few paltry plastic boxes, I've expanded to several Crates of Joy. One is so big that it has wheels on the bottom and I nearly put my back out every time I lift it into the boot of my car. Even this is at overflowing stage. I am the Imelda Marcos of crafting supplies.

The thing with crafts of all kinds is that you never quite have the right bit, no matter how many types of paper you have, or the number of dies, or snippets of ribbon. Your self-adhesive crystals will never be quite the right size or hue. There is always one more thing that will make your project just perfect. I thank God every day for eBay, The Range and Hobbycraft.

The other thing is that your house is never again your own. Or tidy. I try very hard to keep things contained but, invariably, it spreads from the living room to the dining room, consumes the table, a lot of the floor. I sometimes do local craft fairs if the stands aren't too expensive and then every spare inch is taken up with home-made greetings cards or little pillow boxes containing a few chocolates. I make fancy wrappers for chocolate bars too which always go down well.

I load up all my stuff and drive back to Mum's where Dad, without a word of complaint, heaves my crates down the garden to the summerhouse for me.

'I thought before we settle we could wander into the High Street and have a look in Sew Easy.' An independent craft shop that we both like to frequent. 'What do you think, love?'

'Is there anything you need?' I venture.

'Well...' Mum says. 'You know how it is.'

Indeed, I do.

'Perhaps we could get a coffee too.'

'I'm game.' So, mustering my aching legs once more, we walk down into the town together.

The High Street is busy as it always is on a Saturday. At one time, the place was a bit in decline. Like so many high streets there were too many charity shops, too many estate agents, too little of anything else. Now it's had a welcome resurgence. There's a lovely artisan baker, a few new cafés that are slightly more upmarket, a couple of vintage boutiques and, most important of all, a nice craft shop.

Mum and I head straight for Sew Easy – our need for bits of glitter, lace, buttons and glue more pressing than our need for caffeine. It's a really lovely shop and the owner has managed to pack in plenty of treats to help her compete with the aforementioned big craft warehouses that so often are a threat to small businesses. She tries to cater for the needlework crew and papercraft addicts too. There's also a reasonable-sized section for knitting and crochet. A big workroom takes up the top floor where the owner runs all kinds of craft classes and drop-in sessions. Occasionally, she has ambassadors from the big crafting companies come along and do demonstrations. I tell you, if I was at home during the week, I'd never be away from the place.

Mum and I spend a good half an hour just browsing. Later, I have to motivate myself to do something to submit to this American company, so I pick up a few bits and bobs that catch my eye. I justify spending too much money on crafting supplies by having a very small shoe and handbag collection.

I pay for the stuff in Mum's basket too as she does so much for me and won't usually let me spoil her. Then we go across the road to a new café for coffee. It's a warm day and we sit in the window with our lattes to watch the world go by. Even though we've eaten a monster breakfast, we gamely find room for a cake each. It's really nice for us to spend time just being friends rather than her looking after me as she normally does.

'I'd love a shop like that,' I confide to Mum. 'I'd be in heaven. It would be my ultimate dream.'

'One day, Christie. You never know.'

'The rents are too ridiculous now. It would terrify me to take something like that on.' But it would be great, in theory. I could do the same as this shop, run demos and courses. Stock all the pretty things that my heart desired. Mind you, I'd probably end up buying more myself than any of my customers. 'You'd have to have a load of money behind you.'

'You do really well when you have a stall at a craft fair.'

'I know, but there's not much money in selling bits and bobs or cards. But I feel I could really make a go of a business like that.'

'Why not start an online shop?' Mum says.

'Because I know absolutely nothing about e-commerce.'

'You could find out,' Mum says, ever practical. 'Everyone's doing it, so it can't be that hard. That boy of yours knows more about computers than you can shake a stick at. Get him to help.'

Hmm.

'Start small,' she continues. 'Maybe specialise in dies or paper. I don't know much about it, but we could give it some thought.'

It's certainly an idea. It would give me an outlet for my own craft projects and maybe bring in an extra bit of much-needed cash. Finn and I manage OK on what I earn, but there's not a busting amount left over. I can't afford to send him on all the school trips they set up these days. The week-end in London wasn't too bad, but they go off skiing now or to flipping Orlando! There's no way I can pay for that. When I was at school it used to be a day at Alton Towers if we were lucky. Once we went to Hampton Court. What if he stays on for sixth form? Who knows what they get up to there now. Finn never says that he feels as if he's missing out, but it would be nice if we actually had some spare cash at the end of the month so I could treat him.

There is only one snag. When would I actually get time to do it? By the time I get home from work I'm fit for nothing, and I try to spend my spare time at weekends with Finn as we're like ships in the night during the week. Still.

'I'll Google some sites and see what's out there,' I tell Mum. 'See if it's viable.'

'Have a look on YouTube too,' Mum says. 'There are lots of people demonstrating crafts on there. Some of them good. Some of them rubbish. I believe you can earn good money from the adverts on there.'

I laugh. 'When did you become so internet savvy?'

Mum laughs too. 'It's one of the many benefits of being retired, you have time on your hands to play.'

'I look forward to it,' I say with a heartfelt sigh.

'Come on.' Mum drinks up. 'We have some serious crafting to do this afternoon. We'd better make a start.'

Chapter Twelve

So Mum and I spend a wonderful afternoon in the summerhouse making cards and bits. A couple of hours in and the floor is drowning in off-cuts of paper and ribbon. I'm churning out paper hearts, flowers and butterflies on my die-cutting machine while working out in my head what I'm going to do with them. I've also cut out pennants for bunting. Every now and then I stop to look up and appreciate the view. It's a gloriously sunny day full of the hope of summer. We had a mild winter and the ducks are showing a few early babies the ropes. The swans that have been on this stretch of river for years glide back and forth.

The summerhouse is a fair old size – big enough to harbour a sofa and two chairs. It's light, airy and you can throw open the doors yet still be sheltered from the breeze in here. Dad set a wind vane in the shape of a swan on the top which seems to bring him an inordinate amount of joy.

'North-westerly today, Christie,' he'll say, rubbing his hands together.

Never sure what the right response to that is, so I tend to stick to, 'Lovely, Dad.'

It's looking a bit shabby now. The sofa is sagging where it shouldn't and the walls are covered with hand-stitched hangers – Mum's creations – which are looking more than a bit faded now. Still, they give a good home to the spider population of Stony Stratford.

Mum keeps threatening to buy some Farrow and Ball paint to spruce it up, but never seems to get round to it. I'm sure Dad's relieved as it would take him away from precious tinkering time.

While we cut and glue, Mum disappears to make tea at alarmingly regular intervals and you'll never go faint for the want of a biscuit here. Mum and I work together in quiet companionship. She puts the radio on and we listen to Dermot O'Leary even though Mum declares the music all too modern for her. We have a lovely, relaxing after-

78

noon and, for brief periods, I even manage to stop worrying about Finn and how he's getting on in the big smoke.

Every now and again, I look up from my card making to see my lovely dad pottering about in the garden. It looks as if he's deadheading flowers or something. Dad isn't the best or the most enthusiastic gardener – that's Mum's department – but he makes a stab at it. He gives us a wave and Mum blows a kiss back which warms my heart. This is what I wanted for myself. It's their golden anniversary next year and they seem to be more in love, more content than I've ever seen them. I feel sad that Liam and I didn't have enough between us to stay the distance and grow old together. It's hard being a single mum, especially when Finn's dad is on another continent. Every decision falls on me. Every bill falls on me. Every worry, mine too.

'Let's see what you've done,' Mum says, peering over the glasses perched on the end of her nose.

I show her the card that I've been working on. It's a design for a thank you card and I've tried a few complicated techniques to make it look simple – if you know what I mean. I've die-cut a scalloped circle and mounted a fancier lace-edged circle on top of that. Then I cut a heart with some gorgeous shabby-chic paper and made another heart-shaped aperture in the middle. I covered that with clear acetate to make a window which I've filled with glass beads.

She lowers her glasses. 'That bit in the middle looks proper fancy.'

I've finished it with a double flower in the shape of a daisy on one side and have cut out a senti-

79

ment pennant which says *Follow Your Heart.*

'Thanks. You think it works?'

Mum nods. 'Very much so. I don't think you realise how talented you are, Christie.'

'I've done this for my home décor project.' I hold up the banner I've created for spring. I've die-cut a dozen bits of bunting and, inside that, there's a small square for each letter – the letters are Victorian style and have lovely embossing. Then I've decorated the bunting triangles with an abundance of die-cut and cinched flowers in fresh pastel colours. Finally, I've embellished them with pearls. Then I mounted them on some twine. I've had Mum winding away on her little die-cutting machine, churning out flowers too.

'That's gorgeous,' Mum says. 'Look how you've worked your magic with those petals.'

'You're biased though,' I remind her. 'Is it really good enough to send off?'

'It's perfect. I think they'd be mad not to have you.'

'So, I've just got the gift wrapping to do.' And make a couple of dozen cards for my craft sale at work next week. Simples!

'Stay here for dinner, then you can carry on until late. What have you got to rush home for?'

'The cats,' I say. 'They'll need feeding at some point.'

'We'll send Dad round. If he's feeling energetic, he might cycle up there.'

As if he knows we're talking about him, he walks past the summerhouse and waves again which makes me smile.

Then my phone pings and it's a text from Finn.

Missing you, Mum. Xx.

'Aw.' I show my mum.

'He's a good boy.'

'And a home bird. I bet he's feeling homesick.' I blow out a breath and text Finn back. 'I miss him too.'

'Of course, you do. You're his mother. It never ends.' She looks up from her die-cutting. 'Even though I see you every day, I still think of you when you're at work.'

'You soppy old thing.'

'I stand guilty as accused,' she says. 'There's only one thing that takes your mind off it.'

'What's that?'

'A nice gin and tonic. How about it? I'll get your dad to make one for us.'

'Sounds like a plan.'

We have two gin and tonics. Then a third. I'm not sure it improves my crafting, but I manage to finish my gift-wrapping idea. As the company has 'contemporary' in its title, I try to do something clean and simple, not fussy. I choose a lovely ochre-coloured paper with flowing script on it to wrap a tissue box I've pinched from the kitchen. Then I make a little envelope in brown craft paper to stick on the front. I embellish that with some twine and a flower with a water crystal glued in the middle. Then I die-cut a selection of hearts – can't live without my hearts – differing in shape and size using some pretty patterned papers that I've been itching to incorporate into a design for a while now.

It all goes together really nicely – which isn't

always the case. When I sit back and look at the neatly wrapped box, I'm quite pleased with it. But then I'm also slightly squiffy on gin and my judgement may be somewhat compromised. Dad cycles up to feed the cats who are probably fast asleep on my bed and haven't actually noticed that I've been out all day.

Mum makes spaghetti Bolognese and some garlic bread for dinner which is about as exotic as Dad can cope with. And I have a glass of red wine out of their wine box in the fridge to go with it.

My post-dinner crafting session is somewhat more reckless than it was earlier. Mum and Dad sit amid the glitter and ribbons in the chairs in the summerhouse and doze. I look at them with love and admiration. This is all that I crave, this cosy domesticity and companionship. I don't want anyone who's going to bring heartache and drama into my life. At forty-two, am I too young to have given up on men? It would have to be someone really special for me to disrupt my life with Finn.

When Mum wakes up, she says, 'Stay over tonight, love. Don't go home alone. Your bed's always made up.'

In fact, my childhood bedroom has hardly changed at all.

'*Britain's Got Talent* is on later,' Dad says, as if that's a clincher.

I've had too much to drink to be able to drive now, anyway, and I'd have to make Dad turn out to take me home as, of course, they wouldn't hear of me getting a taxi. Plus I hate the thought of going home to an empty house.

'OK.' I'm such a pushover. I know that I'll get

tea in bed in the morning too which, frankly, is more of a draw than *BGT*.

So, we watch telly while I continue crafting and my Mum disses the acts, proclaiming them all rubbish. Then I go to bed in the room that still has all my teddies on top of the dresser. Though my posters of Jason Donovan have, thankfully, disappeared.

I text Finn before I go to sleep. Then I take one of the teddies down off the dresser and give him a cuddle. Jingles bear was my favourite until I was eleven and started secondary school. It was at that point I decided I was too old to sleep with a teddy and weaned myself off him. I've never quite got over my guilt for doing that. I stroke him lovingly. He's faring quite well considering he must be about thirty-five or so himself. He has soft, brown fur, a smiley face and kind eyes. He smells exactly as he used to. There are times when I think it would be nice to move back in with Mum and Dad and have them look after both me and Finn. I snuggle down, my arms wrapped round Jingles, and think that growing up and becoming an adult is very overrated.

Chapter Thirteen

I'm on the coach again. It's a miserable, grey morning and it's bloody cold. My heart is in my boots. I do wonder whether I can continue to do this for the rest of my working life. It's exhausting.

Finn got back from London at about seven o'clock last night and he'd had a great time. He was bubbling over with enthusiasm, but I could see that he was tired too. If he hadn't already been in trouble for missing school, I would have been very tempted to let him lie in this morning. Dad is probably going to have a devil's own job getting him up.

The coach appears in the distance and I brace myself for another day. I get my preferred seat, which is a bonus – but there's still no Susan. The seat next to me stays empty and, strangely, I find myself looking forward to seeing if Henry Jackson gets on the coach at Hockliffe.

He does and he comes down the coach to the empty seat. 'No Susan?'

'No Susan,' I confirm.

'Can I sit or am I am in danger of a serious breach of etiquette?'

'Be my guest.'

'I have a bribe.' He sits down and shows me a brown paper bag. 'Breakfast seedy flapjack things. Extraordinarily healthy. Allegedly.'

He has already sussed that I am a weak-willed woman. I take one out of the bag. When Toni comes to offer us coffee, she raises one eyebrow at me and grins. I hope Henry didn't notice.

'I had to go up to Norfolk at the end of last week,' he says as he juggles his hot coffee and his flapjack. 'Production problems at the printers. Nightmare.'

I don't tell him that his absence was noticed.

'Did you have a good weekend?'

'OK,' I tell him. 'I spent most of it with my

parents. My son, Finn, was away in London.' I'm sure he doesn't want to know that most of the time I was getting squiffy with my mother and cutting out hearts, butterflies and flowers.

'Oh,' he says. 'I was home alone too. Maybe we could have gone out together. If you find yourself at a loose end again perhaps we could go for a walk or something. I need to explore this area at some point. A local guide would be useful.'

'Well...'

'I could give you my phone number.'

'Er...'

He reels it off and, despite not having thought this through, I tap it into my phone. I don't offer mine which I'm not sure is a good thing or a bad thing.

'I go up to see Kyra every other weekend, so I'm not around much,' he adds. 'It's difficult because I don't have a base up there now. We have to go and stay with my parents.'

'Do you get force-fed cake every hour by your mother?'

'Yes.' He laughs.

'Me too. I'll swear I've put on a stone in two days.' I'm not joking. I'm sure my blouse was harder to do up today. That still won't tempt me to repeat the jogging incident. Perhaps I'll give my parents' Wii Fit a go. Though I can't say I'm keen.

'You look great,' Henry says and we both flush.

Then he chats about this and that and nothing in particular all the way to my stop on the Embankment. I find myself arriving at work with a smile on my face.

'What are you grinning at?' Robyn asks when I swing into the office. She puts a coffee down on my desk. 'It's Monday. You're not allowed to be cheerful.'

'I sat next to Henry again today,' I tell her as I strip off my coat. 'I think he's growing on me.'

'Well, I never.'

'He might have asked me on a date.'

'Might?'

'It was a bit vague. He suggested a walk one weekend. But then he said he needed a local guide as he didn't know the area. Does that sound like a date?'

'I'm not sure.'

'Me neither. I took his phone number.'

'That's a promising start.'

I laugh. 'I suppose so. He's complicated though. Recently divorced. Quite acrimoniously. Not sure if he still carries a torch for his ex as he talks about her a lot. His daughter is still up in Manchester, so he goes there every other weekend.'

'At your age, you're never going to find anyone without baggage.'

'Thank you for that, Robyn.'

'It's true. Live with it.' She shrugs. 'How many forty-odd-year-old blokes do you know who don't have some issues?'

I sag. 'That's what makes me think it's all too much effort.'

'You'll know when it's right,' Robyn says. 'I thought I was happily married when I met Imogen and it was being like hit by a bolt from the blue. I'd never looked at another man before, let alone a girl. Yet I knew from that first hello I needed to be with her.'

'Wow,' I say. 'You're lucky. I've never felt like that.'

'I'm not sure most people do.'

How depressing to go through life and never know what that feels like, to believe without a shadow of a doubt that you've met your soulmate.

'None of the obstacles in front of us mattered,' she continues. 'We both felt it and just knew we had to be together. It caused a lot of hurt and I'll always be sorry for that, but my life wouldn't have been worth living without her.'

'That's just so romantic.' I actually feel like a good blub. I sniff back my tears. 'Well, thanks for that, Robyn. That's really set me up nicely for a boring morning of preparing your document bundles.'

The Robster laughs. 'Thankfully, I'm not in a rush for it.'

This is one thing about my job, the bosses are all so good to me – not just Robyn. Where else would I find that? They're great about me having time off if I need to do something for Finn – like taking him to the doctor or if he's in a school play. Though I have to say that Finn avoids all forms of performance arts like the plague and only appears in anything when he's press-ganged. I get good money here too and, let's face it, this is a growth industry. I'm on a proper contract – not one of those zero hours things. I have nothing to complain about.

The only thing is that this is the least creative job in the world. There is nothing remotely arty about it. Sometimes I feel as if I'm split into two.

There's my creative side and my logical side and never the twain shall meet.

'Right.' Robyn rubs her hands together. 'Are you ready? Shall we kick the ass of some of this law shit?'

I sit at my workstation, engage my logical brain and say, 'As ready as I'll ever be.'

Chapter Fourteen

I've brushed the dust off my parents' Wii Fit – quite a thick layer of it – and have set it up in our living room. I've taken the precaution of drawing the curtains. None of our neighbours or innocent passers-by need to see this. I am in leggings again. Finn and I stand in front of the television. All the crafting detritus has been moved from the floor so that we don't accidentally jump on it. We are poised with the controllers in our hands.

'This is instead of jogging?' my son asks.

'I thought I would die if I jogged again.'

'I quite liked it.'

'You can jog to your heart's content. Please do. I thought exercise in the comfort of my own home would suit me better. Plus you like computers, I thought you'd go for this too.'

He shrugs. 'Cool.'

'There's all kinds of things to choose from. I thought we'd do something from *Sports Resort*. Twelve different sports on a tropical island,' I read out, hopefully. 'It might be the closest we ever get to one.'

Finn doesn't look keen. 'What else have we got?'

'Dance Party Pop Hits. Zumba Workout.'

'There's a law against people under thirty doing Zumba. Males in particular.'

'It's good for you.'

Finn raises an eyebrow.

I move on. *'Disney Sing It?'*

'Give me a break, Mother. I'm doing this under duress as it is.'

'They *are* Nana's choice.' I look at the rest of the games. *'Wii Fit Plus.'*

'Sounds way too healthy.'

With much faffing, I manage to turn it on and set up the balance board as instructed. A message on the screen says, *It is 2791 days since your last session.*

That's quite some time by anyone's reckoning.

Your weight seems a little different from when you last stood on the balance board.

'Did that thing just call me a tub of lard?'

'Harsh,' Finn says. 'But I think it did.'

'We could do yoga or something called *Penguin Slide*. You're a penguin on an iceberg trying to catch fish to eat.'

'Let's save that delight for another time.' His face says, Maybe never.

'There's jogging.'

'No jogging.'

'Dance Party Club Mix.'

Finn chuckles. 'Go Nana.'

'I bet she picked that up by mistake.' Even I grimace at the last one. *'Farming Simulator.'*

'For real?'

'She must have bought that for Pops.'

Finn says. '*Sports Island* it is then.'

'We have a choice of–'

'Just pick one, Mum, and let's get this over with. We've been stood here doing nothing for about twenty minutes now.'

'Wakeboarding. How about that?'

'Whatever.'

With rather more difficulty than seems necessary, I start the game.

'You know that I'm going to whoop your arse again?' my son says.

'Language, Finlay.'

Another ten minutes later and, with much swearing – this time from me – we've set us up with 'Mii' characters. Seriously, who makes these names up? Due to pressing a lot of wrong buttons, my *cartoon representation of myself* appears to be short, fat, blonde and wearing specs. It will have to do. Finn has marginally more success. Finally, we're good to go. I'm exhausted and stressed before we even start. I could have been halfway round the park by now.

I turn to Finn, who's wearing his best bored expression. 'Ready?'

He shrugs. 'Bring it on.'

As soon as we start moving, the cats run away in sheer terror and flatten themselves under the dresser in the dining room. Eric barks his interest in joining in.

Finn and I take it in turns to be pulled behind a virtual speedboat, encountering various obstacles. Finn sails through them all accumulating many, many points. I, on the other hand, appear to have a penchant for drowning my short, fat, blonde Mii self. Eric has a barking frenzy and runs round in circles on the rug, chasing his own tail. I know how he feels.

After three rounds my son wins and, grinning broadly, says, 'Right. What next?'

We opt for archery. I'm no better at it than wakeboarding. It's fair to say that my aim is, at best, erratic. I miss most of the targets. Finn doesn't.

'You know if this was real life, you'd have shot both of the cats by now,' he observes.

'No one likes a smart-arse.' I gnash my teeth.

Next up is *Snowboard Slalom*. I manage to miss all of the gates as I slither and slip in an un-controlled manner down a virtual mountain – that surely must be some sort of achievement? At the bottom, I get a verdict of 'unbalanced' and have burned two calories for my pains. No wonder these things end up in the loft.

We try several more games with no more success on my part. When it's over, and my arse is soundly whooped, Finn and I collapse on the sofa. I can fully understand why these things went out of fashion.

'Let's not do that again,' Finn says. 'It was humiliating. For you. Not me.'

'You're right.' The only thing that's aching is my right arm from waving the controller around. The dog, exhausted by excitement, is sound asleep. 'Perhaps we're not cut out for exercise.'

'It's not making my headache go away either.'

I frown at him, instantly on my default setting of worried. 'I should take a trip to the health food shop and get you some supplements.'

'A tub of Heroes might do it.'

'Nice try,' I say. Perhaps I should take him to a homeopath or a chiropractor. He might be allergic to something or have a vertebra out of joint. That can give you headaches. 'Ready for some dinner?'

He nods and, feeling more knackered than I should, I serve up the casserole that Mum has left in the slow cooker. And, because I'm exhausted from all the effort on the Wii, I eat two bread rolls and a KitKat for my half a dozen calories burned. I heart exercise. Not.

Chapter Fifteen

Later, when we've finished dinner and Finn and I are curled up on the sofa for the evening, I ask, 'How was school today?'

My son looks up from his task. 'Boring.'

The entire living room floor is, once again, covered in card-making detritus. Because I spent so much time on the projects for the Contemporary Crafts company over the weekend, I'm a bit behind on my card-marking target. I've booked a space in the boardroom at work for Thursday lunchtime and, currently, don't have enough to take in to sell. The most annoying thing was that when I looked at the projects in the cold light of day on Sunday – hangover and all – I decided that they really weren't good enough to send off. In fact, I had a massive attack of self-doubt. How could someone like me dare to send off my very amateur designs to a proper company? They'd probably have laughed me out of the place. Anyway, I think the deadline was today and I've missed the chance. There's no way I can do anything better now. Time not exactly wasted, but ... well ... you live and learn.

'Make the most of your school days,' I tell my son. 'Don't waste your education.'

'I'm not getting an education. I'm fodder for teachers who are marking time until they can draw their pensions.'

'So young and so cynical.'

Finn grins. 'Yeah. Such a rebel. That's why I'm sitting here cutting out butterflies for my mother when I could be holed up in my bedroom surfing dubious websites.'

'Finlay!'

'It's cool. I don't mind helping. There is something mindlessly therapeutic about it.'

'It's better for you than playing *Call of the Assassin* all night.'

'I could make an argument against that,' he teases.

'Get cutting. I need at least fifty cards in the next three days.'

'Slave driver,' he says. 'Did we even discuss terms?' But he winds the handle of the die-cutting machine and spews out more butterflies.

Then I think, at fifteen, should he be happy to do this? Shouldn't he be slamming round the house, grunting at me and looking at dubious websites as he said? That's what fifteen-year-old kids do.

'Nana says we should run an online shop for

93

craft supplies,' I tell him.

'Huh.' He pulls the sort of face that says he might be interested. 'There must be loads out there.'

'We'd have to offer something different. Do you think we could?'

'It wouldn't be that hard to set up.'

'It might give us a bit of income, some extra money for hols. We might even be able to go abroad.'

'I could look into it.'

The cats have finally deemed it safe enough to come out from under the dresser now that the Wii has been put away. Pixel cat circles a pile of paper and then sits on it. I shoo her off. No one needs a birthday card with cat hair on it. Next to me Eric opens one eye to see if he might be missing one of the cats getting into trouble – the thing he loves the most next to Pop's treat cupboard.

'Mum...' Then there's a long pause and I realise something of note is coming, so I put down my glue and listen properly. Finn frowns. 'I'm finding it really difficult to concentrate at school.'

'Headache?'

'Yeah. And sometimes my vision is going blurry.'

I don't like the sound of that. 'Do you think you might need glasses?'

'I don't know.'

'You managed all right at archery.' I'm still stinging from my cruel pasting at my son's hands.

'Beginner's luck,' he says. 'And it's not blurry at the moment. It sort of comes and goes.'

'Shall I book an appointment for you at Spec-savers?'

'I suppose so.'

We all wear glasses in the family, so I guess it's not unreasonable to expect that Finn would, at some point, need them too. Perhaps that's what his headaches are all about – something as simple as that – and I'm cross with myself that I didn't think of it earlier.

'I'll do it as soon as I can.'

'I hope I don't need them otherwise I'll be not just the smallest kid in the class, but speccy too.'

'I like a speccy kid.'

Finn rolls his eyes. 'Yeah, but you're a sucker for the underdog. You like a stray cat and a flea-bitten rescue hound too.' Eric, quite rightly, looks mortally wounded.

'Whether you need specs or not, you'll still be the best kid in the class in my book.'

Finn smiles.

'Love you to the moon and back.'

'Give it a rest, Mum.'

But when he goes back to cutting butterflies there's a happy grin on his face.

Chapter Sixteen

I do my lunchtime sale at work and sell all of the fifty cards that I managed to produce – with Finn's help. It nets me about a hundred quid. Not exactly going to enable me to put a deposit on a top-of-the-range Merc, but not too shabby either.

I chat to Henry every day on the coach and he

keeps bringing me breakfast treats. I wonder if he's working on the theory that the way to a woman's heart is through her tummy. Then another week is gone. Tonight, Henry catches the coach home which he very rarely does.

'This is an unexpected surprise.'

'Yes,' he says, breathless. 'Managed to get away early.' He flops into the seat next to me. 'Still no Susan?'

'No. I wonder what's happened to her. Toni said she's bought a season ticket too.'

'She might have lost her job or decided against commuting,' he muses.

'Or won the lottery,' I counter.

'Whichever way, her loss is my gain.'

I'm about to take a deep breath and tell Henry that I'm home alone that night as Finn is going out to celebrate a friend's birthday with a group from school. They're going for a pizza in Milton Keynes and he's being picked up at seven and brought home afterwards by the conscientious parents who have organised this. I could sit by my jolly old self with a bottle of wine and make some more cards as planned. Or I could do something reckless and propose a drink in a pub with this man.

While I'm still trying to form the words in my head, he says, 'I'm shooting up to Manchester tonight. It's my weekend with Kyra. I can't wait to see her.'

My heart both sinks and is, simultaneously, relieved.

'That's nice. I hope you have a good time.' Probably just as well as I need to replenish my card stock. It's so long since I've been out on a Friday night that I probably would have got overexcited and embarrassed myself.

'Perhaps when I'm around next weekend, we could go out for a walk or lunch? Or a coffee?'

Ohmyohmyoh. I'm having palpitations. 'Er ... well...'

Now he looks terrified. Perhaps Henry is having palpitations too. 'If you're not busy.'

'No,' I say. 'I'm never busy.'

He laughs. 'That's sorted then. You can choose the place as you know more about the area than me.'

'We could walk along the Grand Union canal and then have a pub lunch somewhere. I know a few nice places.'

'Sounds like a plan,' he says. Then, for the rest of the journey, we're both coy with each other. And at least one of us is wondering what the hell we've done.

When I get home, Finn has had a shower and washed his hair. Clearly, this is Serious Going Out.

'Mum,' he says, all wheedly. 'Can you iron me a shirt?'

'Blimey. Let me get through the door.' I hang my coat up.

'They're coming for me soon.'

'Right, right, right. Keep your shirt on.' I grin at Finn. 'See what I did there?'

But he's having none of it. 'Can you or not?'

'You're pushing the boat out for your mates,' I note. 'Are there young ladies involved in this?'

'No!' He's surprisingly petulant. 'You're always on at me for being scruffy. I'll put a T-shirt on. It's no big deal.'

'I'm only teasing you. Of course I'll iron you a shirt. Which one?'

He stomps off to the washing basket and brings a very crumpled black one back. When I win the lottery, I'm going to get someone in to do my ironing.

'I'm glad you're going out,' I say and I really am. 'You don't do it often enough.' I wish I could afford for him to go out regularly, but even a trip to the cinema costs an arm and a leg these days. Throw in a bucket-sized soft drink and the same of popcorn and you might as well hand over your kidneys too.

As penance for his minor strop, Finn sets up the ironing board in the kitchen. He stands there in just his jeans, hand crossed over his chest while I get pressing. I don't often see Finn without his clothes as the days of the bathroom door being left open are long gone.

He seems so pale and slight. He's all sharp angles and snow-white skin. Perhaps he doesn't get enough sunshine. He's certainly happier indoors than he is outside. Maybe I should try to save up for a holiday abroad next year. It might be doable. I wonder whether Mum and Dad might like to come too. I can't think last when they went further than Cornwall. If we do manage to get our bottoms into gear and start a little online shop, that might bring in enough money.

Handing Finn his shirt I watch as, self-consciously, he slips it on. I don't think that I

98

could love anyone as much as this child and wish he was still at an age where I could give him a cuddle for no reason. It gets harder to do when they're teenagers.

I reach into my purse and give him thirty pounds. 'That's too much,' he says.

'Trust me, it won't be.'

'I think Ollie's parents are paying for it all.'

'Take it just in case.'

'It can be my wages for all those flipping butter-flies.'

I laugh. 'No. This is my treat.'

'Thanks, Mum.' Then he hugs me warmly and, to be honest, that's worth thirty quid of anyone's money. I hold him tightly, stupid tears not far away.

There's a knock at the front door and, reluct-antly, I let go of him. 'This must be your ride.'

When I open the front door there's a slightly frazzled-looking dad standing there. From here, I can see that there are three oversized teenagers squashed in the back of his car.

'This is very kind of you,' I say.

'No problem. I'm Charlie Hemworth. Jake's dad.' He extends a hand and I take it.

'Christie Chapman.' I look back towards the kitchen where I can see Finn hopping around on one leg. 'He's nearly ready. Just putting his shoes on.'

'We might be late back.'

'That's fine,' I say. 'As long as he's with you.'

'My wife and I have booked a table in the restaurant – as far away from them as possible – but we'll be there all the time.'

These are the kind of parents I like. 'Come on, Finn,' I shout. 'Don't keep Mr Hemworth waiting!'

A second later and Finn is standing beside me. I resist the urge to kiss him as there are people watching. 'Have a great time.'

'Cheers, Mum.'

I stand and watch them drive away, even though I know Finn will be willing with every fibre of his being for me to go inside. I don't wave though, so give me that.

When I shut the door, the house seems really quiet. So, it's just me, two cats, a dog, the Creative World channel, some chocolate and a cheap bottle of Chardonnay.

Chapter Seventeen

I change into my PJs, then pour myself a glass of white wine, recoiling slightly at the first sip. Maybe I should have paid a bit more for it. I put some ice cubes into it which may or may not improve the taste. Then I find a small space among the animals who've already made themselves comfy on the sofa and, somewhat grudgingly, budge up to accommodate my bottom. I settle down to watch my crafting guru and role model, Sheridan Singleton, who has an hour-long special on a new die-cutting machine that's just come onto the market. That'll be on my wish list this Christmas.

I watch Sheridan, silky-smooth, smiling and

selling to me as if I'm her very best friend. I love her even though she makes me feel inadequate. She is on telly on a Friday night. I am at home on my sofa in PJs with Elsa on the front even though, technically, I'm probably too old for Disney pyjamas. I'd love to do something like this and be paid for it.

I get my die-cutting machine and my laptop cushion and cut out some hearts and stars while I watch. Taking it all in, I realise that I need to up my game and develop a style. If I want to carve a little niche for myself, I ought to have something special to offer that's unique to me.

Then my phone rings and I tut as I have to put Sheridan on pause. This had better not be some cold-caller wittering on about mis-sold PPI or they'll get the sharp end of my tongue.

'Hello.' I sound a bit more snappy than I'd intended.

'Hi.' A man's voice. Strong accent. Definitely American rather than the usual Indian call centre. 'Am I speaking to Christie Chapman?'

'You might be,' I say, crossly. 'Who needs to know?'

'This is Max Alexander from Contemporary Crafts.'

'Oh,' I say. 'Oh.'

'I have your designs here.'

'My designs?' I frown at the phone, which is ridiculous. 'But I didn't send them.'

The man laughs. 'Well, someone did.'

The penny drops and I sigh. 'That would be my mum,' I tell him. Who else could it be? She must have decided to email the photographs of them

101

on my behalf. Without telling me. I could kill her and kiss her. 'Oh, I'm so sorry. She shouldn't have done that.'

'I'm glad she did,' he says. 'They're very good.'

'Really?' I sit up straighter. 'I woke up the next morning and decided they were rubbish.' I don't need to tell Mr Alexander that they were mainly gin-induced.

'Sure, they were a little rough around the edges, but I can see that you have a lot of potential. I like your style, Christie. It's clean, crisp – contemporary – and fits in with the kind of image I'm trying to create for Contemporary Crafts.' Then he hesitates. 'Just one thing...'

I wait with bated breath.

'Have you ever considering using any of *our* dies?'

'Er ... um...'

'You realise that all of your designs were created with our competitors' products?'

'I didn't even think about it,' I admit. I'm never drinking gin again. 'I can only apologise.'

'You Brits are all eccentric, right?'

'Yes,' I agree. 'Very much so. You'll have to excuse us.' Thankfully, he sounds amused rather than outraged at my mistake.

'If I'm honest...' I cringe even as I say it, 'your products don't have a very high profile here.'

'That's what I'm hoping to change,' he tells me. 'What if I send you a box of our dies? Do you think could create something with those for me?'

'I'll certainly give it a go.'

He laughs again as if it's the funniest thing anyone's ever said. 'I'm sorry,' he adds. 'I love

102

your accent. You sound like Mary Poppins.'

That's a good thing? I can't pinpoint his accent. East Coast probably. But it's soft, gentle, refined. Not one of those southern drawls, anyway. But then my entire experience of American accents has been gleaned via the medium of film and TV.

'I'd need you to turn them around quickly,' Max Alexander says.

'Not a problem.' Clearly, he is unaware that my life is one mad social whirl. Plus I'm more than happy to forgo further fabulous evenings on the Wii Fit to facilitate this.

'You've looked at our website?'

Of course I haven't. Didn't even occur to me. 'Broadly speaking.' I wonder if that translates to 'no' in American.

'We're a very small start-up company and we've made some inroads into the market over here, but I hope that by moving into Europe we can grow quickly.'

'We're way behind the States on this type of paper crafting,' I tell him.

'I'd heard that. Which is why I want to engage a designer in England. Your style and approach is very different to the typical American look.'

'I'm no expert, but I can tell you what I know about the market here. Or, if there's something specific that you'd like researched, I can help with that.'

'That sounds great, Christie. May I call you, Christie?'

'Of course.'

'I'll get some of my products shipped over to you right away and then we'll talk again next week.

Technically, it's after the deadline for submissions but, as I made the rules, I'm sure I can bend them a little. If I get the dies to you as soon as possible, could you turn them round in a week?'

'Yes.' I sound so confident but, frankly, I have no idea how. I do know that I'd be stupid to pass up this opportunity. I'll have to burn the midnight oil.

'I'll send them by express courier. Will you Skype me to let me know when they arrive?'

'Yes.' I've no idea how to Skype either, but Finn will. The man reels off his contact details.

'You have my address for the parcel?'

'Yes.' I can hear the smile in his voice. 'Your mother was very thorough with her paperwork.'

'I'll have to thank her.'

'Please thank her from me too, Christie. I feel quite excited. I hope this may be the start of a long association.'

'Me too.'

'Bye now.'

'Bye.'

We both hang up and then one of us jumps up from the sofa, punches the air and does a happy dance, frightening the cats in the process and sending Eric into a frenzy of barking.

I break out into 'A Spoonful of Sugar' at the top of my voice. I tell you, if he needs Julie Andrews, I can be Julie Andrews.

He didn't exactly say that I'd got the gig, but that definitely sounded promising, didn't it? When I get their products, I really need to pull something special out of the bag.

While I'm still dancing and singing, the phone rings again. This could be Max Whatsisname again. I clap my hands in glee. Then I panic that he might have changed his mind, so I take a few deep breaths to calm myself. And when I answer I put on the most English voice that I can manage.

But it isn't Max at the other end of the line and what I hear brings me to my knees.

Chapter Eighteen

Finn has collapsed. An ambulance is currently taking him from Pizza Express to A&E at the hospital. The temptation to jump right into my car is overwhelming, but I've had two glasses of wine, so I call Dad.

He's at my house ten minutes later and I'm out of my PJs and back in my jeans. Another fifteen minutes after that, we're pulling into the car park at the hospital. While Dad fiddles about feeding the parking meter, I fly inside. Friday night and, of course, A&E is heaving. Half the drunks from the city are up here slumped in chairs, several of them bleeding profusely, the rest of them are effing and jeffing at the staff.

Thankfully, the first person I see is Charlie Hemworth, the dad who took Finn to the city centre. He stands up as he sees me.

'I think Finn's OK,' he says, though his face is white. 'They've taken him straight through.'

I'm both glad and alarmed that Finn has jumped the queue. Does that mean there's something awful wrong? 'What happened?'

Charlie spreads his hands. 'I've no idea, really. One minute he was laughing, eating pizza. The next he was on the floor. It all happened so quickly.' The man looks totally traumatised, as you would if you'd taken someone else's kid out and they, unexpectedly, hit the deck. It's every parent's worst nightmare.

'Thank you for acting quickly,' I say. 'I've got it now.'

'I can wait,' he says. 'My wife took the other children home. I was about to call her.'

'It could be hours. My dad's here too. You've done enough. Thank you.' He's not a parent I know – only to nod at – and, although he's been kind, I don't want to be making small talk to a relative stranger in these circumstances. He sort of seems relieved to be able to leave too.

'You'll ring me and let me know how Finn is?'

'As soon as I hear anything,' I promise.

'I'm really sorry.' Charlie looks as distraught as I feel. 'This is terrible.'

'I'm sure he'll be fine.' But as I have absolutely no idea what's wrong, I'm not really sure at all. 'I'm sorry that Jake's birthday celebration ended like this.'

'As soon as Finn is feeling better, we can do it again,' he says.

'That's very kind.'

At that point, a nurse comes to speak to me and Charlie takes his leave. My dad comes in looking harried.

The nurse consults her iPad. 'You're Finlay Chapman's mum?'

'Yes. Can I see him?'

She nods. 'Doctor's just with him. He'll want to ask you some questions.'

Dad sits in the waiting room, while I follow the nurse through to a cubicle with curtains around it. Finn is lying on the bed. I'm relieved to see that his eyes are open and he still looks like my son. His face is damp with sweat and his hair is plastered to his head, but then it's as hot as Hades in here. There's a slight cut on his forehead.

I go to the side of his bed and grab his hand. 'Are you all right?'

'Yeah. I think so.' His eyes, on closer examination, look a little bit glassy.

'Hello, Mrs Chapman. I'm Dr Rhani.' We shake hands. 'I've had a good look at Finn but can't see anything wrong. Has he fainted like this before?'

'No.' I shake my head.

'Never had any fits?'

'No. Is that what this is?'

'It seems unlikely.'

'He gets a lot of headaches.'

'Does he take any medication for that?'

'Just paracetamol. They don't seem to touch it though, do they, Finn?'

'No,' my son answers.

'Our GP checked him over.' Sort of, I add to myself. 'But he couldn't find anything wrong. He said he needed more exercise and fresh air. That's not made any difference either.' Though I'm not sure that we can judge it on the meagre efforts we've made so far. 'Finn was saying his eyesight has sometimes started to go blurry.'

The doctor looks at my son. 'When's that, Finlay?'

107

'At school. I have trouble seeing the whiteboard.'

'Have you taken him for his eyes tested?'

'I've just booked an appointment for him.'

'It might be something and nothing,' the doctor says. 'He looks well enough now. We'll keep him in overnight for observation as he's banged his head but, all being well, he should be able to go home in the morning.'

You have no idea how thankful I am to hear that.

'Make sure he has a restful weekend,' he adds. 'Maybe keep him off school for a few days.'

Oh, Lord. I wonder what the headmaster will think about that.

It's an hour before there's a bed available on the children's ward for Finn. But, eventually, we're taken up there and he's settled in. It's close to midnight by the time I'm leaving him. The lights have been turned down and he's looking sleepy.

'Are you sure you'll be OK?'

'I'm fine, Mum. Don't fuss.'

I stroke his hair. 'I'm worried about you. I can't have you keeling over in pizza places. Especially when you've not been drinking.'

'Mum!' He manages a smile.

'I'm going now. Poor Pops has been downstairs in the waiting room for hours. He'll be awash with terrible vending machine tea.'

'He should have gone home,' Finn says.

'You know what he's like. He wouldn't go home until he knew you were all right.' What I want to do is lie down on the bed next to Finn, but I should go home too. 'I'll see you in the morning. First thing.'

'OK.'

'Text me if you need anything. Whatever time it is.' I can see that his eyes are tired and I'm sure he'll be sleep within minutes. 'I love you.'

'Love you too,' he says.

Then I go back to Dad and he hugs me while I tell him that Finn's fine and we both have a cry. 'I'll call your mother,' he says and we both talk to her. She cries too.

After that Dad drives me home. We sit and have a cup of tea. I call Liam to let him know that Finn's in hospital, but he seems to be OK. My ex-husband talks about jumping on the next plane, but I calm him down and tell him to wait until we have more news. Which I think is the right thing to do.

Finally, I wave Dad goodbye and climb the stairs, exhausted. I strip off and snuggle into my pyjamas. I can't remember the last time I was at the hospital with Finn. The only time he's stayed in overnight was when he had his appendix removed when he was eleven. I miss him like mad. Even the dog seems forlorn. He lies behind me, sticking to my back like a limpet. The cats, of course, are untroubled by his absence.

There's a picture of Finn and me on my bedside table. It was taken by Mum at their house last summer while Dad was turning sausages into charcoal in the name of barbecuing. Finn and I are both laughing, heads thrown back, beaming smiles. It looks as if we haven't a care in the world.

I put the picture next to me on the pillow, say a silent prayer to a God that I don't really believe in, and turn out the light.

Chapter Nineteen

They keep Finn in hospital, run some tests which prove inconclusive and then, deemed to be fine and suffering from nothing but being a teenager, he comes home on Sunday. Dad and I go to collect him. I settle him in his own bed and Eric curls at his feet and neither of them move all day. I go into full fuss mode, but I think that Finn secretly likes it, despite tutting and protesting a lot. Liam phones a few times and later, when Finn's feeling up to it, they Skype each other.

Finn sleeps on and off most of the day and into the evening. I know that kids of his age sleep all the time, but I'm still worried that there's some underlying problem. What if he goes back to school and keels over there? What if there's no one to act as swiftly as Jake's dad? Am I panicking unnecessarily? Perhaps it was all that jogging and jumping around on the Wii that brought it on. That thing can go right back to my parents' cupboard whence it came.

Speaking of which, my parents visited earlier, armed with a takeaway roast dinner for us and they fussed over me like I fuss over Finn. They too are beside themselves with worry. Finn is their only grandchild and is much adored.

After pacing about all afternoon in a state of indecision, I call Robyn at home to tell her what's happened and that I'm keeping Finn off school for a few days. She thinks it's the best idea. I wonder whether I should call or maybe text Henry to let him know that I won't be on the coach in the morning. He might worry. Or he might think I'm peculiar. I'll leave well alone. We'd agreed to a sort-of date, but that doesn't mean he needs to be involved in the details of my domestic crises.

I leave Finn in bed on Monday morning and call the school to say that he's unwell again. By the afternoon he's looking a little bit brighter, so – still in his dressing gown – he moves down to the sofa. He's not eaten much all weekend from what he said, but I coax him to have some buttered toast and I've made some chicken soup for later. No matter how old they are, the minute your child is poorly they revert to being a baby in your eyes. I stroke his forehead, fretting whether he feels too warm or not.

'I'm fine, Mum.'

'Well enough to go to school?'

His smile is wan.

'I thought not. Let me fuss over you then.'

Finn throws his arms up in surrender. 'Pamper away.'

'What can I get you?'

He gives me a hopeful look. 'I suppose I'm too ill to be on my laptop?'

'You suppose right, young man. Rest and recuperation. That's what the doctor ordered. The moment you're well enough to play *Call of the Assassin,* that's when you're well enough to put on your school uniform again.'

'You could always bore me back to health with the Crappy Crafts channel.'

'What an excellent plan.' I think that's Finn's way of asking me to sit with him. 'I'll make us a cup of tea and then we can enjoy it together.'

'Joy,' Finn says, but he's still smiling.

I've just brought the tea in from the kitchen when the doorbell rings. Standing there is a small courier with an enormous cardboard box.

'Sign here,' he says, shoving his machine under my nose. Then he dumps the box on my hall floor before hotfooting it back to his van. I wonder what on earth it is, then remember what happened to me on Friday night! In all the trauma with Finn, I'd quite forgotten.

I heave the box into the living room and plonk it on the rug in front of the fire. 'Look what I've got,' I say to Finn.

'Special delivery?'

'All the way from the US of A.' With a bit of huffing and puffing and brute force, I tear open the lid. 'I had a bit of news of my own while you were in the hospital.' I stop tearing and turn to Finn. 'A man from Contemporary Crafts called me. He liked my designs.'

Finn's eyes widen and I find myself feeling quite emotional telling him. Tears prickle behind my eyes and I blink them away. Perhaps it's because the weekend has been so fraught or perhaps it's because I've found something that I could be very good at.

'I didn't get the gig yet, but all of this stuff is from the company. He wants me to create something using their products.'

'That's well sick, Mum.'

'I take that as a compliment.'

112

'Yeah, watch out Sheridan Singleton, there's a new kid on the block. Well, a middle-aged woman.'

'Enough of that, Finlay Chapman.'

'Should it scare me that I know the names of all the presenters on a craft channel?'

'Yes,' I say. 'It should.'

I pull everything out and spread it on the rug. It's like being a kid in a sweet shop. 'Oh, look at these, Finn.'

There are dozens of different metal dies – every size and shape you can think of. I'm going to have such fun! There are pads of pretty crafting paper, glitter, glue and all kinds of embellishments. Christmas has come early this year!

'Cool.' Finn slides onto the floor next to me and helps me to take all the bits and pieces out of their wrapping. 'This lot should keep you quiet for a while.'

Then I sag. 'But he wants me to get my designs back to him by the end of the week. I'll never do it by then.'

'Of course you will,' Finn says.

'My heart's not really in it with all that's going on.'

'I can help,' Finn says.

'You're supposed to be resting.'

'All it takes is turning a handle to die-cut the pieces. How hard can that be? You're the one who needs to provide the creative spark. Does it matter who cuts the bits out? We could get Nana round too.'

I'm not sure. It all seems too much at the moment. All I want to think about is getting Finn well again. Nothing else matters.

'What are we going to do, otherwise? Watch other people making crafts on telly?'

I have my wobbly head on. 'I'm not sure.'

'Step up to the plate, Mother,' Finn urges. 'This could be your one big chance. Don't let me blow it for you.'

'It's not you …

'It is. I'd feel like shit if you didn't do this because of me.'

'Language, Finlay.'

He brushes aside my admonishment. 'You know you have to do it. If we do start our own online shop, it would look so much better if you could say you were a designer for a craft company. We'd probably be able to stock all their stuff too.'

'I hadn't really considered that.' I look at my son. 'You are clever.'

'So you'll do it?'

I'm all of a dither. 'I said I'd Skype the man in America to let him know the stuff is here. Perhaps he could give me a few extra days.'

'What's his name? We could look up the company. Or have you done that already?'

'Of course I haven't. You're the brains in this family.'

Finn smiles. 'It means I get control of the laptop.'

'There's not too much wrong with you, Finlay Chapman.'

Despite being completely manipulated by my child, I go to get the laptop.

Chapter Twenty

When he has the laptop, the first thing that Finn does is Skype his dad again and reassure him that he's getting better, surely but slowly. And that's fine by me. My heart does go out to my ex-husband. On the screen, Liam's face looks drawn and worried. Whatever our differences, it must seem like a very long way away when your son is ill.

'Dad says he wants me to go out there on holiday when I'm better,' Finn says when he finishes his call.

'Sounds like a good idea. It would be nice for you to see where he lives now.'

'Maybe in the summer holidays? He said he'd send a ticket.'

The thought of Finn going on a plane by himself to Dubai fills me with dread. 'Let's see what happens.'

'That's mother-speak for "not on your life".'

I ruffle his hair. 'You know me too well.'

'I'll be sixteen by then. I'm old enough.'

'I know. I'm just a worry-pot.' Then I try a distraction technique. 'Let's look up the Contemporary Crafts company. I should Skype this man.'

It works. Finn taps in their website and we view their full range of products. They've certainly sent me a decent selection. More importantly, I find out that Max Alexander isn't *a* man, he's *THE* man. Oh, my. He's only the CEO of Contemporary Crafts. Yikes!

'Do you want to contact him now?'

'I should.' I'm terrified now that I know who he is.

'Give me the address,' Finn says. 'I'll see if he's online.'

I hand over the paper I scribbled it on and Finn enters it. 'He's here,' my son says. 'Shall I call him?'

I nod before I can think better of it.

A bit of tapping and a few moments later, a man pops up on the screen and Finn pushes the laptop in front of me. It all happened so quickly I haven't prepared what I want to say.

'Hi,' he says over space or whatever. It feels as if he's in the living room with us and I find that quite disconcerting. This man is a stranger and, effectively, he's here with me, sitting on my lap on my sofa. 'Nice to see you, Christie.'

If this is Max Alexander then he really isn't what I'd imagined at all. He's younger, for a start. Probably my age when I'd envisaged someone nearer to sixty. And he's handsome. Suave, even. He has dirty-blond hair which is greying at the temples and cropped short. His lips are full, his cheekbones sharp, chin strong. He wears it all in a slightly rugged way that suits him. There's a deep line on his forehead that indicates that he frowns a lot. I'm not sure if the shadow of stubble on his face is fashionable or if he just hasn't shaved. His eyes are the most piercing pale blue and they're staring right at me through the screen.

For a moment, I'm lost for words and I feel Finn poke me in the side and manage, 'Hello.'

116

I can only see Max's head and shoulders, but I can see that he's wearing a white, round-neck T-shirt beneath a light grey sweater.

'I take it the package arrived?' he says.

'Yes, it did. It's lovely. Thank you.' Finn pokes me again. 'I'm very excited to be working with your products.'

'I put a catalogue in there too and there's more on the website which you can have a look at. Just ask if you need anything else.'

This is the moment that I should press him to extend my deadline. I should explain to him that my son has been in hospital and I'm more stressed than I've ever been. I could tell him that I don't feel up to this task and call it a day. But none of it will come out of my dry mouth. Instead, I just sit and gape.

I wish I'd combed my hair or put lipstick on or something. Anything. I hope he can't see too far into our rather small and cluttered living room. Then I wonder why that matters. Is it because the sight of this man has made my heart race and has revved up all kinds of hormones that were previously lying dormant?

'Can I help you with anything else, Christie?'

'I ... er ... no ... I should be going.' I try a laugh and sound like a lunatic. 'Lots of crafting to do.'

'Good. I look forward to seeing your designs.'

'Yes. Designs. Right.' I'm in danger of going into gabbling mode. 'Thank you for all this.' I gesture to the heaps of dies, card and whatnot scattered all over my rug which, of course, he can't see.

'We'll speak soon.'

'Yes. Bye.' Then he's gone.

Finn is staring at me. 'You've gone all sort of weird and goggle-eyed, Mum.'

'Have I?'

'Nothing to do with the fact that Max Wotsit looked a bit like that James Bond bloke, Craig David?'

'Daniel Craig,' I correct.

'Yeah, him.'

'Did he?' He did. Very much so. 'I think we'll have another cup of tea.' Though I think a double brandy might be more in order.

'Nana and Pops have just pulled up outside.'

'I'd definitely better get the kettle on then.'

So my parents have come bearing food parcels again and, when he's had a cuppa, Dad takes the poor dog – who has been sorely neglected in the walkies department – out for a long hike. Mum and I sort through the goodies that Max Alexander has sent.

'Blimey,' Mum says. 'He must have been quite impressed to do this for you.'

'I still haven't had words with you about sending them off without me knowing yet.'

'You hide your light under a bushel, Christie,' she says, unabashed.

'I have no idea what that means, Nana,' Finn notes.

'It means that she should get her finger out and crack on with these designs. She's got a deadline to meet.'

'We can die-cut things while Mum designs them, can't we, Nan?'

'We can. Come on, Christie. We haven't got all day.'

118

But we do have the rest of the afternoon and well into the evening. Working together, I tell Mum and Finn what I want cutting and with what paper and they set up a little production line, churning out flowers, hearts, butterflies, speech bubbles, sentiments and all manner of things. I make two designs then we have a break for dinner and Mum warms up the casserole she's brought. Dad does the washing up and then sits in the corner looking at the newspaper while Finn, Mum and I carry on. As my fingers fix and fiddle, putting flowers together, colouring them with inks, adding pearls, crystals and whatnot, I can feel my excitement rising. This could be a big break for me and I should grasp it with both hands.

But do you know what makes me feel happier than that? When I look over at Finn, head bowed over the die-cutting machine, working away, I can see the colour coming back to his cheeks, the life to his eyes and I know in my heart that he's going to be all right.

Chapter Twenty-One

Monday. Coach. Commuting. Meh.

I slump into my usual seat. After a week at home with Finn, getting back to my routine this morning was more difficult than ever. Still, I managed to get my designs done for Max Alexander and sent in. I emailed them off at midnight before falling into bed, knackered. It's not like me to blow my own trumpet, but I have to say that I was quietly pleased with them. All I can do now is wait to see if Max Alexander thinks they're good enough to make the grade. I did my best and it's now out of my hands.

So Finn goes back to school. I go back to work. Life returns to normal.

To ease the pain of my early start, I'm going to need an awful lot of coffee this morning, I can tell you. More than likely chocolate too. Toni better keep my caffeine levels topped up.

Henry gets on the coach at Hockliffe. He sits next to me. 'I missed you,' he says. 'Everything all right?'

'My son's been ill,' I explain. 'He's OK now though. Back at school. Grumbling about it.'

'Ah. A sure sign they're well when they complain about everything.'

'That's what I thought.'

'I did wonder though. I would have called, but I don't have your number.'

'No.' This is my moment to give it to him, I think. If I pause any longer it will look rude. So, slightly hesitantly, I tell him and Henry taps it into his phone. I feel another line has been crossed. Now we have each other's phone numbers. I realise that in these days of Tinder and Grindr and whatever – where you can hook up with perfect strangers for a shag without strings – that this is one small, rather middle-aged, step, but it feels like a giant leap for me.

'I've been bringing breakfast every day, just in case,' Henry says.

And something about that makes me feel really

sad. I don't like to think of Henry being alone at home, missing his daughter, bringing breakfast treats for a woman who may or may not arrive. I don't know if he's getting up any earlier in the morning, but he still looks as dishevelled as ever. His dark hair is messy, his tie is all askew, one of his shirt buttons isn't done up properly. He's like the kid in the class with scuffed knees and a plaster holding his glasses together.

'Today, you have wholemeal muffins. I'd have eaten it for my lunch, otherwise.' He hands me a paper bag.

'Thank you. That's very thoughtful of you.'

'I'm not seeing Kyra this weekend. Are we still OK to meet up?'

Was this when we were supposed to be going out for our walk and lunch? Yikes.

Perhaps he sees the terror in my eyes as he says, 'It's all right if you can't make it.'

'I confess with all that's been going on, I'd completely forgotten.' I realise that I haven't told Henry about my flirtation with international crafting – perhaps that's the wrong term giving that my heart still hasn't quite recovered from seeing the rather dashing CEO of said crafting company.

'We could reorganise,' he suggests.

'That sounds like a good idea. I feel that Finn and I could do with a quiet time together. Would you mind if we give it a miss for now?'

'No, no,' Henry says. 'That's fine. Whenever you're ready.'

'I'm absolutely knackered and it's only Monday.'

He laughs. 'I know how you feel. This doesn't get any easier.' We both delve into our bags and take a bite of the muffins. 'Finn's all right now, though?'

'Yes,' I tell him. 'I think so.' I took him to the opticians last week and he had an eye test and that thing where they puff air into your eyeballs that everyone hates. They took a picture of the back of his eye or something too and he came out with a clean bill of health and no glasses. Finn was delighted at that and I can tick another thing off the list that's not wrong with him.

'How's your job going?'

'Yeah. OK,' he says. 'Still feel like the naive northern lad up in the big smoke. I'm sure I'll get over it.'

'Still missing home?'

'Like you wouldn't believe.'

Then we eat our muffins and talk about nothing in particular. For a Monday, the traffic is relatively light and we reach the Embankment stop only ten minutes after our scheduled time. A miracle.

'I'll see you tomorrow,' Henry says, and his smile makes me feel a foot taller.

Chapter Twenty-Two

The Robster and I sit and have two coffees in the staff lounge. Yes, we have such a thing. It's done out like an ultra modern library and is full of leather-bound legal books. Not a romance novel in sight. Pah.

I think Robyn realises that I need to be gently cajoled into the week as she's being very kind to me. While we recline in our shock-orange seats, I tell her all that has been happening.

'No wonder you look so tired,' she concludes.

And I am. It would take little encouragement for me to lie down on the floor under the coffee table and go to sleep. I wonder if anyone would actually notice?

'When did you last have a holiday?' Robyn continues. 'And I mean a proper holiday, not just time off looking after Finn.'

'Christmas probably. Like you.'

'Yes, but I went to the Bahamas for two weeks. What did you do?'

'I didn't go to the Bahamas for two weeks.'

'My point exactly.'

'I don't have Bahamas money.'

She grimaces.

'I'm not complaining,' I add quickly. 'You pay me well for what I do. It just doesn't stretch to extended breaks in the Caribbean.'

'If it was up to me, you know I'd pay you double.'

'I'm well paid,' I reiterate. 'It's just that it costs a lot to bring up a kid.' Despite being small in stature, Finn isn't far off being a man. If he does scrape through his exams and has a chance at university, I'll have to think about putting money aside for that. I know what Robyn's saying but, at the moment, holidays are a long way down the list.

'If there's anything I can do, you know that you only have to ask.'

'I do.' I smile tiredly at her. 'I'm fine.'

'How are things going with Henry?'

I shrug. 'He's nice enough.'

'Damning with faint praise.'

'I was supposed to be going out with him this weekend, but I've just cried off, but I'm not sure if I've done the right thing. I want a quiet time at home with Finn. I've probably no need to be, but. I'm still worried about him. Plus, I haven't even told Finn about Henry. I can't just spring another man on him – if you know what I mean.'

Robyn glances at her watch. 'I hate to do this, but we'd better get a move on, otherwise our absence will be noted.'

'I'll work through my lunch hour today.'

'We've got a lot on at the moment with the Blake Hotels case but, as soon as the load lifts a bit, you and Finn should try to get away.'

'His dad wants him to fly out to Dubai by himself. Not sure how I feel about that.'

'Couldn't you go together and you check into Liam's hotel for a bit of rest and relaxation? If he couldn't get you a freebie, surely he could give you mates' rates.'

'I hadn't really considered that.' Perhaps that would be a possibility. If Finn could stay with his dad and put me in the hotel, it might be doable. I'd only have to find the cash for my flight if Liam pays for Finn, plus some spending money.

'You should go on a date with Henry too. Risk it. Isn't it time that you had a little fun in your life that doesn't involve glue and ribbons?'

That makes me laugh. If only all my problems were craft-based.

I work like a mad thing and I don't think about Henry Jackson or Max Alexander or anything other than the document bundles for Blake's Hotels *v* Experiential Development all day. I nip out for five minutes for my meal deal and eat it at my desk. It's a lovely warm day, the tantalising promise of summer alive in the air and it gives my spirits a lift. My life isn't all ha-ha-hee-hee but I do have a lot to be thankful for.

It's four o'clock when I look up from my paperwork again and my caffeine levels must be dangerously low. While I'm in the kitchen Finn rings me and, immediately, my heart goes into panic mode.

'Is everything all right?'

'I don't know,' he says. 'You've got an email from Max Alexander.'

Now I panic some more but in a different way. 'What does it say?'

'I don't know, Mum. I haven't read it. I didn't like to. I just saw the heading.'

'It could be bad news.'

'It could be good,' Finn counters. 'I thought you'd want to know straight away.'

'Read it.'

'Are you sure?'

'Do it.'

'OK.' I can hear his fingers tapping and I bite my nails while I wait. It seems to be an awful long time before he says, 'Oh.'

'What? What? What?'

'Are you sitting down?'

I'm not, but I say, 'Yes.'

'You're in,' Finn says with a laugh. 'You've only done it, Mum.'

'Oh, my.' I wish I *was* sitting down. 'What does

it say?'

'Not much,' Finn tells me. 'Well done. Great design. Blah, blah, blah. He says can you call him tonight to discuss the details.'

I feel wobbly all over. This could be the break I need. I can't begin to tell you how wonderful it feels to have someone like Max Alexander believe in me. If it wouldn't frighten the lawyers – who tend to be people of serious disposition – I'd run round the office doing a happy dance.

'We should celebrate, Mum,' Finn says.

'We should.'

'I'll tell Nana.'

'Great.' Mum too will be overcome with joy. Especially as she's the one who engineered all of this. I pull myself down from the clouds and turn my attention to my son. 'How have you been today?'

'Cool,' he says. 'Bit tired now.'

'Have a nap on Nana's sofa.'

'I'm not four,' he says, indignant.

That makes me smile. 'I'll see you later.'

I hang up and stay in the kitchen for a minute trying to compute what Finn said in my head. I've done it. Max Alexander has chosen me to be the UK designer for his craft company. Then I go back to my desk and don't do another stroke of work. Instead, I sit in stunned silence and, beaming in a slightly weird manner to myself, stare out of the window and wonder what happens next.

Chapter Twenty-Three

We celebrate my success at Mum and Dad's house with cottage pie and a bottle of cava that Dad popped to Budgens to pick up especially. The evening is so mild that we sit out on the little decking area in the lee of the summerhouse by the river, quite a sheltered spot, the perfect place to sit and watch the sun go down. The ducks are busying themselves before they settle for the night. Two of them nestle in Mum's geraniums which drives her mad as it flattens them. I think it's a small price to pay for having such a lovely outlook. On the other side of the riverbank, the evening dog-walkers stroll along the path and Dad will be taking Eric and Trigger to join them soon. I might even go with him.

Mum lifts a glass to me. 'To my very clever daughter,' she says with a tear in her eye.

'Our girl has hit the big time!' Dad is beaming.

'I hope that it leads to amazing things for you.' Mum again.

'I'm just going to be doing some designs for them,' I counter. 'It's not going to change my life.'

'You never know,' she insists.

'To Mum,' Finn says and we all drink a toast. Then Finn pulls a horrified face. 'Bleurgh. Why do people drink this?'

'Never underestimate the recuperative power of bubbly drinks,' I tell him. 'I'll have yours.' I take another swig even though it's a school night. 'Anyway, thank you for sending them in, Mum. Even though you did it without my knowledge and you really shouldn't have.'

'Mums always know best,' she says and holds out her glass to Dad for a refill. That will be her all giggly in ten minutes.

'I suppose I'd better call Max Alexander.' Even saying that makes my tummy flip in an odd way. 'What time is it in Washington DC?'

'Is that where it is?' Dad laughs. 'You jet-setter.'

'I'm not sure that one phone call to the States makes me a jet-setter, Dad. But I live in hope.'

Finn taps into his computer. 'It's lunchtime.'

'I can't call him. I'm too nervous.'

'You should send an email back, at least,' Finn says. 'Show that you're keen.'

'Thank you, my business guru. I'll do just that.' My son hands over the laptop. I take the time to read Max's email again and still can't quite take it in. I type an email.

Thank you, Max. I'm so thrilled. I'll speak to you tomorrow. Tomorrow, when I've had time to digest all this. *Thank you again. Christie.*

I show it to Finn.

'Perfect,' he says. 'Eager but not too gushy.'

I press send. There, that's it. Gone.

I'm just about to close up the laptop when one pings right back. *I've just got back from a meeting,* it says. *Are you available to Skype now?*

'He wants to Skype me,' I tell my audience.

'I can't cope with all this technology. We used to see this sort of thing on *Star Trek* and now it's here,' Dad says with a bewildered shake of his

128

head. 'I'm going to walk the dogs. Come on, boys.' The dogs fall into step with him.

'Can I do that here?' I ask Finn.

'Of course you can.'

'Right.' Technology is not my strong point either. 'I'd better get on to him.'

'I'm going in to get a cardigan,' Mum says. 'Do you want some tea?'

'Yes, please.'

'I'll set you up and then I'll go and help Nana.'

'You're a good boy.'

Finn grimaces. 'Leave it out, Mother.'

'You were OK at school today?'

'Yeah. Bored. But not ill.'

'I worry.'

'You shouldn't.' He gets Skype set up for me. 'There you go.'

A few minutes later and Max Alexander is on the screen. He's wearing a crisp white shirt and a dark grey tie which is loosened. His hair is tousled and he runs his hand through it again for good measure.

'Hi.' He grins at me. My mouth goes dry. 'Welcome on board.'

'Thank you.'

'I'm so glad that you've accepted my offer. I loved your designs and I'm pleased you were able to turn them round so quickly.'

'Me too.'

'I'll send you a contract through in the next day or two. But, basically, I'll require four designs a month – a scrapbook page, a card, a mixed media item and something we call "One Die Wonder" which is probably self-explanatory. You'll get new

129

dies every few weeks and a delivery of paper, ad-hesives, embellishments and such every quarter.'

That doesn't sound too taxing. I can cope with that. The thought of getting all those new goodies is quite exciting.

'I'm setting up a training programme now. We tend to call it a retreat, but you'll get a thorough briefing in all our products and those of our partners. I'll let you know the dates as soon as I have them. It's usually a week long and there'll be about ten other designers with you. They're mainly from the States, but there might be a few attendees from other parts of Europe. We're just waiting to finalise the list.'

Now my head's starting to reel a bit and it's not down to Dad's cava. Training programme? I hadn't expected that. 'Training programme?' I venture.

He laughs. 'Don't look so worried.' I'd forgot-ten that he could see me too. 'You'll have great fun as well as learning all about us and our ethos. We put you up in a very nice hotel, give you some good food and you'll take home more crafting products than you can lift.'

'Right.' My heart's pounding now. 'And this is where?'

'Our office is just a short ride out of the centre of Washington DC and the hotel is in the same street.'

In Washington DC. Wow. Gulp.

'Have you been out here before?'

'No,' I admit. 'Never.'

'Our capital city is very beautiful. You'll love it.'

I'm sure that I would.

He frowns. 'You have a passport, right?'

'Oh, yes.' One that's gathering dust in the back of a drawer in my hall cupboard.

'I'll leave you to think about all that,' Max says. 'It must be a lot to take in.'

He's not kidding.

'I take it that it's late evening there?'

'Yes.' Sort of.

'Sleep tight.' There's a hint of a smile at his lips. 'Goodnight, Christie.'

'Goodnight,' I say.

Then he hangs up or logs off or whatever the correct term is. I sit there in the silence of my parents' garden and the gathering night and wonder what to do now. There's no way that I can go. How can I leave Finn and trot off to Washington for a week? Especially now. How could I take a week off work? Max didn't mention who'd pay for my airfare. What if I have to stump up for that? How much is it to fly to Washington these days? I've no idea.

I put my head in my hands and try to think. I imagined that they'd just send me some products and leave me to my own devices. I had no idea that it would be so ... so what? So formal, I suppose. Or so much commitment.

Finn comes out carrying the tray of tea, Mum in his wake. He puts it down on the table. 'Did that go all right?'

'Yes,' I say, trying not to sound as flat as I feel. But it didn't. How can I tell them that and burst their happy bubbles as well as mine?

Chapter Twenty-Four

Finn has another headache, so blinding that it makes him sick. I keep him off school for the day. The school secretary rings me and demands a sick note from the doctor. I roll my eyes, take it on the chin and make an appointment with our GP. Which, obviously, means Finn missing even more school and me taking time off work.

We see a locum this time and he looks little older than Finn. However, while I explain what's happened, he seems to pay a lot more attention than our own doctor. When I've finished talking, he gets up and examines Finn. He listens to his chest, checks his eyes, takes his blood pressure – all manner of things.

'How are you feeling now?' he asks Finn.

'Tired,' Finn says. 'All the time.'

'Headache?'

'Always there,' he tells the doctor. 'Sometimes worse than others.'

'His chain-eats Paracetamol,' I chip in. 'But it makes no difference.'

'Back at school now?'

Finn nods.

'No more fainting?'

'No.'

'I see that Dr Jessop recommended fresh air and exercise. How's that going?'

Finn and I exchange a guilty look. Probably

one abortive session of jogging and a jump round the living room on the Wii Fit doesn't really count. 'Small steps,' I confess. Perhaps I should get me and Finn Fitbits to use. They're all the rage, aren't they?

The doctor frowns at his screen. 'You've been in here a lot over the last year. I think it's about time that we ran some blood tests. See if we can't find if there's any underlying problem.' He looks at Finn kindly. 'How does that sound?'

'Cool,' Finn says.

'Could it be migraine?' I suggest. 'I took him to the opticians and there aren't any problems with his eyes.'

'Let's make a decision when we get Finn's bloods back. I'll see if we can get you straight in with the nurse to save you taking more time off school.' He calls the receptionist and then says, 'Sorry, but there are no appointments free until next week.'

'That's fine.' At least something is being done. The locum writes out a sick note which seems completely pointless other than to appease the school, but there you go. 'Thank you, doctor.'

If I hurry, I can drop Finn off and still be in work by lunchtime if I catch the train.

While I'm at work Max Alexander sends me the details of the training retreat in a chatty email. Not only is it in Washington DC but the next one is in a week's time and he wants to book me on that. I suppose that, quite understandably, he wants to strike while the iron's hot and all, but how can I possibly do it? Does he not realise that

I have a full-time job and responsibilities? How can I just drop everything and scarper out there?

An hour later the chatty email is followed by a quite legalese contract – and I know about these things. There's nothing untoward in it but, if I sign this, then I'm committed. And I want with all my heart to do so. But how can I?

It's a lot of work and it would mean going away for a week. Soon. By myself. Finn is due to have his blood tests. I don't even know how I'll raise with Robyn that I'd like time off – though I'm owed a bucket load. Suddenly, the joy has gone out of this and I'm just anxious. Mum and Dad are thrilled. So is Finn. But, frankly, I'm terrified. My heart is heavy and my brain doesn't seem to be able to come up with a solution.

While I'm sitting, head in hands, trying to make myself think clearly, Robyn comes over and drops some papers on my desk. 'This needs doing for Blake Hotels versus Extremely Dodgy Development Company.' Then she stops short. 'Are you all right, Christie? You've got a face like a wet weekend.'

'Thanks.'

'You know what I mean.'

'I've got a lot going on,' I tell her.

'Finn's OK?'

'Yes. Sort of. Just stressing about his blood tests.'

'You need a night out on the town, lovely,' she says. 'When did you last let your hair down and have some fun?'

'I had cottage pie and cava at Mum and Dad's the other night.'

'I'm not entirely sure that counts,' is her view.

134

She perches on the edge of my desk. 'Look, Imogen and I are going out tonight. We're just going to Chinatown for a meal, nothing fancy. Why don't you join us? It's ages since you've seen Imo.'

'The last time was probably your Christmas drinks party.'

'Too long then.'

'I don't want to play gooseberry, if you two were planning a date night.'

'We weren't. It was just some food and a few drinks. She'd love you to come.'

I'm hesitant. It would mean missing the coach home and paying for another train journey.

'Stay overnight with us,' she says, as if reading my mind. 'Phone your mum and tell her to put the dinner in the dog, for once. Finn can stay with them for one night. It won't hurt him.' She puts her hand on my arm. 'I know he's a bit unwell at the moment, but you can't wrap him in cotton wool. You can't be there for him 24/7 and, if you don't look after yourself, you'll collapse in a heap too.'

'I know. I know.' I feel close to tears.

'I'm not getting on your case,' Robyn says. 'I want to help. Good Chinese food and copious amounts of Tsingtao beer are very therapeutic.'

'It's sounding better by the minute.'

'Make that call,' Robyn says. 'I'm your boss. I command it.'

That brings a smile to my face. 'How can I refuse when you put it so nicely?'

She grins at me. 'Imo's at home. I'm sure she'll have something in her wardrobe to fit you. I'll get her to bring in some jeans and stuff so that you

135

don't have to party while looking like a legal secretary.'

Suddenly, a girls' night out sounds like a great idea and, when Robyn drifts off again, I pick up the phone to call Finn.

Chapter Twenty-Five

So, after work, Imogen brings me in some designer jeans – which fit much better than my own Asda ones – and a posh shirt with kingfishers on it. I apply another layer of make-up in the staff loos and feel trendier than I have in years.

I ring Finn again. 'Are you sure you don't mind?'

'Go out and have fun, Mother.'

'I can get a train home now if you want me to.'

'I'll see you tomorrow,' he insists. 'Nana's just putting dinner out.'

'What are you having?'

'I don't know. Some sort of carb fest.'

'I love you.'

'Bye, Mum,' he says and hangs up.

Robyn, Imogen and I head out to Chinatown. It feels like we're entering a different world as we go under the traditional Chinese arch in Gerrard Street. The strings of red lanterns stretch across the street, swinging in the breeze and giving the street a party atmosphere. Arm in arm, we pass the colourful shops and supermarkets selling anything from ready-cooked crispy ducks to Bruce Lee T-shirts. Even at six o'clock it's buzzing down here with tourists and the after-work crowd.

We manage to get a table in Robyn and Imo's favourite restaurant and the waiters make a fuss of us as they're regulars. I think it must be nice to have a regular restaurant where they all know you. I'm not sure that the McDonald's on the A5 counts, which is Finn's go-to place. They order a whole heap of dishes that we all dig into: wonton soup with warming ginger, soft Beijing dumplings filled with spicy minced pork, gong bao chicken in a delicious sweet and sour sauce, lavished with chillies and crunchy peanuts, the accompanying dan dan noodles sublime. The food disappears too quickly, the beer flows.

My friends laugh and giggle together. Imo flirts outrageously with me while Robyn tuts. Three beers in and it feels as if a heavy weight is starting to lift from my shoulders. Imo has us in stitches doing impersonations of some of her celebrity clients and I can understand what Robyn sees in her. She's fun, feisty and fearless. All that I aspire to be. Robyn looks at her with such love in her eyes that I feel a pang of jealousy. No one has ever looked at me like that. I don't think I've ever truly loved or have been loved. Liam and I had our own half-hearted version of it and, to be honest, we did our best. But I didn't realise at the tender age I got married that this kind of love could exist.

Three hours later we pour ourselves out of the restaurant and into a cab. We go back to Imo and Robyn's place in Hampstead. It's one of those enclosed by a high brick wall and gates that only open if you know the pass code. It has huge windows and a flat roof and is the polar opposite

137

to my cosy little Victorian terraced house. Inside, it's like a show house. And, at this point, I think I'm glad that our homes are so different. As befitting the gaff of an interior designer, Robyn and Imo's house is the ultimate in good taste. The garages are at ground level and when you enter the front door you then go up a flight of stairs lit with pink lights to the main living area. The kitchen, dining area and living room is one big space that flows seamlessly. They have real oak floors, white leather sofas, one of those big arc lamps that are so trendy. There's an ultra-modern woodburner at one end of the living room and Imo lights it. Instantly, the room feels cosier. In the kitchen, Robyn pulls out some shot glasses and a bottle of toffee vodka. The units in here are white, high-gloss and the cooker looks like something off a spaceship. There are no bowls of dog biscuits or cat toys on the floor. Note to self: I must never, ever invite them to my house.

We make ourselves comfortable on the sofa in front of the warming fire and have a few shots. Imo curls up on the cashmere cushions and is soon asleep.

'Have you had a good evening?' Robyn asks as she snuggles against me.

'Brilliant.' My eyes are a bit gozzy and my limbs feel all spongy and nice. 'You're right, I really needed it.'

'There's something else on your mind though,' Robyn says. 'I've known you long enough to be able to tell. Spill the beans to Aunty Robster.'

Perhaps the drink has loosened my tongue as I forget that, essentially, I'm talking to my boss and tell Robyn, my friend. 'There was a call-out for designers in a craft magazine a few weeks ago. I did some designs and thought nothing more of it, but Mum sent them in.'

'Good old mum.' Robyn tops up our glasses and we hit the vodka again.

'The long and the short is, I've been chosen.'

Her eyes widen. 'Seriously?'

'Yes.'

'You clever old stick. I knew you had it in you. We should wake Imo and celebrate.'

I hold her arm. 'There's a snag. The CEO wants me to go on a training course – a retreat – as soon as possible.'

'Not unexpected.'

'It's next week.'

'Ah.'

'And it's in Washington DC.'

'Well.' Robyn puts on her thoughtful face. 'There's no doubt we've a lot on at work, but we could fiddle things around. You've got loads of holiday due to you – even I know that – and a week isn't the end of the world.'

'I've taken so much time off with Finn that I feel really guilty going.'

'Don't,' Robyn says. 'You've given the firm eighteen years of sterling service. Now it's time for a little payback. We'll cope.'

'You make it sound so easy.' More vodka. 'I can't bear to leave Finn either. He's just not right. They keep saying it's just to be expected for a lethargic teenager addicted to computer games, but I'm not so sure. He has blood tests booked for the week I'd be away.'

'Your mum can take him, surely?'

'Yes, but–'

'You're a person too, Christie. Everything you've done in the last fifteen years has been for Finn. You've never had a chance like this before. It's something you're good at. Do it for you.'

'I've never even been on a plane by myself before. The thought terrifies me.'

Robyn holds up her glass. 'A few shots of this is all the courage you need. It's not that difficult, Christie. Don't let being afraid hold you back in life.'

'That's what I love about you,' I say. 'You're so wise.'

She leans forward and kisses me on the cheek, tenderly, her lips lingering. 'Then you must do exactly what I say.'

'So you think I should go?'

'With all of my heart.'

'You need to look at the contract for me.'

'Will do.' She grins goofily at me. 'Does this mean that you're going?'

'Yes.'

'Excellent. That's the spirit. Faint heart never won crafting designing contract. We need to toast this.' She fills up our glasses and we chink them together.

'You also need to appreciate that if I drink any more vodka you will get absolutely no work out of me tomorrow.'

'I can live with that.'

We knock back the shots. 'To you, Christie,' she says. 'My beautiful friend. May this be the start of something big.'

And perhaps it's because I'm in a haze of alcohol but, right now, I feel as if I could conquer the world.

Chapter Twenty-Six

Robyn and I have massive hangovers and spend the entire morning groaning at each other and vowing never to drink again.

'It was fun though,' I tell her as we meet in the kitchen for another caffeine hit. 'We should do it again.'

'Never,' she says.

That makes me giggle and the noise reverberates in my head. Gah.

Robyn raises an eyebrow. 'You're still planning to do this training thing? I don't want you going back on your decision in the cold light of the day.'

'I'm not.' I get a shiver of terror as I say it. 'I'm definitely doing it.'

'Good. Now let's both go and pretend to work.'

I do actually manage to be quite productive once I get going and I catch a later coach home to assuage my guilt at being fit for nothing for the first few hours of the day. It's a nice surprise to see Henry sitting there.

'Hello.' He moves so that I can take the window seat.

'Hi.' I flop down, exhausted.

'I missed you this morning,' he says as we move off into the traffic on the Embankment, heading north and towards home.

'I went out on the razzle with my boss,' I explain. 'Well, she's more friend than boss. We had a heavy night. I stayed over at her place. I'm worn out though. I can't cope with alcohol and a late night these days.'

'Not the party animal any more?'

'I don't think I ever was.' I remember all the vodka shots we knocked back last night and my stomach roils just a little bit.

'Were you celebrating?'

I pause. It didn't quite start out like that but, by midnight, I'd say that we were. Plus I haven't actually shared anything about my crafty leanings with Henry. Men, generally, aren't interested in that stuff. Then I think, why not? I should blow my own trumpet every now and again. If I don't, then who else is going to do it? 'Yes,' I say. 'We were.'

'Big contract at work?'

'Not exactly.' I get a little flutter of excitement. 'A big contract for me. I've been taken on by an American craft company as their UK designer.'

'I know nothing about that sort of thing,' Henry admits, 'but it sounds like a big deal.'

'It is. For me.'

'Then we should go out for a drink to celebrate.'

'It will have to wait until I've forgotten how dreadful this celebration made me feel.' Then Henry smiles and there's a bit of sadness in his eyes. He clearly thinks that I'm giving him the brush-off again. 'But I'd really like that.'

He brightens instantly. 'Good.'

'The only snag is that I'm going to America for a training course.'

'Oh,' he says.

'It's all been a terrible rush, but the company are keen for me to get started as soon as possible. It might be as early as next week, if I can get it all organised at such short notice.'

'That sounds great.'

'Can we put it on hold until I come back?'

'Of course. Anytime.'

As we push slowly through the rush-hour traffic and turn onto the M1, I look at him properly and I think that he really is a nice, kind man. I should make time to go out with him. We enjoy each other's company on the coach – perhaps it could be more than that. If he keeps asking and I keep saying no, then he might give up and, as you're now well aware, there has been precious little romance in my life. If this is the new me and I'm embracing new challenges in my life then, surely, I should grasp this opportunity too.

Chapter Twenty-Seven

I sign the contract. I book a flight. Contemporary Crafts are paying for the ticket. Premium economy! Yay. Go me. I get lots of emails from Max Alexander. I take the week off work as holiday. I'm all ready and packed. I'm truly outside my comfort zone.

I've also spent an inordinate amount of time preparing 'retreat swaps' as instructed in my email from Max – little gifts for each of my fellow designers that say something about where we're from. I managed to get little canvas bags from eBay and have decorated them with a flowery interpretation of the Union Jack in a Cath Kidston print and some charms. I picked ones that I felt represented both me and England – a teapot, a butterfly, a cat and 'handmade with love' stamped on a heart. Then I put in a pack of I Heart London tissues, a small bar of Dairy Milk and a pretty notebook. Is that all OK? I've nothing to judge this against and hope I've hit the right note.

Now it's stupid o'clock on Sunday morning and I'm having a last-minute faff while Finn, still in his pyjamas, is lying arms above his head on my bed. Eric is trying to burrow his way into my case.

'Stop it, dog,' I say, to no avail. I'm folding something that doesn't really need to be folded, so, exasperated at myself, I just stuff it in my case. 'I could stay at home, Finn. It's not too late for me to cancel.'

'It is,' he points out. 'Pops is coming to pick you up for the airport in about ten minutes.' He props himself up and sighs. 'Go. Do this for you, Mum.'

'That's what Robyn said.'

'Then listen to her.'

'You'll be all right with Nana and Pops?'

'I spend most of my week with them, anyway. Plus Nan's a better cook than you.'

Can't really argue with that.

'What about the cats?'

'They don't care whether we live or die.' Pixel lifts his head and looks at me in utter disdain as if to confirm that Finn is quite right. 'They'll be fine. They'll lie on your bed and never move.

Pops will come in every day to feed them.'

'You'll look after the dog?'

'Eric will be in heaven all week. He'll have un-limited treats and walks. He only gets neglected when we look after him.'

Not exactly neglected, but he certainly gets fewer walks and immeasurably fewer treats. 'I don't want to leave you to have your blood test by yourself.'

'Mum, a nurse is going to stick a needle in me. It'll take a minute. Probably less. Nana will drive me there.'

'You won't forget to go?'

'No. I won't forget to shower every day either or wash behind my ears.'

'Clean pants too?'

'It's a given.'

'I'll miss you.'

'It's a week, Mum. You'll be back before you know it.'

A car pulls up outside.

Finn gets off the bed and looks out of the window. 'That's Pops now.'

'I'm not ready.'

'Then you'd better stop fussing and get a move on,' Finn says. 'I'll let him in.'

My son goes downstairs. I make sure for the tenth time that I have all my retreat swaps packed, then hurriedly shove everything else in my case. I'm in a state of mass panic. I have no idea what to take. Will it be casual or will they be all dressed up to the nines? The only advice Max gave was to leave lots of space in my case as there'd be a lot of products to bring home, but that's not really much use.

A moment later, Dad pops his head round the bedroom door. 'I'll lift that for you, love. It looks like it weighs a ton.'

'I'm supposed to be packing light.'

'Ah. Like your mother does.'

With a bit of huffing and puffing, I close the case and lock it. With a grimace and a jokey hand on his lower back, Dad hefts it and takes it to the car. I'm on the verge of tears already. I've never flown long-haul before. The furthest I've been is Spain and that's just a few hours. This is a proper flight.

'You could come to the airport with us,' I say to Finn.

'That would be really dull and I'm not dressed,' my son says, oblivious of my need to have him there. 'You'll only make a scene.'

Teenage-speak for I'll want a hug and cry until I've got a blotchy face and my eyeballs are fit to fall out of my head.

'When I've had my breakfast, I'll walk Eric round to Nana's.'

'If you feel faint or anything, you'll tell Nana right away?'

'Yeah.'

I embrace him in a bear hug whether he likes it or not. 'I love you,' I say to Finn. 'I'm going to miss you like mad.'

Less grudgingly than usual, Finn hugs me back. 'Have a blast. Kick the arse of the other crazy crafting ladies.'

'Language, Finlay.' I let him go. 'I'll call you every night.'

'I'll be fine. Stop worrying.'

'I'm a mother. That's my job.'

'If you stand here stressing, you're going to miss your flight. Or at least make Pops drive over thirty miles an hour to the airport.'

He has a point. So with one last kiss, which he doesn't wipe off his cheek, I go and join my dad in the car.

'I'll be back soon,' I say to Finn.

'I'll come with Pops to the airport to meet you,' he concedes. Which is his way of saying that he'll miss me too.

At the airport, I have two glasses of wine in the departure lounge even though it's way too early and I have sworn off strong drink. It doesn't make me feel any less terrified, but at least I go through security without hitch or panic attack and now I know which gate my plane is going from. While I'm pondering why air travel has to be so daunting, Finn texts me.

Have a great time, Mum. You've been gone for three hours now and I'm still alive. F

Cheeky.

I send him lots of kisses and don't mention that I've been drinking. I think, briefly, about texting Henry and reminding him that I won't be on the coach next week, but my courage fails me and I don't. I look round duty free and buy nothing. Then I go, way too soon, to the gate and sit there watching other people board who all look like seasoned travellers and not scaredy cats.

Eventually, it's my turn. When I get on the plane, I sit in my comfy seat and have another two glasses of wine – very small ones – then I stop. I should watch a film or have a sleep or something and not booze myself into oblivion. After all, I don't want to arrive in Washington a bit squiffy and whirling my bra around my head while shouting 'woo hoo' and singing 'I Will Survive'.

This is my Big Chance and I Must Not Blow It.

Chapter Twenty-Eight

Max Alexander told me that there would be a driver to meet me at the airport, but when I finally get through customs and into the airport, the man himself is standing there waiting for me with a sign that says, *Welcome to the USA, Christie Chapman!*

I stop dead in my tracks. I know that I've seen this man on Skype, but I hadn't quite expected him to look like this. In real life, he's so handsome it hurts. He's wearing a black linen shirt, open at the neck, and dark blue jeans. Nothing out of the ordinary, but it's the way that he wears them and I can't even tell you what that is as my brain seems to have been scrambled. There's a presence about him, an aura. Perhaps this is what charisma looks like. This is a busy airport with a thousand people around, but I'll swear that there's no one here but him. And I wonder if this is something similar to how Robyn felt when she first saw Imogen.

He's scanning the crowd and hasn't yet noticed me, but then his eyes fall on me and his face breaks into a smile. I like that. 'Christie,' he shouts and holds up a hand.

Willing my legs to work properly, I make my way towards him. 'Hi,' I say, sounding ridiculously shy. 'What a welcome party. I hadn't expected you to be here.'

'I don't do this for all my designers, you know,' he says with a twinkle in those piercing blue eyes. He looks at me as if he's drinking me down. 'Only the chosen few get a personal welcome.'

Before I go weak at the knees, thankfully, Max takes my case from me and puts his hand under my elbow while he steers me through the crush of people and towards the car park. 'Did you have a good flight?'

'Perfect,' I tell him.

He glances at me again, those eyes taking in everything, and I wish that I'd gone to the cramped bathroom on the plane and put some more make-up on or combed my hair or generally done something to make me look like less of a skank.

We get to Max's car, which is a sleek black Mercedes, and he loads my suitcase into the boot.

'I'll take you straight to your hotel, so that you can check in,' he says as we sweep out of the airport. 'Are you feeling jet-lagged? If you're not too tired, we could go to dinner later.'

I'm feeling like a woman who's having an out-of-body experience. Is that the same as jet lag? But I feel I can't miss out on this opportunity. 'I'd like that.'

'I can show you some of the sights of our city by night. It's a fantastic place.'

149

We hit the freeway or the highway or whatever they call it here and it all looks so strange and American, yet so familiar from all the television programmes I've watched over the years. 'I can't believe I'm actually here,' I say.

He laughs. 'It's great that you could come. I know it was short notice.'

'I'm really looking forward to it.'

'Good.'

We chat about nothing in particular until we reach a more suburban area. When we turn into a broad, tree-lined street, Max points out a low white building with big windows. 'That's the office.' It's a nice-looking place and attached to it is a small warehouse.

'You'll be having your training there all week.' Another hundred metres or so and he swings into a forecourt on the opposite side of the road. 'And this is your hotel.'

It looks very swanky. Distinctly more upmarket than the usual Travelodge or B&B that I normally stay in.

A porter comes to the car and Max jumps out to give him my bag. Then he escorts me into reception and helps me to check in as I look round in wonder. The hotel has an old-fashioned style, a quiet buzz. The foyer is all plush carpet, towering pillars and blood-red leather sofas. I feel as if I should whisper. A few minutes later and I have my keycard in hand.

'We'll have an early dinner so that you can get a good night's sleep. It will be a busy week.' He checks his watch. 'I thought we could do Italian? Casual. Wear jeans. I'll pick you up here at six?'

'Sounds good to me.'

Then he's gone and I make my way up to my room which, I kid you not, is the size of my flipping garden. I'm on the tenth floor and have a lovely view across the city. It's all decorated in delicious shades of chocolate and vanilla with dark wood furniture. Across the bottom of the bed is a beautiful, embroidered oriental throw. This is, by far, the nicest place I've ever stayed.

I unpack quickly and I phone Mum and Dad to let them know I've arrived safely. Then I speak to Finn.

'Did you get an upgrade?' he asks.

'No.'

'Huh.' He's not impressed by that.

'Premium economy was nice enough and the hotel is really lovely. My room's huge. I'm thinking about holding a party here.'

'Cool.'

'I'll call you tomorrow when I get home from my training. Get up early in the morning,' I warn. 'Don't make Pops pull you out of bed.'

'OK.'

'I miss you all,' I say.

'Don't,' Finn instructs. 'Have a good time. You deserve it.'

'I'll call every day.'

'I'm going now. You're getting slushy.'

So my son hangs up and I have a little cry. This is the first time that I've left him for any length of time and it feels so strange.

Mustering myself, I run the biggest, deepest bath you can imagine and then lower myself in with a grateful and heartfelt, 'Ahhhh'. I am tired now and there's nothing quite so revitalising as a long, hot bath.

I wash my hair, slather myself in the complimentary body lotion and then get myself ready for my dinner with Max. I'm feeling slightly overwhelmed by it all, and I hope that agreeing to dinner with my boss was a good idea.

Then, too quickly, six o'clock is here and I take the lift down to the foyer. Spot on time, Max has already arrived and the beat of my heart goes up a gear when I see him waiting for me. I feel slightly underdressed in jeans even though these are my very best pair. Mine are from Primark whereas Max's would appear to be designer label. But I've put on a pretty white shirt with tiny, multicoloured hearts on it and, besides, it's too late to change now.

He's smiling again as I walk towards him and it does weird, weird things to me.

'You look great,' he says and he sounds sincere. 'Ready?'

I nod and he leads me outside. This time it's another flash car and someone else is driving. Max holds the door while I slide into the back seat, then he climbs in next to me. And I try to keep my nerves in check.

Chapter Twenty-Nine

The restaurant is homely and busy. My jeans are fine. Max recommends the chicken parmigiana and orders a bottle of Barolo.

'You're the only overseas delegate who was able to come out to this session,' Max says, leaning close so that I can hear him above the general hubbub. 'So I want to spoil you.'

He'll get no complaints from me.

'It also gives me the time to tell you more about my company and my plans for the future. Though I'll come in and introduce myself again in the morning to the rest of the team. I have big plans for the UK and I want you to be fully versed.'

The food arrives and it's delicious. A good call by Max. However, I do look at all that tomato sauce and wonder if a white blouse was the best choice. I resist the urge to tuck my napkin in my neck like I used to do for Finn when he was smaller.

The wine is smooth and heavy and I'll have to watch what I drink as it's going down too well. I don't want to pass out at the table. It's not really the impression I'm hoping to make. Sip, Christie, sip!

'How long have you been crafting?' he asks.

'Most of my life, on and off. My mum is well into crafts. Anything you can think of: knitting, crochet, painting, soft-toy making, origami, cross-stitch, embroidery. She's done it all at one point. And, as an only child, I did it all too.'

Max smiles. 'Me too. My parents ran a popular craft barn in our local area. It's long gone now. It was sold on to a big corporation, but they demolished it to make way for new office space.'

'That's sad.'

He shrugs. 'They'd call it progress, I guess.'

I notice his hands on the wine glass and his fingers are long with impeccably manicured nails. His watch is probably worth more than my poor, clapped-out car.

'My brother Don and I used to help behind the counter at weekends. Mom used to do the demonstrations and make-and-take sessions. Dad ran the admin side. It was a great little family business. They wanted to retire, but I wasn't ready to take it over from them. However, Don said he wanted to take over the reins. He only ran it for a year more and then took the decision to sell up. I don't think his heart was really in the business. He was offered a good sum for it, but I think it was a mistake now.'

'What did you do?'

'I joined a big creative arts company based in New York. I had a great time working for them and climbed my way up to marketing director. When Mom and Dad died they left me some money and I decided it was now or never if I wanted to set up on my own. So I bit the bullet and started Contemporary Crafts and we've been going now for just over two years.'

'That's very brave of you.' Makes my ambition to start a little online business seem quite modest.

'The competition is tough here. There are a lot of craft companies but we're holding our own. In a small way.' He laughs at that. 'I'm not going to lie to you, Christie. Trading conditions are hell, but I want to expand. I'd heard that the UK market is still, largely, untapped.'

'I'm sure this area of crafting could be grown.' Does that sound suitably businesslike?

'That's what I was hoping you'd say.'

'I'm really keen,' I tell Max. 'I think that I could help you. I have lots of ideas.'

'We'll talk more as the week goes on,' he promises. 'For now, tell me a bit more about yourself. That was your son who answered the phone?'

'Yes. That's Finn. He's my only child and he's fifteen now. And he's very proficient at die-cutting butterflies.'

We both laugh.

'It's not often you hear that,' Max concludes. 'But I was the same. I earned my pocket money by getting crafting kits ready for my mom.'

'Me too. Now I've passed it on to Finn.' I take a sip of the Barolo. 'He's a good kid. My mum and dad help me out a lot with him. He's staying with them this week. It's the first time I've been away without him.'

'You should have brought him.'

'I think the school might have objected to him taking holiday in term time.'

'Ah.'

Max doesn't need to know about the ongoing battle I'm having with them.

'No Mr Chapman?' he enquires.

'No.' I shake my head. 'Divorced for about five

years now. We still get on quite well, but he's remarried and lives in Dubai. So he's not really in our lives on a daily basis.'

I wonder if there's a Mrs Alexander. There's no wedding ring on Max's finger, but then not all men wear them. He's too perfect not to have been snapped up, I think.

Then I meet his eyes and say honestly, 'The lack of romance in my life is probably why I spend my evenings watching Creative World and making cards.' I don't want to mislead him and make out that I'm some shit-hot crafting demon when everything I do has, up to now, been very low-key.

'That's a terrible admission, Christie.'

'But true.' I hold up a hand. 'Don't get me wrong. I love it. Me and Finn are a tight little unit. There's not a lot of room in it for anyone else.'

'I understand.'

'Crafting has been my saviour,' I tell him, 'but I'm very much an amateur. Occasionally, I take a stall at a craft market, but mostly I sell my stuff to friends and colleagues.'

'The majority of people who are big noises in this business started out that way.'

I think of super-smooth Sheridan Singleton and wonder if she's ever stood in her wellies in the freezing cold rain behind a market stall. I expect not.

'I don't want you to think I'm anything I'm not.'

He looks at me over his glass. 'I believe that you're underestimating your talent. Your designs were head and shoulders better than anything else that was submitted.'

'Really?'

He nods. 'You have a real flair for it and your designs are fresh, young.'

That's good to hear. 'I do a bit of a blog too,' I tell him. 'But I don't devote enough time to it. I could do more.'

'If we can support you with that, I'll make sure it happens when you're ready to step it up.'

'Thank you.'

He pushes his plate aside and sits back. 'Shall we have coffee? You're looking tired now, Christie. I was going to give you a whistle-stop tour of our city, but that can wait until another evening.'

Much as I'd like to extend my evening with Max, I have to confess that my eyes are feeling a bit rolly and that mahoosive bed in my room looked very comfortable. Plus I won't have to share it with two duvet-hogging cats and a farty dog.

'I'd really love to see Washington, but the sensible side of me says that I ought to go back to the hotel. I want to be as fresh as a daisy tomorrow.'

He smiles at me and calls for the bill. Then we get in the big, flash car again and he whisks me back to the hotel.

When we pull up outside, Max turns towards me and says, 'I hope you've enjoyed our evening, Christie. I'll see you in the morning.'

Then he leans forward and, for one mad minute, I think that he's going to kiss me. But, instead, he reaches past and opens the door for me. My heart decides to pound anyway.

I catch his eyes which are glittering in the darkness and say, 'Goodnight, Max.'

He grins at me. 'Goodnight, Mary Poppins.'

Chapter Thirty

If I was jet-lagged last night then I am in a total state of shock this morning. It's just hit me that I'm in America and I have important stuff to do. I'm missing Finn like mad and I'll try to talk to him at lunchtime when he'll just be getting home from school – hopefully. Even though I'm sure he'll be none the worse for me not being there. I manage a light breakfast in the hotel, despite my stomach being tight with nerves. Then I walk across the street to the offices of Contemporary Crafts. My mouth is dry even though I've downed three cups of coffee and two glasses of water.

The receptionist greets me warmly and takes a few minutes to check me in. I have a look round me while she taps into her computer. The offices are bright and stylish. On the walls there are huge photographs of projects using the Contemporary Crafts dies.

A moment later, a young woman in a smart suit arrives and shakes my hand. 'Welcome to Contemporary Crafts, Christie,' she says enthusiastically. 'Max has told us a lot about you. I hear you're from England.'

'Yes.'

'Well, I sure hope you enjoy your time with us.'

I follow her to the lift and am taken up to the first floor. As we walk along the corridor past a large office, I catch a glimpse of Max inside and he looks up.

'Hey,' he says. 'Good morning. Did you sleep well?'

'Yes. Thank you.' Like the dead. I didn't even notice that my usual menagerie weren't in bed with me.

'Come in.' He waves me into his office. 'I'll take it from here, Donna.'

'Sure.' Donna disappears.

I shout, 'Thank you,' to her retreating back.

'How do you like this?' Max asks, holding up a hand to show me one of the designs I submitted to him in full Technicolor on his wall.

'That's lovely.'

Laughing, he says, 'Yeah. It is.' Then he slips on his suit jacket. 'How do I look? I want to make a good impression on my new designers.'

'I'm sure they'll be bowled over.' It's a dark grey suit, slim-cut, worn over a white shirt with a black tie. It's very flattering. I wish I'd dressed up more, but at least I'm not wearing jeans. I hope all the other ladies aren't Sheridan Singleton lookalikes.

He takes my arm and ushers me down the corridor. 'I'm going to be introducing the company and then you'll have your first crafting session. We have some of our partner companies coming in to show you what they're made of.'

'I'm terrified,' I admit.

'Don't be. You earned your place here. Relax and enjoy it.'

We swing into the room together and I'm surprised to see it decorated with balloons and streamers. On the back wall there's the American flag and, right next to it, the Union Jack. There's

159

a buffet table full of cake and cookies and some of the other ladies are already tucking in. It feels more like a party than a training session. There are ten desks set out and each one has a decorated place name, notebook and pen.

Donna is at the front and claps her hands. 'Ladies, if you can take your places we can introduce ourselves and then our CEO, Max Alexander, would like to say hello.'

Duly we go round the room and say a little bit about ourselves. As Max told me, all the other designers are from different parts of the USA – I'm the only one from the UK. It terrifies me that they all seem so professional. Some have their own successful blogs with thousands of subscribers, a few have their own craft channels on YouTube or have done television work. I can hardly bear to tell them that I'm only a newbie who happened to be in the right place at the right time.

When it's my turn, I say, 'I'm Christie Chapman from England. I've been crafting all of my life, but this is my first opportunity to do something more formal with my skills and I'm really grateful for the chance.'

I get a little round of polite applause, as everyone else did, and my fear subsides a bit.

Then Max stands at the front and tells us about the company history and I try to listen to him and not just gape at him inanely. I find his handsome face far too distracting. Plus I try not to think about his smile or his gorgeous eyes or of us having dinner together last night or him taking me to the hotel in his flash car. I wonder what the other ladies would think about that?

160

When he's finished, he leaves the room with a wave to us all and then a designer comes in and gives a presentation. She's clearly very famous in America as all the other designers go into raptures. I knuckle down, concentrate and try to learn as much as I can.

Every now and then a bell goes and I quickly ascertain that's the signal that we're to be given treats. Paper, dies, glitter, embellishments are loaded onto us and some of the ladies burst into tears at such generosity while I try to hang on to my British reserve. It is all rather overwhelming and, by lunchtime, I'm wishing that I'd brought a considerably bigger suitcase.

The day goes by in a blur of crafting, cake and creativity. I cause hysteria by asking for a cup of tea rather than drink the soda that's on tap. But I feel that I'm holding my own among my fellow designers. There's a quiet air of competitiveness and I'm glad that I've spent so many hours watching the Creative World channel. As it turns out, it was time not wasted!

Chapter Thirty-One

That night we're taken to an elegant restaurant in the upmarket and historic area of Georgetown and I'm glad that I've packed a few nice things to wear. I've chosen a dress in pink chiffon courtesy of TK Maxx and it's perfect for the setting. Pastel-coloured flowers and candles adorn the tables in the cream dining room. The crystal glasses shimmer in the light. The flute of champagne that I drink before dinner goes down very nicely.

I had, literally, ten minutes between finishing our sessions and changing for dinner in which to call home and check that all was fine. It was. Thank goodness. As it will be too late when I get back from dinner, I promise to FaceTime Finn tomorrow.

My fellow designers are all friendly and I sit next to a lady called Mandy from Arizona.

'Is he not the hottest thing you've ever seen?' She nods towards Max – the only man among us. Tonight he's wearing a dinner suit and looks very debonair. I'm seated at the other end of the table away from him. Shame.

'Yes,' I agree. I could hardly do otherwise.

'He's always in the trade magazines here,' she intimates. 'Always with the prettiest woman on his arm.'

'No Mrs Alexander?'

She swigs her wine, then shakes her head. 'No. Never married. A confirmed bachelor if ever there was. I've heard he likes to play the field.'

'Oh.'

Mandy shrugs. 'If I looked like that, honey, so would I.'

We giggle at that – perhaps a bit raucously, as Max glances down towards us and raises an enquiring eyebrow. I feel myself flush red.

'He's a very genial host though,' I counter. 'I've really enjoyed today.'

'This is my second training retreat,' Mandy

162

says. 'They're a great company to work for. You won't find better. Max is generous to a fault. I wish he'd give my husband some tips.'

More giggling.

Mandy tells me that she has her own YouTube channel and I vow to have a look at it. Maybe this is something I need to do myself. I tell her about home and what it's like to live in England to which she confesses she's never been out of the USA and rarely out of Arizona. Mandy vows to visit London one day.

Then, after a sumptuous dinner, we exchange the gifts we've all crafted and my little bags of Englishness go down very well. All too soon, it's time for us to leave.

As we're heading out, Max takes my arm and guides me to one side. 'Wait here for me,' he says, hurriedly.

'OK.'

Then he strides off to say goodnight to all the other designers and I'm left standing alone and more than a little awkwardly in a corner of the foyer.

When I begin to wonder if he's forgotten about me, he comes back and says, 'Are you up for a whistle-stop tour of Washington?'

'Now?'

'It's beautiful at night.'

My heart gives a little surge of joy. 'That would be lovely.'

His too-blue-to-be-true eyes twinkle when he answers, 'I thought so too.'

Chapter Thirty-Two

I think my dad was right. I am an international jet-setter now. At least I feel like it as I'm driven through the late-night streets of Washington DC in the back of a limousine. Seriously. Max pours us both a glass of champagne from the bar on board and we sit back to take in the sights. The traffic is still busy and I'm not entirely sure where we're going and, to be perfectly honest with you, I don't care. I'm happy just being here with Max and a glass of champagne. I could even do without the champagne.

Max strips off his jacket and loosens his bow tie. He undoes the neck of his shirt and sits back with a sigh. I'm mesmerised. He lifts his glass and proposes a toast. 'To international relations,' he says.

'Indeed,' I respond and we clink glasses. If my mum and dad could see me now!

'Ready for your personal tour of the sights?'

I laugh. 'I think so.'

The driver weaves in and out of the lanes of traffic and Max points out various buildings and landmarks as we go. 'That's the National Space Museum,' he says. 'It's a great place to visit. Your son would love it.'

'He would. Finn's a complete space geek.' I get a pang of longing for my son and hope he's OK at home without me. Though, no doubt, Mum will be force-feeding him cake.

'You'll have to bring him with you next time.'

I had no idea that there would be a next time, but it's heartening to hear Max talking like this. We turn into Constitution Avenue and I recognise the outline of the US Capitol building illuminated against the evening sky. The driver turns and parks the car.

'May I present the Washington Monument,' Max says.

'Wow.' The brightly lit icon needle stretches high ahead of us.

'Have you got comfortable footwear?'

Thankfully, I'm all for flats these days. 'Yes.'

'Would you like to walk?'

'I'd love to.'

'We'll meet you back here,' Max tells the driver. 'But we may be a while.'

It's almost sunset as we climb out of the limo, but the evening is still warm, balmy. Max grabs his jacket from the back seat.

'Here. Put this round your shoulders.' He drapes his tuxedo around me and I accept it, gratefully, even though I'm not really cold. The faint scent of his aftershave lingers on it.

'Thank you.'

Together, we set off towards the monument. There are plenty of tour groups around with their guides giving them their spiel, but Max and I walk in silence up to the base. We take in the monument and I snap some truly inadequate pics on my phone. Max continues my tour and we stroll slowly alongside the reflecting pool that I've seen so often in films. There's not a breath of air and the water is as still as a millpond, the last vestiges of the sunset echoed perfectly in it. Ahead of us, the Lincoln Memorial looms impressively in the landscape.

'This is magnificent,' I say.

'Isn't it. This is a good city to live in,' Max tells me. 'Like anywhere, it's not without its problems, but I've been here a while now. Long enough to call it home. I can't see me moving anywhere else.'

'You weren't brought up here?'

'I was born in New York, but I've lived in several different states. What can I say? My parents liked new challenges.' He grins at me. 'But I've been here for the last ten years.'

'I assumed you'd always lived here.'

'No.' He laughs. 'And my grandparents were Scottish. I keep meaning to trace my family tree, but I haven't got to it yet.'

'One day.'

'We all need to know where we come from, right?'

'I suppose so.'

'You enjoyed today?' Max asks.

'Yes. Very much so.'

'Good.'

'I learned so much more than I expected. My head is buzzing with ideas. But I feel like a rookie compared to some of the designers.'

'Don't undersell yourself,' Max says. 'Every single one of you brings something different to the table.'

We reach the Lincoln Memorial and it's every bit as grand as I could have imagined. There are couples sitting hand in hand on the steps and, in a move that seems so very natural, Max takes mine in his as he leads me up towards the impressive statue of Lincoln. We take a few turns around the legendary president and then go to sit on the steps ourselves. Max leans back and our arms touch. I feel a tingle all through me and wonder if he felt it too.

The sun has gone, but the moon is high and bright. The Washington Monument is reflected in the mirror of the pool and it's a wonderful sight.

'This is a very beautiful city,' I sigh. It also feels ridiculously romantic, sitting here with this handsome and charming man. Max is so close that I could turn and kiss him right now. And, believe me, the temptation is very strong as I'm experiencing feelings that I haven't had in a long, long time. Then I recall what Mandy said, that Max Alexander is a player who likes a string of beauties on his arm and it would serve me well to remember that. He probably dates supermodels and the like. He might be being attentive, but that's his job. It's in his company's interests to keep me sweet. What else would he see in a middle-aged, single mum?

He stands up and takes my hand again, tucking it into the crook of his arm. 'Let's see some more.'

I'm happy to oblige.

We walk back through the Constitution Gardens and up to the White House. It looks reassuringly solid and I take some more photos through the railings.

'There's a great bar in the hotel right across the street, if you'd like a nightcap?'

'That sounds as if it would round off the evening nicely.'

Max laughs. 'I love the way you talk. I could listen to you all night.'

I sigh and think darkly, That could easily be arranged.

So, we leave the wondrous sights of Washington behind and head to the hotel that Max has earmarked. We go down into a subterranean bar. It's all plush and rich, red colours with a dark wood bar. It has an air of old-world seduction and I feel as if I'm stepping back in time. As befitting the Washington vibe, there are framed caricatures of famous politicians on the wall. The lighting is low, the conversation noisy. Max steers me to a booth.

'I recommend the Old-Fashioned Lafayette,' he says as he scans the cocktail menu. 'It's like a Manhattan but with Dubonnet rouge.'

I have no idea what any of that means. I'm a dry white wine kind of girl.

'It's good,' he assures me as I hesitate. 'You'll like it.'

'Then I'll accept your recommendation.'

The waiter comes and Max orders. I sit and watch him. I've never been out with anyone like this before. He's so assured, so confident and oozes masculinity. My ex-husband and I grew up together and had quite a sheltered life. He'd have been so out of his depth in this situation – as am I. I'm so used to doing everything myself – even making the smallest of decisions – that it feels nice for someone to take control for once.

We drink our cocktails, which are most potent. Then we have another. We laugh and chat and talk about everything and nothing. It feels as if we're old friends but, perhaps, that's the power of cocktails.

'As much as I hate to, I should call the driver,' Max says when we've drained our second glass. 'You have another busy day tomorrow.'

I could sit here all night with Max, which both thrills and worries me. No matter how much Old-Fashioned Lafayette I drink, I should keep both feet firmly on the ground.

The car comes for us and as we get in I give Max his jacket back, though I'm reluctant to part with it. We're both quiet on the journey home and, shortly, we're back at my hotel.

'I've had a lovely evening,' I say. 'Thank you so much for taking the time. I know you're a busy man.'

'The pleasure has been all mine,' he says smoothly.

Then, before I can think better of it, I kiss him chastely on the cheek and skip out of the car.

When the driver pulls away, Max turns and watches me out of the back window.

Chapter Thirty-Three

In the morning I have a slight Dubonnet-induced headache and I don't even know what Dubonnet is. I text Finn to tell him I love him and miss him. I get two kisses in reply. Better than nothing. I'll try to catch him this evening when he's not at school. Then I call my parents who tell me that all is well. I chat to them more about what I did yesterday, including my twilight tour of Washington DC, but omitting the bit where I had cocktails in a late-night bar with my boss and wanted to snog his face off. I don't want them to think that I'm having too much fun.

I spend all day in the classroom again. We have lots more cake and even more treats and my mountain of crafting goodies continues to grow at an alarming rate. I'm going to have to go out and buy another suitcase at this rate, or even charter my own jet. Some of the top experts in their field come to talk to us and I find it all so inspiring. Their energy and passion for their products is infectious and I'm trying techniques that I've never even heard of before. A woman shows us how to apply ink straight to the dies, or use them to cut foam and create your own stamps. Something I would have never thought of before. One of the most well-known designers in the States comes in to lead a session. She has a grungy/inky style and I learn that making crafts doesn't need to be neat and precise. A whole new world has opened up to me and, by the end of the day, I'm ripping card, shaping flowers, inking edges, flicking glitter around. It's all very liberating.

The only downside is that I don't see Max all day. Perhaps he's busy or maybe he feels as if I've had more than enough of his time. It's nice that he singled me out to give me a tour of his city, but I don't tell any of the other ladies where I went last night. I'm sure there would be more than one of them who'd like to have been sitting in a bar on Max Alexander's arm drinking cocktails until the

170

wee small hours. Then I think maybe tonight one of them will be and depress myself intensely. Gah.

A surfeit of caffeine has swayed away my headache and I've tried one or two of the baked goods that are rolled in at regular intervals to try to boost my sugar levels. I think it works, so I join the general feeding frenzy and have some more.

We're given a project to complete during the afternoon using a new set of dies that the company are launching in the market. These dies are called Elegant Afternoon and are based around an art-deco motif created by one of their top designers in the USA. I make a stylish card with Tiffany blue card stock and use silver glitter paper to cut out an ornate frame which I mount on the card, embellishing it with pearls and cut-out blooms and my signature paper hearts. I think Audrey Hepburn would approve. At the end of the day I'm awarded first prize and my confidence is given a much-needed boost.

The other ladies decide that they're going to take taxis into Georgetown for dinner and ask me to join them. I agree as I don't want to be left in the hotel alone. Late afternoon, when our little fingers are crafted to the bone, we leave the conference room together to head back to the hotel. As we're walking down the corridor, I peep into Max's office and glimpse him standing, staring out of the window over the street. He's talking on the phone and doesn't see us as we pass. Meh. There goes my chance to chat to him today, I suppose.

In my room, the very first thing that I do is FaceTime Finn. I can't tell you how much I'm missing my boy.

171

'Hey, Mum,' he says and waves at me on the screen.

'Hello, love. Is everything OK?'

'It's fine. Don't stress.'

'You're not fed up at Nana and Pop's?'

'I'm overfed. Does that count? Nana doesn't know what low carb is.'

'Neither should you,' I say. 'You're a growing boy.'

'What are the other women like?' Finn asks, trying to divert me.

'Nice,' I tell him. 'They've all been very kind. They all seem so much more experienced than me, but I'm holding my own. I got first prize for a card I made today.'

'Way to go, Mum!'

'I know. I feel like I'm back at school.' Although, I was always rubbish when I was at school. How's the headache?'

'Not so good,' Finn admits. 'I came home a bit early this afternoon. I'm going to bed soon.'

'You haven't forgotten your blood test?'

'No. It's in my phone and on Nana's calendar next to the fridge. We're all on the case.'

'Maybe we should give swimming a try when I get home.'

'Maybe we shouldn't,' Finn says.

I decide not to pursue the subject. 'Is Eric missing me?'

'No,' Finn says. 'He has The Cupboard of Forbidden Treats to occupy him.'

'Ah.' Then I catch sight of my watch. 'I'm sorry this has to be short, but I'd better be going. I'm having dinner with the other ladies tonight.'

'Cool. Have you seen anything of the James Bond-looking guy yet?'

'Yes,' I admit. 'He took me on a sightseeing tour of Washington DC last night. We rode around in a big limo and had cocktails at a swanky bar.'

'Oh, yeah?' Finn says. 'And here's me thinking that you're working.'

'It wasn't like that, he was just being kind as I'm the only overseas designer. Don't tell Nana though or she'll be buying a wedding hat.'

'Your secret is safe with me, Mother.'

'You should come with me next time. We went past the Space Museum. It looked amazing. I bet you'd love it here. Anyway, I must go. Love you to the moon and back.' I've said that since he was about five and there's no way I'm stopping now just because he's a teenager.

'Love you more,' Finn teases.

I hang up and hurriedly get ready.

In a bustling part of Georgetown I have a lovely dinner with the ladies. The restaurant is in an old house and I have cheese-stuffed meatballs which may be the most calorific thing I've ever eaten. I follow it with Key lime pie just to make sure that I'm hardly able to move when I get up from the table. The meal is taken at a slow pace and we have plenty of time to talk more about where each of us is from and how we got started in crafting. Although we're all of a similar age, we're quite a diverse group too. Most are married with children, a couple are resolutely single and have lots of cats. I'm the only single mum with a teen-ager and a full-time job. They all wonder how I'm

173

going to fit this in. I wonder that myself.

By nine-thirty, we all decide that we need an early night and order taxis to take us back to the hotel. Half an hour later, all my make-up is off, my hair's in a scrunchie so it doesn't turn into a tangled mess in the night and I'm in my comfiest Disney PJs with Minnie Mouse motif. I'm sitting on my bed, trying to digest my enormous dinner and flicking through what's on the hotel television channels to find something to watch for half an hour before my head hits the pillow.

There's a knock at my door and I mute the TV. I forget to look through the security spyhole and assume it's one of the other women, so I'm surprised when I open the door to find Max Alexander standing there.

'Hey,' he says.

I stand there frozen with shock in my pyjamas, not knowing whether to cover myself or to brazen it out. At least I'm not sporting rollers or a face pack. But I could easily have been.

'Oh, I'm sorry,' Max says, when he takes in what I'm wearing. 'You're ready for bed.'

Max, on the other hand, isn't ready for bed. He's wearing a grey cashmere sweater and jeans and looks as if he's ready to head out to a jazz club or something.

'I thought you and Minnie might like to step out.' He supresses a smile. 'I don't mind a three-some.'

That makes me flush even more and I blurt out, 'We went out to dinner in Georgetown,' as I sort of fold my arms across my chest, aware that my nipples are unfettered and may be quite

174

excited to see him. 'Then we all decided that we needed an early night.'

Max's expression is apologetic. 'I should have thought this through.' He leans on my doorframe. 'I was tied up with meetings and calls all day and didn't manage to get along to say hi. I just thought I'd swing by to see how today went and see if you wanted to go for a nightcap again. You could tell me how the retreat is going.'

'Right,' I say. 'Let me put some clothes on. Give me five minutes.' Who wants to go to bed when I can have another night out with a hot man? Not me.

'No, no, no.' Max holds up a hand. 'It was rude of me to come up here unannounced. I can only apologise. I should have called first.'

'My time is yours,' I tell him. Suddenly, I'm desperate to spend some time with him and not curl up for a sad single's early night. 'I need five minutes. Literally. Maybe ten. I'll see you down in reception.'

'Go to bed,' he says with a shake of his head. 'We'll catch up tomorrow. There's plenty of time.'

But there isn't, I think. We're on Tuesday already and I fly home on Friday. There's hardly any time at all. But what can I do? I don't want him to go, but I've no idea how to keep him here. If I offer him a drink out of my minibar that would sound so wrong. It would be me, him and a great big super-king-size bed.

'Goodnight, girls,' he teases.

I *so* need to reconsider my nightwear.

Max turns to walk away.

This is my moment to stop him. 'What about

175

tomorrow night?' It's out of my mouth before I can stop it.

He looks back at me and purses his lips in thought. 'Do you like pasta?'

'Love it.'

'I make a mean lobster linguine with chillies. Come to my apartment for seven. I'll send a driver for you.'

'Thank you.'

He looks as if he's about to add something else and then thinks better of it. Instead, he smiles sadly and says, 'Goodnight, Christie.'

'Goodnight.' I close the door and lean against it. 'Damn, damn, damn,' I mutter to myself, when I really mean 'Stay, stay, stay.'

Chapter Thirty-Four

I didn't sleep. Of course I didn't. I lay there awake thinking of all manner of things, not just Max Alexander. Although, I'll admit he did feature quite heavily. I might as well have got dressed and gone out on the town with him. Damn and double damn.

All the other ladies look quite chipper this morning, as if they've benefitted hugely from their early night. Perhaps they don't have a stupid schoolgirl crush on the CEO of Contemporary Crafts that kept them tossing and turning until dawn.

We have a talk by one of the gurus of the American crafting channels. Debby Huntly is as glossy and as smooth as Sheridan Singleton but with an East Coast accent of some sort. I get a pang of envy. Sheridan would not be languishing in cartoon pyjamas if her hot boss turned up at her door late at night. Gah.

Debby's demonstration is done at breakneck speed and I have trouble keeping up. Even three cups of strong coffee don't kick-start my brain. When it comes to creating our own project, I put in a feeble effort and, deservedly, do not get first prize. I could kick myself. I've come here to get everything that I can out of the week – this is my big break, the opportunity of a lifetime. I'm a minnow in a pond of ... whatever fish are very big. And I'm annoyed with myself for being too tired to focus. I'm no expert in jet lag, but maybe that's catching up with me too.

At lunchtime, I rush out to the nearest store to buy a bottle of wine and some chocolates to take to Max's tonight and I get butterflies in my stomach just thinking about it. I choose the nicest ones I can find in the hope of making a good impression on my host. Then I hide them in my handbag so that none of the other women see them and think I'm drinking and eating alone.

Maybe it's the quick blast of fresh air or the good talking-to I gave myself, but I fare much better in the afternoon. Yet every time we turn to our own projects my mind drifts to tonight. What am I going to say? What will I wear? Having never eaten lobster before, will I even like it? I answer none of these things by the time five o'clock comes and it's time to leave for the day.

The other ladies are going out for dinner

together again and I make my excuses. How can I tell them, though, that I'm having dinner with Max Alexander – at his apartment! I realise what a difficult situation this is creating for me. These are lovely girls who've been so friendly and I don't want to lie to them.

I stagger back to the hotel, laden down with more crafting goodies. I'll have enough to open my own shop at this rate. Back in my room, I check in with Finn and Mum and Dad. A big fat nothing has happened since I've been gone and I should just stop worrying about everything so much. My phone pings and it's a text from Henry Jackson.

Hope you're having a great time.

Is it terrible to admit that I haven't even given him a thought this week? And he's such a nice man. I quickly text back.

Brilliant. Thank you. Very productive. See you on the coach! I debate adding kisses, but don't. They might be misconstrued as something more than being friendly.

As time is marching on, I quickly get changed. Jeans and a nice shirt. I don't want to look as if I've made too much effort. But, then, I don't want to look as if I haven't made any at all. So I do put on my make-up extra carefully and get the GHDs to work on my hair. I opt for my modest heels instead of the Converse I've been wearing all day. I'm ready and waiting in reception when the car arrives for me.

It's only a short ride to Max's apartment and the driver drops me off at the door. This is a smart and quiet street of apartment buildings, lined with trees. Some have old-fashioned façades, but this one is quite modern – red brick, but with an ultra-modern steel porch over the front door. It looks as if it could be quite a fancy address. There's a long line of buzzers inside the foyer and I find Max's and press.

A second later he answers, 'Hey.'

I lean forward and self-consciously talk into the speaker. 'It's Christie.'

'I'm not expecting anyone else,' he says with a laugh. 'Come up. I'm on four.' And he gives me the number.

Heart in mouth, I take the lift and then find Max's apartment a couple of doors down the corridor. He's already standing on the threshold waiting for me.

Tonight he's wearing a black T-shirt and grey linen trousers. His feet are bare, his hair damp and it looks as if he's just got out of the shower. He wears casual as well as he does smart.

'Glad you could make it,' he says and I'm thrilled that he looks genuinely pleased to see me.

Then we have that moment when neither of us know how best to greet each other. We've got past the handshake stage, but I'm sure we've not yet reached a hug. I risked a chaste kiss with a couple of cocktails down my neck, but I can't be that brazen fully sober. I'm pleased to see that Max has a moment of shyness, because every time I've seen him so far he's been cool, sophisticated and in control.

So we both stand there a bit awkward and then I hold out my gifts. 'Just a little something for having me.'

'Thank you.' He takes them. 'I'm delighted you

179

could be here.'

I don't mention that I'm missing a dinner with my fellow designers and feel as guilty as hell about it. Max heads towards the kitchen and I follow him.

'Can I get you a glass of champagne?'

'Lovely. Thank you.'

'Dinner won't be long.'

'It smells delicious.' While Max busies himself at the counter, popping the cork and pouring out two glasses, I have a good look at his apartment.

It isn't huge, but it's incredibly stylish. The front door leads straight into the living space and it's all open plan. The kitchen – everything stainless steel and black marble – is to my right. Ahead of me are the lounge and dining areas. There are windows all along the far wall which are covered with white slatted shutters, so that the light is diffused. There are comfy sofas in an oatmeal colour with a dark wood coffee table between them and a rust-coloured Indian rug on the floor. His cushions, in toning shades, are beyond tasteful. I wonder if he's had an interior designer in. Surely no man is capable of choosing such exquisite soft furnishings. On the wall there's an enormous television as befitting a bachelor. The dining area has a dark wood table big enough to seat four. I notice that it's set for two and there's a candle, already lit, in the middle. There's an antique sideboard with a large silver mirror above it and, on the end wall, a modern painting of a woman in shades of red, blue and brown. Adele's *25* is playing and the whole place has a mellow air. This would be a good place to relax and I vow to do something to revamp my own home. You would not accidentally sit on a cat in somewhere like this.

Max brings me a glass of champagne. 'Your home is gorgeous.'

'I confess that I had help in putting it together,' he says. 'I have a friend who's an interior designer. This is very much her influence.'

I wonder quite how friendly they are and then check myself. That's really none of my business.

'If it was up to me, it would probably all be black.' He raises his glass. 'To you. And to Contemporary Crafts. Long may you be associates.'

'I hope so.'

'You're enjoying the retreat still?'

'Yes. I'm loving it. I've learned so much. It's going too quickly though.' We have a final dinner on Thursday night and then I fly home on Friday morning. Why is it when you want things to go slowly, they speed by twice as fast?

'I have great plans for the future, Christie, and I'd like you to be involved in them.'

'Sounds intriguing.'

'Later,' he says. 'Now I have some linguine to attend to.'

Chapter Thirty-Five

Turns out that Max Alexander is a great cook too. Sigh. The man must be rubbish at something, right?

The linguine is delicious, all creamy, and the

lobster has a delicate flavour. The champagne is as sparkling as the conversation. We have the chocolates I bought and coffee afterwards. Then we move to the sofas and Max sits next to me. He lowers the lights and, is it just me, or does the music become distinctly more smoochy?

We talk about Max's plans for the business during dinner and I like that he's ambitious. He doesn't say as much, but I'm sure if I play my cards right, the expansion into Europe could involve me. It's also slightly weird to be spending the entire evening talking about crafting with a man. That can't happen that often and it's nice to have such a strong mutual interest. I also find out that Max loves to cook as much as I love to eat. We like the same music and the same films too. If only I could find someone like him who didn't live in another country.

'I admire you,' Max says. 'Managing a full-time job and a kid. Doing this as well.'

'Sometimes it's difficult to keep all the balls in the air,' I admit, the champagne having loosened my tongue. 'But I do it all for Finn. He's my life.'

'I had a great childhood,' he says. 'I always thought that I'd be settled down by now with a family of my own.' He looks at me and I think his eyes are filled with regret.

'Why didn't you?' The drink is making me bold too.

'Never found the right woman,' he says. 'Maybe I played the field too much.' He takes a swig of coffee. 'Don't get me wrong, I've dated some incredible women, but I don't think that they were the type looking to settle down either. Maybe it's

182

too late now.'

'Have you ever come close to marriage?'

'No.' A slightly rueful shake of the head. 'I've recently come out of a long-term relationship.' Then he laughs. 'Well, long-term for me. Meg and I had over a year together, but she was always too high-maintenance, too needy. I was more like a parent to her than a partner. She took it very badly when it ended.'

'Your choice?'

He nods. 'It was the most difficult thing I've ever done.'

'You didn't dump her by text.'

'Part of me wishes I had. I might have saved myself some pain. Instead, I faced it like a man.' Then he's serious. 'I hurt her very badly and I never wanted that. She'll never forgive me.'

I wonder if she's still in love with him.

'I've stayed away from dating ever since. It's all too raw and maybe I'm too wary for commitment now.'

'I haven't been on a date since my husband and I split,' I admit. 'I don't get home from work until at least seven o'clock – my commute takes me two hours each way. Finn and I have dinner with my parents at least three nights a week and I'm too tired to go out any other night. At weekends I just want to be with my son. We never have enough quality time together.'

'It sounds nice though.'

'I don't really know anything else, Max,' I tell him. 'All this, being here, eating lobster, drinking champagne, staying in a fancy hotel, it's all alien to me. I'm a very homely person.'

'That's what I like about you,' he says. 'You're very honest and straightforward. It's a long time since I met anyone quite like you.'

Max moves closer to me on the sofa and my emotions go into overdrive. He takes my glass and sets it on the coffee table. My heart moves into my throat. It would be so very easy now to inch towards him. Then I remember what Mandy said about him being a player. Perhaps this sob story about his ex-lover is all a ruse to make me feel sorry for him. I can't let it cloud my judgement though. This job, this role, is too important for me to jeopardise it. Max Alexander is my boss and I feel compromised by being here. Tomorrow I'm going to have to lie to the other lovely ladies about how I spent my evening and that's not me at all. I *am* honest and straightforward.

'I should go,' I say to Max. 'I've seen the programme for tomorrow and it's going to be full-on.'

'It is,' he agrees. But neither of us move.

'I really *should* go.'

He gently curls his fingers around my wrist and his voice is husky when he says, 'Stay.'

What for? Another drink? Or for the night? What exactly is he proposing here?

'I'll get you back to the hotel before breakfast.'

Ah. He did mean what I thought he meant.

'No one would be any the wiser.'

And that's the rub, isn't it? It would have to be in secret, clandestine, and I don't like the sound of that at all.

'This isn't me, Max,' I tell him. 'I haven't had a relationship in five years. I don't do one-night stands. I never have.' His eyes never leave my

184

face. I wonder what kind of lover Max Alexander would be. I think he'd be tender and sensual. But I'm basing this on so little. He might have a rapacious appetite and throw me round the bedroom like a thing possessed. Suppose he wanted me to do things that a gymnast might struggle with? You already know how easily I get out of puff. The thought terrifies me. If I stayed, it would involve getting naked with Max and I can't see myself doing that at all. I can't go from pasta, to sofa, to bed so quickly. 'You're my boss. It would put me in a difficult situation.'

'Yet you're here,' he points out.

I laugh. 'Don't think that I'm not very tempted.'

'But you're going to turn me down nevertheless?'

'Yes,' I say. 'Have I spoiled the evening now?'

'Well,' he muses, 'I had hoped that it wouldn't end *quite* so soon.'

'I've had a lovely time. The food and the company were both wonderful.'

'However, I should call my driver now?'

'I think that would be for the best.' I feel stupid and unworldly. He's probably used to much more sophisticated women with tightly honed gym bodies who wear cheese-wire thongs and would think nothing of spending the night with him. But I haven't made love in so long that I'm not exactly sure what to do any more. I might be completely rubbish and how embarrassing would that be? I'm not sure I could bring myself to share my curves and cellulite with him.

Not so subtly, he moves away from me and punches a number into a phone. 'Hi, Ben, Ms

Chapman is ready to go back to her hotel now. Thanks.' He hangs up. 'Five minutes.'

'Thank you, Max. I do appreciate all that you've done for me.'

'You're welcome, Christie,' he says. However, I'm sure I detect a distinct cooling of his ardour. 'I'll walk you down to the foyer.'

'There's really no need.'

'This is a great neighbourhood,' he says. 'But not so much at night. I'll see you safely to the car.'

I stand up, awkward again, and grab my handbag as he leads the way out of the apartment and to the lift. We stand in silence as we wait for it.

As we travel down to the ground floor, he says, 'I hope you have a great day tomorrow. You've got Cathy Kubrick coming in and she's a legend. You'll enjoy her session.'

So that's how we'll play it. All chat will be kept to business now.

The car is already waiting when we emerge from the lift and into the foyer. Ever the gentleman, Max opens the door for me.

'I've had a really lovely time,' I say before I get in.

'Me too,' Max agrees.

Then I slide into the back seat and the car drives away. I turn to see if Max is watching, but he's already gone back into his building.

Chapter Thirty-Six

The final day of the retreat speeds by too quickly. Max hasn't been around at all, though I keep hoping he'll come through the door. I'm pretty sure that it was the right decision to go back to my hotel last night, but that's not to say that part of me doesn't regret it. There's a posh farewell dinner tonight that he's hosting, so I know that I'll see him there, at least. I wonder if he'll invite me back to his apartment again and my tummy flutters at the thought.

Still, I have a lot to keep me occupied. We have some great sessions at the retreat – as they've all been – and I have my crafting mojo back. I made a little box that would be fabulous for wedding favours. I made it in pearlescent white paper and decorated it with a cut-out silver tiara and some feather detail. Then I crafted a heart-shaped photo-frame, decorated with blossoms and sprigs of leaves and edged with lace. I manage to focus and make some of my best work. I win two fab prizes – a selection of pigment inks in glorious hues and a heat gun with a little case of glittering embossing powders. I know if you're not a crafting person this may cause you to glaze over, but to crazy crafting ladies this is catnip. There's lots of whooping and hollering as more gifts are showered on us. I'm tempted to join in, but can't quite bring myself to let go. Too British by half.

When I get home, I'm going to have a renewed effort with my blog and I've certainly got lots to talk about and plenty of tips and projects to show my few followers. I really want to push on and try to organise an online shop, with Finn's help. Perhaps that's going to have to wait until after his exams as I want him to concentrate on his GCSEs. Still, it gives me a little excited buzz. At the end of the last session, we are deluged with more products, after which we all toast each other with Prosecco and there's lots of sobbing and exchanging of addresses. I shed a few tears myself. This week has been a roller coaster of emotions. I'm proud of myself simply for being here. It's given me an amazing boost in confidence and a renewed enthusiasm.

And then there's been Max Alexander.

Sigh. I don't really know what to say about how I'm feeling towards him. He's the total package and I've experienced emotions with him that I thought I never would. But It's Complicated, as they say. He's my boss. He's way above my league. Plus, even if there is chemistry between us – and I'm pretty sure there is – then what would he really see in me long term? My life is on a completely different plane to his. He'd probably only want a few nights of fun, but I'm not sure that I'm brave enough to risk that. I don't think I'd come out of it feeling enriched. I think I might be scarred. This is my last night here though. If he asks me to spend the night with him again, what will I do? Should I resist again or should I think sod it and throw caution to the wind for one night? But what if he's absolutely fantastic in bed and I experience the best sex I've ever had and fall hopelessly in love on the spot? It happens! Or is that just in films? He's already said that he doesn't want to become emotionally entangled with anyone. He couldn't have made it any more clear. If that's the case, will I then hanker after him for ever, spending my nights tortured by my un-requited love? More sighing.

I've no doubt that, in different circumstances, we might have had something going for us. Perhaps I'm kidding myself. Maybe he just likes to make a conquest on every retreat.

Then that's it. First thing tomorrow morning, I'll be packed up, on a flight home and heading back to good old Blighty and harsh reality. Some of these ladies have been on more than one retreat, but I have no idea if I'll ever be offered another chance to come out here. I can only hope so.

Yet I'm so looking forward to going home and seeing my family too – I'm missing Finn like mad – but part of me doesn't want to leave so soon. I'd be happy for this to go on for ever. I've been spoiled and cossetted to the nth degree and it would be nice if it didn't have to end. See what my head's like? However, it is what it is. Nothing can change that now.

Along with the other ladies, I haul another load of crafting stuff gifted to us by Contemporary Crafts and their partners to the hotel – for the last time. I think I'm actually going to have to leave all my clothes here in order to take it all home. Then my new friend Mandy says, 'I have my car with me. I can throw everything in the trunk. I'm happy to give you my spare suitcase, if that will help you.'

'That's so kind. I never expected to be taking so much back with me.'

'It's always like this. Next time, you'll know. Do you want my luggage?'

'I'd love it. But how can I return it to you?'

She waves a hand, dismissively. 'No problem. Gives me the perfect chance to buy new. I'll unload and bring it to your room.'

'Thank you.'

'I knocked last night,' she says as an after-thought. 'When we got back from dinner. We were having a drink in the bar and I thought I'd see if you wanted to join us. There was no answer.'

'Maybe I was in the bath,' I say. But I know that I sound guilty.

I'm sure that Mandy looks at me in a way that says she doesn't really believe me, but perhaps I'm simply feeling a bit mean for duping them when they've been so welcoming. I wonder what they'd say if they knew I'd been to Max's apart-ment for dinner? I wonder what they'd think if they knew there'd been infinitely more than that on offer? I daren't mention it to Mandy as I don't want to hear that's what he does at every retreat – single out someone for special attention. I feel slightly sick thinking it.

I get ready for dinner, putting on the poshest dress that I possess. It's black, tightly fitted and flatters my curves. At least, I think it does. I had it for a work do a few years ago and it hardly ever gets an airing. I take extra care with my hair and make-up. Then I put on the pair of tottery heels that I've brought with me. Going all out for this one!

Before I leave, I call Finn's mobile but there's no answer. I bet he's run out of credit. So I try my parent's landline which also rings out – which is odd at this time of night. Normally, they'd be well settled in front of the telly by now or, quite possibly, as it's about ten o'clock at home, getting ready for bed. I try Mum's mobile – not really holding out as it's usually in the bottom of her handbag and turned off. She's the only person I know who can make a ten pound credit last about two years.

As I'm about to give up, Mum answers. 'Hello, love.'

'Hi, Mum. I was just about to hang up. There was no answer for your home phone.'

'Oh,' Mum says but doesn't throw any light on why that might be.

'I can't stay. I'm dashing out to our farewell dinner, but I wanted to check in and remind Dad that my flight gets in at about quarter past eight, all being well.'

'He'll be there, love. It's on the calendar.'

'Great. Sorry, I can't chat for long.'

'Bye then.'

'I'm not in that much of a rush, Mum. Put Finn on quickly.'

'Oh, right. Er... He's gone to bed.'

'Has he? At this time?' My son is usually very reluctant to have an early night.

'He was a bit tired.' Mum is sounding really odd.

'Is everything OK?'

'Yes, fine. We can talk properly tomorrow when

191

you're home.'

'About what? Has Finn behaved himself? He's not been spending all night playing computer games.'

'Not that I know of,' Mum answers, all cagey.

'He's been going to school without a fuss?'

'Oh, yes.'

'And his blood test went OK? You did go?'

'Yes, yes.' She sounds a bit exasperated with me. 'You go out and enjoy yourself. Dad will be waiting for you. He'll check the flight's on time on the internet.'

That'll be a big thing for Dad.

I can't think what else Finn might have been doing as he's normally so well behaved. It will have to wait until tomorrow, I suppose. 'Tell Finn I love him.'

'Of course.'

'Right.' Even though I can tell that something's not quite ringing true, I have to run otherwise I'll miss the start of the dinner. 'Better dash.'

'Love you, Christie,' Mum says and hangs up.

'I love you too,' I say into a phone that's already dead.

Chapter Thirty-Seven

We're taken by a fleet of taxis into the heart of the city and dropped off at the hotel opposite the White House where Max and I had cocktails the other night after our walking tour of the sights.

The hotel is glamorous and elegant. Everyone is dressed up to the nines. Including Max. He's wearing a black, well-cut suit with a white shirt. His dark blond hair is smoothed down and he's freshly shaven – the usual hint of stubble gone. He looks more handsome than ever and my hormones go into overdrive. I tell you, my poor heart doesn't know whether it's coming or going these days.

We're given a welcoming cocktail when we arrive and I hang on the periphery of the group feeling strangely nervous. Other members of Max's company who we've yet to meet are there too and, surreptitiously, I try to follow him as he moves around introducing them to my fellow designers. Max is working the room. He smiles when he glances up and sees me, but doesn't come over to talk. I don't get to meet the rest of the team. At dinner, I'm seated at the other end of the table from him.

The wine flows and the dinner is divine, course after course of tempting dishes are placed in front of us – crab salad with fennel apple coleslaw, salmon with tarragon butter sauce and parmesan polenta. To top it all, there's a milk chocolate and red fruit tart with raspberry Chantilly cream. As much as I love my mum, going back to her cottage pie and lasagne is going to be a serious shock to the system!

Despite all this lavish food, there's a hollow gnawing pit in my stomach. Every time I let my gaze wander to Max's end of the table, he's chatting away to one of the other ladies – Sandy or Candy or Brandy – and she looks just as smitten as I am. Maybe tonight she'll be the one taken

193

back to his apartment. I feel sick and it's not due to the richness of the food.

After dinner we have drinks in the bar and I think about brazening this out and going up to Max. I'm crushed that he's spent the entire evening just blanking me. I down my wine to give me some Dutch courage and just as I'm about to gird my loins to march over and say 'hello' to him, I'm thwarted.

Another man comes to stand in front of me. 'Hi.' He holds out a hand for me to shake. 'I'm Dean Steadman. I work for Max as his executive vice-president of marketing.'

'Hello. Nice to meet you.'

'This is my wife, Martha.'

There's a pretty and very slim blonde on his arm. I shake hands with her too and say, 'Hi.'

'I'd normally be around all week for the retreat,' Dean says, 'but we're only back from honeymoon yesterday.'

'Oh. Congratulations.' They both look at each other in an appropriately loved-up manner. They obviously make a great couple. 'How fabulous. Where did you go?'

'The Maldives,' Martha says.

Dean and Martha tell me about their wedding and honeymoon. It all sounds idyllic, yet I have to try not to look over their shoulders to see what's happening with Max and his posse.

'I wanted to meet you as I'm going to be your manager at Contemporary Crafts,' Dean tells me.

That pulls me up short and I don't know how well I hide my surprise. I'm actually going to be working with this man, not Max? Suddenly, he has all of my attention.

Dean smiles encouragingly. 'Max has shown me your designs from this week and they're great. I love them.'

'Thank you.'

'It's wonderful to have you on board. I look forward to working with you. Hopefully, we can make some inroads into the UK market. Anything you need in terms of support or materials, don't hesitate to email or pick up the phone. I'll do my best.'

My heart plummets to my tottery heels. So I'm not even going to be dealing directly with Max? This man is going to be my contact in the company. Though I'm shocked, maybe that's a good thing. I can have a purely professional relationship with Dean and not feel compromised. I should have known that I wouldn't always be dealing with the head of the company. What was I thinking? I don't know, but it doesn't stop me from feeling disappointed that, going forward, my contact with Max might be, at best, minimal.

Dean tells me more about the company and some of the excitement comes back, though the punctuation of laughter from the other end of the room is somewhat distracting. Eventually, Dean and his lovely wife shake my hand again and move on. I'm left standing alone. This, surely, would be the moment for Max to come and talk to me. But he stays put and I go to find another group to latch onto.

At the end of the evening, the fleet of taxis arrives for us and I realise that time is running out for me. Max has successfully avoided me all evening and has made his point. It's been a lovely evening, nevertheless, and I feel fired up for when I get home and start designing. Plus, I haven't thrown myself at the company CEO and that can only be classed as a good thing.

We're heading towards the exit when Max finally catches up with me. My spirits soar and I do wish that they wouldn't.

'I hope you've had a great time with us here, Christie.' There's warmth in his voice, but there's no little spark present as there previously was.

'I've thoroughly enjoyed it,' I tell him honestly. 'This has been one of the best things that I've ever done.'

'I'm glad to hear it. And you've met Dean?'

'I have. I look forward to working with him.'

'He's a fantastic guy. The best. Anything you need, just ask him.'

'He said.'

Max steps back from me. 'I hope you have a good flight home and I'll be in touch.'

'Thank you, Max.'

He nods and moves on to say more or less the same thing to Mandy who's standing next to me. I feel bereft. I know that it was me who made the choice to go home last night, to tell him that anything more would be too complicated. It seems as if he has taken me very much at my word. I feel sick at his aloof manner. It's as if he's taken one of my paper hearts and has scrunched it up and thrown it on the floor at my feet.

We're ushered towards waiting taxis and I hang back, wondering if anyone else will be climbing into Max's limo with him tonight. But everyone else gets into the taxis too and I see Max heading to his car alone. I'm standing in line waiting for the last taxi and I see Max turn to look towards me. He hesitates for a moment, but then he carries on and slides into the back seat. His car pulls away. So that's how it ends. I've had a fabulous time, but I can't help but feel deflated too. Would I have thrown caution to the wind and spent the night with Max tonight? I guess I'll never know. Yet I can't help feeling slightly hurt that the choice wasn't mine to make. I wish we could have parted on more friendly terms.

It's hugs all round when I get back to the hotel, and more tears. I pack as soon as I get back to my room, grateful that Mandy has kindly donated her suitcase to me. I don't know what I would have done otherwise. Then I lie in bed awake all night, staring at the ceiling. The room's too hot and I'm restless but I can't bear the air conditioning. The cold air on my body just makes it too sensitised and in places that I really don't want sensitised. Gah. It's a good job that I don't have a mobile phone number for Max because I'd be seriously tempted to call him. And that would be wrong. So very wrong.

Chapter Thirty-Eight

My eyes are full of grit when I get up a scant few hours later to catch my flight. As the taxi pulls away, taking me to Dulles International, I look across at the Contemporary Crafts office which is all in darkness and I wonder if I'll ever come back here.

Check-in is at ungodly o'clock and I spend my time before departure sitting in a soulless airport café staring at a cup of coffee, unable to stomach anything. Eventually, it goes cold and I push the cup away from me.

On the flight, I try to sleep but it eludes me. I'm squashed in my seat next to an enormous man who's spilling over onto me. Unlike me, he soon drops off and, when he does, he snores like a train. I put in my earphones in an attempt to drown out the sound and let a film pass by my eyes but can't take in the plot or who's who or even begin to care. Each hour takes me further away from Max and what might have been. Each hour takes me closer to home and my lovely boy, who I've missed so desperately. I wrestle with that quandary all the way to Heathrow.

It's not yet dark when I land and negotiate immigration and customs, but it's distinctly cooler than Washington was and I wish I'd left a jacket out of my case. I feel woozy and wrung out. Long-haul travel is not the best fun I've ever had and I feel decidedly dazed when I step out onto the concourse.

My dad, my dear, dear stoic and steadfast dad is standing there in his aged corduroy jacket that Mum is desperate to give to the charity shop and I could almost cry. I'm shocked at how elderly he looks, peering in a slightly bemused way into the crowd, searching for me, unaware that he's being observed. He is my knight in shining armour and is the best father anyone could have. I should remember that any man I might get involved with in the future would have to match up to him.

Then he turns and sees me and, for a moment, his face lights up. A second later, it's replaced by an expression of anxiety and I hurry towards him. I notice that Mum's right behind him and it's nice that they've come out together. Finn's not here, but maybe he's got a better offer than coming to the airport to pick up his old mum.

When I reach Dad, he says, 'Hello, love,' and his voice is gruff. He pulls me into a bear hug and it feels as if he never wants to let go. Eventually, he releases me. I'm sure they're pleased to see me, but his face is grim.

I turn to Mum and see that her eyes are brimming with tears.

'What?' I say, heart in my mouth. 'What's wrong?'

'It's Finn,' she sobs. 'He's all right.'

He can't be or why would they both be in this state? And why isn't he here then?

'He's in hospital,' she continues.

My world goes all wobbly. 'Has he collapsed again?'

Mum nods. 'Last night.'

'Why didn't you tell me?' Now I know why she was sounding so weird on the phone.

'We didn't want to worry you, love. What could you do? It was too late for you to get another flight back. Dad and I thought it was best if we waited until you were back.'

'Is he there by himself?'

'I stayed with him last night,' Mum says. 'Dad was there all day. We only came to collect you

199

together as Dad was so worried that I didn't want him driving alone. Finn's quite comfortable.'

'Have they said what it is?'

'They're doing tests,' Mum says. She and Dad exchange a nervous glance.

'Is it bad?'

'They don't know yet, love.'

'Take me straight to the hospital.'

Mum hugs me again. 'He's in the best place.'

And I should be with him. At this moment, my boy is ill and I feel like the worst mother in the world.

Chapter Thirty-Nine

I dash onto the children's ward at the hospital, leaving Mum and Dad sorting the car out. I know my way here as it's the same place where Finn was just a short while ago. The nurse shows me to his bed and my heart nearly stalls as I see him. He looks so small, so young, lying there dozing. Just a child.

Bending down, I stroke his hair and he wakes up, unsure, for a moment, where he is. 'Hey. How are you?'

'Hi, Mum,' he says, blinking himself awake. He looks relieved to see me.

'I'm never letting you out of my sight again,' I say.

Finn pushes himself up. 'That could be embarrassing for both of us when I need a shower.'

I could cry at how brave he's being.

'What about when I'm on honeymoon?' he quips. 'That could be seriously awkward.'

'You're never getting married,' I tell him. 'I'm going to keep you at home, for ever.'

'I'm glad you're back,' Finn says and I hug him tightly. 'Did you have a good time?'

'Yes.' I think of gadding about all the time Finn was ill. 'I should have been here for you.'

Finn shrugs. 'You can't be here 24/7, Mum. You've got to work.'

But I'm still wracked with guilt. I sit down by the bed and Mum and Dad catch up with me.

'All right, Finn?' Dad asks.

Finn nods. 'Bored more than anything. I had an MRI scan while you were collecting Mum. I think they said I'd get the results tomorrow. I'm not sure.'

'I'll double check,' I tell him. An MRI scan? That doesn't sound good.

A minute or two later, the nurse comes to join us. 'Doctor wants to see you in the morning, Mrs Chapman. He'll be able to give you more information then. Finn's doing well though. You should go home and get some sleep. We're looking after him.'

'I'll stay,' I say.

'Go,' Finn insists. 'I'm only going to go to sleep again. Come back in the morning.'

'Have you spoken to your dad?'

'Yes. He's FaceTimed me a few times. He wants you to ring him.'

'OK.'

'We'll take you home, love,' Mum says to me.

201

'It's best if you get some rest. You'll be weary after your long flight and Finn will be absolutely fine.'

'I want to stay until he's asleep. Why don't you go and get a coffee? I'm sure I won't be long.'

So Mum and Dad say their goodbyes to Finn and go to the visitors' lounge down the corridor to get a coffee.

I pull my chair closer to the bed and hug and kiss my boy. 'You OK?'

Finn nods.

'I'll be back first thing,' I say, 'so that I can speak to the doctor.'

He slides down into the bed and I tuck him in, my heart breaking. I would switch places with him in an instant. I sit beside Finn stroking his hair, watching his sleepy eyes roll with tiredness until he falls asleep. Then, when I'm absolutely sure that he's settled for the night, I search my parents out in the waiting room and they both look exhausted. Clearly, they need a good night's sleep too.

'Is he all right?' Mum wants to know.

'He's fine. So brave.' That makes me have a little cry and Mum joins in.

Dad pats us both, murmuring, 'There, there,' over and over.

Then they take me home. The house feels horribly empty without Finn. Eric isn't even here as he's still at my parents' house. I go to bed but don't sleep. Instead, I watch the clock round until five o'clock. Then I get up and, after a cursory shower, haul myself back to the hospital.

Chapter Forty

A few hours later and Finn and I are sitting side by side on his bed, still on the children's ward. An emergency has delayed the doctor's rounds and I've nearly chewed all my fingernails off.

'Stop fidgeting, Mum,' Finn says.

'Sorry, love.'

'It'll be all right,' he assures me. 'I'm fine.'

But I don't think he is. All this time of having my concerns ignored has culminated in this and I have a dread feeling in the pit of my stomach. 'I know,' I say.

A nurse comes along. 'Sorry for the delay, Mrs Chapman.' I've given up correcting anyone, as it seems so unimportant now. 'Ten more minutes and Doctor will be here.'

'Thank you.'

I squeeze Finn's hand. 'Not long now.'

Yet it's another half an hour before the young doctor stands before me, looking at Finn's notes on an iPad. He's not smiling. He rubs his chin. 'How are you feeling today, Finlay?'

My son shrugs. 'OK.'

He nods. 'That's good.' He purses his lips before he speaks again. 'I'm afraid that it's not great news,' he says to my boy.

My insides turn to ice.

Then he looks at me. 'Finlay has a brain tumour, Mrs Chapman.'

It's a good job I'm sitting down, otherwise I would have fallen down. It feels as if the doctor has punched me in the stomach. Finn's sitting on the bed next to me and I see that all the colour has drained from his face. I put my arm round him and squeeze. The ward seems to go hot and cold, everything shifts a little and I wonder, for a moment, whether I might actually faint.

'I'm really sorry,' the doctor says. Even though it's his job to be the bearer of bad tidings, he looks as if he wishes he was somewhere else. 'There's no way to dress it up.'

I struggle to speak, but I have to pull myself together for Finn. 'What does it mean?'

'Finn has a growth in the frontal lobe of his brain, in the pituitary gland. Right here.' He touches the front of Finn's forehead. He looks more comfortable to be back on the safe ground of clinical explanation. 'It's the gland which controls a lot of functions in the body. The result of Finn's tumour is that he isn't producing enough growth hormone and he isn't making any cortisol either.'

'Oh, God.' My hand goes to my mouth. I have no idea what some of those terms even mean, but it doesn't sound good. All I can hear clanging in my head is 'brain tumour'. Isn't that everyone's worst fears? My poor, poor Finn.

'The good news is that we hope we've caught it early and can correct it with drugs,' the doctor adds, looking relieved that he has something positive to add. 'But he'll have to take them every day, probably, for the rest of his life.'

'He won't need an operation?'

204

'I can't guarantee that,' the doctor says, cagily. 'The tumour is in a difficult position and we'd rather leave it alone, if we can. We're going to monitor Finn closely, make sure the tumour isn't growing and we'll see how he responds to the drugs.'

Finn is sitting there white-faced, but is coping with the news remarkably well. I feel as if I'm the one who's falling to bits. I can't believe that we've been told all this time by our stupid GP that there was nothing wrong with him. I think of forcing Finn to go jogging and jump around on the Wii Fit when all the time he's had a bloody, bastard brain tumour and no one has cared.

'What's caused it?'

'That's very difficult to say, Mrs Chapman. There's no history of it in the family?'

'Not that I know.'

'Sometimes, it can be behavioural or environmental factors that can cause changes in the body which push the cells into a cancerous state.'

I wrack my brains to think if there's anything I've done that could be causing it. Is it where we live or what we eat? Is it too much bloody *Call of the Assassin?*

'In children, that's rarely the case. Sometimes, it's just unlucky that your genes mutate.'

Unlucky. I'll say so.

'We'll refer you to a specialist clinic in London, but for now, I'm going to order all the drugs that Finn will need and one of the nurses will come and talk through it all with you, so that you know what to do.' The doctor makes eye contact with me. 'It's *very* important that you fully understand

205

it all, Mrs Chapman.'

Finn and I sit there stunned. Out of all the things that I might have expected, I hadn't expected this.

The doctor closes his iPad. 'Any questions?'

I shake my head. Millions, I think. But I can't form the sentences right now. And there are questions I want to ask while Finn isn't here. All that I can do for now is look at my child who is ill, hope that the doctors know what they're doing and pray that he gets better soon.

Chapter Forty-One

A few days later and Finn is home. The fridge is full of drugs. Finn managed a bit of breakfast and we're now both curled up on the sofa. I'm watching Creative World. Finn is asleep. Eric is asleep on top of Finn. The cats are asleep on top of Eric.

On the screen, my crafting heroine, Sheridan Singleton, is demonstrating how to make some special summer bunting. On the one hand I don't give a flying fuck about summer bunting – my child is ill. What else could possibly matter? On the other hand, all this talk of dies and paper and glitter is bringing some normality back to my life. There's nothing like a bit of craft distraction to take you away from your troubles for an hour or so. If I concentrate on the screen, it stops me from thinking that my son's brain, through no fault of his own, has gone completely haywire.

At the moment – and for the foreseeable future

– it seems as if we have troubles aplenty Chez Chapman. I have to give Finn injections every day and it terrifies me. My hands shake with nerves. The act of piercing my child's skin with a needle is the worst thing I've ever had to do. Finn bears it with a stoicism that makes me want to lie on the floor and weep. I jab him with a growth hormone and he has hydrocortisone and thyroxine tablets. Then he has to go back to the hospital for regular testosterone injections. I can't do that one as the needle is alarmingly large. My poor, poor boy. This is how it's going to be from now on and I'm sure we'll both get used to it in time. But, for now, we're both traumatised.

Without my lovely parents we would never manage. They've been running backwards and forwards, cooking, cleaning, collecting prescriptions and generally being as caring as they possibly can. They adore Finn and this has been such a terrible shock for them too.

Robyn has also been absolutely fantastic about giving me time off work. She sent flowers for me, plus a get well soon card and a box of sweetie goodies for Finn. It's really wonderful how people have rallied around to help us. I offered to work from home, but she said that I should focus solely on Finn, so they've taken on a temp to help cope with my workload and I couldn't be more grateful. I'm planning to have at least a couple of weeks off to see how we manage and Finn still has a lot of hospital appointments at the moment. I think all of my friendship favours are used up now, but Robyn knows that it's for a critical cause. She is outraged on my behalf. Which is lovely because

I'm exhausted by emotion and the only one I'm embracing is fear. Robyn says that we should sue the arse off the GP who so soundly brushed off my concerns for so long – her words not mine. With her professional head on, she's drafting me a letter to send to them and I'm so grateful as I couldn't face doing it myself. As this point, I'm just grateful that Finn is alive.

I texted Henry to let him know about Finn and that I wouldn't be around for a while and he sent a kind message back. Who knows what will happen there.

The school couldn't have been nicer. I think they're also feeling dreadful about questioning the frequency of Finn's absences now. The head-master sent a personal note and a bunch of cards have arrived from his school friends too and, though they've asked to visit, I don't think Finn's quite up to it yet.

Liam is being great too. He's Skyping Finn every day and is currently trying to organise his duty roster so that he can come home for a visit as soon as possible. I try to assure him there's no rush now that we know Finn isn't in imminent danger. There might come a time when I need him to be here more for Finn, though neither of us say that to each other.

My dear son stirs and I carefully lift the menagerie from him. 'What have I missed?' he asks, sleepily. 'Has Sheridan Singleton sworn live on air?'

'No, she hasn't,' I tell him with a tut. 'She's as saintly as ever.'

'Does she know that, when I'm better, you're

coming for her?'

That makes me laugh. 'There's not so much wrong with you, Finlay Chapman.'

'I'll be OK,' Finn says, suddenly serious. 'You don't have to worry.'

'Of course I have to worry. I'm your mother. First line of the job description.'

Finn sits up. 'I don't feel sick or anything,' he says. 'Just tired. And cheesed off.'

'I've got some craft projects to do.' In fact, my deadline is fast approaching and I haven't even thought about what I'm going to do. I haven't spoken to Max since I got back either. Why would I with another manager in place now? A couple of days after the retreat, Max sent a round robin email to everyone to say how wonderful we all were, blah, blah, blah. But, on a personal level, there's been nothing. Something else to be filed under the heading Cocked Up.

Dean, however, has called a couple of times to see how I'm getting on and throwing in some ideas and suggestions. I haven't told him about Finn's situation. It's something I'll just have to deal with. Dean's really nice and I think we'll work well together. He's not Max though. Dean and I will never exchange longing looks, late night cocktails or anything like that. Perhaps just as well. I'm never likely to make a fool of myself with Dean.

I slide my attention back to Finn. 'You could help me to do some die-cutting.'

'Mother, I'm fifteen years old and I have a brain tumour, I should not be spending my days cutting out daisies.'

'You're right,' I say. 'What do you want to do?'

209

'Play *Call of the Assassin.*'

'No.' I've banned Finn from computer games. 'I don't want it to fry your brain.'

'My brain already appears to be fried.'

'I don't want you to do anything that might damage it. I...'

'Worry!' Finn completes.

'I do.'

'So, if I can't play on the computer, what's the chance of me going out for hot chocolate then?'

I grin at my beautiful boy. 'Better.'

'Take me for hot chocolate and I'll help you to die-cut daisies and butterflies and stuff later and I won't even complain.'

'You have a fabulous career in sales ahead of you,' I say. 'Get dressed then. See if you can remember what the shower looks like first.'

'Hilarious,' Finn bats back as he drags himself from the sofa and heads for the stairs. His pyjamas hang from his hips and he's too thin. He looks like a strand of spaghetti.

While my son reacquaints himself with the bathroom, I turn to put Sheridan on to record and then turn off the telly. I wander into the dining room to look at the suitcase full of crafting swag that I brought home from America. With all that's been going on I haven't even had a chance to open it yet and it's still where my dad dumped it when he dropped me off.

Sitting on the floor next to it, I again offer a silent thank you to lovely Mandy who gave this whopper case to me and saved my bacon. I flick the lid open and the sight of all the delights in front of me lifts my flagging spirits. There's a wide selection of dies, more adhesives than I have things to stick together, a dozen different sorts of ribbon and washi tape, card stock, rubber stamps, embossing folders and powders, and several little tools that might well be useful if only I could remember what to do with them. I've missed doing this over the last week or so and I should get started again to capitalise on all that I learned on my retreat. There's a little sharp pang of longing as I think of Max again. I wonder how things would have turned out if I'd agreed to spend the night with him. Still, a bit too late to dwell on that now. The story of my life.

Now we're on opposite sides of the Atlantic, Max doesn't even know what's going on in my life. And he doesn't need to. As long as I fulfil the terms of my contract and I turn my projects in on time, then all will be fine.

I feel soothed as I sort through the papers, the dies and all the bits and bobs we were given. Sometimes I forget how much I enjoy this or how therapeutic it can be. After a few minutes, I can feel some ideas percolating in my head. I put some colours together and pick out spools of pretty ribbon that might come in handy. I get a little rush of excitement which has to be a good sign. When Finn and I come back from our little coffee shop outing, I really should get cracking.

Chapter Forty-Two

We have a leisurely visit to our favourite coffee shop, Piano Man & Co, in the High Street. We even strolled down there with Eric, and Finn ate a hearty burger for his lunch which I was pleased to see.

Back at home and, true to his word, Finn sits at the dining room table with me and cuts out paper hearts, leaves, flowers and butterflies without complaint. For my home décor project, I'm going to create a series of wall-art pieces depicting all the seasons with a fabulous set of leaf-shaped dies that are in my stash. From my new paper cache, I've picked out white and silver for winter, fresh greens for spring, the colours of ice cream, sun and sea for summer and a range of browns and burnt oranges for autumn. I think it will look great. Fingers crossed. In the background I have Creative World on for inspiration. Finn has his earphones on listening to the Foo Fighters, but we sit and work together companionably.

After our walk to the High Street, Finn has a little pinkness back in his cheeks and I think that we should start to take a gentle stroll every day on his road to recovery. It's hard to know what he can and can't do. Having pushed him so ill-advisedly into doing exercise, I'm now terrified every time that he moves.

While I'm musing, I hear the mention of a

familiar name on the television and my head snaps up. I can't believe my eyes. Abandoning my dies, I dash back to the living room and stand and stare, transfixed, at the screen. Finn stops what he's doing and joins me.

On screen with Sheridan Singleton is Max Alexander – as large as life.

'That's the head of Contemporary Crafts, right?' Finn says.

I nod, the power of speech having deserted me.

'Welcome to London, Max,' Sheridan smooths. 'We're delighted that you could join us on the Creative World channel. We're becoming *big* fans of the Contemporary Crafts products.'

'Thank you, Sheridan. It's a pleasure to be here.'

I get a surge of joy and anxiety in my stomach. Max is here in London. He's barely sixty miles away from me. But he hasn't phoned or emailed to tell me so.

'Max,' Sheridan continues, 'your company might be the new kid on the block in the UK, but it's making a massive impact in the crafting world on this side of the pond.'

'We're trying to create a fresh, new look that will appeal to crafters here and we've taken on a great designer to help us do that.'

That's me. He's talking about me. At least, I think he is. He might have taken on another better designer for all I know.

Sheridan looks to camera. 'I'm going to demon-strate a clean, simple card while you talk us through the products I'm using.'

'Sure thing,' Max says.

And I'm mesmerised. I don't really take in any of it and I'm glad that the telly is set to record as I can watch it again later. Who knows what Sheridan's doing, but I can't tear my eyes away from Max.

'Phone him,' Finn says. 'When he comes off air.'

'No, no, no.'

'He'll like that. Tell him he looks cool.'

I glance at Finn. 'He does, doesn't he?' I can only see Max's top half as they're both standing behind a desk, but he's wearing a white, round-neck T-shirt under a dark grey sweater. His blue eyes are stunning in the studio lights and the camera clearly likes him.

My son laughs. 'You've gone all red, Mum!'

'I'm a woman of a certain age,' I tell him. 'We all do that.'

'Woo, hoo. I'm going to tell Nana that you fancy your boss.'

'You'll do no such thing.' I'm still mesmerised by Max. 'This is a purely professional relation-ship.' The more I tell myself that, the better.

If I'm being honest, I do feel somewhat deflated that he hasn't contacted me. Even if it was just to let me know that he was going to be on the television here. Oh, well. At least he gave me a mention, if not a name check.

I watch the rest of the segment and there's a certain chemistry between them. Lots of flirting on her part. Huh. I think that I could have done a better job of demonstrating the products than she did though. Perhaps she wasn't giving it her full attention but, quite frankly, her card isn't anything to write home about. But then that might just be sour grapes on my part.

'Thank you, Max,' she says sweetly. 'We'd love to have you back next time you're in the UK.'

'I'd love to be here.'

Then there's the sales pitch for Contemporary Crafts and Sheridan moves on to another product range called Beyond Paper which features MDF die-cuts. I turn off.

'I should get back to work,' I say to Finn. 'We're due at Nana's for dinner soon. I'll take the rest of this with me to finish off. Do you need a sleep?'

'I might chill out on the sofa for a bit,' he says and he shoves the cats out of the way to lie down. Instantly, Eric joins him. Within minutes, they've both nodded off.

I sit down at the dining room table and stare at my project, but my concentration is shot to pieces. All I can think of is Max being in London.

Chapter Forty-Three

About half an hour later and I'm still gazing into space when my phone rings and makes me jump out of my skin.

I look at the call and can see that it's Max phoning me. Instantly, I go into panic mode and I keep staring at it until the voicemail is in danger of clicking in before I can speak. When I do press to answer, my mouth is dry as I say, 'Hello.'

'Hi, Christie,' he says, sounding less assured than usual. 'How are you?'

'I'm fine, thank you.'

'I'm sorry that I haven't been in touch since you've been home, but life has been very busy.'

'Same here.' I'm coming across more crisply than I mean to, but I genuinely don't know how to play this.

'I called because I wanted you to know that I'm currently in London.'

'Ah. I'm ahead of you there.' For something to do with my hands, I shuffle the paper around in front of me. 'I've just been watching you on television.'

'You have?' He laughs. 'How did I do?'

'Very good,' I tell him and there's finally some warmth in our conversation. 'I'd give you a job.'

'This is a flying visit. I'd meant to contact you ahead of leaving but ... well. You know how it is.'

I do.

'I'm free tonight,' he continues. 'I'd like it very much if you could come down and join me for dinner.'

So he does want to see me. I thought that now I was reporting directly to Dean we'd have little or no contact and I'm alarmed that my heart soars at the thought of seeing Max again when I really don't want it to. There's nothing on earth that I'd love more than to have dinner with him, but what can I do? I can't leave Finn. What if he collapses again and I'm not here?

'I know it's short notice.' Perhaps Max senses my hesitation. 'But it would be great if you could be make it. I'm staying at The Shard and I've taken the liberty of booking a table at the restaurant for this evening.'

The Shard. Blimey.

'I can book you a room to stay over. A separate room,' he adds hurriedly. 'That would give us more time to talk.'

My emotions have a good old wrestle while I grip the phone and work out what I'm going to do.

Max says, 'Are you still there?'

'Yes. Sorry.' With a heavy heart, I continue, 'I'm sorry, Max, but Finn is poorly. Really poorly.'

'I didn't know.'

'I'm still trying to get my head round it myself, that's why I haven't mentioned it to Dean. There's a lot been happening since I got back from the retreat. I have to be here with Finn.'

'I'm really sorry to hear that, Christie.'

'Thanks. It makes things really difficult and, for that reason, I can't come to London tonight.'

'Oh.' If I'm not mistaken, he sounds as disappointed as I feel.

'Maybe another time.' I don't really want to enter into a discussion or any further explanation about this as I feel I might cry. To be honest, I try to say the words 'brain tumour' as seldom as possible.

'Yes,' he says. 'Of course. I understand, perfectly. I hope Finn gets better soon.'

Max doesn't need to know the details. As long as I deliver my projects to a good standard and on time, this really isn't anyone else's business.

'Have a great time in London,' I say.

'I will.'

'I'll send my projects through to Dean soon. I'm working on them now.'

'If you need extra time...'

217

'No,' I say. 'It'll be fine.' I don't want him thinking I'm flaky before I've even started.

'Excellent. I look forward to seeing them too.' Then there's a difficult little pause. I don't think either of us want to end the conversation, yet what else is there to say? 'Well ... goodbye, Christie.'

'Bye.' Quickly, I hang up.

Then I turn to see Finn standing with his arms folded across his chest. 'Please tell me that you did not just turn down dinner and a night in London with that man?'

But both Finn and I know that's exactly what I did.

Chapter Forty-Four

It's late afternoon and we're at my parents' house and Mum is making a lasagne to cook for to-night's meal – one of my boy's favourites. Not that they're indulging him, of course. Finn and I are sitting at the kitchen table while good old Dad's making us both a cup of tea.

'Mum's boss asked her to go down to London tonight,' Finn says, quite loudly. 'He wanted her to go to The Shard and stay overnight and every-thing.'

Quite frankly, I'm not sure that anyone needs to know what 'everything' might involve. 'Finlay,' I hiss. 'No one likes a telltale.' My son pulls a face at me.

'The Shard, eh?' Dad says, impressed. 'I fancy

218

having a look at that myself. You can go right to the top. I bet you get a great view of London up there.'

'Yeah, but she said *no*.' My dear son, I feel, is more pointed than necessary.

Mum turns to stare at me as if I've lost my mind, spoon poised mid-stir. 'You did what?' she splutters.

'Surely, it's not that earth-shattering?' I glare at Finn. 'In different circumstances, I would have loved to have gone.' It remains unsaid that I don't want to leave Finn, but we all know that's why I'll be spending the evening at home instead of gallivanting off to London.

Mum's face darkens and my mum never gets cross. 'This is your job, Christie. You've been given an amazing opportunity and you've said no?'

'What else could I do?'

'Go,' Finn chips in.

'This chap's an important contact, Christie. And he really looked after you in Washington. You said so yourself.'

Though I did give them all the abridged version. No mention of lobster linguine or developments thereafter.

'If you want this to become more of a permanent thing, then you should make the effort to be there.'

'If you won't listen to me, then listen to Nan,' Finn pleads.

I'm feeling backed into a corner. 'I don't want to leave you.' There, I've said it.

'You can't wrap me in cotton wool, Mum,' he insists. 'I'll stay with Nan and Pops.'

Now it's my turn to put my foot down. 'Look

219

what happened last time I went away.'

Mum tuts at me.

'She's right, Christie,' Dad says and Dad tries never to have an opinion on anything if he can avoid it. 'You love doing this and you never know where it might lead. It sounds as if this Max is a very powerful man. Who knows what he could do for you.'

I lower my voice and speak as if my son's not here. 'I have to put Finn first.'

'It's one evening,' Finn says. 'You're going to have to go back to work full-time soon. They won't let you stay at home with me for ever. I'll have to go back to school too.'

He has a point.

'It's not only important that you're there, Christie,' Mum adds, 'but you need a break too. It's about time you had some fun.'

I feel myself flush and Finn smirks at me. I shoot him my most threatening glance. *Fun* is definitely not on my mind.

'You could quickly grab some things and Dad will run you to the station.'

'I will, love,' he agrees. 'You could be there in a couple of hours.'

I can feel myself weakening. As much as I'd like to convince my traitorous heart otherwise, I'd love to see Max again. I thought that he was giving me the cold shoulder. It looks as if I was mistaken.

'This could be considered as bullying,' I tell them.

'It's for your own good, Christie.' Mum again. 'Finn will be fine with us.'

I chew at my lip, anxiously. 'So you think I

220

should call him back?'

'Yes!' They all say together.

'He might have made other plans by now.'

Mum looks up from stirring the cheese sauce she's returned to. 'Well, you'll never know until you phone him, will you?'

'If he's still available, I could have dinner and then come home on a late train.'

'I'd rather you didn't travel at night by yourself, love,' Dad says. 'Unless you want me to come down with you and wait.'

'You can't do that, Dad.'

'It's no bother.'

'Have dinner and stay,' Mum says, firmly. 'It will do you good. I bet somewhere like that's got a swimming pool and everything.'

I have no idea whether it does or not. I've never stayed in one of the posh London hotels before. 'OK. OK.' I hold up my hands. 'I surrender. I'll ring him now.'

So I wander out into the garden – away from flapping ears – and I call Max back.

'Max, it's Christie,' I say when he picks up. My heart is pounding and I rush on before I lose my bottle. 'If that offer for dinner is still on the table, then I'd like to accept.'

'Right,' he says, sounding surprised. 'Perfect.'

The words almost stick in my throat when I say, 'Perhaps I'll need a room too.'

Chapter Forty-Five

I make Finn come with me to say goodbye at the station. 'You must text me every hour,' I instruct as I get out of the car. 'If you don't I'll...'

'Worry,' Finn finishes.

'Yes, I will. Promise me.'

'That won't be weird at all,' he protests.

'I won't go unless you promise me.'

He holds his hands up in surrender. 'OK. OK. I know when I'm beaten.'

'Do it or I'll rain terrible punishments down on you.' I hug him tightly.

'He'll be fine with us,' Dad says, but I still feel like crying when I get on the train into London.

An hour or so later, by the good grace of London Midland trains and the Northern Line, I'm outside The Shard. This is the tallest building in Europe and the slender pinnacle of glass stretches so high into the sky that I can't see the top of it from inside my cab. It also means that the taxi driver can't get a signal for me to pay by credit card and I haven't got enough cash. We drive round a bit more until he picks up wi-fi – by which time he's very cross and I'm close to tears again – and I pay my fare.

I go up to reception on the thirty-fifth floor and queue for ages as there's one person on the desk and a wedding party are checking in. This is not an auspicious start and I'm aware that time is ticking

222

on. I'm due to meet Max shortly and I'd like at least to change into my dress and fluff my hair before then. Finally, I get to my room, frazzled and anxious. As I walk inside, the blinds rise automatically and I'm treated to the most amazing view across London. The room is glass on three sides and I can see the broad swathe of the Thames, Tower Bridge and the Tower of London on the other bank. I'm ashamed to say that even though I live so close to London and travel in nearly every day, I don't know it very well at all. This is an area of breathtaking beauty and it's a shame that I won't have more time to explore it.

I lie on the bed, stretched out in a star shape, and drink it all in. As my stress levels are coming down, for the second time since I left home, my phone pings.

Still alive! Finn texts.

I smile and text back. *Cheeky. I love you. xx*

While I have my phone out, I text Max to let him know that I've arrived.

I'll meet you in the Gong bar. Fifteen minutes? he replies. *Level 52.*

I quickly drink the hot, green tea that's in a flask on the desk – why wouldn't you? – and enjoy the view again. Then I change into my LBD and hurry up to the fifty-second floor to meet him.

My stomach's fluttering with anxiety as I walk out of the lift and into the bar. I've never been one of those women who are confident enough to walk into a place by themselves without an attack of nerves.

The bar is dark, oriental-themed, and opens out onto the swimming pool at one end. It's the most glamorous thing I've ever seen and a glimpse into a life that I don't know. The view is spectacular and the lights are starting to come on all over the city, making it look like a fairytale land from this dizzying height. Max is sitting at the bar and my knees shake as I walk towards him.

He's in the black suit that I've seen before with a silver-grey shirt open at the neck. He already has a cocktail. His face lights up when he sees me. I'm sure it does.

As I approach, he stands and holds out his hands. Touching my arms, he kisses both cheeks lightly. 'I've remembered that when I'm in Europe, it's two kisses, not one.'

Frankly, I couldn't care less about the etiquette, I just like the feel of his lips against my skin. 'This is an amazing place.'

'It is,' he agrees. 'I slept in the clouds last night. Literally. Which floor are you on?' I tell him. 'Ah. Just down the hall from me. You have a good view then?'

'Right over the Thames.'

'I wish I were able to stay here for longer,' Max says. 'It's been many years since I was a tourist in London.'

'I was thinking the same thing. I work on the other side of the river behind the Embankment, only a few minutes from here, yet I rarely see outside my office.'

'Maybe one day we'll both do something about that,' he suggests.

I get a welcome image of Max and me wandering round the city like tourists – taking in Covent Garden, the South Bank, the London Eye.

'Sounds like a plan.'

'What can I get for you?'

'I seem to remember you have very good taste in cocktails.' I think back to our late night in the bar in Washington and flush slightly. 'I'll have whatever you recommend.'

'Old romantic that I am, I'm having the Romeo and Juliet. The menu says it's inspired by Shakespeare's Globe theatre which is, apparently, nearby.'

'It's very close.'

Max shrugs, regretfully. 'If only I had more time.'

The cocktail is gin, raspberry purée and Earl Grey tea with a twist of lemon, and hits the spot.

Max chinks his glass against mine. '"If music be the food of love,"' he quotes, '"play on."'

I smile. 'Cheers.'

'Not a big fan of the bard?'

I shake my head. 'Not really. Shakespeare has always left me cold. I'm more of a Bridget Jones kind of girl.'

That makes him laugh.

'It would have been a sin not to see you while I was here,' Max said. 'I'm glad that you could come.'

'Me too.' Neither of us mention that the atmosphere was a little frosty between us when I left Washington to head for home.

'Let's have a nice evening,' he says. 'I can fill you in on some things that have been happening in the business.'

We chat while we drink our cocktails and Max orders another. Halfway into my second one and

I'm just beginning to relax when Max says, 'There's someone joining us. I hope you don't mind.'

Before I can answer, he's on his feet again. 'Ah. Here she is.'

When I turn, I see Sheridan Singleton gliding towards us – THE Sheridan Singleton – and I'm robbed of speech.

While I gape, Max holds out his arms and embraces her like an old friend. Over his shoulder, Sheridan eyes me up and down.

When they part, he says, 'Sheridan, this is Christie Chapman. She's the bright new designer I was telling you about. Fortunately, she was free to join us for dinner. I thought it would be the perfect opportunity for you two to meet.'

Sheridan looks as if she might have liked advance warning of an interloper. Me too, I think. Did I harbour the hope that this might be a cosy little dinner for just me and Max? Of course I did. So this is to be strictly business after all. Well, I guess that makes things a bit less complicated. For me, at least.

'I'm a big fan,' I manage to say to Sheridan. 'I watch all of your demonstrations on Creative World.'

'Thank you,' she says, coolly.

I'm in awe that I'm even in the same room as her. She looks less impressed. This has the potential to be so awkward. Despite having made the effort to be here, maybe I should offer to disappear now and leave them to it. Sheridan, it seems, was also expecting a duet rather than a trio.

While she scans the cocktail menu with Max –

not a woman to let a man pick her drink – I take the chance to have a good look at her. In the flesh, so to speak, she's more beautiful than she is on screen. She's glossily sophisticated, wearing an emerald green silk sheath dress and her long, dark hair swept up in some effortless chignon. My little black TK Maxx number that a minute ago made me feel like a million dollars now feels cheap and shabby. I wished I'd had time to have my hair done or my nails. Or an entire face and body lift.

We sit at one of the tables by the swimming pool instead of at the bar – Sheridan, I would guess, is not a bar-stool type of woman. Max turns his charm up and perhaps we both decide to make the most of this, as the atmosphere thaws slightly. When we're all on the mutual ground of our love of crafting the conversation flows much easier.

We're just finishing our cocktails, ready to go through to dinner, when Finn texts me again.

Yep. Still here.

'Excuse me,' I say to Max and Sheridan. 'That's my son texting. He's sworn to text me every hour.'

I tap a couple of kisses back to Finn.

'I'm not normally so paranoid, but he's poorly at the moment,' I confess. 'I'm worried about leaving him.'

'Nothing serious?' Sheridan asks.

'Well...' I hadn't actually meant to share this, but they might as well know what we're dealing with. 'He's just been diagnosed with a brain tumour.'

They both look genuinely shocked.

'I had no idea,' Max says.

'It happened when I got back from Washington,' I tell him. 'He's fine. For the moment. It's taken a

227

long time to get a diagnosis, but now he's on the proper medication.' Instead of two paracetamol and a prescription for fresh air. 'And he's being closely monitored.'

Sheridan puts a hand on my arm. 'You must be frantic.'

'I'm a mother. You wish it was you and not them.'

'Is he your only child?'

I nod. 'It's just me and Finn.'

'That's hard.'

'I have a lot of support from my parents. They're very good to us.' I slip my phone into my bag and drain my cocktail. 'I'm sorry about the interruption.'

'Don't be,' Sheridan says. 'It's only natural. I'd be out of my head with worry.'

I don't think I need to tell her that I am.

'You mustn't hesitate to call him, if it puts your mind at rest.' Sheridan links her arm into mine. 'Dinner?'

'Lead the way,' Max says.

As we turn and head towards the restaurant, Sheridan says, 'I have two boys. Dylan and Buddy. I'm on my own with them too. They're eight and six.'

'That's a lovely age.'

'Yeah?' Sheridan laughs. 'Mine are a real handful.'

'I'm lucky that Finn's a good boy. He's probably handling this better than I am.'

I glance over my shoulder to see if Max is following and I can't read the expression on his face but he's certainly deep in thought.

Chapter Forty-Six

The dinner is superb. I have a risotto of langoustines, chorizo and parmesan, followed by halibut with samphire and lemon. Is it wrong to say that part of me is still missing Mum's lasagne though?

I'm desperate for a dessert as the previous courses were sooooo small, but neither Max nor Sheridan are partaking and I don't want to seem greedy. There are lots of lovely things involving chocolate which are calling me. I sit on my hands. This is why Sheridan is as slender as a reed and I am not.

Max tells Sheridan of his plans for the business and, when she asks, I go through my crafting history, trying to make it sound more interesting than it is.

'My mum taught me all my crafting skills too.' Sheridan smiles kindly at me. 'We have a lot in common.'

I look at us both and think that, apart from an overriding love of crafts, we don't have much in common at all. She is self-assured, successful and sophisticated. I'm … well, I am what I am.

'Thank you for coming into the studio today. It's been a lot of fun finally meeting you, Max,' she says, coquettishly. 'There's a great buzz around Contemporary Crafts. I've been hearing a lot of good things about your company and its ethos.'

'Thank you, Sheridan,' Max answers.

'And we should definitely have you as a guest presenter more often,' Sheridan says. 'Our sales went through the roof on that segment.'

He laughs. 'Any time. You'll have to pull some strings for me.'

'That may be possible,' Sheridan says with an enigmatic smile. She glances coyly at both of us, playing to the gallery. I guess if you're used to presenting to a camera all day long, it must sometimes be hard to turn it off. 'It hasn't been announced publicly yet, but I've just bought a major share in the company. I have some *fabulous* plans for the future.'

'That's great,' Max says. 'You'll be exactly the right person to take the channel forward. We should have more champagne to celebrate.'

'Not for me.' Sheridan puts a hand over her glass. 'I must be going. I need my beauty sleep. I'm on air at ten in the morning.'

Max stands. 'I'll walk you back to the foyer.'

'Stay.' She pushes away from the table. 'Both of you have a glass of fizz in my honour.' Sheridan smooths down her dress. Two hours later, she still looks as fresh as when she arrived. Her lipstick hasn't even moved. She must put it on with super-glue.

I stand up too and Sheridan embraces me. 'I hope Finn gets better soon.'

'Thank you. We both have everything crossed.'

'I'm sure we'll meet again soon,' she says. 'I look forward to seeing your designs for Contemporary Crafts. Max tells me you're very talented.'

'I don't know about that,' I mumble.

'Don't be modest,' she chides. 'Modesty never

got women anywhere.' Then she kisses Max and sashays away from us.

Max sits down again and I join him. He purses his lips. 'I think that went well.'

'She seems lovely.'

He laughs. '"Lovely" isn't often a word associated with Sheridan Singleton. She's a ruthless operator, who you don't want to cross. The whole team are terrified of her. But she's one hell of a lady and I think she's on our side.'

'She seems *very* taken with you,' I tease.

He smiles in acknowledgement. 'And with you. Don't underestimate what she could do for you, Christie. We definitely should have that extra glass of champagne to toast her.'

'I'm game.'

The restaurant is less busy now, most of the diners having left for the evening. Max summons the waiter and, moments later, two fresh glasses appear.

'To Sheridan,' he proposes.

'And Contemporary Crafts,' I add.

'To our special English–American relationship.' We both raise our glasses and drink. Then Max looks at me with a serious expression on his face and says, 'I felt it ended badly between us in Washington. I was crass and behaved appallingly.'

'It doesn't matter.'

'It does,' he insists. 'I was out of line. You were perfectly right. Do you forgive me?'

'Of course. To be honest, I've had more on my mind to worry about.'

'You should have told me about Finn.' Max fixes me with his gaze.

'We're managing.'

'I could have helped.'

I'm not sure exactly what he could have done from Washington DC but I guess it's a nice that he's thinking of us. 'Thanks.'

'Do you need more time to deliver your projects? I can speak to Dean for you.'

The last thing I want to do is fall at the first hurdle. Do you think that Sheridan Singleton would contemplate doing that? 'It's fine,' I assure him. 'I'm on it.'

'Let me in, Christie,' he says, gently. 'I can be a friend as well as your employer.'

I soften. 'It's kind of you to say so.'

We drink our champagne and chat more about the company. I tell Max that Finn and I are thinking of setting up an online shop. 'Could I be a stockist for your products?'

'That would be great,' he says.

'I think your minimum order would be out of my range.'

'I've set up a distributor in the UK and we've put our entry level quite low,' he tells me. 'For now, we need market exposure. Your first order needn't be daunting. It would be another retail outlet for us and that's great. What I can't do is give you preferential terms. I'd have to treat you exactly the same as our regular suppliers.'

'I understand. I'm not asking for favouritism. Just a fair crack at it.'

'Then we should make a deal,' Max says.

Despite enjoying the conversation, I let out an involuntary yawn.

'Time to hit the sack,' Max says. 'I have an early

flight tomorrow.'

'You're not even staying for a few days?'

'I'm going straight to Italy in the morning for some meetings there.'

'When will you be back in London again?'

He looks at me and I see sadness in those mesmerising eyes. 'I don't honestly know, Christie.'

Finn texts me again. *Still here and going to bed now. See you tomorrow, Mum. xx.*

'My son,' I say by way of explanation.

'I hope he'll be OK.'

'I hope so too.'

'If there's anything I can do to help – anything – let me know. You're under enough pressure, I don't want to add to it.' Max picks up his key card. 'I'll escort you back to your room.'

We leave the restaurant, his hand under my arm. We stand close together in the lift listening to the plinky-plonk music and not quite looking at each other, but the small space is crackling with electricity.

When we reach our floor, we both turn towards my room and he walks me to my door. 'This is it,' I tell him.

'Then I should say goodnight.'

'Thank you for a lovely evening,' I say. 'And for the room. It's stunning.'

'My pleasure.' Max steps towards me and goes to brush my cheek but, right at that moment, I turn awkwardly and our lips meet. And I don't know what happens next but, instead of jumping apart as we should, he moves closer and kisses me deeply until I feel as if I'm melting inside. The intensity of feeling, I think, takes us both by

233

surprise. I cling to him and his mouth is hard on mine, his breathing ragged.

It would be so easy to ask him to come into my room. So very easy.

Whatever happens we can't stay here in the corridor snogging like lovesick teenagers. Someone might see us.

Max breaks away from me. 'I don't want a relationship,' he says. 'I have to make that very clear, Christie. This would be about now, about tonight.'

Instantly, that brings me crashing back to earth.

The truth is that I'd like nothing more than a relationship with this man, but I can't just spend the night with him on those terms. Part of me wishes that I could. Yet I don't want to be someone who gets a booty call every time he's in London. I'm better than that. I hoped that Max was too.

'I'm trying to be honest with you,' he says, sensing my hesitation.

I take a step away to put some distance between us. 'Goodnight, Max,' I say. 'I hope you have a pleasant flight tomorrow and a successful trip to Italy.'

He lets his hands fall from my arms. 'I'll speak to you soon.'

He walks slowly down the corridor away from me and I watch him go. At his door, on the other side of the lift to mine, he turns and lifts a hand to wave.

I wave back, which fails on a million levels to convey what I'm feeling. Then I go into my room before I change my mind.

Chapter Forty-Seven

I lie in my bed in my glass room. About one in the morning, I watch as the clouds slowly roll in, engulfing the sights of London and softly pressing against the windows. I feel as if I'm way up in the sky, floating, floating.

Max is a few doors away from me and I wonder if he's sleeping or whether he's watching the clouds swirl round us. I could go to him. Would it be that difficult? Ninety per cent of me thinks that it's a really great idea. Some parts of that ninety per cent haven't had fun in a long, long time and are very keen. But ten per cent of me – that little sensible nagging bit – is saying that it would be a bad, bad idea. Currently, that's the bit that's winning. It could go either way though.

I'm helped in my decision by the fact that I'm wearing my Matalan's-finest Minnie Mouse pyjamas again. If I'd planned on being a seductress, then I should have gone to Next or somewhere and treated myself to something a bit flimsy trimmed with lace. I can't really turn up at someone's door hoping to wow them with Minnie Mouse on my chest, right? In my rush to get down here, I admit that I didn't really think this through. I suppose I could put on the hotel's complimentary waffle dressing gown over my birthday suit, trot along the corridor and flash him when he opened the door. Some women could do that. I

235

eye the dressing gown for several long minutes, wracked with indecision. Nope. I'm not one of them. I just don't have the bottle. What if Max laughed? I'd shrivel up and die on the spot.

Then I realise that I'm giving this way too much head time. Instead, I look at my phone, checking the last message from Finn, and I resist the urge to text him. If he answers, he'll be cross that I'm worrying. If he doesn't answer then I'll have to go home this minute. Neither is practical.

So I get up and put on the waffly dressing gown over my jim-jams and help myself to green tea from the replenished flask. Then I sit in the armchair by the window and watch the beautiful clouds as they ebb and flow, sometimes allowing me tantalising glimpses of the river or Tower Bridge below. Eventually, the clouds clear and the sun starts to rise. I take some pictures on my phone which are not as crap as they might be.

I think I must have dozed off for a few minutes as I hear a noise by my room door and start awake. By the time I've roused myself and go to it, there's a note on the floor that's been pushed underneath. I pick it up.

It's on the hotel notepaper and simply says, *Dear Christie, It's been great to spend time with you. I hope I might see you again in Washington one day.*

I snatch the door open and am just in time to see the doors of the lift closing and, I assume, Max leaving. What shall I do? I can't really chase after him in my nightwear and, by the time I've got dressed, he'll be in a cab and on his way to Heathrow. What would I say, anyway? What would I do? Would we have another snog or would we stand there awkwardly? Who knows?

Instead, I text him and say, *Sorry to have missed you. Have a safe journey. We'll speak soon.* Then I wonder if I should put any kisses. And I do. *xx.*

I look at his note. His handwriting is meticulously executed, strong. At least if he left a message this proves that he was thinking about me too. Doesn't it?

I'm wide awake now and I still daren't text Finn at this hour. He'll definitely be in the land of nod. So I decide to make use of the facilities. When am I ever going to get a chance to stay somewhere like this again? So I grab my swimsuit and head up to the pool. There's no one else there when I emerge from the changing room and I hit the cool water and do some lengths. A bit of physical exercise seems like a good thing to get rid of some of my frustrations. When I'm breathing heavily and my muscles are protesting at the unaccustomed exertion, I lean on the edge of the infinity pool and gaze out. This is the highest swim I'm ever likely to have. I text Finn a photo and he pings one back. *Still alive. Have fun.*

I follow my swim with a hearty cooked breakfast in the TING restaurant. Calories out, calories in. I watch the trains, thirty-odd floors below, looking like a model railway as they trundle in and out of London Bridge station. I wonder about the people on the trains. Are they like me, struggling to keep a roof over their heads, struggling with the illness of a child or their loved ones, struggling with relationships? Struggling, struggling. Soon it will be back to school for Finn and back to commuting for me. Can't say that I'm looking forward to it.

Chapter Forty-Eight

When I check out of the hotel, I get into a cab that I can't really afford and ask him to take me to my office. Robyn nearly has a heart attack when she sees me at her door.

'Well, shut the front door,' she says. 'Look what the cat dragged in.' My friend comes to give me a great big bear hug and I sink into her arms. 'I've missed your ugly mug around the office.'

'I've missed your pithy banter.'

'What are you doing here?'

'I'm not here to work,' I tell her.

'Perish the thought.'

'I've got time for coffee though.'

'Let's do it.' She closes the folder on her desk and we go through to the kitchen where I make us two good, strong cups of espresso and we lean against the counter to drink them.

'So. Tell all,' she says. 'What are you doing in town looking slightly smug and a little blissed out?'

I can't help but grin. 'I've just spent the night at The Shard. Courtesy of Max Alexander of Contemporary Crafts.'

'How very exciting.'

'Not in the biblical sense,' I add hastily.

'How very dull.'

'It could have happened.' I get a little flashback to our kissing in the corridor. 'But, well ... I was a complete wuss and bottled it.'

'And now you're regretting it?'

'No. Yes. Maybe.'

Robyn raises her eyebrows. 'For a minute, I hoped you were here to entertain me with tales of wanton sexual activity in the manner of the *Kama Sutra*.'

''Fraid not.'

She feigns crippling disappointment.

'I can't do one-night stands, Rob. I'm too old. Too lacking in self-esteem. He's as hot as you like and I have more wobbly bits than Jabba the Hutt.'

'We could have a discussion about that, but maybe the truth of the situation is that you have more respect for yourself?'

'Let's go with that,' I agree. Though at three o'clock this morning, I would have happily given it up in a heartbeat. 'I don't know when, if ever, I'll see him again.'

'You could sort of do with a boyfriend who's around,' Robyn suggests. 'Dinner is slightly tricky transatlantic style. Maybe hooking up with Max Wotsit isn't the best plan. Have you heard anything from the guy on the coach?'

'Henry Jackson?'

'That's the one.'

'Not a thing,' I admit. 'I've barely given him a thought.'

'You've had a lot on your mind. Compared to dealing with your son's brain tumour, finding a new bloke is probably quite low on the list.'

'Tell me about it.'

'How's Finn doing?' Robyn asks.

'He's great. Such a good kid. He's coping with

this so amazingly, while I'm in bits. I made him text me every hour last night to check that he was OK.'

'I hate to raise this,' she says, reluctantly. 'And I certainly don't want to put you under pressure, but...'

'When am I coming back to work?'

She nods. 'We've got a big case on and I could do with you here.'

'I think Finn will be ready to go back to school next week and I guess that I'll be looking to shift the temp out of my desk too.'

'She's done a great job,' Robyn says, 'but she's not you. We'll need all hands to the pump and it will be good to have you back.'

Part of me is terminally reluctant, but I know that I have to prise myself away from Finn and come to work at some point. It might as well be now. 'Shall we make it a date? Next Monday nine o'clock?'

'Suits me. Don't rush it though. We need you desperately, but if you don't think you can manage we'll muddle through somehow. I don't want you stressing.'

'I think it will help to get some sort of normality back in our lives.'

'You'll cope all right? I expect Finn's still backwards and forwards to the hospital?'

'Yeah. Regular injections of testosterone for him.' From now until the end of time, I fear. 'My dear parents will step into the breach once more.'

'They do a fantastic job.'

Tell me about it. 'I couldn't manage without them.'

Robyn checks her watch. 'I'd better get back to work.'

'I should go home too. I've been away from my boy for too long.' I give Robyn a hug. 'Thanks for being so understanding.'

She shrugs. 'It's what friends are for.'

'I'll see you first thing on Monday morning.' We both grimace as I say it.

'Give my love to Finn. Tell him he has a fabulous – and virtuous – mother.'

I laugh. 'Maybe I'll just stick with the fabulous bit.'

Then I hurry out and head up to Euston station, eager now to get home to my child.

Chapter Forty-Nine

The rest of the week flies by and, on the following Monday morning, I'm back in the twilight world of the commuter and waiting for the coach. I'm quite depressed about it. I don't think I'd mind so much if it was a gloriously sunny summer's day, but it's not. The weather greeting me on my first day back is grey and grizzly. The sort of day when you have no idea what shoes to wear or whether it's cardigan or jacket weather. If it stays like this, I'll be cold all day. If the sun comes out, I'll roast. You can't open the windows on the coach and sometimes the air conditioning is all skewed, adding to the boiling-hot/freezing-cold dilemma.

My fellow commuters and I lurk at the stop by

the end of my road and grumble. One or two of them who sit closest to me comment on my absence. They assume I've been on holiday. I don't tell them otherwise. Though they must think I've been to Margate or Morecambe rather than Mexico or Mauritius, as I haven't got a tan. I should have slapped on some fake stuff. Mind you, the last time I did that I needed new bedding.

To compound matters, the coach is late, which makes me even more glum. At least when I get on Toni is ready with a cup of coffee for me and, more importantly, no one else has laid siege to my favourite seat while I was absent. If that had happened, I think I might have cried. Toni is as cheery as ever and I'm delighted to see her. I whisper to her what has really been happening and she makes sympathetic tutting noises while I recant my tale of woe.

'Henry's been missing you,' she confides. 'He's been right miserable.'

'I sort of stopped returning his calls,' I confess. 'I've just had too much on my mind to think about anything else.'

'It will perk him up no end when he sees that you're back.'

And, when he climbs onto the coach a short while later, I can tell that Toni's right. I watch as Henry makes his way down the coach. His face looks as miserable as I feel. Then, when he sees me, he breaks into a broad grin.

'You're back!' He swings into the seat next to me. I think if circumstances allowed, he'd give me a big hug. 'I've been so concerned,' he says. 'I

242

just didn't like to keep calling when you had so much on your plate.'

'It's OK.' I understand perfectly. People just don't know what to say when you tell them that your kid has a brain tumour and there are only so many bad news calls that a stranger can take. 'It seems to be under control now. Fingers crossed.' I have *everything* crossed, if I'm honest. 'Finn has gone back to school today.' Which I think was traumatic for both of us. My dear boy certainly seemed very reluctant to get out his school uniform last night in readiness. Dad is going to have one hell of a job getting him out of the door on time. I check my watch and text Finn. *Don't oversleep. Mum xx.*

Wide awake. Now, he texts back.

'I haven't got any breakfast for us,' Henry says. 'I sort of stopped buying anything. I can start again tomorrow, if you like.'

'That would be nice.' I'd forgotten what a pleasant man Henry is. He's handsome too, but in a different way from Max Alexander. Henry looks like a scruffy schoolboy, but there's no doubt he has a charm. His smile is disarming and warm. He's easy company too and I don't turn into a complete jibbering jelly in his presence which is also nice.

Toni brings Henry a coffee too. 'Happy again now?' She winks at him and he flushes.

'I have missed you,' he confesses when she moves away. 'The journeys have seemed a lot longer without you.'

'How are things with your daughter?' I ask, in an effort to dodge the compliment.

'I've been up there quite a lot while you've been away,' he says with a sigh. 'She's missing me terribly. Playing up a bit for the ex. I'm trying to see her as much as I can.' He lets his guard down for a moment and I can see the sadness in his eyes. 'This isn't really how I imagined living my life. I don't know how much longer I can do it for. I take my hat off to you for enduring this day in, day out. It's killing me.'

'The first five years are the worst,' I say in an effort to make light of it. Thankfully, he laughs.

'This is why I've missed you. Tomorrow, I'll bring us an extra-special breakfast,' he promises.

We chat the journey away and we vow to try to catch the same coach home. I wave as I get off at the Embankment. I'm half an hour late. Not the best start to my resumption of work. Robyn, it seems, couldn't care less about my tardiness. She's just relieved that I'm there at all.

'Thank God,' she cries and almost falls on me, hugging me tightly. 'Are you all right?'

'Surviving.'

'That's good enough for me,' she teases. 'Get your coat off and get cracking. We've got masses to do. I might not even give you a lunch break.'

'Baptism of fire,' I comment.

'I'm joking. You take it easy. Break yourself in gently.'

'Thanks, Robyn. I will.' It's amazing how a few weeks off can make you feel so rusty.

'Good to be back?'

'No,' I tell her truthfully and we both laugh.

But that's really the last time I get to draw

breath all day. We're manically busy dealing with an impending court hearing and I spend my day stuck in my chair, on the phone, bashing out witness statements. Lunch is a slightly squashed Mars bar that's in my desk drawer and two coffees. I'm so busy that I miss my coach home and am barely going to make the next one.

And that's pretty much how the rest of the week goes. Commute, work like a mad thing, miss lunch, dash for coach, catch by skin of teeth, commute, eat dinner without tasting it, snatch an hour with Finn, fall into bed. Repeat for five days. By the end of the week I'm almost dizzy with exhaustion.

On Friday evening, Robyn comes to sit on my desk as I'm gathering my coat and bag. 'I'm sorry that today's been so manic.'

'It's fine.' I stifle a yawn. Every bone in my body is urging me to sleep.

'It's been a shit week really.'

'Yeah.' Can't argue with that.

'I'm worried about you. As a friend.' Robyn frowns at me. 'Are you really going to be able to do this?'

'I don't know,' I confess. 'One week back and I'm shattered.' It was bad enough before, but now I've got Finn's illness to handle I feel right on the edge. Plus, if I'm really honest, I resent every minute that I'm away from my son. It might sound stupid, but the distance feels just too far. If anything happened to him, at school or while he's at home alone, I can't get there for well over an hour, even if I take the train. If I worked locally, or for myself, I could be a lot more flexible. He's about

245

to start his exams and I want to support him through those too. Currently, I'm able to rely heavily on Mum and Dad, but they're not getting any younger. What if they were ill too? God forbid. There's absolutely no slack in my system and that worries me more than I'd like to admit.

'I don't want you to keel over,' Robyn says while all this is knocking round in my brain.

'I'm sure I'll get into the swing of it again after a few weeks.'

She doesn't look convinced. Perhaps because I don't sound it. 'I'd rather have a bit of you than nothing at all. I've been thinking, what if we let you go part-time or offered you a job share? Would that work out better for you?'

The thought sounds very appealing. 'Could I even do that?'

'I don't know,' Robyn says. 'The temp we had was OK. I could ask her to come back. If that's what you want.'

'I don't know,' I admit. My brain's too tired even to consider working out the pros and cons.

She sounds tentative when she suggests, 'Should we give it a go?'

I could lie down on the floor and weep with relief. If I'm finding it hard coming back now, when the days are long and light, just wait until winter arrives and I'm leaving in the dark and getting home in the dark. That's soul destroying.

'What if you did three days rather than five?' Robyn offers. 'Would that suit you?'

'I'd have to think about the money,' I tell her. It would be really difficult to lose a good chunk of that. But is lifestyle more important than that?

246

Finn needs me and I wonder if we could manage on less. 'Can I do some figures tonight?'

'Take as long as you need, Christie. I'm trying to help. I don't like to see you drowning.'

Drowning. That's exactly how I feel, yet I hate to admit that I can't juggle it all.

'I love you.' I give her a big hug. 'And I'll think about this all the way home and all tonight. But now I have to run for my coach.'

Chapter Fifty

When Dad picks me up, I'm nearly on my knees. To compound my return to commuting, the traffic was truly terrible. We were at a standstill on the M1 for over an hour and now it's eight-thirty and I'm so hungry that I could bite my own legs off. As I got a different coach home from Henry, I did – at least – manage to have a bit of a doze.

Dad twists in the driver's seat and scrutinises me. 'You look knackered, love.'

'Thanks, Dad.'

'Your mum's got Mary Berry's fish pie on. That'll put hairs on your chest.'

'I'm not sure it's hairs on my chest that I need.' A fortnight under a duvet wouldn't go amiss.

Before he drives off, he pauses to ask, 'Are you sure you can keep doing this, Christie?'

'What?'

'Commuting. All this work.'

'I honestly don't know, Dad.'

'Finn being poorly is taking its toll on you too. Understandably.'

'I really struggled at work today,' I confess.

'I'm not surprised. The journey alone must be exhausting. I did it for a few years myself. Wild horses couldn't make me do it again.'

I think when you're in the commuting groove, then you just get on and do it on autopilot. It's when you have a break that you realise what a monumental pain in the neck it is. 'My boss suggested that I could go part-time or do a job share.'

Dad pulls into the traffic. Clearly he has one eye on the fact that if he doesn't get a move on Mum's fish pie will be singed and he'll get a flea in his ear. 'That sounds like a good idea.'

'In theory, it is,' I agree. 'In practice it would mean a big cut in salary.' My contract with Contemporary Crafts is fantastic, but it isn't particularly lucrative – not yet. And it's temporary. What if I get to the end of the year and Max – or Dean – decides that he doesn't want me any more? Then I've given up a crucial part of my income. What would I have to fall back on? 'Robyn is being really kind to suggest it, but I'm not sure that I can juggle my finances that much.'

We drive in silence the rest of the way and Mum hugs me when I get to their house. She looks worried too and it's clear that she and Dad have been having a conversation about my welfare. No matter what age your children, as a parent, it seems as if you never stop worrying about them.

My boy, still in his school uniform, is lying full length on the rug in the living room, books open in front of him. Eric, dead to the world alongside him, is twitching his paws in a dream where he's probably chasing one of the cats. Finn has one eye on the television rather than his books and I should nag him about concentrating while he revises, but I can't. I couldn't care less what his grades are in IT or geography or whatever. There's more to life than great GCSE results. His exams are soon and, if he doesn't know it now, he probably won't. This is a terrible time for him to be unwell, but when was life ever neatly planned?

He looks so young, so much smaller than he should be for his age, that it makes my eyes fill with tears.

'Hi, Mum,' he says, turning round.

'Hello, love. How was school today?'

'Rubbish,' he says. 'Crappy week really. Though everyone was nice about me being back. Good day at the office?'

'No. Also rubbish.'

'Crappy week too?'

I nod and don't even tell him off for saying crappy.

He chews the end of his pencil. 'I've been thinking. We need a change of lifestyle.'

I can't help but smile. 'Sounds like a plan.'

'We should get this online shop up and running. If it takes off then you could give up your job in London.'

'It's something to think about,' I agree.

Then Mum shouts. 'Dinner's ready!'

'Come on,' I say to Finn. 'Mary Berry's fish pie waits for no one.'

Mum's set the table in the kitchen, so we eat in there and Finn chats about his day while picking the prawns out of his dinner. I notice that I've got an extra big helping – clearly I must look as if I'm in need of bolstering up. At the moment, I couldn't agree more. The thought of getting up again on Monday to go into London and repeat the week I've had fills me with dread. Even the thought of seeing Henry on the coach doesn't do much to lift my spirits.

When we've eaten dinner, Dad is tasked with washing up and Finn returns to his television/ revision session. I dry up for Dad, but we don't talk much.

When we've finished he says, 'I'm going to say goodnight to Big Bertha.' The ongoing project that Dad has in his workshop.

Mum rolls her eyes. 'His other woman.'

Dad heads down the garden, a spring in his step, while Mum and I take a cup of tea into the conservatory.

'I think it's actually warm enough to sit outside.' I've spent all day cooped up, only seeing the sun from inside an air-conditioned office and feel desperate for a bit of fresh air. Summers come and go and I feel as if I see precious little of them. 'Let's go down to the summerhouse.'

Mum throws open the doors. 'Hmm. Take a blanky. It's not as warm as it looks.'

I pick up the rainbow-coloured crocheted number that's slung over the back of the sofa. This is the closest we've got to a family heirloom. I remember Mum spending months and months doing this when I was about eleven. There are a few rows from me in among the shell stitch pattern too.

Mum and I wander down the garden together. We sit inside the summerhouse, so that we're sheltered from the breeze. Me huddled in the blanket, Mum in a good, thick cardigan.

'You could do with a fire pit,' I say to Mum. 'On the decking.'

'Don't give your father ideas.' She waves a hand, dismissively. 'He'd be cutting down trees willy-nilly before you could say boo. He'd probably set the summerhouse alight. Remember when he got ten foot flames off the barbecue because he'd covered everything in lighter fuel? Never trust a man with fire. They get giddy.'

Despite Mum's reservations, I think I might buy him one for Christmas. He'd be in his element. Dad's never happier than when he's chopping things up or setting fire to them.

'We've got a little fan heater in here, if you're chilly.'

'I'm fine. Honestly.' I snuggle into my blanket. It's cosy in here, if a little cobwebby.

'You can't go on like this, you know.' Obviously, Mum's been rehearsing this conversation in her head. 'I'm sorry that I sent those projects off. I should have thought. You've got more than enough to cope with. It was silly of me.'

'Don't be sorry. That's the best thing that's happened to me in a long time.' I get an image of Max's handsome face, the touch of his lips on mine. 'It's given me a nice boost. And, to be truthful, it's something that I'd rather be doing with my future. The world of – often pointless – litigation is definitely losing its thrall.'

'I don't know how you do it,' Mum says.

251

I touch her arm. 'With lots of help from you and Dad.' I draw my knees up and wrap the blanket round them for comfort more than warmth. 'Robyn has said I can go part-time. I think she realises that it's all a bit much for me at the moment. I'm just trying to work out how feasible that is.'

'Dad and I have been thinking.'

That way danger lies.

'You can have some of his money,' she says, the words rushing out. 'It's only sitting in the bank earning nothing. What good is it to us?'

'I can't take that.' My parents aren't big spenders, but Dad's payout is their rainy day money. 'You might need it for something.'

'I always wanted to do a cruise,' Mum says. 'A big, posh one. But I can't be bothered now. I've seen all the places I need to. I like the Lake District. You know where you are with the Lakes. And your father doesn't like foreign food.'

I laugh at that.

'It's much better that you use it,' she continues. 'It will all come to you eventually, anyway. Might as well have it now.'

'Mum...' I can't bear to think about them not being around. 'Don't talk like that.'

'We want to see you happy, Christie. You and Finn. You need to be here for him. If we can help you with that, then so be it. That's what being a parent is all about.'

I get up and wrap my arms round her. 'Thank you.'

She strokes my back. 'There's no need to feel you have to be superwoman, you know. Your generation think that you can do it all and have it all. Being a mum is a full-time job and Finn needs you more than ever.'

'He's coping so well.'

'On the outside,' Mum says. 'You don't know what's churning round on the inside.'

'He seems all right to you though?' The sad thing is that, now I'm back at work, Mum and Dad will see him more than me.

'He seems fine. Very brave. I'm really proud of him. But this is a lot to deal with. On top of everything else, he's got his exams to worry about. There might be times when he needs you more than he likes to admit.'

'You think I should talk to Robyn and tell her that I'll go part-time?'

'If she's offered it, then you should definitely try to make it work.'

It seems a really scary thing to do. Almost like cutting an umbilical cord. I've been at that job for so long, it's difficult to prise my fingers off it. But I have to do it, don't I?

Chapter Fifty-One

With a hug, we both leave the summerhouse. Mum goes indoors to find her knitting and, still wrapped in her blanket of many colours, I wander back up the garden path past the apple trees to the forbidden sanctuary of Dad's workshop. He built this place himself probably thirty years ago and it's a proper man shed. It smells of oil and paint and wood shavings.

I knock at the worn door and stick my head inside. 'Only me.'

It looks like one of those old-fashioned iron-mongers in here. There's a place for everything and everything has its place. There are rows of screwdrivers, drill bits, pliers. Next to them, a rack of shelves filled with half-empty cans of paint matching every shade of decorating that's ever been done in their bungalow. My dad is not a man to throw anything away that 'might come in handy'.

'Hello, love.' Dad glances up, adjusting his glasses. 'Mind you don't get your clothes dirty.'

Honestly, you could eat your dinner off the floor in here, but Mum makes him wear an ancient green overall as she's paranoid about dirt. I tiptoe inside.

Dad's standing there, bent over his bench, glasses perched on the end of his nose. I think of the family photos of him as a younger man, handsome, slim frame, a full head of hair. Now his hair is thinning, white and there's a little pot belly due to my mother's love of producing dinners that contain as many carbs as possible. He still has a look of Michael Caine about him though. Well, I think so.

'Everything all right?'

'I've just been talking to Mum.'

'Ah.'

'Thank you for the offer of help. I don't know what to say that begins to tell you how grateful I am.'

'Go on with you,' Dad says. 'You need it more than we do.'

'I know ... but ... it's a lot to give me.'

'So your mum won't get her cruise or the new kitchen she mithers on about.' Dad gives me a kindly smile. 'There's more in life to worry about, love.'

I wrap my arms round my dad and hug him. Even thinking that there's a way out of my daily drudge seems to lift a huge weight from my shoulders.

'We only want you to be happy,' he adds. 'You and Finn.'

'Thanks, Dad.' Then I see that he's crying. 'Don't cry.'

'If anything happened to Finn ... or you.'

'We'll be fine. Honestly. We both will.' I hug him tightly. 'We'll get through this.'

He lets me hold him for a little while, then he steps away and takes out his hanky to wipe his eyes and blow his nose. Embarrassed now, he turns his attention back to the engine he's fiddling with.

'How's it going with Big Bertha?'

'Oh, lovely,' he says. 'She's coming on nicely.'

I think he's been saying that for the last ten years. If I'm being truthful, we try not to ask Dad too much about Big Bertha as he can bore for England about it. I tell you, he swoons with delight if a packet of screws or something arrives through the post for it from eBay. He could tinker in here for hours and I'm not entirely sure what he does. I've never seen anyone treat a lump of metal with such love and affection. Everything Dad does is executed with meticulous care and precision. This is no exception.

Tonight, I'm prepared to indulge him. He has been the best father anyone could ever hope for. He's always there, always steadfast. He's not a drinker – half a pint of mild is his limit. He's not a womaniser – unless you count his soft spot for Katherine Jenkins. He goes all pink when she's on the telly and I don't think it's because of her angelic voice. He's always put his family before anything else. I'm only disappointed that I haven't found that kind of man in my life.

While Dad tells me about grinding out valves, I let my mind wander. I might have said that I'd indulge him, but I didn't say that I'd concentrate. Max Alexander would be terrible husband material. He's in the wrong country for a start. I should make up a checklist of qualities that are essential in a man. 'Same country' should head it. Closely followed by 'Same age bracket, sane, solvent, sober, steadfast and, not strictly essential, stylish'. Does Max fix this bill?

'I'd better be getting you home,' Dad says into my reverie. 'Bertha can wait until tomorrow.'

'I love you, Dad.' Now I'm the one who's filling up.

'I love you too, Christie.' He hugs me again. 'What silly billies we are.'

'Yeah,' I sniff.

'It'll all come right. These things do. You've just got to relax and accept what the universe brings.'

'That's a bit airy-fairy for you, Dad.'

'Mum makes me watch *Lorraine* every morning.'

'Ah.'

Dad wipes his hands on a rag. 'Ready then?'
I nod.

'We'll get this sorted out,' Dad says. 'Don't you worry. Those doctors know what they're doing. You're right. That boy of yours will be fine.'

Then suddenly it's as if a dam breaks inside me. All the pent-up anger and anxiety and exhaustion bursts free. I step into Dad's arms and he holds me as he used to when I was a child – when I'd skinned my knee or bumped my head or fallen out with a friend or had done any of the things that seemed so important then but are so very trivial now – and I cry my eyes out.

Chapter Fifty-Two

On Monday, before I lose my nerve, I tell Robyn that I would like to do a job share.

'Could you do Monday to Wednesday?' she says. 'I'll phone the temp agency to get the woman back who's been covering your work. She's been quite good.'

The thought of not having to get on the coach more than three mornings a week makes me ecstatic. 'That would be great,' I tell her, gratefully. 'Are you sure we could operate like that?'

'We can give it a damn good go,' Robyn says.

'When could I start?'

'As soon as we can get someone into cover the other days. A month or so?'

'Sounds good to me.' Just four more weeks of

the daily commute. I could weep with relief. It can't come quick enough.

'How's Finn doing?'

'OK. We're back at the hospital soon for yet another check-up.' Now they've actually diagnosed his condition, I can't fault how thorough they're being. Something that has my blood back to a gentle simmer rather than a rolling boil. 'I can try to schedule the appointments on my days off so that it doesn't interfere with work as much.'

'Do what you have to,' Robyn says. 'We'll cope. Shall we get to it?'

So the rest of the day goes by in a blur again and soon the clock is heading towards five. Finn has sat the first two of his exams today and it's probably just as well that I haven't had time to stress about that too. His GCSEs seemed ages away – just something else to fret about on the horizon. Then, suddenly, boom, they're here. I put a little note into his school blazer pocket with a bar of chocolate and I sent him a text before each one. He did all right in his mock exams, but that was before everything unravelled. I can only hope that he's done enough work to scrape through so that he can carry on into sixth form.

I'm still trying to type with one hand and put my cardigan on with the other, as I'm rushing out of the door. I bask in a few moments of welcome sunshine while I wait for the coach on the Embankment. Before we know it, summer will be over and, this year, I've barely even noticed it. I didn't see Henry this morning, but he texted me to say that he would try to catch the same coach home. I didn't have time to reply.

When I get on, he's already sitting in what we now term 'our' place and I squeeze in next to him.

'I thought I'd treat us.' He delves into the brown paper bag he's holding and pulls out two cans of ready-made gin and tonic and two plastic glasses.

'Very civilised. I approve.' He pours one for me and, timing it with the swaying of the coach, hands it over. 'Are we celebrating anything in particular?'

'The fact that it's summer. The fact that I've survived commuting for so long. The fact that you're back at work and I no longer have long, lonely journeys in the morning.'

I laugh at that.

'And to your son's health, of course.'

'I'll drink to that.' Despite being out of a can, the gin is cool and fresh on my tongue and hits the spot right away. 'Good job I don't have to drive at the other end.'

'What's it like being back at work?'

'Awful,' I admit. Then I think that I might as well tell Henry my news. 'I've just been talking about it with my boss. I'm going to work three days a week for a trial period. With all of Finn's appointments and the travelling, I'm just finding it too much. Plus, to put the tin hat on it all, there's my design work now.'

'I remember you telling me about that and we still haven't celebrated.'

I sip my gin. 'I think it's going to take up a lot of time. I want to do it properly or I might as well not bother.'

'It sounds as if I should get my bid in early, if I want to see you.'

'Yes,' I laugh. 'Mrs In Demand. That's me.'

He takes a deep breath. 'Are you doing anything this weekend? I'm not going up to see Kyra, so I'll be home alone.'

Part of me feels this is too much to cope with on top of everything else, but the hopeful look in his eye has me vacillating. Henry seems keen to take this further, but I'm not sure that I'm ready to do that. I like him as a companion – very much so – but do I really want any more from him? It's always the way, isn't it? I've found someone who sets my heart racing and my hormones surging who's completely unattainable. Then someone else – someone right here, right with me – is eager to take our friendship to the next level and I'm keeping him at arm's length. Oh, fickle heart!

'Nothing heavy,' Henry adds, quickly. 'We could just go for a walk and a coffee. I feel I don't get anywhere near enough exercise now that I'm stuck in an office all day.'

Before I can think better of it, I say, 'Yes. I'd like that.'

Frankly, he looks as shocked as I am that I accepted.

'Wow,' he says.

To be honest, I don't think he could look more stunned if I'd slapped him across the face. He was clearly expecting another rejection.

'I can pick you up, so you don't have to drive,' he rushes on. 'Is there anywhere particular you'd like to go?'

'I don't know.' I try to think but my mind won't comply. 'Let me come back to you on that.'

'I confess that I've been Googling the local

260

hotspots. Why don't I surprise you?' he suggests.

'That would be nice.'

'OK. Consider it done.' Then he settles back in his seat and we drink some more gin and it makes me smile to see that Henry really is as pleased as punch.

Chapter Fifty-Three

Finn and I are having dinner at home. This is one of Mum's craft club nights so Dad was dispatched early to bring a casserole over to put in the slow cooker. One of Delia's little numbers. Even in the height of summer, my mum doesn't consider salad to be a Proper Meal.

My son and I sit opposite each other at the kitchen table, the dining room being completely swamped with crafting detritus. It's good to be home in our cosy little house, warm with the scent of the casserole. Eric sits at my feet, ever hopeful. The cats are curled up together on top of the boiler, fast asleep. The sun has disappeared and, as befitting a British summer, it's raining now – big, fat drops – and the sky is as dark as night. Good job we've got a nice, warming dinner rather than lettuce. Poor Eric won't be getting his walk tonight unless the rain stops. My dad takes him out in all weathers, but I'm definitely a more fair-weather dog walker. He'll have a quick run round the garden instead and be none the worse for it. Then I notice that Finn is picking at his food and looks pale.

'Are you OK?' I ask.

'Just tired,' he says.

'School all right? How did your exams go?'

Finn shrugs. 'All right, I suppose. Maths wasn't that difficult. French was a bit *merde*.'

'Language, Finn. You're not *too* tired?'

'No more than usual. It's just that the days seem really long. I'm totally knackered by four o'clock. I wish it was like nursery where they put you down for a little nap in the afternoon.'

'You used to hate it then. All the other kids would be conked out and you'd be screaming your head off.'

'I was young and foolish then,' Finn says.

'We'll have a word with the doctor at your next appointment. It's only a week away.'

'Cool.'

'You're probably going to be a bit up and down until you settle on your medication,' I try to reassure him. 'Soon you'll have your old mum at home more to look after you.'

'I can't wait.' His voice is loaded with sarcasm, but he gives me one of his cheeky smiles to soften his words.

'I'm going to do some crafting tonight.' The deadline for my projects is rushing up.

'I'll help,' Finn says, affably.

'Don't you have any revision to do?'

'Yeah, but I'll give it a rest for an hour or so. I said I'd Skype Dad too. So what can I barter for cutting flowers and stuff?'

'Washing up?'

'Done,' he says. 'When I'm a millionaire, the

first thing that I'll do is buy you a dishwasher.'

'I look forward to it. Can I put in a request for a Mercedes too?'

'You can try,' he teases. 'I'll call Dad while you wash up.'

'Eat some more for me first.'

'I'm not five.'

'I know but you're still a growing boy.'

Grudgingly, he picks up his fork. Then, before he goes to leave the table, I think that I must broach The Matter of Henry with him. 'Finn...'

He glances up from pushing his dinner around, perhaps alerted by the sudden seriousness of my tone.

'I want to talk to you about something.'

'What have I done?'

'Nothing.' I laugh. 'Don't look so guilty.' I wonder if he's got cigarettes hidden in his bedroom or has been looking at porn on the laptop.

'What, then?'

I feel myself gulp and my throat tightens. 'I've been sitting next to a nice man on the coach,' I say. 'Henry.'

Finn raises an eyebrow.

'We've become quite chatty.'

The other one joins it.

'And now he's asked me out.'

'Way to go, Mother.'

'It's not like that,' I add, quickly. 'We'd just be friends.'

'Does he know that?'

That makes me chuckle. 'I'm not really sure.'

'And you're telling me this, why?'

'I'd like your approval.'

'You have it.'

'He's not going to be moving in anytime soon,' I rush on.

'I'm pleased to hear it.'

'It's well … he's been asking me a lot and I keep saying no.'

'You thought that he'd stop asking if you didn't say yes.'

'Yes.'

'I had the same issue with Bridget Willets in year nine. I gave up in the end.'

'So you can understand my worries.'

'Of course.'

'And you don't mind?'

'What about Max Alexander? He's the one who makes you go all silly when you talk about him.'

'He does not!' Finn gives me The Look. 'Well, only a bit.' I start to clear the plates for something to do. 'But he's not here. He's in America and how would that work?'

'Where there's a will and all that.'

'Sometimes there's too much to overcome,' I say and hope that's the subject closed.

'So where's Henry taking you on this date?'

'I don't know yet. He said he'll surprise me.'

'That way danger lies,' Finn says sagely.

Chapter Fifty-Four

To tell you the truth, the weekend comes round way too quickly. It's Saturday morning and, even though Henry isn't picking me up for another hour, I'm already anxious.

I'm making myself a camomile tea – which I don't really like – in an attempt to calm my nerves. Finn comes into the kitchen, still in his pyjamas, still yawning. He's been busy with exams all week and looks exhausted. I'd so much rather be spending time at home with my boy. I don't know what I was thinking of agreeing to this.

I give Finn a hug and Eric wags his tail in welcome. 'Can I get you some breakfast?'

'Just some toast, please, Mum.'

'We've got bacon. I can do you a sarnie or some eggy bread.'

He flops into a chair. Another yawn. Eric goes to curl beneath his feet. 'Toast is fine.' Then he stares at me. 'I thought you were going on a date today?'

I put some bread in the toaster. 'I am.'

'Then why are you dressed like that?' He takes in my cropped white jeans and pink checked shirt, my white sandals, my pale lemon sweater tied round my shoulders. 'What's with the whole Wisteria Lane goes to a rodeo look?'

My face falls. 'You don't like it?'

Finn grimaces. 'You look like you're going to

work on a farm or something.'

'You're not too far off, actually.' My son waits for me to enlighten him. 'Henry's taking me to an alpaca experience.' He said that it was going to be a surprise, but caved in and told me what he had planned when he realised that I'd have no idea what to wear. I'm not sure that telling me made much difference.

Finn recoils. 'Say again?'

'We're going to a farm that specialises in alpacas and we're going to walk them.' Finn's toast shoots out of the toaster and I butter it.

'Right.' My boy scratches his chin. 'If you don't mind me asking, what exactly is an alpaca?'

'It's like a llama, but cuter. I think.' I confess that I had to look up alpacas when Henry organised this for our first outing together.

'What kind of date is that?'

'It's the kind of date that middle-aged people who are jaded with life have.'

'Can I remind you that the other bloke took you to dinner at The Shard and you had cocktails and came home with a big grin on your face? I'm not sure that alpacas are going to do that for you.'

'I like animals. It will be fun.'

'I'm afraid the jury's out on that one.'

'Besides, the visit to The Shard wasn't specifically for me. That was only because Max happened to be staying there.' I give Finn his toast and he tucks in. 'Max Alexander is in an entirely different league to Henry. Henry's just ... normal.'

'You're not selling him well.'

'He's nice,' I tell Finn. 'I'm nervous enough going out to an alpaca experience. I don't think I

266

could cope with anything more glamorous.'

'If I ever get a girlfriend, remind me not to take her to a farm on a first date.'

'She might love you for it.' I have some more camomile tea, which at the moment doesn't seem to be making a blind bit of difference to my anxiety levels. 'It's different. I'm not exactly sure where we're going, but there's a really nice farm called The Alpaca Place not far away that has a gorgeous shop and a tea room.' And sells lots of ruinously expensive hand-crafted alpaca scarves and knitting kits. They also do crochet workshops using their yarn which I'd be interested in too. Thank you, Google. 'It looks lovely. I could be in my element.'

Finn looks unconvinced.

I go and rest my hands on his shoulders and kiss his hair.

'Mum!' He tries to brush me off.

'You will find someone to love,' I tell him. 'You'll know her when you see her.'

'Enough with the slushy stuff,' he says. 'You're putting me off my toast.'

'I'm only trying to help.'

Then Finn's suddenly serious. 'Do you think anyone will ever love me? With all the things that are wrong with me? I'm not going to end up on *Undateables*?'

'Oh, Finn.' Tears instantly spring to my eyes. 'Look at you. You're the most handsome boy on the planet.'

'I think you might be biased, Mother.'

'You are. But, more importantly, you're beautiful on the inside.'

'That's the sort of thing Nana says.'

'And she's right. I don't want you to even worry about it. Of course you'll find someone to love.'

'It's not that easy though, is it? Look at you. You're great and yet you've been on your own since Dad went.'

'That's partly out of choice,' I remind him. 'Partly because I don't have the time.'

'And partly because you spend your nights in watching the Crappy Craft World channel and cutting out paper hearts.'

Some of that rings true. As I've said many times before, paper hearts are never going to get broken.

'I'm putting my toe back in the water of dating today.'

'With a bloke who thinks alpacas are where it's at.' He rolls his eyes. 'I don't want you to end up sad and lonely.'

'Thanks for that, Finn.'

'You know what I mean.'

'Finding someone to be with is easy. Your generation do it with phone apps. I won't lie to you, finding someone to love who loves you is much harder. But I have no doubt that you'll meet a great girl and fall in love and get married. Then, if you know what's good for you, you'll give me half a dozen grandchildren.'

'I'd like to travel the world a bit first,' Finn says. 'Maybe go out and see Dad.'

'I can live with that.' That makes us both laugh. I wrap my arms round him and he lets me. 'You're handling this brilliantly. I'm so proud of you. I know it's all difficult and new, but this –

the injections, the medication – it will all become a way of life. In a few years, you won't even think about it. It will simply be a part of your daily routine and your partner will accept it as such.'

'Sometimes I'm scared, Mum.'

I feel Finn's slight shoulders shake as he cries and I hold him tight. 'My brave, brave boy.'

When he's had a good cry, he sniffs away his tears.

'I can stay here today,' I say. 'I don't have to go out with Henry. He'll understand if I ring and cancel. We could do something together. Something that doesn't involve exercise or crafting. You name it.'

'No, no,' Finn says, wiping his nose on his sleeve as he used to do when he was a toddler. 'Go. I'll be fine. I'll do a bit of work for next week's exams, then I'll take Eric round to Nan and Pops.' He turns and, though he's still red-eyed, grins at me. 'I wouldn't dream of coming between you and your alpacas.'

I cuff him round the head for his cheek and then hold him tight.

Chapter Fifty-Five

The doorbell rings and, when I open it, Henry is standing there. He looks shy but just as untidy as he does on the coach. The only difference is that his mad hair is under a beanie hat, even though it's a nice, sunny day. He's also wearing a checked shirt and jeans. We could be a matching pair.

'I thought I was going to be late,' he says, flustered. 'My satnav had a devil's own job of finding this place and then I couldn't get a parking space.'

'It's always a nightmare here,' I tell him.

'We'd better get going.' He glances at his watch. 'Time and alpacas wait for no man.'

'Come in for a second and say hello to Finn before we dash off.'

So Henry comes inside and looks around. 'Nice house.'

'Don't look at the mess,' I instruct as I take him through to the kitchen. 'These boxes aren't usually here.'

Finn is fiddling about on his laptop, deep – or feigning to be – in concentration.

'Finn.' My son glances at me. 'This is Henry.'

My son holds up a hand. 'Hi, Henry.'

Henry does the same. 'Hi. Nice to meet you. Your mum's told me a lot about you.'

Finn shoots me The Look.

'All good,' I insist.

'It was,' Henry agrees. 'Sorry about the hospital stuff and the exams.'

'It's cool,' Finn says, nonchalantly.

'We'd better get going,' I say. 'The farm might be a bit tricky to find. You'll be OK while I'm out?'

'I'll be fine,' Finn says. 'I've advertised that I'm having a wild party on Facebook. What could possibly go wrong?'

'I'll come straight to Nan and Pops' when I'm back.'

'Don't rush,' Finn says. 'We can manage without you for a few hours. Have fun with your *alpacas*.'

I hope I'm the only one who can hear the loading in that word. If Henry does then he shows no sign of it.

'I'll see you later. Be good.'

'Laters,' Finn says with a wave. 'Don't do anything I wouldn't do.'

'Bye, Finn,' Henry says. 'I hope to see you again.'

When Henry turns away, Finn mouths, *'I don't fancy his chances!'* and I wag a warning finger at him.

Henry's car is nice. Because I know absolutely nothing about cars, I can't tell you what it is. But it's very smart and, quite honestly, quite a bit tidier than Henry.

We head out of Wolverton and into the wilds of Buckinghamshire. Now I'm confused as The Alpaca Place is in the opposite direction. Maybe this one will have a lovely shop and tearoom too.

'I hope this is good,' Henry says. 'One of the girls at work said her and her husband did it last Christmas and it was great. They had mulled wine and mince pies, but we've just got tea and cake after our walk.'

'Sounds good to me.'

Settling back in the seat, I let the scenery go past my eyes. Soon we're heading out of the environs of deepest, darkest Milton Keynes and into the green, gently rolling countryside beyond. We live, I think, in a beautiful part of the country and I don't get out and about enough to embrace it. Perhaps Finn and I could take up hiking. Then I remember it might nearly be as energetic as jogging. Hmm. Maybe not.

271

We drive through small, picturesque villages with ponds and thatched houses with roses round the door – Newton Longville, Drayton Parslow, Stewkley – all dreamy English village names. Half an hour or so later, we reach our destination.

'Here we are,' Henry says.

The drawing of a smiley alpaca on the sign to the farm sort of gives it away.

We bump and thump down the potholed farm track and I fear for the suspension of Henry's smart car. Finally, car still just about intact, we turn into a farmyard at the top of a hill. This is a proper farm, not the theme-park type experience I'd predicted. We park in the yard amid the cluster of green, corrugated-iron farm buildings. There's an old, brick farmhouse that looks as if it's been here for hundreds of years, but in the fields beyond I can see the distant outlines of the alpacas and wonder what the original farmers would think of this modern addition to the livestock.

A number of people, our fellow alpaca walkers, I presume, are already assembled. A few have entered into the spirit and are wearing colourful, Peruvian-style summer hats. There's one man in a colourful poncho, even though it's a nice day and he's probably too warm. I'm glad Henry went down the checked-shirt route and nothing more extravagant. Even in my white jeans and pink shirt I feel a bit overdressed as they're all distinctly more casual than I am. We join them and register our arrival, shaking hands with the smiling farmer as we do. He is younger than I'd imagined, ruddy-faced from the outdoors lifestyle with hair that clearly has been untroubled by a comb for some time.

'This looks great,' Henry says, taking in the farm and surroundings. 'Just the thing my ex and I imagined for ourselves.'

'Oh.'

'We always wanted a smallholding, to get away from the rat race. You know how it is.' He surveys the countryside, the rolling fields, the endless sky, drinking it in. 'That's why I wanted to come here. Check it out. This would have been perfect. Look at the views.'

'Gorgeous,' I agree. And it is. A hundred different shades of green stretching into the distance until it meets the blue of the sky.

'Helen's family were from farming stock.' Henry is clearly a little put out by that. 'It's in the blood, isn't it? I think that's why she wasn't happy with me. We had a three-bed detached on a modern estate. Not her thing at all. She wanted a farmhouse. She wanted rolling fields.'

'Don't we all?' I say in a teasing manner, to try to add some levity.

Henry doesn't bite. 'Mind you, the bloke she's with now works in the motor industry. That's not exactly green, is it?'

'No.' I give up trying to be funny.

'She wanted to live off grid,' Henry continues. I'm not even sure what that is.

'That's what she wanted. What we both wanted.'

He sounds quite bitter that it wasn't what either of them got. Oh, dear.

'Ladies and gentleman,' the farmer says. 'Are you ready to meet our wonderful alpacas?'

273

'Alpacas,' Henry mutters almost to himself as I trot along behind him. 'Maybe we'd have stayed together if we'd had alpacas.'

Chapter Fifty-Six

We head off along a muddy path, clearly trampled by the feet of many animals and not just alpacas. I pick my way through the puddles trying not to get my white sandals dirty and wishing that I had a pair of scuffed trainers in my handbag. I didn't really envisage muddy fields or think I'd need hiking boots for my date. My focus was, I have to admit, entirely on a tea room and a shop selling alpaca goodies. Why could we have not just gone out for a nice lunch?

The alpacas are hiding out in a stable at the end of a field and when the farmer calls them, they all come at a canter to the fence. They're quite pretty-looking creatures with long necks, pom-pom hair and smiley faces. Each one is named and the farmer introduces us to them all. He tells us that they don't spit but they puff air at you if you get too close, they might kick which will give you a nasty bruise, they don't like being stroked and go mental if anyone touches their pom-pom hair. Frankly, if I had hair like that, I think I'd go mental if anyone touched it.

Then it's crunch time. In turn, the farmer harnesses them all and we're handed our own alpaca. Mine, Molly, is pure white and has particularly great hair. She's very skittish and keeps bouncing away from me.

'Hold on tightly to her,' the farmer warns. 'She'll settle down in a while. Don't let go of her lead or she'll be off.'

'Right.' I strengthen my grip on the canvas tether attaching me to said frisky alpaca. She bounces a bit more.

'Last time it took us an hour to catch her.'

'Naughty Molly,' I coo to her. 'We'll be all right together won't we?' She turns doleful eyes on me and gives a shake of that pom-pom hair. I can't tell whether that was a yes or no.

The farmer frowns. 'Are you sure you can manage her?'

How the hell would I know? Not having had any previous alpaca walking experience. 'Er ... I'll give it a go.'

'Shout if she's too much for you,' the farmer says and marches off.

'Right.' Molly and I regard each other with mistrust.

Henry's alpaca, Baron, is a golden brown colour and is much bigger than the others. I'm thinking he's the alpha male and needs watching too. He looks like trouble.

'This is great fun, isn't it?' Henry says, his mood momentarily lifted.

'Lovely.' Molly runs round in a circle and comes back to where she started, tangling me up in the lead.

The others set off while I'm still unravelling myself.

We head off down towards the open fields, passing ducks, pygmy goats, two Shetland ponies and a huge pig called, not surprisingly, Peppa. The sun is shining and there's a gentle breeze to ruffle the alpaca's hair. I'm hanging onto Molly as she's trying to keep pace with the alpacas at the front. I didn't know that alpacas were competitive.

All the alpacas are jostling for position and Henry's big boy clearly wants to be right at the front, so he's striding away from us. Molly and I are struggling to keep up with him – especially as Molly now seems to have given up on jogging and stops every two seconds, finding every single daisy and weed fascinating. And I'm wearing dainty sandals instead of Suitable Footwear.

I tug at her lead and try to urge her on so that we're not left behind. 'Come on, lovely.'

There's quite a gap opening up now and, to catch up, I have to do the awful running thing – which, as you know, I never quite mastered. Molly keeps braking quickly and nearly has me on my backside more than once. No one else seems to have such a reluctant beast.

When I do catch up with Henry, he has a dark expression on his face and barely looks at me.

'Are you OK?' I ask Henry, slightly out of puff.

'Fine,' he says, crisply.

Blimey. He seems to be down in the dumps again. 'Are you not enjoying it?'

'Of course I am.' Bit snappy.

'I thought you might be regretting it?'

He sighs. 'My only regret is that this place isn't mine.'

'Well, it's a lovely day for it,' I say, trying to cheer him up. 'Imagine it here in the winter. It would be waterlogged and as bleak as hell.'

'I suppose so.' He stares longingly at the fields. 'But then I'd be at one with nature and not spending half my life on a bloody coach.'

Can't really argue with that one.

The alpacas jostle along happily, stopping to eat the grass whenever the fancy takes them. I think they're actually taking us for a walk rather than the other way round. We go down the hill, through a wild flower meadow alongside a stream and, finally, take a path shaded on one side by tall trees. Henry and I fall into step beside each other, courtesy of Baron and Molly. He's still a bit morose but I have to remember that he's only recently divorced and is bound to get black moments.

'This is lovely,' I say. 'The perfect way to spend an afternoon.'

Reluctantly, his smile comes back. 'Glad you're enjoying it.'

I am, but I can't help but notice that there's no chemistry between us. Henry is pleasant company, no doubt, and he's handsome too. I saw one of the other ladies casting a sideways glance at him just a moment ago. But the air doesn't crackle around us. Is that a bad thing? I don't yearn to touch him, to run my fingers through his hair, to feel his lips on mine, his skin against my skin. Would life be a lot easier if I had a relationship with someone like Henry? I try not to think of Max Alexander's mouth, his laugh, his devastatingly beautiful eyes.

Then, as I'm clearly concentrating on Max and not Molly, she decides to take off. There's no warning, one minute she's trotting along happy to accompany me in my not entirely appropriate reverie, then next it's as if she's in the Grand National.

'Whoa,' I shout. 'Whoa, Molly!'

She's having none of it.

We're positively at a gallop now, Molly's hair flying in the wind, me staggering behind her in my silly sandals, desperately trying to keep up. I have no idea where she's heading. It looks as if she's chasing something but, if she is, I can't see what she's seeing.

'Good girl,' I yell. 'Good girl!'

She's not a good girl. She's an evil bitch. I know it. She knows it. I manage to look back and the rest of the group are standing stock-still staring agog at me and the runaway alpaca. Only the farmer is bounding his way over the field towards us. Startled-looking sheep scatter in our wake.

I'm determined not to shout for help or to let go of her. I'm hanging on for grim death to the bolting alpaca. Then I can see that the grass is petering out and we're into a muddy area by the stream. But, worse than that, we're coming up to a barbed-wire fence. This is shit or bust. I can't let her drag me through that. She'll hurt herself and shred me too. So I try my hardest to bring her to a halt by hauling on the lead. This thing is the size of a small horse, and more wilful, so it's no mean feat.

At the last minute, Molly swerves, which wrong-foots me, the farmer heads us off and grabs at her halter. She brakes hard and stops dead. If this was a driving test, it would be the perfect emergency stop. I don't fare quite so well. I'm leaning back and, suddenly, with no tension on the lead, I

278

stumble forwards and end up doing a full face-plant right into the mud.

'All right, girl?' the farmer asks.

I assume he's addressing me and not the smug-looking alpaca with a glint in her beady eye. 'Yes, yes.' I stand up and gaze in dismay at my sandals, my once-white jeans, my mud-spattered shirt, face, hair. I favour a mud-wrestler. A beaten one, at that.

'Let's get you back to the house,' the farmer says, looking me up and down. 'She's never done that before. Well, just the once. Or twice.'

Molly looks as meek as a mouse now. I give her a wide berth. Give me a cat or a dog any day. I've a good mind to ruffle her stupid pom-pom hair for the hell of it. See how she likes that, eh?

I march back up the field to where Henry is still standing with Baron. He has the good grace to look concerned even though he did nothing to help. 'I thought it best to let the farmer take control,' he says.

'Yes.'

'You're all right though? Not hurt?'

Only my pride, I think, but I say, quite crisply, 'I'm fine, Henry.'

I wonder if Max Alexander would have stood and watched while a stampeding alpaca made fast and loose with me. Then I rationalise that Max Alexander wouldn't be taking me anywhere near alpacas to start with. Maybe Finn was right.

We make our way back up towards the farm-house – everyone else making sympathetic noises and comments, me feeling like a complete idiot. We take the alpacas back to their paddock. With a bit of coaxing – they get a bit freaked out about the hair thing again – the others manage to take off their harnesses and they run free once more. I've had enough of alpacas and keep clear.

As a reward for their tolerance, everyone is given a carton of food and, after a bit of prancing around, the alpacas return to take the pellets from their hands, nipping gently with their teeth as they do. Molly is the picture of innocence, fluttering her eyelashes, gently feeding from someone's fingers.

'This is fun,' Henry says.

I ignore him. I don't want to feed an alpaca. I want to lie down and weep.

'Come to the house,' the farmer says. 'You can get cleaned up.'

I trail after him to the farmhouse and his wife fusses as she finds me a towel and points me towards their bathroom. I still want to cry.

I use some toilet paper to wipe off the worst of the mud. My white jeans are probably ruined, my sandals too. I wash my face, scrubbing with the soap. I'll have to get in the shower as soon as I'm home.

When I can put it off no longer, I emerge from the bathroom, thank the farmer and his wife and go to find Henry.

He's sitting outside the barn at the pop-up café. Among piled hay bales, they've set out garden furniture and Henry is waiting at a table by the door beneath a pink parasol. He stands up when he sees me.

'Can I get you some tea and cake?'

I want to go straight home, but also feel that I

could be mollified by cake.

'I see you've managed to get most of the mud off.'

'Yes.'

We both have tea and a slice of home-made Victoria sponge. Conversation is stilted.

'I'm sorry how it turned out,' Henry says. 'I thought it would be fun.'

'Thank you,' I say to Henry. 'It was a very nice idea. You weren't to know I'd get a hormonal alpaca.'

'Still, I'd love to run something like this.' He has a wistful air about him.

'I'm sure that there's time. If you really want it. You're young. Resourceful.'

He shakes his head. 'It would cost a fortune. Besides, I'm not sure that it does to fill your head full of dreams. You'll only be disappointed.'

'Oh, I don't know about that.' I stuff my cake in my face, but it's just not hitting the spot.

'What I like about you, Christie, is that you're not like that. You're not discontented about everything.'

'I have my days.'

'You're nice, steady, solid,' he says. 'Ordinary.'

Ordinary? Is that supposed to be a compliment?

'My wife wanted everything that was beyond our reach. She was never happy.'

'I'm sorry to hear that.' But my mind's still stuck on 'ordinary'. Is that really how I appear to him? To others? I'm game for anything. I've just taken part in alpaca wrangling. Admittedly, I came off worse, but do *ordinary* women do that? Would they even give it a go? I feel as if the sun has gone behind a cloud.

Henry finishes his cake. 'We could have a pub lunch, if you like. I went on Google. There looks to be a reasonable place just down the road.'

'I should get back to Finn. I don't like to leave him for too long.' I look down at my mud-stained, ruined clothes. 'Besides, I'm not really dressed for the pub, Henry.'

'Oh. Right.' Henry stands and rubs his hands together. Clearly, he's not going to try to persuade me otherwise. Perhaps he has had enough too. 'I'll get you back then.'

And all I can think as I walk back to his car is ordinary, ordinary, ordinary.

Chapter Fifty-Seven

Henry drops me off at my parents' house.

'Thank you. I've had a lovely time.' Apart from the mud, obviously.

He looks as if he might like to come in with me, but I don't want him meeting my mum and dad now. I want a shower. I want to wash my hair.

I open the car door.

'See you on Monday, then,' he says. 'What do you fancy for breakfast?'

'I've got to take Finn to the hospital in the morning, so I won't be on the coach.'

'Oh. Right. Eating alone then.'

'I'll see you on Tuesday.' I feel a bit awkward. 'Thanks.'

'We should do this again,' Henry says.

Maybe he's feeling rueful about spending our time together regretting what he and his ex-wife did or didn't do. Perhaps he's feeling bad that I was dragged up hill and down dale and he did precious little to help. Or possibly he's realising that calling a woman 'ordinary' isn't the best compliment you can pay her.

'Yes.' But even to my own ears I sound non-committal.

'I hope Finn's OK.'

'I'm sure he'll be fine,' I say. 'I probably just worry too much.'

'Understandably.'

I get out of the car. 'Bye, then.'

'Bye, Christie. I've had a great time.'

'Me too.' I feel as flat as a pancake.

Then I stand and watch as he drives away, giving him a slightly fake cheery wave.

Chapter Fifty-Eight

Everyone's in the garden when I get back from my date. They've set up camp outside the summerhouse. Dad's snoozing, sunhat over his face, his paper discarded in his lap, Eric and Trigger curled up in the shade of his chair. Mum's knitting under the parasol – another jumper for Eric – and Finn is stretched out on a blanket on the grass with his laptop. The temperature is climbing nicely now and, if we're lucky, we'll soon be in the region of 'shorts weather' as my mother calls it.

'Hi.' I make Dad jump.

'You're back early, love,' he says, trying to blink himself awake. 'We hadn't expected you so soon.'

Eric runs to me barking and wagging his tail as if I've been lost to him for five years rather than a couple of hours. I ruffle his ears.

'Hi, Mum.' Finn glances up. 'What happened to you?'

I spread my hands. 'Molly the alpaca, one; Christie Chapman, nil.'

Mum looks up from her needles. 'I thought you were having lunch out.'

'Like this?' I toss a cushion aside so I don't get it dirty and sit down on the chair with a sigh. 'It didn't quite go according to plan.'

She frowns at me. 'Did your date not go well?'

'Yes,' I say. 'It was lovely. Until my frisky alpaca pulled me over in the mud. It was kind of downhill from there onwards. We did have cake though.'

'Were the alpacas all that you'd hoped they would be?' my son asks, tongue firmly in cheek.

'Don't you be cheeky to your old mum, Finlay Chapman,' I admonish and he laughs. 'The alpacas were adorable. Sort of. Some of them. You'd love them, Dad.' But then my dad likes anything with four legs – probably better than most humans.

'I won't be getting a wedding hat then?' Mum says.

'No.' I shake my head, sadly. 'I think he's still hung up on his ex-wife.' And he didn't come to my rescue when I needed him to. 'He'll make a nice friend, but nothing more.'

284

'Shame.'

'It's one of those things.' I'm trying to be philosophical about it. I don't mention that I might have contributed to the slightly negative result of our date by still being hung up on Max Alexander too. I think the outcome would have been very different with Max. He'd have been my knight in shining armour, he'd have wiped the mud from my face. I can picture him carefully unbuttoning my blouse, helping me out of my jeans...

'You've not had any lunch?' Mum asks.

I snap back to the present. My nice fantasy about Max Alexander disappears.

'No. No.' That'll send my mum into a flat spin. She can't understand how you could possibly miss a meal and not starve to death.

She puts her knitting aside, instantly. 'I'll make you a sandwich while you get a shower.'

'Can I borrow some clean clothes?'

'I did your ironing this morning,' Mum tells me. 'There'll be something in there.'

'Thanks, Mum.'

'No problem.' Mum's on her feet already. 'Cheese all right? Or I've got some nice Yorkshire ham.'

'Cheese is fine.'

'Finn, would you like some cake?'

'You gave me cake less than fifteen minutes ago, Nana. I'm good.'

'You're a growing boy,' Mum shouts over her shoulder as she hotfoots it back to the kitchen, hurrying to make my sandwich before I fade away.

Dad puts his sunhat back over his face and I go

to lie on the blanket next to Finn. 'Have you had a nice time?'

'Great,' he says, rolling onto his side and squinting into the sun. 'I spent the morning killing twenty-three people and a few dragons while being force-fed cake by Nana.'

'I forgot to tell her that you're restricted to playing on that thing for an hour.'

He grins at me. 'That's what I was relying on.'

'I'll balance it later by making you cut out butterflies.'

'I can't wait.'

'Did you manage to squeeze some school work into your action-packed morning?'

'Yeah,' he confesses. 'I did.'

'You feel prepared for next week's exams?'

Finn laughs. 'I wouldn't go that far.'

'It doesn't matter, you know,' I tell him. 'Just do your best.'

'Do I look worried?' Finn says.

'Probably less so than me.' I sigh at him. 'Shall we take the dogs into the meadow together after I've had my lunch?'

'If you can cope with all the excitement after your alpaca walk?'

'After hanging onto a frisky alpaca for an hour, I can manage anything.'

Finn laughs. 'I'm sorry it didn't work out with that Henry. He seemed like an OK kind of guy.'

'He is.'

'Apart from the checked shirt.'

'I thought you'd clock that. It could have been worse. There was a man in a Peruvian poncho.'

'Count yourself lucky then,' Finn says.

286

'I do.'

My son props himself up on his elbow. 'Dating looks like crap.'

'It is at my age. When you start, it will be brilliant fun.'

Finn looks sceptical. 'Yeah. All fun and games until someone's heart gets broken.'

'It's an inevitable part of love,' I tell him. 'Very few people are lucky enough to get it right first time. You'll love, you'll lose, you'll lick your wounds and you'll love again.'

'It sounds really scary,' Finn says. 'Perhaps there are some benefits to not growing up properly.'

I put my arm round him and pull him in for a rare cuddle. As no one can see us other than Nan and Pops he doesn't shrug me off.

'You've remembered that we're at the hospital again on Monday morning?'

'Yeah. You gave me the note for school.'

'And you remembered to hand it in?'

'Yeah. I even did that.'

'You're a good boy. Do I ever tell you that?'

'Yeah. We're cool on that front. Here's Nan with your sandwich.'

Sure enough, Mum is trotting down the garden holding a tray, Eric at her heels in the hope of errant crumbs. I give Finn a last squeeze and retreat to the shade of the parasol. It looks as if my shower will be delayed.

'Here you go, love,' Mum says. 'Some home-made lemonade too.'

The taste of my childhood.

'Thanks, Mum.'

'Never you mind,' she says, sitting beside me.

287

'Someone nice will come along. You mark my words.'

'I live in hope.'

'Hey, Mum,' Finn shouts. 'Forgot to say. There's an email in from Contemporary Crafts. Do you want the laptop?'

'I'll look at it on my phone. Thanks.' My heart skips a beat as I access my mail and see Max's name in the subject line. But it's a round robin to all the design team and not a personal mail just for me. Max is letting us all know that the new range of dies that we were shown at our training retreat are now in stock and are on the website. I click through to the link, ostensibly to look at the dies, but I can't help but linger on the photograph of Max on the home page. Which is just as pathetic as it sounds. But I curb the urge to reach out and stroke the image of his handsome face. Give me some credit for that.

Chapter Fifty-Nine

Monday, and Finn and I are sitting in the waiting room at the hospital in London. Finn is dressed again after his scan and I buy us both a drink from the vending machine while we're waiting. Tea for me, cola for Finn. My boy is playing *Tomb Runner* or *Zombie Invasion* or something equally unpleasant on his phone.

Mum and Dad have come up with us today, on the train. They've gone off to look at the Victoria and Albert Museum, which isn't too far away. If all goes well – fingers crossed – I'll go straight into work after our appointment and they'll take Finn home. He doesn't have an exam until tomorrow morning, so he can use the time to revise.

This clinic deals with many different kinds of cancer and leukaemia. It also caters for different ages of kids. There's a waiting room downstairs for the younger children with Little Tyke toys and a colourful soft play area. Up here, where we are, caters more for teenagers, with a pool table, computers, musical instruments, board games and stuff. All pretty cool. Finn never really minds waiting here as there's plenty to keep him occupied. Also half the patients are in pyjamas as it's a ward too, but no one bats an eyelid.

Opposite us, another mum and her daughter are waiting for an appointment too. The girl has a scarf on her head instead of hair. But then, most of the children in here are bald or sporting caps of some kind. Despite that, she's as pretty as a picture. Her eyes are wide, violet, and only the dark shadows under those young eyes and her fragile-looking frame hint that she has a serious illness. I wonder how far she is into her treatment and when she can hope for her hair to come back.

She smiles shyly at Finn and he blushes beet-root red.

'Have you had to come far?' I ask the mother.

'Bedford,' she says.

'Oh. Not far from us. We're in Milton Keynes.'

'Ella and I like to go shopping there, don't we?'

'Yeah,' Ella says, never taking her eyes from

Finn. 'I like Hollister.'

If I'm honest, she looks like a Hollister kind of girl. Petite, trendy, doesn't mind shopping in the dark.

'Have you been coming here long?' I ask.

'Six months now. Ella has non-Hodgkin's lymphoma. We're almost finished with her treatment.'

I don't know much about that, but I think it has good survival rates. I hope so, she's too young, too pretty to have something terminal.

'We could play pool,' Ella says to Finn in an admirably bold opener.

My son turns to me, the look of a rabbit caught in headlights in his eyes.

'We'll probably be waiting for ages yet.' I give him an encouraging look.

'I warn you. I'm good,' Ella says.

'I'm rubbish,' Finn says, conceding defeat before he starts, but he stands up anyway and I feel my heart swell for him. Together they go to the pool table.

'What's your son here for?'

'Brain tumour,' I tell her. 'On his pituitary gland. He's just had another MRI scan. They're hoping to control it with drugs.'

'Ah,' she says with the air of someone who's been there before.

Laughter comes from the direction of the pool table. I'm not an aficionado of the game of pool but, from here, it does look as if Finn is taking a pasting. It also sounds as if he and Ella are getting on just fine. Knowingly, her mum and I grin at each other.

When we're called in, Finn puts down his pool cue and follows me. We sit down next to each other in the consultant's office. We've been here too many times already. He's the person over-seeing Finn's treatment and, no doubt, we'll be regular features for some time yet.

I'm sure, at home, Mr Darby is a barrel of laughs. In his office, he is a man who looks as if he bears the weight of the world on his shoulders. I guess if your day job is always dealing with sick kids, your sense of humour must take a battering.

As always, Mr Darby looks serious. He perches on the desk in front of us.

'How are you feeling?' he asks Finn.

'OK,' he says. 'I get tired a lot.'

'Finding the injections all right, Mum?'

I nod. 'Obviously, I'd rather not be doing it, but I think Finn and I are both getting used to it.'

Mr Darby folds his arms across his chest. 'I've got your scan results.' He indicates the image of my son's brain which is up on a lightbox on the wall. 'Sorry, Finn, but it's not good news.'

Finn and I sit up straighter.

The consultant crosses the room to the image. 'See here?' He points to a shadowy mass. It looks like some sort of alien growing in my son's head. Finn visibly pales and I wish I'd left him outside for this bit. It's too much for him – for anyone – to take. I grip his hand. I wish he was still playing pool with Ella and didn't have to go through all this.

'Here's the tumour. We'd hoped that we could leave it alone for as long as possible, but it's in-creased in size. Only slightly, but enough to worry

291

me.' Mr Darby frowns. 'The medication hasn't been enough to halt its progress and my feeling is that we're going to need to take it out.'

It's as if someone has punched me in the guts. My tea makes a bid for freedom and, for a moment, I think I'm going to be sick on the floor of the consultant's office.

'If I'm being frank with you, Finn, I don't know how much longer we can delay an operation,' Mr Darby continues. 'Do you understand?'

Finn nods.

'Good boy.' He comes back to sit on his desk. 'With your consent, I'd like to go ahead with it as soon as we can.'

Perhaps I was being too optimistic, but I thought that it wouldn't come to this. I manage to say, 'With the drugs and injections and monitoring, I hoped that Finn would be all right.'

'That was my hope too,' Mr Darby says.

'There's no other way?'

'We could try a course of radiotherapy,' he says. 'But my feeling is that it would simply delay the inevitable. The tumour is growing at quite a rate. If it were my son, I'd rather have it out than in.'

Right.

'There is some good news,' Mr Darby adds. 'Not all brain surgery requires us to go through the skull. Where your tumour is means that we can do all of the operation through Finn's nose.' He turns to my son. 'We'll have to take some skin from the thigh to repair the inside of it. So you will have a great scar that'll look like a shark bite but it's a lot simpler this way.'

Good, I think, that sounds good. And it makes

me realise how your perspective changes when you think that your son having nothing more than a 'shark bite' scar on his thigh is a blessing.

'How soon?' I croak out.

'We're probably looking at a month or so. This is a big operation and I need to assemble my team.' He closes his folder. 'Ready to bite the bullet, Finn?'

But we're both too shocked to respond.

Chapter Sixty

We all go to a nearby Pizza Express afterwards and I tell my parents the verdict. We sit there in stunned silence. Mum looks like she might cry at any moment. Dad too.

Somehow we manage to order food, though, I suspect, none of us feel like eating.

'We'll do something wonderful every week until your operation,' I tell Finn. 'What do you fancy doing? You can draw up a list.'

He looks up from his pepperoni and hot green peppers, tears in his eyes. 'A bucket list? I'm not going to die, am I, Mum?'

'No,' I say, emphatically. 'You're not allowed to. I just thought it would be nice if we had some treats to look forward to. It might help to take your mind off things. We can do anything you like.'

But Finn isn't mollified and I could damn my own eyes for even hinting at a bucket list.

293

'Why do you think I've got this, Mum? Is it because I played too much *Call of the Assassin?*'

'No,' I say. 'I'm sure it's not. It's just awful bad luck.' How does anyone get cancer? Unless you're a sixty a day smoker – when your chances of getting it must go up considerably – it simply seems to be a cruel and random disease.

'We'll be here for you every step of the way, Finn,' Dad says. 'You can count on that. If I could swap places with you...' Then he runs out of words, choked.

'Are you going back to work, love?' Mum asks.

I shake my head. 'Not now.' Even though that had been my plan. 'I'd be fit for nothing. I'll phone Robyn in a minute. She'll understand.'

'Can I stay off school tomorrow?'

'What about your exams?' My head's spinning as I try to work out the implications of this. 'I'm going to have to talk to the headmaster.' How can Finn sit something as important as his GCSEs with this hanging over him? I know that I'd be in no fit state. 'By the time you have your operation and are fit again, it will be the summer holidays.'

Finn brightens. 'I'll look forward to that bit.'

I clutch his hand and even though we're in public, in a restaurant, he lets me. 'You're going to be OK,' I tell him. 'You have my word on it.'

But the truth is, I only hope that I can deliver on that.

We all go home and, as we've eaten a big meal, my mum only forces sandwiches and cake on us for dinner. As is to be expected, we're all subdued – even the dogs can tell and come to lie at our feet and don't pester for a walk. We all sit and watch *EastEnders*, which is as miserable as usual, and *University Challenge*. And my eyes only mist up a bit when I think that Finn will probably never sit in one of those boxes and be quizzed by Jeremy Paxman. He's missed so much school and, though I'm sure they'll give him work to do at home while he recuperates, I wonder if he'll ever catch up.

'Let's shout random foods at Jeremy Paxman,' I suggest. 'That will cheer us up.'

So Finn and I spend a pleasant few minutes yelling 'Sausages!' and 'Cornflakes' in response to questions on cytogenetics and fascist dictatorships.

'If you shout "Gershwin!" in answer to every question, one day it will be right,' Dad advises from behind his newspaper.

So we give that a go too.

'I forgot to tell you,' I say to Finn when we have exhausted the delights of comedy foodstuffs and 'Gershwin!'. 'I took Ella's mum's phone number. We thought we might meet up when they come over to Milton Keynes shopping.'

'I've already hooked up with her on WhatsApp,' Finn says, shyly.

'Smooth work.' I hold out my hand for a high five, but Finn's having none of it.

'Grow up, Mum,' he snaps. 'It's nothing.'

'You seemed to get on well, though. She's nice, isn't she?'

The pink cheeks again. 'She's OK.'

'Maybe you could go out together before you have your op?'

He shrugs.

'Just don't take her playing pool.'

He has to laugh at that. 'Is there a pool game on Nana's Wii Fit? I *so* need to practise. She seriously whooped my arse.'

Nana look glances away from *University Challenge*. 'Language, Finn.'

Both Finn and I giggle. He snuggles into me and I hold him tight as I did when he was a baby. No matter how big he is, he'll always be my baby. Then I cry, but I don't let him see my tears.

Chapter Sixty-One

I'm still in a state of shock when I get up the next morning to go to work. It all feels as if it's happening to someone else, so goodness only knows how Finn feels. I heard him crying in the night, so I went to lie down next to him on his bed. Eric and the cats joined us too, so what little I slept was on about two inches of mattress. Now I'm aching all over and feel as if I've been in a fight. A fight that I lost.

I leave Finn in bed and tiptoe round as I get ready. He's not going to school today – sod the exams. He's in no fit state. Dad is coming over for breakfast and then he'll take Finn back to their house for the day. I so wish that I didn't have to work for a living as I'd like nothing more than to stay here with my brave boy.

Still, needs must. On autopilot, I do what I have

to do and then kiss Finn goodbye. He stirs in his sleep, but doesn't wake. Eric gets back on the bed with him. I'm so tempted to do the same.

Yet, too soon, I'm standing on the pavement waiting for the coach, yawning, yawning, yawning. The coach comes, Toni gives me my coffee, the same ritual every day. Henry gets on at Hockliffe.

This morning's breakfast in a bag is butter croissants, still slightly warm.

'I shoved them in the oven for five minutes while I was shaving,' Henry explains.

'They're lovely.' He's even put a piece of kitchen roll in the bag so I can wipe my buttery fingers. He's so kind, yet I'm not sure I've forgiven him for calling me 'ordinary'.

We head for the motorway and another day in London. Everything seems so much harder than it should be at the moment, as if there's a great weight pressing down on me. My chest is tight, my heart heavy. When a buttery croissant fails to move you, then you know that things are bad.

'I'm sorry about Saturday,' he says. 'It was a bit of a crap date.'

'It was fine,' I insist. 'The alpacas were lovely.'

'I know, but I banged on about Helen far too much. Even I realise that.'

'Maybe you're still not over her,' I suggest. 'It might be just too soon.'

'No,' he says. 'I have moved on. I'd had a row with her the night before over Kyra. Usual thing. She's off all the time with her new man and Kyra is left with my parents. They're going to Vegas now for a fortnight. If they're going on holiday, I don't know why they can't take her with them.'

I really don't know what to say. I've no doubt that it's important to Henry, but it all seems so very trivial compared to what Finn's going through.

'Here I am, doing it again.' He gives himself a facepalm. 'I'd like to try again. If you would. We could have a pub lunch somewhere.'

'I've got a lot on at the moment, Henry.'

'And now you've fallen out with me.'

'I haven't,' I tell him. 'It's Finn. We had some bad news from the hospital. He's going to have to undergo surgery. I need to be there for him.'

'That's terrible, Christie. I should have asked.' He looks mortified.

'You weren't to know. It was a bit of a bolt from the blue. I'd been expecting them to say that everything was all right.'

'I don't know what to say. If it was Kyra I'd be out of my mind. It's too shitty for words.'

'Indeed.' Couldn't have put it better myself. 'Let's put that date on hold. But I could do with a friend.' It's the best I can offer.

'You're bearing up very well,' Henry says. 'I'd be completely in bits.'

But I am in bits, I think. Just on the inside, where it doesn't show.

At work, I lean against Robyn in the kitchen and she wraps her arms round me. 'You look knackered and you haven't even started.'

'I am. I'll have that coffee as strong as you like.'

She unpeels herself from me and pours us two cups. 'Shit news about Finn.'

298

'I know. I just hadn't prepared myself for it. Apart from the tiredness, I really thought he seemed to be improving.'

'Maybe it's for the best. Get it sorted once and for all.'

'I'm trying to stay positive for Finn's sake. You know that it will mean me having loads more time off work?'

'We'll cross that bridge when we come to it. Have you got a date for the op yet?'

I shake my head. 'The consultant said it would be about a month.'

'Good. We'll flog you to the bone before then.'

'He's had to miss his exams today. Art and geography.'

'If you want art, you can buy it. And who needs fucking geography, anyway? We have Google maps.'

'None of it seems important.'

'I know, honey.' We hug again, then Robyn pushes me away, crosses her arms. 'But he's getting good care now. At least they're on it.'

'I know.'

'This is a very poor distraction technique, but how was the date with the llamas?'

'Alpacas,' I correct.

'Whatever. I nearly texted you yesterday, but thought it was too obvious that I was being nosy.'

'It was OK,' I tell her.

'Just OK?'

'Yeah.' I sip my coffee, lost in thought. 'I think Henry's still hung up on his ex. Plus, he called me "ordinary".'

'What?'

'He said he liked me because I was nice and ordinary.'

'Fucker.'

'Am I?'

'Of course, you're bloody not.'

'Is that how I present to the world?' I'm sure that people don't look at me and see the ambition boiling below the surface or the steel coil that runs through me.

'You're the most extraordinary woman I've met,' Robyn says with an exasperated tut. 'Most people would have crumpled with all that you've been through, yet you're still standing.'

'Just about.'

'If that Henry can't see how fabulous you are, then he's not the man for you. I keep telling you, girls are much better. You should try a bit of pink.'

'To be honest, I don't care if I spend the rest of my life alone, sitting on my sofa in a slanket and one of those big, single slippers as long as Finn's all right. I'd sacrifice my happiness for his in a heartbeat.'

She holds me again. 'I know you would. That's because you're bloody brilliant and I hope that you both get your happy ending.'

'Me too.'

'Now let's go and do some legal shit and make like it matters.'

That brings a smile to my lips. 'Have I ever told you that you're the best boss there is?'

'You have. But it doesn't hurt to tell me more.' Then Robyn is serious. 'I love you, you know?'

'I do.'

'Whatever happens, I've got your back.'

'Thanks, Robyn. That means a lot.' I know how lucky I am to work for someone like Robyn. At least that's one area of my life that I don't have to worry about.

Chapter Sixty-Two

When I get home there are piles and piles of boxes in the hall. 'Whoa,' I say to Finn. 'What's all this?'

'I forgot to tell you. It arrived this morning. Pops helped me to carry it through to the dining room.'

'There's more?'

'Loads,' he says and we both go to have a look.

'Oh, my God. It looks like Del Boy's flat in here.' There are boxes everywhere. The cats are asleep on top of them. 'What is all this? Is it even ours?'

'It's all from the UK distributor of the Contemporary Crafts products. Are you sure you didn't order it?'

'Ah.' I do remember now getting a little carried away during a late-night clickclickclick shopping session for our new online website which we haven't done anything about yet. 'This is all for our non-existent shop.'

Now it's Finn's turn to say, 'Ah.' He scratches his head.

I look at it, stunned. 'I don't know what I was thinking.'

'Your boyfriend will be pleased that you're single-handedly helping to keeping his company afloat.'

'He's not my boyfriend, Finn. He's my boss.' Now I scratch my head. 'This isn't funny. This is madness. I've clearly forgotten that our house isn't exactly the size of Buckingham Palace. Did it come in a flipping pantechnicon?'

'Yeah,' Finn says. 'It was a pretty big lorry. I thought it was a new sofa.'

I glance at the labels and feel a bit queasy. As Finn said, it's all from the company which is distributing Max's Contemporary Crafts products across the UK. I'm sure my order is small fry to them, but all these boxes are a big deal to me. 'What am I supposed to do with it all?'

I know that we all have a tendency to get carried away with late-night online shopping – especially when a glass or two of the old Chardonnay has been taken – but when I was happily filling my online basket I hadn't quite envisaged a delivery of this magnitude.

'There's only one thing we can do,' Finn says. 'I guess we'd better start that online shop.'

'How can we at the moment?' I could weep. Really, I could. 'The only thing we need to concentrate on is getting you right.' Ordinarily, I'd be totally excited by this, but I'm overwhelmed. It feels like one more thing to deal with and, despite me having good intentions at the time, I could do definitely do without it.

'It will be a good distraction,' Finn says. 'It's going to take us hours to sort through this to see what there is. Don't look so stressed, Mother.

This is cool. We can put Fancy Nancy on the Crappy Crafts channel and chill out while we have a look at what we've got.'

'What would I do without you?'

'Let's hope that you don't find out,' Finn quips.

'Don't say that.' I get palpitations at the thought. 'Don't even think it.'

'I'm cool, Mum,' he says calmly. 'I'm dealing with it.'

'You're the best kid ever.'

Finn glows. 'Does that mean I get to raid the secret stash of decent chocolate that you hide from me?'

I give a teary laugh. 'Yes. If it will make you happy.'

So I take my coat off and try not to panic about how many boxes there are or how high the invoice will be when it arrives. Then I make us that well-known delicacy cheese on toast, as I've given Nana the night off cooking. We curl up together on the sofa, eating our supper on our laps. Sheridan Smith is on the telly and I can't believe that I've actually met her in real life.

'I still think that you could do what she does,' Finn says.

Then, as he starts on my chocolate stash, we begin opening the boxes and discovering the delights inside. There are dies, dozens and dozens of them, inks, papers, embellishments. I might have gone completely overboard, but there's no doubt that I've ordered many Gorgeous Things. And I've hardly made a dent in the personal stash that I brought back from Washington.

After an hour, we've barely scratched the surface. 'You shouldn't be doing this,' I say to Finn. 'Shall we watch a film instead?'

'We can do. As long as it's not one of those soppy rom-coms or women drifting about in bonnets.'

'You decide.' Courtesy of my mother we have a huge range of DVDs that she picks up from the charity shop. 'You can even choose one that I have to watch behind a cushion.'

'Cool.' Finn casts aside the box of dies on his lap and crouches down to flick through the DVDs.

I don't know how you can look at the back of your teenage son's head and feel a rush of love for him, but I do. 'I want you to have fun, Finn. You've got too much stuff to deal with. Can't you have a meal out with your friends? Or you could have a film night here. I'll stump up for some pizza.'

He turns to me and his cheeks go pink. 'I've something that I want to ask you.'

'What? You know you can talk to me about anything.'

'Can I take Ella out? I've been messaging her and I think she'll say yes.'

'Of course.' My heart could burst with happiness for him. He's on the verge of finding his first love and I couldn't be more delighted. 'You could take her to the cinema and have something to eat afterwards – Nando's, maybe.'

'I can do some die-cutting for you to earn the money.'

'I'm happy to treat you.'

'Don't get overexcited, Mum,' he warns. 'You're like Nana. I can see "wedding hat" in your eyes.'

'I'm just pleased. She seems really nice. I think it would be a lovely thing for you both.'

'Can I say Saturday to her?'

'Yes. I'll take you down there. I hope her mum can bring her over from Bedford.'

'It's no big deal,' Finn says but, before he turns back to the task of selecting a DVD, I can see that he's grinning like a Cheshire cat.

Chapter Sixty-Three

There's a big meeting of the partners in the office today. They're all closeted in the boardroom and no one knows what's going on. Even Robyn is un-usually coy. I wonder if they're buying out another legal firm.

I've just finished delivering coffee to them all and am back at my desk when Max calls me. When I see his name come up on my phone, I nearly go into meltdown.

'Hey,' he says. 'Did you get your delivery? I spoke to the distributor and they said you'd con-tacted them.'

'I did. Thank you. Though I was slightly alarmed by quite how much I'd ordered. I'll have to show you my house one day. The cats are very lucky as there's no chance of swinging them round in it.' Being American, I'm not sure he has a clue what I'm talking about. 'It's small,' I add by way of explanation. 'Very small. And it's currently stacked out with cardboard boxes with Contemporary

Crafts written on the side.'

'Ah. I hope it gives you the motivation to start your online store. We need as many retail outlets for our products as possible in the UK.'

'How's it going?'

'Good. The distributor seems to be doing a great job. I've finalised a deal with one of the craft magazines to supply the cover-mounted dies that they give away.'

My mum and I are a big fan of those. You can't beat a magazine with a freebie.

'It will give us a lot of exposure. However, the main reason for my call is to say that I'll be in London on Sunday. One day only. I'm on my way to the Creativity and Crafting World fair in Frankfurt. It's the biggest one in Europe.'

I've heard of it, of course, but I've never been lucky enough to go.

'I fly in late on Saturday night and on Sunday I'm free until four o'clock. Then I have to go back to Heathrow to catch my flight. Can you have lunch with me?'

Immediately, my hormones are scattered and my heart does a conga. Would Finn be all right for the day with Mum and Dad? I'm sure he would.

'I'm sorry. I seem to be developing a habit of springing this on you at short notice.'

'I think it will be OK,' I say. 'Let me talk to Finn.'

'How's he doing?'

'Not so good,' I admit. 'He's going to need surgery.'

'Oh, man.' There's a heavy silence and I feel as if he's searching for the right words. When he speaks again, his voice is full of sympathy. 'I'm sorry to hear that.'

'We all are.' I don't want to go into details here or I might cry again. I'm doing a lot of it. 'Let me speak to him and see if he's OK about me leaving him for the day.'

'He can come with you. I'd like to meet him.'

'That's very kind, Max. I'll put it to him.' Not sure he'll want to play gooseberry to his mother. 'I'll call you back.'

'Let me know if there's anything I can do to help. I want to help.'

'I appreciate that, Max.'

'I hope you can make it,' he says.

And, as I hang up, I feel exactly the same.

Chapter Sixty-Four

The weekend is here before I know it. Work was manic, commuting was hell, Henry was … Henry. You know how it is.

'So we've both got hot dates this weekend,' Finn says, beaming. 'Go us.'

'Except mine isn't a date,' I hasten to point out. 'It's work.'

Finn makes a W sign at me with his fingers. 'Whatever.'

'You could come with me. Meet Max.'

'No one needs to have their fifteen-year-old kid in tow on a date. Sorry, work assignation.' He gives me a knowing look.

'You don't mind me leaving you?'

Finn rolls his eyes. 'Don't make me tell you again.'

'You should go and get ready,' I say. 'You don't want to be late.' I find my handbag and produce a Boots bag. 'I popped out yesterday lunchtime and bought you this.'

He takes the bag and peers inside. 'Aftershave?'

'I know that you don't really shave, but you could spray it on.'

'Cheers, Mum.' He looks unconvinced.

'You want to smell nice. Gone are the days when washing is enough.'

'If you say so.'

'It will look like you've made an effort. Do you need a shirt ironing?'

'Nana did it for me.'

Good old Mum.

While Finn goes upstairs for a shower and I get the ironing board out again. Mum might have done Finn's shirt but my laundry basket still looks as if a family of ten lives here. And a particularly dirty family at that. So, that's my night's entertainment sorted. To ease my pain, the ironing will be accompanied by a glass of cheap white – just the one as I'm driving later to pick Finn up – and a good dose of rom-com.

Half an hour later, Finn comes down. His hair is washed and styled, giving him an air of One Direction. I'm sure he'd love it if I told him that. And it's obvious he's used the aftershave. I start to cough.

'Very funny, Mother.'

'You're not supposed to use the whole bottle.'

'I only sprayed it on like you said. Is it too much?'

'Well, no flies will land on you.'

'You're doing great things for my confidence. Shall I wash it off?'

'Sometimes, less is more. Come here.' I beckon him into the kitchen and get a flannel from the top of the laundry pile and dampen it.

'You're not doing that,' he says, backing away.

I grab him and rub vigorously round his face as I used to do when he was small, making him howl with laughter. It has the same effect now. I scrub at his cheeks and Finn shrieks.

He's breathless when I've finished. 'You are so humiliating, Mum.'

'You don't smell like a tart's handbag now,' I tell him. 'You smell divine.'

'Yeah. I just look like I've tried to exfoliate myself.'

'You look great. The most handsome boy ever.'

'I hope Ella agrees.'

'Just be relaxed. Have a nice time. Don't try to be something you're not.' Advice that has got me precisely nowhere in my life. 'What movie are you seeing?'

'I can't remember. Something girly. I let Ella choose.'

'Good start.'

'We'd better get going,' he says, grabbing his jacket off the hook.

I stop him as he heads for the door and straighten the collar of his shirt. 'You look so very grown up.'

'Don't cry, you'll mess up your mascara.'

'I'm wearing industrial-strength waterproof stuff these days.'

'I'm nervous,' he admits.

'Don't be. You'll breeze it. If you want to hold her hand in the cinema or kiss her, just do it naturally.'

Finn looks horrified. 'I am *totally* going to ignore that you even said that.'

So I drive Finn to the big multiplex by the football stadium and drop him off outside the busy cinema. I see Ella standing waiting and hope she hasn't been there long. She's wearing a strappy floral dress and has a pretty matching scarf tied round her head. She looks like a little china doll. They make a lovely couple.

Finn turns to me. There's excitement in his eyes, but he looks anxious too. 'Wish me luck.'

I lean forward.

'Don't kiss me,' he says, panicked.

'Sorry. I forgot myself.'

'Close call, Mother. Close call.'

'I'll pick you up at eleven. No later. Ella's got to go back to Bedford.'

'It's not the moon.'

'Less of your cheek.' I give Finn fifty pounds. 'Have a nice time.'

'I won't need all that.'

'You will. Make sure you pay for Ella too.'

'I love you, Mum,' Finn says. Then he hops out of the car and rushes towards his first date.

I sit in the car, oblivious to the double yellow line, and grip the steering wheel. If anything terrible happens to him, if he goes into the operation and doesn't come out, then I know that he's had his first taste of young love. Then I give the industrial-strength waterproof mascara another battering.

Chapter Sixty-Five

I do the ironing, ration myself to one measly glass of wine and watch the clock round until it's time to pick up Finn. Even Sheridan Singleton proves to be no distraction, though I am watching her on repeat – the segment she did with Max – over and over. I can't believe that I'm going to see him again tomorrow.

I call Liam and we talk about arrangements for him coming over and discuss Finn's condition more thoroughly while he's well out of earshot. I try to reassure him, but I can tell that he's distraught that he's so far away.

At eleven o'clock, as arranged, I pull up outside the cinema again to collect Finn. As I get there, I see Ella giving him a peck on his cheek. I swear that Finn has grown a foot in the last few hours. Ella's mum jumps out of her car and comes to say hello. 'Young love,' she says.

'Tell me about it.'

'It's nice,' she says. 'It will give them both a bit of a lift. I'm sorry to hear about Finn's operation.'

'Fingers crossed,' I say. 'He's coping really well.'

'Sick kids are amazing,' she says. 'They seem to have an inner strength. I see it in Ella every day.'

'I hope they'll be able to spend some more time together.'

'We'll make sure that they do.' Then she goes to get Ella and Finn climbs into my passenger seat.

'How did it go?'

'Cool,' he says.

'That's it?'

He breaks into a grin. 'I think I'm in love.'

I laugh. 'That's better.'

'I feel all weird,' he says. 'Trippy. Is that love?'

'Yes. It probably is. Though how do you know what "trippy" feels like?'

'Get a life, Mum.'

By the time I'm pulling away from the kerb, he's already texting Ella. When he looks up, his face is all serious and he asks, 'Can you know what love is at fifteen?'

'I met your dad at that age.'

'Yeah. Look how well that turned out.'

'I got you out of it,' I say. 'So not all bad.' We exchange a wry glance. 'Sometimes people grow up together and sometimes they grow apart. You just have to try to make the best of it.'

'Do you think he'll come over when I have my operation?'

'Definitely,' I say. 'I spoke to him earlier. He's just trying to put everything in place.'

'Can he stay with us?'

'I think he'll probably want to go to a hotel,' I say. 'But we'll see.'

'It would be nice to have him home again,' Finn muses.

312

'If that's what you want, then we can ask him.' Even though I don't relish sharing a bathroom with my ex. If it helps Finn, then I'll do it.

Chapter Sixty-Six

Early on Sunday morning, Dad drops me off at the station and I get the train into London. I meet Max at The Ritz, where he's staying. It's posh and I'm glad that I put on my best trousers and a nice, flowery top.

He strides towards me down the long gallery and his face breaks into a smile when he sees me. Even though we've stolen a kiss together, we'll still unsure of each other and make a hash of greeting each other. Max takes my hand and sort of pulls me into his chest. I give him the sort of affectionate pat I normally reserve for Eric and want to give myself a facepalm for being so ridiculously gauche. My heart, however, is less inhibited and throws its doors wide open.

'It's great that you could come,' he says. 'It's a beautiful, sunny day in your capital city and I thought we'd make the most of it. I've pushed my flight back so I don't have to be at the airport until eight o'clock and I've taken the liberty of booking us afternoon tea here. Are you happy with that?'

'It sounds wonderful.'

'I thought it would be a suitably British thing to do.' Max looks very pleased with himself.

'I just wish I'd dressed up more.'

'You look perfect,' he says. 'We have a reservation for later this afternoon, until then, I'm at your mercy. Let's do tourist stuff.'

'OK.'

'Lead the way.'

We go out into the street and I turn towards Green Park. 'We can walk through the park to Buckingham Palace and then on past Westminster and the Houses of Parliament. We could go on the London Eye, if you like.'

'It sounds like a plan.'

With a chivalrous gesture, Max offers me his arm and I gladly take it. Together we turn into the green oasis of the park which is busy with people in deckchairs basking in the glorious sunshine. We take it at a slow pace, savouring the stroll until we end up at Buckingham Palace and join the throng of tourists. Taking our turn, Max takes a selfie of us both laughing and posing outside the palace gates. Leaving the crowds behind, we carry on through St James's Park and I'm glad that I brought my London A–Z as my navigation of this area is a bit rusty. We cross the Blue Bridge and walk past the spectacular plume of the Tiffany fountain up to Duck Island where the park's resident group of great white pelicans live. Then we come out of the park and onto Whitehall. We're lucky enough to catch the changing of the guard on Horse Guard's Parade, the brilliance of the red uniforms and the brass helmets picked out in the sun.

This is great,' Max says. 'I've never done it before. I'm always in too much of a rush.'

'I love the pomp and ceremony in London. Isn't

it always the way that you take something like this for granted when it's on your own doorstep? I always seem to be chasing my own tail too.'

'How are things going with Finn?'

'Not great. I didn't want to say too much on the phone, but he's got to have brain surgery. In a few weeks' time.'

'I'm sorry to hear that, Christie.'

'We're managing,' I tell him. 'He's finishing a few of his exams. What he feels up to, really. He's already managed to do a couple, but it's not fair to put him under such stress.' Thankfully, his headmaster agreed too and Finn can go in as and when he feels up to it. 'I've decided not to worry about his school work and try to have some sort of treat or outing every week until then. I think I should I bring him up here for the day. This is definitely something he should see.'

'He could have come with you. I'd love to meet him.'

'He graciously declined,' I say. 'I know you offered, but I wasn't sure that having a fifteen-year-old boy as a hanger-on was really your kind of thing.'

Max laughs. 'I admit that I'm not the most child-friendly of people, but that's only because I haven't had much practice. I'm willing to learn.'

I don't know if he says that for my benefit, but it makes me blush anyway.

'He's a great kid,' I say to hide my discomfort. 'But I am biased.'

'You're managing your work?'

'It's tough. I'm not going to lie to you.'

315

'You weren't overwhelmed by the training retreat?'

'No, no,' I lie. 'It's given me some great inspiration for designs.'

'And for kick-starting your online store.'

'Yes.' I don't tell him that I've had to put that very much on hold.

'Ask Dean for whatever help you need. He's a great guy. I want this to be fun for you, Christie. We want to get these products out in the UK market place, but I don't want to see you struggle. If we have to put your input on hold, then that's fine by me.'

'That's very kind of you.' But part of me knows, despite what Max may say, that this is crunch time for me. No matter what's going on in my personal life, I have to prove that I can cut it as a designer. But how can I do that when my child is ill and needs my full attention?

By now we've reached Westminster and the grandeur of the Houses of Parliament and Big Ben. We cross the grey, winding Thames by Westminster Bridge and the wind whips my hair. Despite the thoughts whirling in my head, we're more relaxed in each other's company now and, somehow, I go from linking my arm through Max's to holding his hand.

The queue for the London Eye is as long as usual, but we chat while we wait. Max tells me more about his family and his childhood and the more I hear, the more I like him. When our pod comes round, Max helps me on board and we inch our way smoothly skywards, the fabulous vista of London opening up before us. I point out various landmarks to Max and he takes photographs on his phone. Then he asks me to pose for one and I smile shyly.

'I wish that you could come to Frankfurt with me,' Max says. 'It's the biggest craft fair in the world.'

'I've heard about it, of course. But I've never been.'

'I suppose it's too short notice.'

I nod, sadly. 'I'm afraid so. I have work tomorrow. My parents would need to look after Finn and I want to be with him now.'

'I understand.' Max smiles, apologetically. 'I was being stupidly spontaneous.'

I wish that I could be too. There's definitely an appeal to stupid spontaneity. But I'm not that kind of woman. I'm a woman trying hard to keep a dozen different balls in the air and I can't just stop juggling and let them fall to the floor. I can't simply jet off to Frankfurt at a moment's notice. Though part of me wishes that I could.

Chapter Sixty-Seven

We retrace our steps until we're back at The Ritz. The afternoon tea at the Palm Court is wonderful, all that it should be. The surroundings are opulent – a gilded ceiling, gold cherubs, glittering chandeliers and cascades of seasonal flowers. The sandwiches are tiny and delicate. The cakes a mouthful of heaven. There's a background of tinkling piano and a lovely buzz of conversation. This is a perfect romantic setting. And, most obviously, there isn't an alpaca in sight.

I try very hard not to compare it to my date with Henry as that wouldn't be fair. It was a totally different day out altogether. They are both nice in different ways. I have some more champagne. Hmm. I think that says all that needs to be said.

'Today has been great,' Max says. 'I feel very British now. Thank you.'

'My pleasure. That's the Christie Chapman Abridged Tourist Experience.'

'It's provided some much needed rest and relaxation.'

'You'll be able to hit that craft fair running,' I tease.

'I'll have you know that they're very arduous.'

I don't ask whether Sheridan Singleton will be there. If Max wanted me to know then I guess he'd tell me.

'I hope it goes well for you.'

'Perhaps next year we can plan it better and you could join me out there.'

'I'd like that.'

Then we have some more tea and cake and, too soon, it's time for Max to go. We leave the table and he walks me to reception.

'I'll get them to hail a cab for you.'

'I've got a tube ticket,' I tell him.

'Please, let me treat you to a little luxury.'

'You've already done that. It's been lovely. I've only ever had afternoon tea at my local garden centre before. I think I'll bring Finn here too.' To hell with the budget.

'I'll contact you when I'm back in the States,' Max says.

'Good luck in Frankfurt. Knock them dead. In a good way,' I add, in case he doesn't quite understand.

'I will.'

Then he kisses me. Right here in the foyer of The Ritz. Warmly, lingeringly on the lips. He tastes of strawberries and champagne and my head swims.

'We keep doing this,' he says with a laugh when he breaks away.

'Yes.'

'One day, maybe one of us won't have to rush away.'

'One day.'

Max walks me outside. The evening is still balmy. The doorman hails me a cab and, as he opens the door, Max brushes my cheek with another kiss.

'I hope I'll see you again soon, Christie.'

'I hope so too.' Yet I wonder how long it will be before I see him again. I climb into the cab, the door is closed and the driver pulls away into the ever-present traffic on Piccadilly.

Chapter Sixty-Eight

Is it statistically correct that Mondays come around more quickly than any, other day? No matter how hard I try to hold it back, here it comes again. I am the King Canute of the commute.

The alarm goes off and I lie here trying to get my eyes to oblige with the whole opening thing. They're not really having it. To be honest, despite an entire night having passed, I feel as if I've been asleep for about ten minutes. The alarm hasn't troubled Eric and I have dead legs as he's still conked out on them, but the rest of me feels weird too. I go to move, but my body is as heavy as lead. I lift my head from the pillow, but it just flops back down again. I'm always tired, yet today I'm tired beyond tired. It's as if my muscles have turned to blancmange in the night and I ache everywhere. Even my eyelashes feel heavy.

With some considerable effort, I sit up and shift Eric from my legs. He grumbles and curls up again next to Lily and Pixel. Sitting on the edge of the bed, I try to gather my thoughts and some energy.

I know that I had a busy day, yesterday, out and about in London with Max, but it must be a sure sign that I'm getting old that it has wiped me out quite so comprehensively. Oh, I wish I could lie down and go back to sleep for another few hours. But it's not to be. The siren call of the coach won't go away and I have a busy day in work waiting for me.

But, as I force for myself up, my legs buckle beneath me and I find myself in a crumpled heap on the rug. I feel dizzy, disoriented and can only conclude that I must be coming down with something. There's no way that I can go into work feeling like this.

It takes me a minute or two to even summon the strength to climb back into bed and I snuggle down under the covers. The next thing I know, Finn is shaking my arm. 'Mum, Mum!' He has a worried look on his face. 'You've overslept.'

'What?' The light is hurting my eyes.

'It's half eight. Pops is here to take me to school.'

'Oh.' I peer at the clock to make sure that it isn't Finn who's wrong.

'Are you all right?'

I let out a heavy breath. 'I don't think so. I might be coming down with something.'

'Shall I ring Robyn and tell her you're not coming in today?'

I nod and that hurts too. 'I think you'd better. Her number's in my phone.'

He finds it and punches it into his mobile. 'What shall I tell her?'

'Tell her I'm sorry and that I'll call her later.'

'OK. Do you want me to stay at home? I can look after you.'

'Have you got exams today?' I can't even re-member.

'Yeah, but nothing important.'

'It's a lovely thought,' I say to Finn. 'But you should go to school. All of your exams are im-portant.'

'I'm going to be worrying about you now,' he protests.

'Just do your best. Even if you can scrape a pass, it will be one more thing out of the way.'

'Are you sure?'

I nod. 'Ask Pops if Nana will come over later.'

Finn frowns at me. 'What else can I do for you?'

'I'll be fine. I just need to sleep.' Even talking to

Finn is taxing.

'I'll text you in my break,' he says.

'Thanks. Love you.'

Finn disappears and a minute later Dad knocks at the bedroom door. 'Finn says you're not well, love.'

'I feel terrible, Dad.'

'Best you stay there, then. I'll bring your mum back when I've dropped Finn off at school.'

'No rush. I'm going to go straight back to sleep for a couple of hours if I can. I might feel better then.'

'She'll probably bring some soup or something for your lunch. How about that?'

'Sounds great.' Though the thought of even lifting a spoon is quite daunting.

'I'd better go or Finn will be late for school,' Dad says. 'I've fed the hound.'

I didn't even realise that Eric had moved. 'Thanks, Dad. Love you.'

Then, as he leaves, I pull the covers over my head and remember nothing more.

Chapter Sixty-Nine

I'm still asleep when Mum rocks up at lunchtime. She comes into my room and strokes my hair.

'Hello, sleepyhead.'

I try to rouse myself. 'What time is it?'

'One o'clock. Have you slept all morning?'

'Yes. I guess so.' I still feel as if I'm having an

out-of-body experience. 'What time did you get here?'

'A little while ago. I'm just heating through some home-made chicken soup. Can you manage some?'

Suddenly, I feel hungry. 'Yes. I think so.'

'Want it on a tray?'

'I should come down.'

'Sure?'

I nod. 'Just give me a few minutes.'

So Mum goes back to the kitchen and I push myself out of bed. I feel slightly stronger than I did first thing, but still like I've been hit by a truck. Pulling on my dressing gown, I head to the bathroom and give my teeth a cursory scrub. Then I pad downstairs and see that Mum has already put a small bowl of soup on the coffee table in front of the sofa. The fire is on, even though it's summer, and the living room feels lovely and cosy. I sit, slightly dazed on the sofa, rubbing my eyes.

The scent of the soup is warm and comforting and makes me feel a bit better already, then she joins me. I take a sip. 'This is good.'

I manage to eat most of the contents of the bowl before pushing it away. Mum inspects it to see how much has gone.

'It was lovely,' I say. 'My stomach's feeling a bit delicate, that's all. I want to take it easy. I'll finish the rest later.' I pull my crocheted blanky over me and slump onto the cushions.

Mum tuts, but softly. 'You need looking after.'

'You do so much for me already. It's probably just a bug or something.'

Mum puts down her soup and looks at me,

directly. 'I don't think so, Christie.'

'I'll be fine,' I say. 'I just need a couple of days to regroup.'

'You're burning the candle at both ends. You know that Dad and I don't like to interfere,' she says. 'You should live your life as you want to, but this has to stop.'

'I've got a lot on, that's all.'

'Too much,' Mum says. 'I wish I'd never contacted that blessed craft company.'

'I'm glad you did.' Otherwise, I would never have met Max. 'It's been a highlight in a pretty bleak period.'

'That's as may be, but it's too much,' Mum continues as if I haven't spoken. 'Look at all this.' She gestures at the stacks of boxes that I still haven't entirely unpacked. I have to agree, it does look a bloody mess. They seem to stare at me reproachfully. 'You're trying to hold down a difficult job in the city. And there's all that commuting. Back and forth, back and forth. That's enough to make you dizzy. I'm worn out just thinking about it. You've taken on all this crafting stuff – which you're very good at, I might add. You're talking about opening an online shop too. All this on top of Finn's illness. It's too much, Christie. Way too much.'

Tears fill my eyes. 'I know. I know.' I only have to glance towards those damn boxes to realise that.

'I've been thinking.' Mum moves from the chair and comes to sit next to me. She takes my hand and strokes it, absently. 'Why don't you give up your city job?'

'Because it pays my bills.'

'I know you're not earning much from your crafting yet, but we could work on that. When Finn's all better.' She sighs at me. 'Right now, your boy needs you here.'

A lump comes to my throat.

'It's a terrible thing he's going through, Christie. He wants his mum.'

'I'm going to go part-time soon and that's a big cut in our income. With the best will in the world, we can't live on fresh air.'

'I know and I've talked to Dad about that.' She takes a deep breath. 'Resign from your job. We'll help you financially.' I start to speak, but she holds up a hand. 'That's what families do.'

'If I give up my PA job completely, it would leave a massive hole in my money. How would I be able to keep the house on?'

'We talked about that too. You could rent it out – short term. You and Finn could come to live with us for the time being. When we're sure he's fully fit again, then you can try to increase your income from crafting.'

I wipe a tear away. 'It's a lot to think about.'

'It seems like a no-brainer to me.'

I laugh – a snotty bubble laugh. 'That sounds like something Finn would say.'

'You'd need to talk to him, obviously.'

Looking round my front room, I wonder if I could give all this up. Boxes notwithstanding. It's all very well for Mum to say to move in with them and, no doubt, it's a kind and thoughtful suggestion. However, in reality, they live in a tiny bungalow. They've got three bedrooms, but there's one double and the world's tiniest single. Could we cram our lives in there? What about Eric and the cats? Could they come too? I love being with Mum and Dad and couldn't manage without them, but does that mean I'd want to be there 24/7? Isn't being back in the same bedroom you had when you were fourteen a bit of a backward step when you're forty-odd?

'I'm just trying to help, Christie.' Mum is teary too now. 'Dad and I don't want to see you both struggling. Don't cry.' She fishes in her pocket for a tissue and then dries my damp cheeks. 'Promise me you'll think about it. You're no good to Finn if you're poorly too. You have to be strong for him. We all do.'

'I'll think about it,' I swear. 'You're right. I have to do what's best for Finn.'

'And what's best for you too, love. Don't forget about that.' Then she holds me to her as she did when I was a child and we have a little cry together.

Chapter Seventy

Even though I'm completely exhausted, I lie awake all night thinking about what Mum said. It's true that I can't go on like this. Something has to give. My focus has to be Finn and paying the bills. I love doing my crafting and the opportunities that it could offer in the future are exciting. But I have to consider the here and now.

Mum advised me to give up my job in London, but how can I do that? I'd have to rely on them to support me and move back home.

As dawn is breaking, I make my decision. I have to give up the crafting side of things. I can't live on what might be and part of me wonders if I'm just hanging on to that for the tantalising glimpses of Max that I get. If he wasn't in the picture would I still be doing this? I'm a sensible, middle-aged woman with a poorly son to support, I should stop acting like a lovelorn teenager and kick this infatuation in touch. If I don't see Max at all, don't speak to him, don't contact him, then I'll soon get over this. When Finn's recovered from his operation and has the all-clear, maybe I could settle down with someone like Henry Jackson and my life wouldn't be any the worse for it.

I get up, go down to the kitchen and make a cup of tea. Eric and the cats get an early breakfast. Then I sit at the table and stare at my mobile phone. I'd call Max, but Washington is five hours behind us, or something like that, and he'll be in bed – or out partying. I can't call him now. Besides, if he tried to persuade me to stay, then what chance would I have of resisting his charms? Zero, that's what.

So I pull the laptop towards me and compose an email. I keep it light, chatty. I tell him that it's with great regret that I must give up my place on the design team to concentrate on my job and Finn. I tell him that I'm very grateful for the opportunity and that I've really enjoyed working for him, however, the timing just isn't right for me. I wish him well with the future success of the company and then I send it before I can think twice about what I've done.

After that, I sit with my face in my hands and cry. No more Max, no more cocktails at swanky hotels, no more fabulous boxes of crafting swag, no more getting on a plane to fly to America, no more meetings where my heart races with delight at seeing him. Yet it's the right thing to do. I know it is.

When I look up, Finn's standing at the kitchen door in his dressing gown, yawning. 'What are you doing up at this hour? I thought you weren't going into work?'

'I'm not,' I say. 'I couldn't sleep.'

'And you're crying.'

'Only a bit.'

He comes to sit opposite me. 'You're not crying about me, are you?'

'Yes and no.'

'I'll be all right, Mum. I promise.'

'I know.' I dry my eyes. 'Do you want some breakfast? I've bought a nice packet of granola.'

'Granola? You're kidding me.' Finn stares at me with disdain. 'If I've got a brain tumour, surely I deserve a bacon buttie?'

That makes me laugh. 'I'm trying to introduce us to healthy eating.'

'I like your chances of trying that one on Nana the Carb Queen.'

'True. I'll put the grill on.'

'I don't want you to worry, Mum.'

'OK. I'll stop instantly.'

Finn gives me a look and then grabs the laptop. 'Wait...' I realise that I haven't closed down my

328

email account.

'Whoa,' he says when he sees what I've sent to Max. 'Why did you do this?'

'You weren't supposed to see that.'

'Then why did you leave your account open? Do you know nothing about security online?'

'Clearly not.' I take the laptop from him.

'It's a bit late now,' Finn observes. Quite rightly.

Then I sigh, ahead of my explanation. 'I had a long chat with Nana yesterday and this is the upshot. I'm trying to be superwoman, Finn, but I have to accept that I can't do it all.'

'Why didn't you give up your crappy London job? You hate it.'

'I don't hate the job.' Not really.

'You hate commuting though.'

'I know, but the truth of the matter is that's the job that pays well. I have to consider that. At the moment, I'm pulled in too many different directions. I want to be here for you.'

'You love your crafting.'

'I know, but if it's right for me, then the universe will provide what I need.'

Finn looks agog. 'You don't seriously believe that?'

No, not really. I'm a firm believer in the fact that the universe will generally dump shit on your head when you can least cope with it.

'I thought we were going to open an online shop and everything. Look at all the stuff in the dining room.'

'We were never going to have time, Finn. All you need to concern yourself with is getting better. That's going to take all your time and energy.'

'Phone Max up and tell him that you don't mean it.'

'What's done is done.'

'I bet Nana goes mental when you tell her.'

'I'm sure she'll be supportive of my decision.'

'She flipping won't! You're bonkers,' is my son's conclusion. He shakes his head. 'I'll never understand women.'

And that gives me a moment of lightness in what feels like a very bleak time.

Chapter Seventy-One

I have the rest of the week off work and am feeling much better by the end of it. Max, having seen my email, has phoned every day. Sometimes more than once. To my eternal shame, I haven't taken any of his calls. What exactly would I say that I haven't already covered?

My mum did, of course, think that I'd made the wrong decision. But she doesn't know the whole story. Plus she sees nothing wrong with me and Finn moving back in with them, whereas I do. She did tut a lot and throw dark looks in my direction. Dad retreated to his workshop. Even the dogs stayed out of the way. Finn occasionally tore his eyes away from the television long enough to say, 'I told you so.'

As I'm leaving for work, the postman catches me. 'Here you go, love,' he says. 'Probably all bills.'

'Thanks.' I take the pile of letters to save until I get on the coach. After a quick flick through, most of it is, indeed, bills or bumph. There's only one letter that catches my eye. I open it quickly. Finn's operation is in two weeks' time. I knew that this was coming, but seeing the date in black and white still shocks me. Two weeks. I don't know whether to be relieved or terrified. I'll tell Finn when I get home tonight. No point stressing him before he goes to school.

Now I'm back in the office sitting at my desk, working away, trying to catch up with the backlog that I abandoned while under the weather. I didn't see Henry on the coach this morning and he hasn't called or texted either, but maybe that's for the best too. I have enough complications in my life now.

To be honest with you, I feel sick. I've burned my boats with Max and I feel like such a failure. I don't really want to talk to anyone today, so I'm keeping my head down, being busy, busy, busy. I don't think I've ever felt quite so miserable. I look round the bright, bustling office, but I'll swear that I feel the walls closing in on me. I have an overwhelming urge to rip my clothes off and run out along the Embankment in the nuddy. Needless to say, I squash it down. I need to get on with my work and think about nothing else. Not Max. Not what might have been. Nothing.

Somehow, I manage to focus. As I'm tapping away at my computer, booking hotel rooms for an upcoming conference on insolvency litigation that all of the partners are attending, Robyn comes to my desk.

331

'Can you come to my office for a minute?'

'Yeah, sure. Just let me finishing this booking or you'll be sleeping on the street next week.' Then I look up at her and see that her face is wearing a very serious expression. 'Is everything OK?'

'I need a word.'

'Oh.'

Then she turns and heads back to her office, leaving me a little bit stunned. I bet I know what this is about. They've been so tolerant here of my continuing absences due to Finn's illness and now mine, that I bet even Robyn has her limits. And I appreciate that I've pushed them – but what can I do?

I hurriedly finish the bookings and log off. Then I dash into Robyn's office and, even though she's a mate, my heart's in my mouth. I wonder why we couldn't have done this over a chat with coffee in the kitchen.

'Shut the door,' she says.

Clearly, not good.

'Have a seat.'

I drop down into the chair opposite her at the desk.

'I'm really sorry, Robyn,' I launch in. 'I know that I've had loads of time off recently, but I'm doing my best. I know that I'll need more time off when Finn has his operation, but that can't be helped. I've dropped all my crafting commitments so that I can concentrate just on this job.'

She sits there and says nothing.

'Thank you for being so supportive,' I add. 'You're a good friend and an even better boss.'

'You're making this even more difficult,

Christie,' she says.

'What?' I can feel panic rising in me. 'What's so difficult?'

'We had a partners' meeting while you were away and we had to make some difficult decisions.'

I don't like the sound of this. I don't like the sound of this at all.

'I worried all weekend about how I was going to broach this as I know what you're going through. It couldn't come at a worse time.'

'What couldn't?'

'We're going to be making some redundancies.'

I hear myself gasp in shock. Robyn's face is white.

'I'm sorry, Christie. Really sorry.'

My head is on the block? Is that what she means?

'Perhaps it's for the best,' Robyn continues. 'I know that things are going well with your crafting. This might be the push that you need.'

A push? I actually feel as if she's just pushed me off a fifteen-storey block of flats. 'I've given up all my crafting work, so that I could concentrate on this job,' I tell her again, my voice faltering. 'I need the income. You know my situation.'

'I do,' she agrees. 'And, believe me, I did all I could to keep you. I was outnumbered, Christie. The rest of the partners ... well ... let's say that they didn't feel quite the same.'

'They wanted me out? After all these years?'

'I don't think that they understand our special relationship.'

It seems that I may have taken it for granted too.

'You'll get a generous pay-off,' Robyn rushes

on. 'We'll pay you until the end of next month and there'll be a lump sum. A sizeable one. At least, I managed to secure that for you.'

'Thank you.' What else can I say? I can hardly cite being a model employee when I know how much time I've taken off recently and how much they've had to rely on temps. But I never, ever thought in a million years that they'd get shut of me just like that. 'When am I to go?'

Robyn clears her throat. When she speaks her voice is shaking and she looks on the verge of tears. 'I hate to do it this way, but it's protocol.' She can't even meet my shocked gaze when she adds, 'You can clear your desk out now, Christie.'

'Oh.'

'No point prolonging these things.'

'I guess not.'

Wow. Not entirely sure what to say now.

'Keep in touch,' Robyn says. 'I want to know how Finn is. And you, of course.'

'Yes.' I can't bring myself to tell her that his operation is coming up soon.

She stands up from her desk and comes to hug me. I step into her embrace, but we both feel so brittle that we might break.

'We'll always be friends,' she says.

'We will.'

Yet we both know that what we had is irretrievably broken.

Chapter Seventy-Two

I walk out of Robyn's office, clear my desk and leave the building. I don't say goodbye to anyone. What's the point? Who would care? If Robyn can do this to me, then I realise that you can never trust even what you think are the firmest of friendships.

I sit on a bench on the Embankment, dazed, until the coach comes. Henry isn't on it and, from tomorrow, I'll no longer be a commuter. I'll text him and tell him, so that he doesn't sit and wonder about where I am – like we both did when former commuter Susan disappeared. I speculate how much I'll get back from cashing in my season ticket. It will probably be quite a few quid which will come in handy.

I say out loud, 'I'm unemployed,' and bile rises to my throat. I've never been out of work in my life and I only wish that Robyn could have given me a hint of what was coming so I could have made better preparations.

Dad picks me up, as usual, and takes me to their house. Mum has made chicken and mushroom pie with a golden puff pastry topping. My stomach churns simply thinking about eating it. We all sit down at the table and Mum, Dad and Finn tuck in. It takes all my effort to lift my knife and fork.

I spent my entire journey home on the coach

staring out of the window at the traffic and wondering how I was going to tell them my news. It seems like one thing too many for us to deal with.

'You're not eating, Christie, love,' Mum says. 'Not hungry?'

I put down my cutlery without using it. 'Not really.' I look at them all. 'I had some bad news today.' *More* bad news. They look at me expectantly and the words stick in my throat. 'I've been made redundant.'

Everyone stops with their forks midway to their mouths and looks at me in shock. Much as I did when Robyn broke the news to me. The enormity of my announcement is just hitting home.

'It would have been nice if I'd been given time to sort something else out, but I was turfed out today.' That hurts as much as the actual redundancy.

'Oh, love,' Dad says. 'That's terrible.'

'I am a bit gutted.' Understatement. I daren't even give vent to my true feelings.

When Mum finds her voice again, she says, 'You get straight on that phone to the chap in America. Tell him you've changed your mind.'

'I can't do that, Mum.'

'Plan A obviously didn't work. You'd better put Plan B into action.'

I push my plate away. 'I haven't actually got a Plan B.'

'Then Dad will put the kettle on and we'll come up with one.'

I thought about this all the way home on the coach too. 'I can't call him. It's not fair.' Perhaps it's pride, but I can't see me having that conversation with Max. 'He's probably found someone else by now.'

'But they won't be as good as you,' Finn says, ever loyal. 'You've got to give it a chance, Mum.'

My timing in life is terrible. Always has been. Always will be.

'I'll get the local paper,' I say. 'Sign up with a few agencies, too. There are bound to be jobs in Milton Keynes.' I sound so brave, so convinced. Inside, I feel as if I'm in freefall.

'We'll sort it out,' Dad says. 'Don't you worry, love.'

Everyone tells me not to worry, but how can I not? Wouldn't anyone with this lot on their plate stress a little bit? And I haven't even told them that the date for Finn's operation has come through. That can wait another day or two until they've had time to digest the latest shock. I want to sit down with Finn and tell him on his own when I'm feeling calm too. If we both go to pieces, that would be a disaster.

Then I realise that there is a silver lining in this. I reach over to Finn and hug him. If I'm at home before his operation, then we'll have a lot of time together. 'This does mean that we can spend time working on your "To Do" list.'

'I haven't even written it yet,' Finn admits.

'You'd better get a move on then.'

I'm not even going to consider how much it costs. I only hope that Robyn is true to her word and that they've given me a good redundancy settlement. I've been there for aeons so, surely, I should be in for a few quid? I'm going to take Finn out of school too. Sod the exams, sod the headteacher, sod everything. I want Finn to have as many lovely memories as he can before his operation, in case– I stop my mind from going there.

'Let's go into the garden,' Mum says. 'It's a lovely evening.'

I hadn't even noticed the weather. It might be sunny outside, but it's raining in my bloody heart. Isn't that what the old song said? Something like that.

'Ray, can we leave you with the washing up?' Mum says.

'Of course you can, love.' We always do. I think, bizarrely, my dad finds it therapeutic.

'What sort of things do you think you might like to do?' I ask Finn.

'Dunno.' He scratches his head. 'I know it's a bit of a kid's thing, but I wouldn't mind doing the tour of the Harry Potter studios.'

'That seems easy enough. We can go on the train from here.'

'Don't know what else,' he admits.

Mum picks up the pad by the phone. 'We can have a brainstorming session in the summerhouse.'

'Steady on, Mum.'

'With a gin and tonic,' she adds. 'To facilitate the process.'

'Now you're talking.'

'I'll have a beer,' Finn says, hopefully.

And instead of telling him no I say, 'You can have *one*. Help yourself from the fridge.'

Finn's eyes light up. 'Cool. Way to go, Mum. Last week, you were trying to force-feed me granola, now I can have beer. Lovin' this mixed-message parenting style.'

'Don't push it, Finn,' I say. But at the moment he can ask for whatever he likes and I'll agree. He knows that. I know that.

I just want him to be happy. And, more than anything – more than my crappy job, more than paying my bills, more than any man – I want him to be around.

Chapter Seventy-Three

The next morning, I see Finn off to school. These are the last exams he's doing. Dad comes as usual and we walk the dogs together. We take them up to the top end of Milton Keynes and walk through the Ouse Valley Park – which is one of my favourite areas of the city. Dad is great company, as always. Over the years he has developed a well-honed sense of when to speak and when not to. Today, we do Not Much Speaking. Eric and Trigger run ahead of us, playing together, as we walk through the fields. Then we go through the narrow tunnel under the Grand Union Canal and come out onto the towpath above us. We stroll along the canal, stopping to watch some narrowboats going through the locks, before heading to one of our favourite watering holes, the Barley Mow pub at Cosgrove.

Dad goes to the bar to order some tea while I get a bowl of water for the dogs. It's a warm, sunny day and we sit in the garden. The dogs have a drink and then hide in the shade of our picnic bench. I think what I'd normally be doing now, stuck in an air-conditioned office, bashing away at my computer – and I miss it. I've longed to be able to give up my job, but not in these circumstances. It just seems weird to have had the rug pulled from under me so swiftly. And by someone I considered a good friend too. That stings.

A few minutes later, Dad appears bearing a tea tray. 'Biscuits too,' he says. 'Don't tell your mum. She'll feel like she missed out.'

We take time pouring our tea, unwrapping our little caramel biscuits and letting the sunshine warm us.

'It'll be all right,' Dad says. 'Redundancy feels terrible. They should have a different word for it, for a start. But think of it as opening new opportunities for you.'

'I just slammed the door shut on that,' I point out. Max hasn't called for the last few days. Perhaps he has, finally, given up on me. Even now he could be looking at one of the other applicants to slot into my vacant place on the design team.

'Finn is your priority now,' Dad says, snapping his biscuit in half and giving a piece each to Eric and Trig.

'I know.' A sigh. 'His hospital appointment came through yesterday. It's barely two weeks away. I'd been gearing myself up for a longer time to prepare.'

'That's quick,' Dad says. 'Best to get in and get it over with.'

'I haven't told him yet,' I confess. 'I thought I'd do it tonight.'

'He'll handle it,' Dad assures me. 'He's being brilliant about it all. But I wouldn't expect anything less from Finn.'

'He's a good kid,' I agree. 'I sort of imagined that we'd have more time together to do some of the things that he hasn't done. Stupid things. We might go on the Harry Potter Studio tour. I've got a friend of a friend who works there and I'm hoping they'll be able to swing me tickets at short notice. It's worth a try. I don't know what else. What should teenage boys do that they might miss if...'

I run out of words.

'He'll be fine,' Dad says. 'I'm sure of it.'

Yet how can we be sure? It's a serious operation. Probably as serious as they get. I didn't discuss percentages with the consultant, but I wonder what his chances of pulling through are? Probably best if I don't know.

'Shall we wander back now?' Dad stands up and stretches. The dogs take it as their cue to come out of hiding and run round his legs.

I muster myself too. Before we set off, Dad gives me a bear hug. 'You're not alone in this, Christie. We're here to support you. Whatever you need, just ask.'

'I couldn't manage without you.'

'You don't have to,' Dad reminds me.

Back at home, I grab a sandwich for lunch. No meal deal today. While I eat I stare at the piles of boxes in the dining room. I should sort these out and return them to the distributor. If he'll take them back, that is. God, that's going to cost me a fortune, but can I even afford to keep them now? Maybe I should call him and explain what's happened. Perhaps he'd understand. However, the more I think about it, the less able I am to pick up the phone.

Instead, I ring Henry. He answers after two rings.

'Hi,' I say.

'Hi, Christie. I missed you on the coach this morning. All OK?'

Hmm. 'Not really.' Biting back the tears that come too readily, I continue, 'I lost my job. Yesterday.'

'Oh, hell. On top of everything else? Do these people have no soul?'

I try to make light of it. 'The upside is no more commuting. Yay!'

'What will I do without my travelling companion?'

'Oh, there'll be someone else there taking my place. Probably by the end of the week.'

'It won't be the same,' Henry says.

'No. Well. I just wanted you to know.'

'Thanks for calling.' Then he hesitates. 'I'd like to see you again, Christie. Could I take you for lunch one day?'

'I've got a lot on at the moment...' It sounds lame even to me.

'I'm actually working from home tomorrow. Dental appointment. I could come over to you.'

I hear myself saying, 'Yes, I'd like that,' when really my brain hasn't had the chance to process it at all.

'I look forward to it.' Henry sounds pleased.

'I'll come for you about noon?'

'Sounds fine.' Perhaps we could walk up to the Barley Mow again. Henry would like that, I think.

'Chin up, Christie,' he says. 'You'll come through all of this.'

'I hope so.'

Then I hang up and stare at the piles of boxes again and wait for Finn to come home.

Chapter Seventy-Four

Late afternoon, Dad delivers a chicken casserole from my mum.

'I'm going to have to do my own cooking, if I'm not working,' I complain. 'I've no excuse.'

'Don't rush into it,' Dad says with a wink. 'Coming over later?'

'Yeah.'

'I'll take Eric back with me and go for a bit of a walk with Trig.'

'You're a star.'

'Good luck with Finn. I bet when you tell him, he'll be relieved.'

'I hope so.'

In preparation, I've bought some nice biscuits, loaded with chocolate – as if they'll soften the blow of news of your impending brain surgery. I have no idea what else to do.

Finn comes home. He looks tired. His face his pale, dark purple shadows mar his eyes. 'I'm knackered,' he announces as he throws his bag on the floor. 'My exams were tough today.'

'You don't have to do any more if you don't want to.'

'I've not got that many left,' he says. 'My results might be rubbish though. I couldn't really concentrate today.'

I hug him to me. 'That's understandable. No one's going to expect A stars from you.' Now I feel bad that he's even gone to school. Shouldn't he be in bed resting up? Whatever I do these days, I seem to get it wrong on every level.

Finn flops into one of the kitchen chairs. 'How was your first day as an unemployed person?'

'Weird,' I say. 'I walked the dogs with Pops. We went along the canal to the Barley Mow for a cuppa.'

'There are worse ways to spend a day,' Finn says. 'You didn't phone Max?'

'No.' I realise that I'm wringing my hands and stop.

Finn is immediately suspicious. 'What?'

'I have something important to tell you.'

He looks horrified. 'You're not pregnant?'

'No! Of course I'm not. I don't want to be discussing my sex life with you – or total lack of it – but it would have had to be an immaculate conception.'

'Nothing else could be that bad. I never want a brother or sister. I'm happy being a spoilt only child. The Big Cheese.'

I sit with him and take his hands. Reluctantly, he lets me. 'The date for your operation has come through.'

'Oh.' His face falls. 'That's quite bad. I'm kind

of wishing you *were* pregnant now.'

'You've only got just over a week to wait though.'

He looks dumbstruck. 'That's not long, is it?'

'No. Probably better than having it hang over you though.'

He nods. Though he doesn't look too sure. 'Any more info?'

'I can come down and stay with you the whole time. There's accommodation for families right across the road from the hospital.'

'Will Dad come too?'

'Yes. I called him earlier. He'll be here too. Now that we've got a firm date, he can organise his flights.'

'Cool. Is he staying here?'

'Well...'

'That means no.'

'We did talk about it, Finn. I promise. But it would be a bit too weird for us both. I think Dad would be happier in a hotel.'

'OK.' Finn sighs in resignation. Perhaps his picture of a happy family reunion has just disintegrated. Something else to beat myself up about.

'Nana and Pops can come with us as well.'

'Road trip to the brain surgeon,' Finn quips, but I can tell by his face that he's worried. Who wouldn't be?

'You're all right about this?' I ask. 'You understand what's going to happen?'

'I do,' Finn says. 'The only question I have is do I really need surgery? Can't I wait a bit longer to see if the drugs work? OK, I'm a bit smaller and a bit more weedy than the other kids, but I'll grow out of it, won't I?'

'I wish it were that simple, Finn.'

'If I don't have it, what's the worst that could happen?'

I take a steadying breath. 'It could kill you.'

He purses his lips. 'So, it's got to come out?'

I think of the alien I saw invading his brain and nod. 'It has.'

Then he shrugs. 'We'd better start on that bucket list then.'

'Some good news, at least. I did manage to get tickets for the Harry Potter tour today. VIP status.'

He fist bumps me. 'Nice work, Mother.'

He'll have no idea how many strings I had to pull for this or how much it's cost me and, frankly, that's irrelevant. I've got them and that's what counts.

'They're for next Monday. More time off school.'

'Is there really any point me going now? I've done what I can with the exams. The rest is in the lap of the gods. And I'm going to be off for ages after my operation recovering, right?'

'Yes. I'll talk to the headmaster tomorrow, I promise. If there's anything you need to catch up on, I'm sure they'll send it to you at home.'

'Great.' He rolls his eyes. 'Dump on the sick kid.'

'Ask me anything you want to, Finn. If I know the answer I'll tell you. If I don't, then I'll find out. I want this to be as stress-free for you as possible. There's no need to be afraid.'

'OK.' Then he glances at the casserole dish on the work surface and says, 'What time's tea? I'm starving.'

I wonder then if he realises the enormity of what's happening to him. And I hope in my heart that he doesn't.

Chapter Seventy-Five

The next day Finn goes to school. I pop in to see the headmaster to tell him that my son's operation has been scheduled and that he won't be coming back to school for the rest of this term. I'm not sure that he'll actually miss much now. They don't seem to do very much after the exams anyway. There's the prom, but Finn was never intending to go. He hates that kind of thing.

Instead, he and I are going to have some fun days out, as I promised. He also has to go into the hospital for pre-op checks. After that, of course, there'll be a prolonged absence. How long is anyone's guess. It all depends on how difficult the operation proves to be and how quickly Finn bounces back. He might not even be well enough to go back to school at the start of term in September. I've explained all this to the headmaster who couldn't be nicer to me. Bastard.

Then I don't seem to have time to turn around before it's nearly twelve o'clock and Henry is due to pick me up. I was hoping for a nice summer's day so that we could go and sit in a pub garden somewhere. Instead, it's tanking it down and the beer garden of the Barley Mow with its attractive canalside view is definitely off limits.

347

You know how sometimes dates with people go swimmingly and it seems as if you're destined to be together from the get-go? Max, for example. Then others are thwarted by bad weather and illness and general disaster. Henry, for example. I wonder if the universe, which is generally not to be trusted, is trying to tell me something.

When I see his car pull up, I run out in the rain and bound straight into the passenger seat.

'Awful weather,' I say. 'That's scuppered my plans for lunch in a pub garden. We'll go into Stony Stratford instead.' I'll simply have to hope that we don't bump into my mother as I haven't told her about my lunchtime assignation with Henry. God help me, I'll never hear the last of it, if I do.

'Good job there are no alpacas on the agenda today,' Henry jokes.

'No.' To be honest, you won't believe how relieved I am that this is an alpaca-free date.

We park in the Market Square and walk up past the library to one of the pubs on the High Street. My favourite is a fifteenth-century former coaching inn, so I hope that Henry likes his history. Of course, now it's all *très* contemporary with stone floors and pesto-infused mash and roasted beetroot served on slate boards in rooms decorated with Farrow and Ball Elephant's Breath paint.

We get a table in the snug at the front of the pub which is busy with lunchtime trade. Thankfully, my mother not among them. We choose from the menu, then my phone rings and Henry indicates that he'll go to the bar to order while I answer it.

When I look at my display, it's Max calling. It must be early in the morning in the USA, if that's where he is. He could be in London again for all I know. My heart starts to pound and I wonder whether to answer it or not. Against everything my brain is telling me, my heart wants to hear his voice. But I hesitate too long, and the voicemail clicks in.

I chew my fingernails wondering if Max will leave a message, until a few moments later a 'message waiting' flag comes up and I punch to retrieve it.

'Hey,' Max's voice says and my stomach flips at the sound of it. 'If you're there, Christie. Please pick up. Talk to me.'

I glance guiltily at Henry's back as he queues at the bar.

'If you're around, Skype me. I'm in the office all day. At home all evening. I'm not pressuring you, but I think we should have a conversation.'

Then there's a pause.

'That's it, I guess. Please call. Bye.'

I hang up just as Henry returns and sits down. My heart is still beating a military tattoo and my hand shakes as I reach out for my glass.

Henry notices and frowns. 'Not bad news.'

'No. My old boss from the crafting company. We have some things to sort out. Work things. It can wait.'

'I'm sorry that you've been made redundant,' he says. 'I know what that's like. It knocks the stuffing right out of you. Even if you hated the job. I suppose it's too soon, but any plans for what you'll do next?'

349

'Not yet. Finn's operation is in a week, so I want to make sure that I spend some quality time with him. In some ways being out of work is a blessing in disguise.' I try to sound as if I believe that.

'You're a brave lady.'

Not 'ordinary' today, then. If I'm truthful, I'm not sure that I can ever forgive him that.

I look at Henry and there's absolutely nothing wrong with him. He's pleasant enough and we chat well together, but there's no spark, no elec-tricity, no stomach flips, no longing. His voice doesn't turn me into a quivering jelly. There's nothing to dislike, but nothing to get excited about either. He doesn't make my heart race or tie my stomach in knots like Max does. Perhaps that's a good thing. He'd be steady, kind, nice. Ordinary.

But the sad thing is that while Henry chats on amiably, I have only half an ear to the conver-sation. I'm thinking of Max. I'm wondering what he'll say to me later, what I'll say to him.

Nothing will ever work with Henry while I can't get someone else out of my head. It isn't fair on him to even try.

Our meal comes and we eat it. Henry tells me about the films he's watched in the evenings when he gets in from work, alone. That makes me feel sad for him, as he's a good guy and deserves someone to share his life with. Looks as if that someone isn't going to be me though.

I push my plate away.

'We can go for a walk if you like,' Henry says. 'It looks as if it's stopped raining for a bit.'

There's a great little route round the back of the

town, along the river and up to Sweet Meadow where Dad walks the dogs, but, somehow, I can't quite face it. I feel as if I've spent enough time with Henry for today.

'I should be getting back,' I say. 'I've got lots to do.'

'Of course,' he says. 'Me too, really. I was just trying to put off doing it.'

He drives me home and when he parks outside my house, I don't invite him in.

'This has been nice, Henry. Thank you.'

'My mornings won't be the same without you.' He pulls a rueful face which makes me smile. 'Can we do this again?'

'Yes. I'd like it if we stayed friends.'

'Ah.' Perhaps that's the worst thing you can say to a man as his smile disappears. 'Just friends?'

'That's all I can offer at the moment.'

'I understand.' He might be putting a brave face on it, but I'm not sure that he really does understand. 'I hope Finn's operation goes well.'

'Thank you.' Then I get out of the car and wave him goodbye, all the while wondering how I'll ever find the courage to phone Max.

Chapter Seventy-Six

I don't call Max. I try several times but, coward that I am, hang up before he answers each time. Instead, I do my very best to forget about him and spend the next week having fun with Finn.

Neither of us voice it, but we both know why we're desperately packing treats into the time while he waits for his operation.

We take the tour of the Harry Potter studios and it's fabulous. Makes me want to read the books all over again. We marvelled at the Great Hall at Hogwarts, walked through Diagon Alley, visited number four Privet Drive and enjoyed a frothy tankard of butterbeer. Finn was in his element.

Mum and Dad wanted some time with Finn too and took him off to a falconry centre where he got to fly an owl, a kestrel, a Harris hawk and a black kite. He was so excited when he came home that he could barely speak and it made me so glad to see it.

In a few frantically busy days in London we also managed to cram in an afternoon tea at Fortnum and Mason, lunch at the Hard Rock Café, a trip on the London Eye, a tour of Madame Tussauds and a matinee show of *The Lion King* which made us both cry.

But now we can put it off no longer. Finn has his bag packed and so do I. We're going down to the hospital this afternoon and I'm checking into the family accommodation. Mum and Dad are coming too and the animals have all been relocated to their house. Dad's organised for their next-door neighbour to look after Eric and Trigger while we're gone. They'll pop in and see the cats once a day to make sure they're all right too.

Dad is driving us to the hospital and they're due any minute.

'Ready?' I ask Finn.

He shrugs. 'I suppose.' My son looks round the

room and I see his eyes fill with tears.

'You'll be back before you know it,' I tell him.

'Will I?'

We both know what he's thinking and my throat tightens with emotion.

'Yes,' I say as calmly as I can. 'I promise you.'

'What if...?' He runs out of words.

'You're coming home,' I reiterate. 'No ifs. No buts.'

'I'm glad that you'll be with me.'

'As if I wouldn't.' I hold out my arms and, without me having to employ my usual emotional blackmail or torture, Finn steps into them. Pushing my luck, I kiss his hair.

'Mum...' he complains.

'You're my brave boy,' I tell him. 'At this time tomorrow, the worst of it will be behind you.'

'Nothing will go wrong, will it?'

'No. Of course not.' I cross my fingers and pray that I'm right. 'You've got the best surgeons possible.' Then, to distract him, 'Have you got the card and mascot that Ella sent you?'

It's a grey, patched Tatty Teddy with a bandage round its head. Cute. And I'm glad that Ella sent something for him to take with him. It was very kind of her.

'Yeah.' He blushes. 'They're in my bag.'

'You can put them on your bedside for luck.'

Dad pulls up outside.

'We're on,' I say.

'Best let go of me then, Mum.'

'Oh. OK.' We smile at each other. 'I wish I could go through this for you.'

'*I* wish you could too,' Finn deadpans.

353

'Come on.' I pick up our bags. 'The sooner we get this over with, the better. I'll treat us both to a nice holiday when you've properly recovered. That'll be something to look forward to.' I got the notification of how much redundancy pay I'll get and, true to her word, Robyn has secured me a tidy sum. It will certainly take the pressure off earning for the next few months while Finn re-cuperates and meant that I could afford all of our outings without worrying.

Dad pops in to get our bags and puts them in the boot. We all climb into the car and set off down the motorway. Mum, sounding completely hyper, tries to entertain Finn with versions of I Spy and other silly games, but Finn's having none of it and stares fixedly out of the window. In the end I shake my head at Mum and she drops the cheerful act and falls silent. We all stay sub-dued until we arrive at the hospital, the enormity of what's about to happen undeniable now.

Mum and Dad go to check us into the family accommodation while I accompany Finn to the ward. There'll be more pre-op tests and Mr Darby, the consultant, is coming to see him later.

'OK?' He nods, but slips his hand in mine. I feel cold, so cold, right down to my core.

We arrive on the ward at the same time as Finn's dad.

Finn drops his bag and runs into his arms. 'Dad!'

Liam lifts him up. 'Hiya, champ. What about that for timing?'

'Have you just got in?'

'Yeah. My plane landed a couple of hours ago.

I've booked into the family accommodation across the road.' He looks up at me. 'Hiya, Christie.'

'Hi, Liam. Good to see you.' And it is. He might be my ex, but he's Finn's dad and he needs him here.

Straight away Finn is settled into the ward and ensconced in a bed near the window. 'After the last week of running around having fun, I'm glad of a lie down,' he quips.

'Very funny.'

'I did enjoy it though, Mum. Thanks for all that.'

I squeeze his hand. 'My pleasure.'

'What time's your surgery, son?'

'Eight o'clock in the morning,' Finn says and I can hear the nerves in his voice.

I stand up. 'I'm going to leave you with your dad. I'd better go over to the accommodation and check on Nan and Pops. I'll be back later.'

'I'll walk you to the door.' Liam falls into step next to me. 'I appreciate this,' he says quietly when we're out of Finn's earshot. 'I'm sorry it's fallen to you to handle it all.'

'I'm his mother.'

'You know what I mean,' Liam says.

'I'm just pleased that you could be here for him.'

'I've got a week's leave. I hope that will be enough.'

'I'm sure it will be a good start. He's thrilled to see you.'

'Thanks.' He gives me one of his boyish grins. 'You're looking good, Christie.'

'You too.' And he does look fit and well.

'Clearly, the Dubai lifestyle suits you.' He's tanned, slim and as handsome as ever he was. He just looks the same as the day we parted. He still has all his hair, not much of it grey.

'It's a good place to be,' he says. 'For now.' He flicks a look back at Finn in his hospital bed. 'This sort of thing makes you take stock of your priorities though. I think when my current contract ends, I'll be looking towards coming back.'

'To England?'

He nods. 'I want to be nearer Finn. Providing that...' He doesn't say what we're all thinking either.

'He'll be fine,' I say, touching Liam's arm. 'Our boy is as tough as old boots.'

'Takes after his mum,' Liam jokes and, obligingly, I laugh.

'I'd better go. Mum and Dad will only be stressing.'

'Are they both all right?'

'Yes. You'll see them later. Shall we take tonight in shifts? I don't want Finn left alone in case he wakes up.' I wonder if he'll manage to sleep at all.

'I'll probably stay all night,' Liam says.

'Me too.'

'This is a bit weird, eh?'

I smile. 'Slightly. But we'll make it work for Finn's sake.'

He kisses my cheek briefly. 'I'd like that.'

Then I wave to Finn and hotfoot it to see my folks. I'll be back as soon as I can as I want to spend every minute I can with my child.

Chapter Seventy-Seven

Liam and I spend all night with Finn. One on either side of his bed. He dozes on and off, but doesn't really sleep. I wish I knew what was going through his mind. When he's awake we play games – Scrabble, battleships, hangman.

Mum and Dad pop in to wish him well. They did not sleep much either. Then eight o'clock comes and he's taken down to theatre. We go with him.

'Good luck, Champ,' Liam says as he's wheeled in.

'Thanks, Dad.'

'You go in with him,' my ex says and I do.

I'm put in full hospital scrubs with my hair tied back and a cap on. I hold his hand while Finn has his anaesthetic.

'It doesn't look a bit like you, Mum,' he says drowsily and those are his last words before he slides into a drug-induced sleep.

The surgery is due to take five and a half hours. During that time we all go back to the family accommodation and sit there, not quite knowing what to do. Mum knits. I try to read a book, but find myself going over the same sentence again and again. I wish I'd brought something crafty to do, but probably couldn't put my mind to it. Dad and Liam are chatting away, catching up on the intervening years. They always did get on well and I suspect the only person who's actually interested in Dad's steam engine is Liam. Daytime television amuses itself in the background. Mum makes us sandwiches in the small kitchen for lunch, but none of us eat them.

Five hours in and I crack. The hospital have promised to call me as soon as he's out of surgery, but I can't sit here any longer, confined by these four walls.

'I'm going back,' I say.

'I'll come with you.' Liam puts down the crossword he's been fiddling with on and off for the last two hours.

'Phone us,' Mum says.

'I will.'

As Liam and I reach the hospital, my phone rings. The ward nurse is on the other end of the line. 'Hello, Christie,' she says. 'Finn's done really well. He's out of surgery now and in the recovery ward.'

'Thank you.' I turn to Liam. 'He's out.'

'Thank God,' Liam breathes. He takes my hand and we run together down the corridor, hope in my heart for the first time.

Finn is groggy when we see him and hooked up to a dozen different monitors in intensive care. He looks small and vulnerable, yet, considering his ordeal, doesn't seem in too bad a shape.

He opens his eyes, but they're not entirely focused. 'Hey.'

I take his hand and stroke it. 'How are you doing?'

'Cool.' His mouth is obviously dry and I wonder if he's allowed some water. The machines beep softly in a comforting way.

'In pain?'

'I don't think so.'

'I'm so pleased. We had a quick word with the surgeon and he said it all went brilliantly.'

'Good,' Finn slurs. 'Because I'm not doing that again.'

Liam and I laugh, tearfully.

'Go to sleep,' I say. 'We'll both be here when you wake up.'

'Love you, Mum.' His eyes are closing already and soon he's gone again. I take a minute to phone Mum and tell her that Finn is doing well, my voice shaking with emotion.

Without thinking, Liam and I hug each other. My ex-husband holds me tightly.

'He came through it.' Liam blows out an unsteady breath.

'Yeah.' I can't manage anything more eloquent.

We take up positions on either side of him again. I rest my head on his bed and soon I can feel myself drifting off to sleep too. He's come through it safely and my heart feels twice the size that it did. I don't think that it could hold any more love for this boy than it does now.

Chapter Seventy-Eight

Finn recovers, miraculously. After two days, he's out of intensive care and on a regular ward. At the end of the week, he's allowed home. He looks battered and bruised, but the alien is out of his brain and he's home.

You can't believe how excited we all are. But I'm terrified of him banging his head getting in and out of the car. I feel he should have a big Mr Bump-style bandage on it, but there's nothing to show how terrible his ordeal was. I rush in to his bedroom every morning to make sure that he's still breathing. However, as the days pass and his strength comes back, I start to relax.

Finn has changed too. He went into the operation as a child, but he's grown up so much. It's as if he realises that he's overcome a major hurdle and has been handed a large slice of maturity in return. I love to see his calm confidence, but also know that the boy I had has gone for ever.

He lies on the sofa ordering me around and I'm happy to comply. We watch films together, the trashier the better. Liam is still here. He extended his leave by a week and is staying at a nearby hotel. Currently, he comes in every day, but soon he'll be heading back to Dubai.

Lovely little Ella comes over to see Finn and brings him chocolate. I make myself scarce, leaving them cuddled up on the sofa watching YouTube videos of bands that I've never heard of. Even Eric is put out and is lying at my feet. Ella and Finn make a lovely couple and I can see that her visit has cheered him up no end. It's good to see that she is looking better in herself too. Her hair has started to grow back and, currently, looks quite punky. I hope that they'll both soon be out of the woods.

I set up to do some crafting on the kitchen table. Something that's been seriously neglected over the last few weeks. I'm so out of practice that I don't quite know where to start. I haven't phoned Max and he hasn't tried to call me again, so that's probably that. All these boxes of stuff are still awaiting dispatch back to the distributor. I look at them again, dearly wishing that I could afford to keep it all. If I'm honest, I've barely given him a thought. I've been so wrapped up in Finn – which is probably just as well.

Finally, I find my mojo and, as I'm cutting out some cards to replenish my stock, Liam comes over. I've given him a key, which was a big step for me, but it's been fine. I hear him saying hello to Finn and Ella but he soon heads into the kitchen to see me.

He throws a thumb back towards the living room. 'It looks like I'm surplus to requirements.'

'Yeah. Me too. I'm busying myself in here. It's good to see though.'

'I thought I'd book my ticket back to Dubai for tomorrow. Do you think Finn would mind?'

'No,' I say. 'He'll understand. I'm just pleased that you could be here for him.'

'I've not been here enough. I realise that. I am seriously thinking about coming back at the end of this contract,' he reiterates. 'I want to be nearer to Finn. I've talked to Jodie about it and, now that our kids are older, she wants them to see more of their grandparents too. Dubai's great, but there's no place like home and all that. This had made me feel a long way away.'

'Near here?'

'Ideally,' Liam says. 'Jodie's folks are only in Northampton, so it would be best. But I guess

361

I've got to go where the jobs are.'

I know that it would be good for Finn to have his dad nearer to him. Even in the same country would be an improvement.

'We talked about going on holiday together when he's better,' I tell him. 'Perhaps we could come out to see you?'

'That would be great. I can provide you with hotel rooms. All you'd have to find is your flight.'

'I'm out of work now,' I remind him. The cost of flights might be an insurmountable object. 'But I'll see what I can do.' Now that Finn is getting back on his feet, I'm going to have to start looking for something to do. I'm enjoying being at home with my boy, but I know that I can't put off rejoining the world of work for too much longer. I wonder for the millionth time whether we should consider renting out this house and moving in with Mum and Dad until I'm sorted.

'Tell Finn I'll come back later.'

'Have dinner with us,' I say. 'We're going over to Mum and Dad's later, if Finn's feeling up to it. His first outing. It would be nice for you to spend your last evening with him.'

'Thanks, Christie.' He looks into my eyes. 'You've been great. I couldn't have asked for more. I do sometimes wonder why we split.'

'We wanted different things, Liam. You yearned to see the world. I'll always be a home bird.'

He smiles. 'I didn't get very far. A few years in Dubai. Hardly the big adventurer.'

'There's time. Maybe you and Finn could do some travelling together in time. I'll hold the fort.'

'That sounds like a plan.'

There's giggling from the sofa and we both roll our eyes. 'I feel that we're moving into a different phase with Finn.'

'An easier one, I hope,' Liam says.

I laugh. 'I'll let you know.'

He kisses my cheek and, it might be my imagination, but there's a lot of affection behind it. 'I'll see you later.'

Chapter Seventy-Nine

Dad's barbecuing tonight. Apparently. Which is generally a terrifying experience. Mum has, at least, managed to wean him off heating the coals with a liberal dosing of dangerous accelerants. She bought him a gas barbie after he set fire to the garden fence once too often and we now don't have to throw all the food in the bin because it tastes of WD40. It's still all blackened to charcoal but no longer a near-death experience.

'Are you sure you're feeling up to this?' I ask Finn for the umpteenth time.

'Yes.'

'I don't want you tiring yourself out.'

'All I'm doing is sleeping or lying on the sofa. I'm fine. Stop fussing, Mum.'

Secretly, I think he likes me fussing. But this is the first time he's been up, dressed and about to go out. I'm worried. My parents have been bringing daily food parcels for us, but I have to wean us all off the habit soon. Well, soonish.

'The main worry is whether or not I'll survive Pop's sausages.'

'I did try to persuade them against a barbecue, but you know what they're like. And it is a lovely afternoon. We should make the most of it. There's not much of summer left. It will be winter before we know it.'

'My mother, the optimist,' Finn quips.

'It's good to see that you're getting better,' I bat back. 'But you will tell me if you get tired. Don't overdo it.'

'OK.'

'You'll be fit to go back to school in September.'

Finn screws his nose up. 'Looking forward to that.'

'If your exam results are good enough, you'll be going into sixth form. That'll be good, won't it?'

He still looks unimpressed. 'What if I fail everything?'

'I don't really know. I'm guessing that you'll have to do this year again.'

Finn looks horrified. 'Is that even legal?'

'I'll need to talk to the headmaster.'

'They can't make me do that, surely? Everyone else will be going into sixth form and I'll be left behind.'

'It might be for the best.'

'For who? Oh man, that's made me feel ill.' Finn clutches his chest. 'I'll swear my heart nearly stopped.'

'Enough of the drama queen. Get Eric and we'll be going. The burgers have probably been on the go for the last few hours.' Dad likes to make sure we don't get E. coli or botulism.

So we bundle the dog into the car and drive over to the hotel to pick up Liam. As it's his last night, he might as well enjoy a beer or two and not have to drive. Then we go over to my parents' house.

Unusually, the side gate is locked, so we can't get in that way and we go back to knock at the front door.

'Only me,' I shout through the letter box.

Mum opens the door and is as hyperactive as I've ever seen her. She grabs a rather startled Finn in a bear hug. 'My lovely, lovely grandson,' she croons at him.

He pulls a face over her shoulder and says, 'Put me down, Nan. I've not just come home from the war.'

Yet, in some ways, we all feel as if he has.

'Come in, come in,' Mum says and shouts, 'Ray, it's Christie and Finn. And Liam.'

'Afternoon, Jenny. Thanks for having me.'

'You're always welcome here,' Mum says, magnanimously.

'We would have gone round the side, but the gate's locked,' I point out.

'You can't be too careful,' Mum says mysteriously.

'About what?' I ask as I follow her into the kitchen.

Dad comes to the kitchen door, pink-faced, wearing one of Mum's flowery aprons and brandishing a barbecue fork. 'Everything's coming along nicely,' he says. 'Soon be ready.'

Which means that it was cooked to a cinder a good hour ago.

'But first,' Mum announces with a flourish, 'we should have a toast!'

That means Dad's been down to Budgens for some cava.

I pick up the bottle. Not the cheap stuff either. 'Is this in aid of Finn coming home?'

'That and Other Things.' My mother is looking very smug.

'Like what?'

'No one's at home to Ms Nosy,' Mum says.

That's me told. I look at Finn and we both shrug. They are probably just excited that everything with Finn is getting back to normal. He hasn't been here for ages now and they're used to having him every day.

Mum fills her best glasses which are already waiting on her best tray on the kitchen table.

'Can you carry it outside please, Liam? I don't trust myself.'

Liam does as he's told and carries the tray outside.

Mum and Dad are both hopping about from foot to foot and making me nervous. They turn and beam at each other, conspiratorially.

'What?'

Then, in a slightly giddy manner, Mum produces a silk scarf and says, 'I'm going to blindfold you, Christie.'

'Eh? What? I don't think so.'

'Don't be a spoilsport.'

'What are you going to blindfold me for?'

'You'll see soon enough.'

'Not if I'm blindfolded,' I point out.

'It's a surprise, love,' Dad cajoles. By which he means 'For God's sake humour your mother!'

'OK,' I say reluctantly. I'm not one for subterfuge. Or surprises, for that matter. I like everything out in the open.

With far too much in the way of theatrics, my mum puts the scarf over my eyes.

'Not too tight,' I grumble.

'Take my hand,' she says. 'We're going out into the garden.'

I do as I'm told. Resistance is futile. All I can think now is that the burgers are going to be well and truly burnt.

Chapter Eighty

Mum has a vice-like grip on my hand. 'Don't trip over the rockery,' she says.

'Not helpful. I can't even see the rockery.'

'Just a little bit more and you can take your blindfold off.'

I move carefully over the bumps and hollows of the garden.

'Right,' Mum says. 'This should do it.' She undoes my scarf and I blink against the sunshine.

'Oh, wow. A new summerhouse.'

'Not a new one,' Mum corrects. 'Not exactly. It's still the same one, but Dad's given it some of his special tender loving care.'

'I'll say so.' It certainly looks like a brand new

summerhouse. 'It's unrecognisable.' Dad's painted it all cream and it looks as if there's a new roof. The double doors are wider and have more glass to let the light in. The windows at either side have been reglazed. 'This is amazing.'

Dad glows with pride.

'When did you manage to do all this?'

'Dad's been working on it over the last few weeks,' Mum says. 'We thought it would be a nice surprise.'

'It's fabulous,' I say. 'I know you love your summerhouse. You'll use it even more now.'

'This isn't for us,' Dad chips in. 'It's for you, Christie. We want you to have it to work in.'

I look at him, stunned. 'You've done this for me?'

'We don't want you going back into an office, love,' Mum continues. 'If we can help you to build a crafting business of some sort, then we'd like to.'

'You're kidding me.'

Dad shakes his head and surreptitiously wipes a tear from his eye. 'It's all yours, love. Do you like it?'

'I flipping *love* it.' This has always been one of my favourite places and now it's positively glamorous too! Already I can see myself settled in here, crafting away. It's the perfect place to run a small business and I could weep with joy. My hands go to my mouth. 'Oh my God.' I look from one to the other. 'I can't believe it.'

My parents look as pleased as punch at their skulduggery. How Dad has managed to do this, I'll never know. But he has and you've no idea how grateful I am.

'You'll build yourselves another summerhouse?' I know how much they've loved this and I don't want them missing out on my account.

Dad nods. 'Your mother has already picked out a little spot. But all in good time.'

I hope that once my finances are back on an even keel, I might be able to help them out for a change.

Finn and Liam have joined us at the bottom of the garden. 'Did you know about this?' I ask my son.

'No,' he admits. 'Way to go, Pops.'

'You're too kind to us.' I hug my parents as hard as I can. 'I love you so much.'

'You deserve a treat,' Dad says. 'Both you and Finn have been through the mill, but brighter days are ahead.'

I look again in amazement at the fancy new pimped up summerhouse, and think that he might just be right.

Chapter Eighty-One

Liam is dispatched to check on the barbecue, after Dad's given him a list of instructions.

The summerhouse is basking in the last of the evening sun. I have to say, it looks very grand. The resident swans come to see what we're up to, hoping for some bread. Gorgeous.

'Go on, inside,' Dad urges, clearly as excited as I am.

The interior wood is painted white, making it feel light and airy. They've put a glass table by the window with a desk lamp, magnifier and swishy office chair. The cobwebs are all gone, along with Mum's old hand-stitched wall hangings. Instead, there's a bank of crisp white storage shelves from IKEA, just waiting for all my lovely crafting products. There's a bright rug on the floor, obviously Mum's touch. The dogs join us and give it a thorough inspection too. Eric tries out the rug for size. Good luck hanging onto that, pooch, when the cats see this place.

'This is fabulous,' I say. 'Is it really all mine?'

They both beam proudly at me.

'Think you'll be comfortable here?' Dad looks concerned. 'I've put extra insulation in, so it will be nice and cosy in the winter. You've got a little heater too.'

'It couldn't be better.' I gaze round, stunned. 'I can't believe you did this without me knowing. I had no idea. Do you like it, Finn?'

'It's great. We can get all of those boxes out of the dining room now.'

It's the first time I've thought that we might actually be able to keep them. Well, maybe some of them.

'How will you manage without it until you get your new one?' I ask. 'You love your summer-house.'

'You need this space more than us,' Mum say. 'Dad's giving up half of his workshop too. We thought you'd need somewhere for stock and things.'

This is the equivalent of Dad donating a kidney

370

to me.

'You can't do that,' I protest. I know how much it will hurt Dad to part with pieces of wood that he's kept for twenty years or more – just in case.

'He's had a clear out.' Mum is triumphant. She's been trying to get him to do this for years. Now she has an excuse.

I turn to Dad, bemused. 'You have been a busy boy. How on earth did you keep this a secret?'

'You mother would have killed me if I'd breathed a word.'

'You know what he's like,' Mum tuts. 'Can't hold his own water.'

'Ted next door helped me,' Dad adds. 'I couldn't have managed it all by myself in time.'

'I had a hand in the painting,' Mum adds, not wanting her contribution to be undersold.

Hugging them both, I say, 'I don't know how to begin to thank you.'

'Make a nice little business for yourself,' Mum says. 'That'll be enough for us.'

'I promise that I'll do my best.'

'I'd better get back to see how Liam's coping with the barbecue.' Dad looks alarmed. 'I think I can smell the sausages burning.'

'I need to finish off the salads too,' Mum says.

'Do you need a hand or can we stay here a minute?' I ask. 'I want to drink it all in.'

'You take your time, love.' She takes Dad's hand and I see her give it a surreptitious squeeze as they go back up the garden with Trigger at their heels. Eric stays with us, stretching out on the rug, head on paws.

When we're alone, I put my arm round Finn's

371

shoulders. 'What do you reckon?'

'It looks like a great place to start your crafting empire. One day, a summerhouse by the river, next, world domination. Watch out Sheridan Singleton, Christie Chapman is coming to get you.'

I laugh at Finn's optimism. 'I wish!'

'You'll phone Max Alexander now, won't you?' Finn asks. 'This puts a whole different spin on things.'

'It does,' I agree. 'But I'll have to take time to think where I want to go from here.'

Finn fidgets in my embrace. 'I've been thinking about my future too.'

'Oh yeah?'

'I don't want to go back to school, Mum. I hate every minute. Even if, by some miracle, I pass my exams, I don't want to go into sixth form. I don't fit in there and I want to start working. I haven't stopped mulling over the idea of an online shop. I had a lot of time lying around in that hospital.'

Stupid tears come to my eyes. One day I'll be able to say or hear the word 'hospital' without crying, I'm sure. But not yet.

'This is an ideal opportunity for both of us,' he presses on. 'We could start a business together. I could do a web design course. Maybe something with e-commerce too.'

It makes me smile to hear my child and his business-speak. This is what watching *Dragons' Den* does for you. 'What about university?'

'It's not the be-all and end-all, Mum. If I've got something that interests me now, shouldn't I go for that?'

'I don't know, Finn...'

'I could run the website and send out the orders. If Pops has cleared out a bit of his workshop, we'd have room. If I did that, it would leave you free to be creative and all that stuff. I'll put a business plan together for you. How does that sound?'

'Is this really my boy? What exactly did they do to your brain during that operation?'

'I'm not a kid,' he says. 'Take me seriously.'

'OK,' I concede. 'I will.'

'We could work together,' he insists. 'You know it.'

'All right, all right!' I hold up my hands. 'One step at a time.'

'It must be better than doing nine to five in an office?'

'It is, but there's also security in a regular income.' Says the person who's recently been made redundant out of the blue. 'If we're going to do this...'

Finn's eyes widen. 'So, you *do* think we could?'

'Well, it's a possibility. But, while we're on the subject, there's something I've been meaning to talk to you about. Nan and Pops suggested we rent out the house for a short time – maybe six months or a year – and move in with them. It would give us some money behind us, a safety net. Could you cope with that?'

'It would be worth it,' Finn says. 'It might cramp my style with Ella, though.'

I grin. There's nothing much wrong with my boy, it seems. 'We'll both have to make sacrifices.'

'Yeah. It's not as if your love life is going to suffer.'

'True fact.' I get a sudden pang of longing for Max, but I push all thoughts of him to the back of my mind. This is a time to rejoice, not to regret.

'We'd better get back to the barbecue,' I say. 'I don't want our bright future blighted by burnt sausages.'

'It's times like this when I'm grateful for ketchup,' Finn agrees.

I take one last look around the beautiful summerhouse and feel fit to burst. I could be happy working here. Very happy.

Chapter Eighty-Two

So we eat burnt sausages, and toast the summerhouse and new beginnings. We all sit out in the garden until late and huddle under blankets for warmth. I'm definitely going to treat my folks to a fire pit or something when I've got some spare cash.

I watch Finn's dad drinking beer and laughing with my son and my parents and feel a tinge of sadness that we didn't make our marriage work. In a bizarre way, Finn's operation has brought us closer together and it's been good for them to spend some time re-establishing their bonds.

The next morning, we pick Liam up again and drive him to the airport for his flight back to Dubai. No doubt he's itching to see his other family now.

Our plans to have breakfast together and say a

leisurely goodbye are thwarted by the unseemly amount of traffic on the M25. So we're hurried and harried by the time we reach Heathrow and Liam has to rush straight through to Departures.

At the gate, he holds Finn tight. 'Good to see you, Champ. Keep improving.' Emotion is choking his voice.

'I will,' Finn agrees.

'Promise me that you'll come out to see me as soon as you get the all-clear.'

Finn turns back to me. 'Can we, Mum?'

'Of course,' I say. 'Your dad and I will fix it up.'

'Thanks, Christie.' Liam's face is sincere when he looks at me and once more I think I see warmth and affection in his eyes for me, which is nice. 'Thanks for everything.'

He hugs Finn one last time and then he's gone through the gate. Finn and I stand and watch until he's out of sight.

'OK?' I say to Finn.

He shrugs. 'A bit shitty.'

'Language, Finn.' I say it to make us laugh rather than out of any real desire to chide him. If I were in his position, I'd feel a bit shitty too. It works and we both laugh. Finn leans against me and I sling my arm round his shoulders. He's been more in need of cuddles since his operation and I'm more than happy to supply them.

'Want to find a café and have a hot chocolate before we head back?'

'Sounds like a plan,' he says.

'It's just you and me again, kid.'

'I'll miss Dad,' he admits. 'But going to Dubai will give us something to look forward to.'

I spy a Costa in the distance and steer him towards it. 'We've got loads to look forward to. You're healthy, happy and have a business to think about. Next year we're going to be millionaires, don't you know.'

Finn chuckles. 'Don't get carried away, Mum.'

'Plus, you have the hottest girlfriend.'

My son flushes deeply. 'Yeah,' he agrees. 'I do.'

'Life is looking good, Finn. Very good, indeed.'

Chapter Eighty-Three

What can I tell you? Life goes on. Finn continues to make fabulous progress. Every time we go back to the hospital for check-ups he confounds the consultant by making such great progress. Even the massive shark bite scar on his leg doesn't look quite so terrifying now it's healing.

Finn didn't mess up all of his exams. By some miracle. He did OK, considering the pressure he was under. A smattering of decent grades, a few less so. But it doesn't matter either way. I'm just so proud of what he's achieved. I agreed that he didn't have to go back to school after he set out the most brilliant plan for him running a little online business selling crafting materials. Let's face it, Finn knows nearly as much about crafting as I do. So we might as well put that to good use. He was adamant that he didn't want to go into the sixth form and, after all he's been through, there's no way that I was going to push him. All I want is that he's happy. He's done enough to get a place at a local college and is hoping to start a web design and e-commerce course in the New Year – two days a week. We'll work round it in the business. I have to say that he's been brilliant, so far.

We move lock, stock and die-cutters into the summerhouse. It's a beautiful, sunny space and I love working here instantly. I have my desk by the window and we set up another one for Finn by the shelves at the other end, so that we each have our defined space. Because I am older and wiser, and pull the bad eyesight card, I bag the best view. It's lovely to look up from my current project, be it a card or a mixed media piece, and see the blue strand of the river winding past, the dappled sunshine through the trees, the swans going quietly about their business.

I can't tell you how wonderful it is to have all my crafting materials beautifully organised around me – everything in its own space and not shoved into every available cupboard and under my bed and in the living room cluttering up the house. With its new garb, the summerhouse is lighter and airier than it's ever been. When the days are warm, we fling open the double doors and listen to the quacking ducks, the sound of the reeds in the breeze and the rush of the river. Bliss. Today we have a shower of sweet September rain and the ducks are hiding under the apple tree. For something that spends a lot of time with its bottom in water, they don't seem to like getting wet when it comes from the sky.

Finn works hard at setting up a website for us

and we call our foundling business Summerhouse Crafts. Cute, eh? Finn even has one of his arty mates draw up a cool logo featuring said summerhouse. The boxes of stock that I ordered from Max stay. On the site, we display a nice range of the Contemporary Crafts dies, paper and adhesives, starting out small as our budget and space allows. However, both Finn and I are secretly pleased to get a steady stream of orders despite doing very little advertising. We seem to have a hardcore of crazy crafting ladies who keep coming back for more of our wares, God bless them. They may never buy me a Mercedes but they might just help to buy me a bottle of wine every week and keep our bank account in the black.

It makes me smile when I look over and see Finn hard at work, tongue out in concentration, packing up orders ready for his daily run to the post office – courtesy of Dad's car. He's thinking that we might start a list of subscribers with a view to offering a monthly craft box and has been going through heaps of supplier catalogues and talking to other companies about the possibilities. It's amazing to see how far he's come in the last year and it makes my heart swell with pride.

My creativity has had a definite upsurge and I'm producing some of my best work – even though I say it myself. Mum is helping with some of the cutting for a ready-to-assemble craft kit that I produce every month and we've got Dad employed making box frames for little artwork projects so that he doesn't feel left out. The epitome of a family business! If I could, I'd have Eric on a doggy treadmill powering the laptop.

Instead, he curls up and spends most of the day asleep on the rug, basking in the sunshine.

Perhaps my new lease of life is down to the fact that I don't spend every waking moment worrying about Finn. That's not to say that my concern has suddenly stopped dead – I'm a mother, after all, right? A selfish part of me is thrilled that he was keen to work with me. At any time of the day I can reach out and touch him. If anything was to go wrong, if he was ill or collapsed – I'm right here. And there's a comfort in that. When your son's been through something as life-threatening as Finn has, you don't easily let go.

But, in case you think it's all work and no play, we also have a laptop set up in the corner and have Creative World on in the background as we work. Well, we have to keep up with the competition.

Mum and Dad bring us tea and biscuits on the hour, every hour and I have to take up jogging after work every day to counteract my increased calorific intake. Yeah, get me. Officially, a jogger. Who'd have thought? I even enjoy it. Sort of. I've signed up for the Milton Keynes 10k run to raise money for the Teenage Cancer Trust, so I've no choice now. Sometimes, Finn joins me – when he's not too busy Skyping Ella.

We rented out the house with surprising ease and for more than we thought. It was tough packing all our belongings into boxes and moving out, but a nice guy on his own moved in straight away. He's working down here for the time being and, if it pans out, he'll move his family down later. He reminds me a lot of Henry, and for a moment I miss our daily chats on the coach. He sent a few texts after Finn came out of hospital to wish us both well, but they sort of petered out and I've heard nothing for a while now. Perhaps it's for the best. I hope he finds his way back north and to the daughter he missed so much.

So now Finn and I are crammed into my parents' house. I have the double bedroom at the front, as I did when I was a child, and Finn is shoehorned in the box room. He has his laptop and seems none the worse for the lack of space.

Finn's medicine fills his nana's fridge and I've shown her how to give Finn his injections so that, some mornings, she does them for him. Which, thankfully, he doesn't mind. It's the only part that I still find difficult and it's nice that Mum can share the load.

Now that Finn's earning his own money, he can take Ella out more and so they're not having to hang round the house for their entertainment. Dad frequently runs them to the cinema in the town centre. Ella is looking lovely. Her hair is long now and pink. This week. She's at a local college studying fashion design and is loving it. She's got her own vlog and a YouTube channel. I don't even know what that means. But she says that I should have one too. Also, she's moved into digs nearby – which is saving on a lot of shuttling backwards and forwards to Bedford. I think because they've both been ill, they're more sympathetic to each other on days when they're not feeling their sparkling best. She's good for Finn and makes him laugh.

For the dog, this was home from home, anyway, so I don't think he's actually noticed that we've moved in permanently. The cats don't care either as long as someone is opening a tin. They dominate the conservatory now – seeing off Trigger if he ever makes a bid for one of the sofas. Eric has already learned this at his peril.

Every morning, we all get tea in bed due to my kind dad. He comes into my room bearing a carefully held mug, his remaining tuft of hair on end, in his favourite worn dressing gown that Mum's been desperate to get in the bin for as long as I remember. If we ever move back to our own home, I'll miss this more than anything. It certainly beats crawling out of bed at an ungodly hour every day to catch the coach to London. *That*, I don't miss!

'You need to contact Max Alexander, Mum,' Finn says over his shoulder. 'We've sold a lot of the stock we had and I want to put more of their products on the website. The distributor says that we need Contemporary Crafts' approval and I'll need to set up a business account with them. I guess we should check that's still OK now that you don't work for them.'

'Yes.' No one could mistake the reluctance in my voice. There's really only one elephant in the room now and that's Max Alexander. We moved all the boxes of the Contemporary Crafts products to our storage area in Dad's workshop and I felt totally guilty as we did. Finn's right. I should contact him. I hope that he'll be pleased to learn how much we've sold and that we have regular customers clamouring for more. After all, they're great products. I just wonder if Max still feels kindly disposed towards me.

'Or I can do it,' he says. 'If it's an issue.'

Finn doesn't miss much.

Could I get away, I wonder, with calling my one-time line manager, Dean? But then that would seem rude. Or I could email? The cowards' way.

A quick glance at my watch tells me that it's about nine o'clock in the morning in Washington. Max will be in the office by now. Perhaps I should email him and suggest a Skype session. My heart races at the thought. Could I even cope with Skyping him? Would he make me ridiculously tongue-tied? I glance at the Creative World channel that's streaming on the laptop and Sheridan Singleton is presenting a project. She's as shiny and as confident as ever. She wouldn't baulk at calling Max. Maybe she calls him regularly, anyway? I feel a little green-eyed at the thought.

'Earth to Mother,' Finn says.

'I'll email him to set up a Skype session,' I say and, before I can think of a reason not to, I tap out a note. I keep it light, friendly. I tell him that I'm sorry I've not been in contact. I tell him that Finn is well. And, finally, I ask him if I can talk to him about business. I press 'send' and then, I guess, the rest is up to him.

Chapter Eighty-Four

Perhaps it's because I keep my fingers crossed, but minutes later, Max responds that he'd love to talk on Skype. With a deep breath I tap in his address and wait for the connection.

Then, there he is, right in front of me on my laptop screen, looking every bit as handsome as ever.

'Hey,' he says, softly. 'Long time, no speak.'

'I'm sorry,' I begin. 'You could probably tell from my email that I've been busy.'

'Great news about Finn, though.' Max smiles at the screen. 'You must both be relieved.'

'That's a bit of an understatement,' I admit. 'You don't realise quite how stressed you are until it stops.'

'And the prognosis is good?'

'Looking very good,' I confirm.

I see my craft project photographed large on the wall behind him and my mind drifts back to the wonderful time I spent in America at the Contemporary Crafts headquarters. I like to think that there's a little piece of me always in his office.

'How's business?' I ask.

'Good. I've been running round Europe trying to secure some deals. All looking positive.'

'You haven't been to London?' I hold my breath because I don't want to hear that he has been here and didn't want to see me.

'No,' he says. 'I'm overdue a trip, I guess. I was talking to Sheridan Singleton a few days ago and she wants to schedule another appearance for me on her channel.'

'That would be great.'

'She asked after you and Finn too. I filled her in with what I could and she asked me to pass on her best wishes when we spoke.'

'That's kind of her.' Perhaps I'll send her an email and tell her about my new company. She'd be a great contact and it proves to me that I'm still not thinking quite straight in that I hadn't considered doing so before. This, at least, gives me an opening.

'I told her that you'd decided not to pursue your design role with us.'

'Maybe I was a bit hasty,' I admit. 'I got to a point where I couldn't see the wood for the trees. Since then, I've been made redundant from my job in the city. I have a lot more time on my hands.'

'It sounds as if you've been putting it to good use.'

I take a deep and juddering breath. 'I suppose you've filled the space now?'

'We have,' he tells me with a frown. 'A very nice lady who lives in Kent joined us. Somewhere called ... *Gravesend*.'

'I know it.'

'Sounds kinda spooky,' Max observes with a laugh. 'She's about the same age as you and has two boys. She was here a few weeks ago for her training retreat.'

'Ah.' There goes my chance of picking up where I left off.

'Have you spoken to Dean recently?'

'No,' I confess. 'I've been trying to avoid making phone calls at all.'

'Let me have a word with him,' Max says. 'I can't promise anything, Christie. But, if there's a vacancy on the team, you know that you'd be my first choice.'

'Thanks, Max. That's nice to hear.' Especially after I've messed him about. 'I have to be honest, it was Finn who persuaded me to call. Having lost my job, I've set up my own little company.'

He grins at me. 'You have?'

I nod. 'Summerhouse Crafts. Finn and I are back at home living with my parents. Hopefully, as a temporary measure. They've set me up with a beautiful, sunny summerhouse in the garden where I can work from. It overlooks the river. I'm very lucky. It's really lovely.'

'I'd like to see that,' Max says.

'I can give you a Skype tour.'

'In person would be better,' he says and my heart pitter-patters. One person I can never imagine in my sunny little summerhouse is Max Alexander. It would be a nice dream though.

'We're starting very small,' I continue. 'Finn has set us up a website and we've sold a lot of the stock I ordered from you already. I wondered whether you're still happy for us to sell your products. The distributor said we need your approval and I'd like to set up an account, if you'll have us.'

'I'd be delighted,' Max says. 'Good for Finn – and you. I'm glad that you've taken that step. I know how hard it is to do.'

'It's nowhere near on your scale, but it feels scary enough.'

'I hope it goes really well for you both and that you get lots more orders for our dies.'

There's an awkward pause. This is the moment when Max and I should carry on with something more personal, I guess. But we don't. It's clear that he doesn't know what else to say and neither do I.

'Well,' I hesitate. 'That's it really.' As we've run

out of business chit-chat and there's nothing more to say between us, then I don't really have a reason to linger any longer. 'I shouldn't keep you.'

'It's been nice talking, Christie.'

I take a deep breath and my courage in both hands. 'If you're ever in London, then I'd love to see you again.' That's the best that I can manage.

'Same here,' he says. 'Bye for now.'

'Bye.'

Then we both hang up. I let out a shaky breath and turn to Finn. 'How did I do?'

'Good. So we can sell the Contemporary Crafts products?'

'We can.'

'Yay!' He gives a little air punch. Then he regards me, openly. 'You like him, don't you?'

There's little point lying to my boy. 'Yes, I do.' Then I panic. 'I didn't sound too flirty?'

'That was totally brazen for you, Mum.'

I feel my cheeks redden. 'Was it?'

'Yeah.' Finn laughs at my discomfiture. 'I hope he takes the hint!'

Chapter Eighty-Five

While I'm on a roll, I tap out an email to Sheridan telling her about my new project and giving her an update on Finn's progress. I apologise for not contacting her and ask if she'd like to have lunch together sometime.

Minutes later, and to my delight, a chatty email

386

comes straight back from her. *I've been meaning to contact you,* it reads. *Let's have lunch. Are you in town tomorrow?*

By town, I'm assuming she means London town and not Stony Stratford High Street. I could easily go up there as I have no pressing projects to complete, at the moment. So I write back that I'm free and, a few emails later, we've fixed up a place and time.

The next day, I try to choose my outfit carefully. I don't want to be TK Maxxed to the hilt while Sheridan Singleton wafts in wearing a Stella McCartney number. But the designer end of my wardrobe is found wanting, so I put on a nice wrap dress I found some years ago in Matalan. Retro is in, right? I'm just glad that it still fits.

Then I head off on the train, leaving Finn in charge of the business for the day. I'm meeting Sheridan in a popular French restaurant in Bloomsbury. I only know it's popular because I Googled it last night. Frankly, I'd never heard of it. I'm early – ridiculously so – which means I can spend a good few minutes having a browse around the attached shop featuring eye-wateringly expensive food and gifts. If the restaurant food is similarly pricey, I can only hope that Ms Singleton is happy to split the bill.

I'm glancing up from a bar of chocolate that costs more than a manicure when Sheridan breezes in. She sees me instantly and comes over, air-kissing me quite near to both cheeks.

'Hello, sweetheart,' she says as if we're long-lost friends. 'Come through. Come through. I'm starving! Are you?'

It's fair to say that only one of us looks as if she has flirted with starvation.

Today, Sheridan is wearing a rose-pink, long-length jacket that looks as if it must be cashmere. She slips it off and drapes it over the back of her chair, revealing a crisp white shirt and designer jeans that fit to touch. The wrap dress that I was quite keen on earlier? Not so much now.

Sheridan pulls out the chair next to her and settles her voluminous handbag on it. Clearly a bag far too expensive to be sullied by the floor. She flicks her lustrous hair back and beams at me. 'Darling, you look wonderful.'

'Thanks,' I say. 'So do you.'

She waves the compliment away. 'I've come straight from the studio. I didn't finish until an hour ago and I'm back on again at four.' She throws up her hands. 'It never ends!' The waiter brings a bottle of sparkling water and pours it. As we haven't ordered it, I'm assuming Sheridan is a regular customer and must always have this.

'First, we need a toast.' She clinks her glass to mine and toasts. 'To your lovely boy. I was so pleased to hear everything had gone well. May he have a healthy and happy future.'

'I'll drink to that.'

Sheridan sips her water as if it's champagne. I try to do the same.

'So, how's he doing?'

'Great. His doctor can't believe how quickly he's bouncing back. He's well enough to be helping me in the business and even has a little girlfriend.'

'How sweet.'

'She's lovely,' I add. 'Very good for him.'

'And he's got the all-clear from the hospital?'

'Not quite yet,' I admit. 'I think that will be a long time coming. He'll be on medication in one shape or another for the rest of his life, but they seem to have it under control now. Thankfully, he's showing no ill effects after his operation.'

Sheridan touches my arm. 'So glad to hear it.'

'Thanks.' I'm moved by her concern.

'Let's order quickly,' she says, brisk again. 'Then you can tell me more about this fabulous new business.'

'It's very small,' I insist.

'The best possible way to start,' she tells me.

So we order. Roquefort, pear and endive salad for Sheridan. I pretend that I'm not even interested in the burger and chips option, and go for prawn, chorizo and avocado salad. Which leaves me more room for Mum's home cooking tonight, at least.

While we wait, I tell her a bit more about how Finn is doing and about Summerhouse Crafts.

'How cute!' she enthuses.

'I've had to leave my house,' I conclude, 'but I think it's a small price to pay and I hope that, soon, we'll be able to move back in when I'm on a more secure footing.'

'You're so brave,' Sheridan says. 'You remind me of myself. Inside, there's a little core of steel and I can tell that you're ambitious.'

I like that she sees that in me, as so few others seem to.

She gives me a direct stare. 'Which is one of the reasons why I wanted to talk to you.'

Our food arrives and we busy ourselves with eating for a few minutes and I try not to over-analyse her last sentence. The food is delicious and not entirely harmed by not being accompanied by chips.

When she's picked at her salad for a few minutes, Sheridan says, 'You know that I bought a major shareholding in Creative World?'

'Yes.'

'It's going to be very exciting, Christie, I can tell you.' She gives a little gleeful clap. 'We're making lots of changes.'

'Sounds amazing.'

'And that's where you come in,' she says, rather coyly. 'I have a crazy schedule. I'm sure you can understand that.'

'Yes.'

'It's so hard to spend quality time with the boys and you know how quickly they grow up.'

I don't tell her that my son seemed to become a man almost overnight.

'It was thinking about what you've been going through with Finn that made me realise this time with them is precious. I'll never get it back. I have you to thank for making me see what's important in life.'

'Oh.' Not a lot I can say to that.

'I want to manage the business more and step away from front-line presenting. I still want to be the face of the channel. Of course.'

Of course.

'But I'm going to cut back on my presenting segments. I do way too many now.'

I don't point out that she's one of the main

reasons I watch the channel.

'We need some fresh blood. Someone with young, contemporary designs.' She takes a sip of her water and sighs. 'To that end, I wondered if you'd be interested in doing a screen test for us.'

'Me?' I think all my breath just left my body.

She gives a tinkling laugh. 'You'd be perfect.'

I sit and blink at her, too startled to speak.

'Have you spoken to Max?'

'Yes. To tell him that I started my own company.'

She reaches across the table and pats my hand. 'You really should get back with him. He misses you. I told him that he was mad, *MAD*, to let you go.' She winks at me. 'And I'm not just talking about business either.'

Having been unable to breathe, I think that I'm now hyperventilating.

'Would you do it?' she asks. 'Come down to the studio next week and let's see what you're made of. If you bring a project to demonstrate, then we'd film it, but not show it live. I'm sure that you'd breeze it.'

'Well ... I ... er...'

'You're a natural, Christie. Of course, you are. Relatable. That's what we call it in the business. You're very relatable. Our ladies at home will love you.'

Is 'relatable' a close bedfellow of 'ordinary'? I feel it may be, but am prepared to gloss over it.

'Will you do it?'

'I ... I ... I'd love to,' I stammer.

'Excellent. I'm sure you won't let me down.' She picks up her water and wrinkles her nose.

'I've had enough of this,' she says. 'We need champagne.'

Sheridan Singleton holds up a hand and orders two glasses of champagne from the waiter who appears instantly at her side, while I sit there, dumbstruck.

Chapter Eighty-Six

'I've got a screen test,' I tell my parents at the dinner table. They both stare at me, mouths gaping. Much as I did when Sheridan put it to me. Even saying it out loud doesn't make it seem any more real to me either.

'Oh, my giddy aunty,' my dad says. 'Our Christie, a film star.'

Bless him. 'Not quite, Dad. But Creative World does get a huge number of viewers. It would be a good move.'

'This *is* the big time.' Mum clasps her hands together over the toad-in-the-hole. 'I can't wait to tell the ladies at the WI. That snooty Mrs Jenners has a son who once played a dead body in *Silent Witness* and we never hear the last of it. Being a presenter on Creative World, well, that trumps a dead body any day.'

'I'm glad you think so.' Finn and I exchange a wearied glance.

'You'll be great, Mum.' My son tries to buoy me up. 'I've always said you could rival Sheridan Singleton.'

'Now, apparently, she thinks so too.'

'You'll have to go shopping,' Finn says. 'You need a killer outfit. Sexy, but not too much cleavage.'

All our heads swivel towards Finn. Even Eric's.

'Trust me,' he says. 'I know what I'm talking about. I'm in love with a fashion vlogger.'

Mum raises her eyebrows and I hide a smile behind my hand. Dad just looks perplexed. I think he glazed over at the word 'shopping'.

'You could do worse than put yourself in Ella's hands,' Finn says sagely.

Mum mouths to me, *'She has turquoise hair.'*

'That would be lovely,' I say. 'We should go to the city together, if she's got time.'

'I'll ask her,' Finn says. 'But she'll be thinking Monsoon not Marks & Spencer.'

I shrug. 'Suits me.' I am currently trying to remain open to new experiences.

'Cool,' Finn says and punches in a text to her.

The Creative World studios are in a warehouse in north London near Camden. I'd better not tell my parents that as clearly they think I'm on my way to Hollywood. I've got a screen test booked for next Monday morning and, I tell you, no one is more shocked than me. At least I only have a few days in which to go into a complete melt-down.

'Next year will be your year,' Dad says, assuredly. 'I can feel it in my bones.'

'I hope you're right, Dad.'

'Hold your nerve,' Mum says. 'It will all come good.'

I don't know if these sayings really mean anything at all, or whether they're simply platitudes, but they're comforting to hear, nevertheless.

I turn to Finn. 'What did you get up to today while your old mother was schmoozing with her best mate Sheridan?'

'I photographed and catalogued all of the remaining stock from Contemporary Crafts,' he says. 'It will all be ready to go on the website tomorrow. I started putting together our next order from them too.'

'Oh.' Hadn't really expected that answer. 'Great.'

'I didn't just sit there staring out of the window,' he chides. 'I've got an empire to build.'

'Go, Finn,' I say.

So we finish our dinner and Dad takes Finn over to see Ella. In the meantime, I pull on my tracky bottoms and go out into the meadow for a jog now that I'm a jogging lady. Eric, not content at already having two walks with Dad, comes along too.

As I pound the path by the river, avoiding the goose poo, I think that we've really turned a corner. Dad's right. If I play my cards right, next year really could be our year. There is, however, the matter of one small screen test to get through.

Chapter Eighty-Seven

I go shopping with Ella. We have two little disasters in Monsoon where she tries to dress me in some sort of boho/hippy/festival mash-up, which isn't me at all. She agrees and we head upstairs towards the sections that are distinctly more middle-aged.

Ella goes through the racks, taking the same care with which a surgeon would approach a heart patient, examining each garment with studious intent, before finding them wanting. Only two or three items find themselves hooked over her slender arm.

In the end, we choose a silk tunic dress in pale blues and silver greys. It has a round neck – no accidental cleavage peepage, as Finn instructed – and three-quarter length sleeves which show off my wrists and won't flap about while I'm demonstrating. It's possibly the most expensive garment that I've ever owned. Actually, it is *definitely* the most expensive garment, etc.

Ella and I stand back and take a good long look in the mirror.

'It says "I'm a woman in control",' Ella tells me, serious expression on her face. 'It says "You can trust me." It says, "I am glamorous, but not frivolous."'

'It says all that?'

She nods solemnly in confirmation.

'Not bad for a hundred and fifty quid then.'

'Consider it an investment.'

I smooth the dress down. 'You think I'll do then?'

'I think you'll knock it out of the park,' Ella says.

'Thank you.' I give her a hug. 'You're a lovely girl and so good for Finn.'

She grins. 'He's cool.'

That might mean she loves him in teenager

speak. I don't know. I hope that they stay together, defy the odds. They've both done that
already and Ella is looking much healthier than
when we first met her in the hospital.

'Let's pay for this and then I'll treat you to
lunch.'

'After that, we'll do shoes,' she says. 'And a
handbag.'

I'd better do well at this screen test as I'm already heavily invested.

On Monday morning, I'm terrified. I spent all
weekend putting together two projects to demonstrate, as requested by Sheridan. They're the best
that I can possibly make them and I used Contemporary Crafts products to show them off.

Seriously, my mother is almost crying when they
wave me off from the house. Finn, Dad, Mum,
Eric and Trigger are all standing on the doorstep
to say goodbye. Only the cats, as usual, couldn't
care less about this momentous opportunity in my
life.

I'm driving myself down the M1 to the studios
of the Creative World channel. I've got my fancy
outfit in the back, plus the matching shoes and
bag. Next to them are my two craft projects, boxed
up and good to go. You have no idea how nervous
I am. I'm not sure that a trip down the motorway
is going to do anything to calm my nerves either.
Of course, Finn, Mum and Dad offered to accompany me, but I thought that I'd be better
doing this alone. I don't think that I could have
borne the weight of their collective expectation. I
need to feel the fear and do it anyway. I think.

I put my iPod on shuffle and let a random selection of Snow Patrol, Adele, The Feeling, Goo Goo Dolls and Del Amitri entertain me while I dice with the tail-end of the commuter traffic. I think, fleetingly, of Henry and how little I've heard from him. But I've got more pressing matters on my mind now. Following Sheridan's excellent directions, I find my way off the motorway without hitch until I turn into the car park of a big warehouse in Camden just left of the famous market. The place looks quite a bit fancier than the term 'warehouse' might suggest. Or maybe I'm just easily impressed. It's modern, white and has trees in steel planters by the glass front door. I park up and text Finn to let him know that I've arrived safely. He sends me one back with *Good luck* and lots of kisses, thumbs up and bouquet emoticons.

I lug my clothes carrier and boxes from the car into the reception. This is similarly smart. Again, all white, with the steel industrial ducting on show and white leather sofas. I give my name to the receptionist and dump my boxes on the nearest coffee table.

A few moments later, a girl comes down to greet me and, helping me with my load, takes me through to the studio. Sheridan is waiting for me and greets me with a hug. Today, she's dressed in a raspberry shirt and black jeans with raspberry patent heels. I can see the concerned glance at my own clothes.

'Don't worry,' I say. 'I have a fancy outfit with me. I just need to change.' I even went to a salon on Saturday and had one of those gel manicure things – a new experience for me – but I don't point that out. In fact, I had two manicures. When I got home, I thought the polish I'd picked looked a bit garish, so I went back and had it done again in a more subtle colour. Double manicure distress.

'We'll have a coffee,' Sheridan says. 'Run through the plan and then, when we go off air, see how the camera likes you.'

She makes it sound so very easy. Before I have time to go into a flat spin, she takes my arm and leads me out of the studio into a café-style area called The Park. It's a great space that's decorated with fake trees and green, high-back sofas and green carpet.

'Finn still OK?' she asks as we join the queue.

'Yes. He seems fine,' I tell her. 'Fingers crossed.'

'I'm so relieved.'

'Me too.'

She buys us each a cappuccino from the counter at the end and we settle into a leafy booth.

'You look worried,' Sheridan says as she sips – miraculously managing to avoid getting froth on her lips. I'm sure I'll be sporting a white, foamy moustache.

'I'm terrified,' I admit. 'This is such a fabulous opportunity that I don't want to mess it up.'

'Of course you won't. You'll be amazing. I have every faith in you.'

I wish that I had it in myself.

'We've got plenty of time to film. We don't go back on air until three o'clock. There's no rush,' she advises. 'Relax, be yourself.'

'Any other tips?' I say this as if I haven't spent all weekend glued to Creative World, making copious notes. I also made Finn, Ella, Mum and Dad sit on the sofa while I practised my demonstration on the pop-up picnic table which had been deployed in the conservatory. They said I did it really well, but then they could be classed as a slightly biased audience.

'Smile,' Sheridan adds, bestowing one of her dazzling beams on me. 'Look as if you're the happiest person in the world. People at home love to smile back.'

I remember doing it myself.

And I get a sudden thrill to think that I'm actually here. I'm not sitting at home on my sofa watching someone else. I'm here. I have my foot in the door. I could be the one beaming out from television screens across the land. I don't know if it's a boost from the strong, frothy coffee, but I feel high, as if I could do anything. I tap my foot waiting for the calm and collected Sheridan to finish her drink as I can't wait to get into the studio and in front of those cameras before this feeling of euphoria wears off.

Chapter Eighty-Eight

The studio is big, bright. Cables snake all over the floor ready to catch the unwary. There's a long white counter at one end, behind it there's a huge, colourful logo saying *Creative World* and a backlit arched window, framed with paper roses. There are shelves on either side filled with crafting projects of all shapes and sizes. Three cameras point at it and there are a number of people standing around on the studio floor, many of them wearing headphones and clutching clipboards. I wonder what they do. I realise that I've never even been into a television studio before and have no idea of the mechanics.

Either side of the main counter there are half a dozen more areas, all set up in much the same manner.

'We set one segment up as we're filming another,' Sheridan explains when she sees me staring round, agog. 'It means that the transitions are seamless. Usually.' She raises her perfectly arched eyebrows. 'But you don't need to worry about that today.'

Before I came onto the studio floor, I was given a dressing room so that I could get changed – think cupboard rather than suite – but it did have my name on the door. Of course, I took a picture of it and sent it to Finn. So now I have on my carefully selected silk tunic courtesy of my fashion guru, Ella. I've fluffed my hair, reapplied my lipstick and, quite frankly, am feeling rather chi-chi. I tell you, I could take on the world in this tunic. What I hadn't considered is that I'd be standing behind a counter and I'll only be seen from the waist up. My fabulous new shoes and handbag are entirely surplus to requirements. Gah. Maybe I'll take them back to the shop tomorrow for a refund.

My boxes containing my projects are set at the end of the white counter and I go to lay out my materials, hands barely trembling. A young, trendy guy puts a couple of bottles of water under the counter and gives me the thumbs up. Sheridan chats to someone else who looks as if they have overall control in that she has a bigger clipboard than everyone else.

'Ready?' Sheridan says as she comes to join me a few minutes later.

I nod and put the final touches to the dies, paper, ribbons and all, laid out before me. We take up position side by side behind the counter.

There's a slightly embarrassing moment when the soundman comes to fit me with a microphone which has to go up my dress and clip onto my neckline. The battery pack goes into the pocket of my tunic. He does the same to Sheridan and she gets an earpiece too.

'The production team give me selling prompts and direction through these,' she explains, and I wonder how you cope with both speaking and being spoken to at the same time.

In front of us are two big televisions on wheels. Sheridan points at them. 'This one shows us what's being filmed. The other shows what's being broadcast. That's on a ten-second delay in case we swear.' She laughs.

Don't swear. Don't swear. Don't swear, I tell myself.

'But today is just for us.' She waves a dismissive hand. 'So we don't need to think about any of that.'

Don't think about it. Don't think about it. Oh, Lord. There seems to be so much to remember.

'Follow my lead,' she says. 'We're just two friends having a nice chat. There's nothing in the slightest to worry about.'

'Right.' My hands are a bit damp now and I rub them together.

'What we hate most is dead air, so whatever you say, just keep talking. Look into the camera with the red light on top. If you forget, the camera operator will wave at you.'

'OK.'

'All you have to do is be yourself.'

The spotlights shine down on us, the camera operators take up their positions and move towards us. A red light comes on above one of them and Sheridan beams directly at it.

'Hello,' she says in her usual bright voice. 'Welcome to Creative World. I'm Sheridan Singleton and today we have a lovely new presenter for you, Christie Chapman of Summerhouse Crafts.' She turns to me. 'Hi, Christie.'

And, of course, all my supercool confidence completely deserts me. I have a moment of blind panic. There's nothing at all in my head. My mouth opens but nothing at all comes out. Nothing. All of my life rushes before me. Is this what they call a 'dry'? If it is, I'm having one.

Sheridan smiles patiently and gives an encouraging nod of her head.

'Hello, Sheridan,' I finally manage, shakily. 'Thank you for having me.'

'Now, Christie, tell us all about the fabulous project you have to show us.'

Then it's as if a dam bursts inside me. I have nothing to fear from this. The world won't end if I mess it up. No one dies. With renewed energy, the words flow and I settle into my rhythm. 'I've created a simple card with an aperture frame and a heart motif,' I say as if I'm talking only to Sheridan. I hold my pre-prepared card up to show the camera. I give them my best winning smile. 'Perfect for someone you love.'

'That's gorgeous,' Sheridan coos. 'You're so clever.'

'I die-cut my card from brown craft paper,' I continue.

'I use so much of that,' Sheridan says, before turning back to the camera. 'We have a lovely pack of ten on offer today. You'll see the details at the bottom of your screen. It's so versatile.'

This is like being a *Blue Peter* presenter. I love it! Living my childhood dream! I was one of those kids who got a Blue Peter badge for making an advent calendar out of two coat hangers and some tinsel. I knew it would come in handy one day.

I pull my carefully selected stash of papers towards me, feeling more comfortable as I handle the materials I'm so familiar with. 'I've chosen a pretty paper and then I'll die-cut my square aperture like so.' I demonstrate the cutting of the die with my machine.

'That's a great piece of kit,' Sheridan says. 'I love mine.'

'It makes cutting so much easier,' I agree. 'And it gives your dies a lovely, rounded edge.'

I remember to show that to the camera too.

'All I do now is attach a piece of cream pearlised paper to the front of the card with the adhesive.'

Sheridan holds up the container, so the camera-man can get a close shot. 'This is one of our best sellers,' she tells the imaginary audience. 'And we have a great offer on them for you today. Our bumper value Sticky Stuff kit contains nine different types of adhesive that will suit all your crafting needs.'

'I've popped some photo corners onto my pretty paper with a little glue and add some strips of foam tape to the back, which will lift the paper from the card, giving it a 3D look.'

'Such a great effect,' Sheridan says. 'Yet so easy. Our phone number is on screen now for you to place your order. Our team is waiting to talk to you. All you have to do is quote the order number...' She reels it off like the pro she is.

She gives a slight nod and I turn the card to the camera once more. 'Now I'm cutting a heart out of the aperture square.' I feed the paper through my machine. 'And another heart in the same pretty paper.' More smiling, more showing. 'All we have left to do is assemble them.'

My hands make light work of it. My posh manicure sparkles in the light. I'm glad that I went for the pearly polish. 'There,' I say. 'One simple card to say I love you.'

'That's great, Christie,' Sheridan says. 'Let's talk through the products you've used today.' So we move to the end of the counter, where all my wares are displayed and Sheridan goes through them with me and quotes prices and I throw in some extra little ideas.

Finally, Sheridan says, 'Thank you for joining us on the Creative World Channel today. We look forward to seeing more of your projects in the future.'

She steps away from me.

'And cut,' someone shouts from the floor.

My co-presenter gives me a hug. 'Nice job.' She smiles at me, in admiration. 'You're a natural.'

'Thanks.' My heart is racing.

'Good to go straight into the next project?'

'Yes,' I say. And I am. In fact, I can't wait.

Chapter Eighty-Nine

'That was great,' Sheridan says when we've completed the next project and the cameras have stopped rolling. 'You took to it like a duck to water.'

'Really?'

She laughs. 'Yes. I don't even need to replay the segment to know that it was fine. Well done, Christie.'

We high five each other.

'Max was quite right with his recommendation.'

'This came from Max?'

'It was his idea. A brilliant one. I didn't take any persuading. Didn't you know?'

'No,' I admit. 'He said nothing to me.'

'We both have him to thank,' she insists. 'So, will you join us as a presenter?'

'Oh my God! You mean it?'

'Of course.'

'I'd love to.'

We both giggle like schoolgirls and Sheridan says, 'Welcome to Creative World.'

While I'm still grinning like a loon, the man comes back and takes off my microphone. Everyone wanders away from the studio floor leaving Sheridan and me alone.

'I'll send you a contract,' Sheridan says. 'You'll be a freelance, rather than employed by us, but we'll guarantee you a certain amount of slots every month. We'll have to sort out the fine print, but my basic offer is this...' She reels off a sum.

It might not buy me a holiday home in Cornwall. Probably not even a beach hut, but it will mean that I don't have to take my superfluous shoes and handbag back to the shops tomorrow. It will certainly help to pay the bills and plug the gaping hole in my income since I lost my job.

'Will you accept?'

'Yes.' This all feels so surreal that I can't quite believe it's happening. 'Yes. Of course.'

I'm a television presenter, I think. Just wait until I tell Finn.

Three hours after I arrived, I come out of the studio feeling punch-drunk and dazed. Sheridan kisses me and someone helps me to the car with all my gear. In my stunned state, I forget to change out of my fancy frock and shoes for the journey home and I'm halfway down the motorway before I realise.

An hour and a bit later, I'm home. I park in Mum and Dad's drive and sit there, still trying to gather my wits. After a few minutes, I get out of the car and go indoors.

'Hi,' I shout. 'I'm home.' Eric bowls out of the kitchen, barking hysterically, and nearly takes my legs out from under me. Clearly, I have been away for decades rather than hours in doggy reckoning.

I make my way through the kitchen and out into the garden. It's a glorious day which is why I find Mum, Dad and Finn having a tea break in the sunshine on the decking by the summerhouse. When I wander down towards them, they all turn to look at me, expectantly.

'I got the job,' I say. 'I'm a television presenter.'

They all jump up and come to give me a group hug. Eric barks some more, although he's obviously not sure why.

'Oh, you clever girl,' Mum says, cupping my face in her hands. 'I knew you could do it.'

I can tell what's going through Mum's mind. She'll be the toast of the WI with a daughter on television. It will be passed on in whispered tones and she'll bask in the reflected glory. Even now the smile on her face is borderline beatific. I can read her like a book.

'Way to go, Mum,' Finn adds.

'I still can't believe it.'

'Sit down, love,' Dad says, a bit damp-eyed. 'Let me get you a cup of tea. I bet you need it.'

'I think a double brandy is more in order.'

'I'll send Dad down to Budgens,' Mum says. 'We can have a drop of cava with dinner.'

There is no greater celebration.

'What now?' Finn says. 'When do you start?'

'I've got to wait for the contracts to come through, but I could be on air by next month.'

'Cool.'

'Apparently, Max Alexander put my name in

the hat,' I tell Finn.

'Then you need to call him.'

'It looks like it.' And that cheers my heart too. I'll Skype him later and tell him my good news. I wonder what he'll think about that. 'How were things at Summerhouse Crafts in my absence?'

'We've had a ton of orders in this morning,' Finn says, proudly. 'If this carries on, we might need to take on more staff.'

'Let's walk before we can run,' I warn.

'Said every successful entrepreneur never,' Finn bats back.

Dad brings me some tea.

'We'll get there in our own good time,' I tell my son. 'We're already off to a good start.'

'I'm so full of ideas that I could burst,' Finn says.

'If this television job goes well, then we might have some spare money to implement them.'

'I'm not giving over all of my workshop,' Dad warns.

'I wouldn't dream of asking you to.' I rest my head on his shoulder. 'You've already done so much. Both of you have.' I drink my tea and Mum goes to make me a sandwich when she finds out that I missed my lunch.

The sun is shining, the sky is blue. I look at my family around me and down the garden at my lovely summerhouse and feel nothing but contentment. This is how life should be, I think. It doesn't come better than this.

Chapter Ninety

When I'm back in the summerhouse, I set up a Skype call with Max and get the now familiar thrill through my body when I see his face on the screen. He's casual today, sporting a pale blue polo shirt and looks tanned. I wonder if he's been away for the weekend. I wonder who with. Still, to business.

'I'm calling to say thank you,' I tell him.

He frowns, puzzled.

'I got the job,' I continue. 'With Creative World. I had a screen test with Sheridan this morning.'

'Congratulations, Christie.' He beams at me. 'It's nothing more than you deserve.'

'I understand the recommendation came from you.'

'She was already a fan,' he says, modestly. 'But I did put in a good word.'

'Well, I'm indebted to you. This certainly will help with our current situation.'

'I haven't given up on getting you back on the team here,' Max says. 'I've been talking to Dean.'

'You've done enough for me. Honestly.'

'I'm glad to hear it.'

'I'll speak to you soon, Max.'

'I hope so,' he answers and then we both hang up.

I sit and watch the ducks scooting past on the currents in the bend of the river and wonder how many times it will be feasible for me to find excuses to talk to him.

While I dwell on this, the phone rings and, as Finn is busy in Dad's workshop, packaging orders, I pick up.

'Do you still hate me?' Robyn's voice.

I laugh. 'Only a bit.'

'I kept trying to pick up the phone and couldn't,' she says. 'I feel so bloody guilty.'

'You don't need to be.'

'Tell me that you're OK.'

'I'm absolutely fine,' I insist.

'I miss your ugly mug,' she whines. 'They've given me some old bat to share with another partner. She hates me. I don't want to snog her in the kitchen over coffee. She has no juicy gossip.'

'Is she any good at her job?'

'Who cares about that?' Robyn says. Then she sighs. 'Look, I need you back. I'm doing everything in my power to get you reinstated. This new ... arrangement ... really isn't working out for me. I'm pining for you.'

'I can't come back,' I tell her.

'Don't tell me you've got another job already,' she wails. 'You're middle-aged. I thought it would take you ages!'

'Ha!' I tease. 'Not so.'

'I should be pleased for you, shouldn't I?' Robyn says, miserably. 'My loss is their gain and all that crap.'

'I've been busy.' I look at the projects spread out all over my desk. 'That's partly why I haven't called.'

'Where are you working now? Some shit, two-bit solicitors who won't love you like I do?'

'I've started my own company,' I confess. 'With Finn. I'm doing all the creative bits and he's running the admin side.'

'Wow.' Robyn sounds impressed. 'You *have* been a busy bee.'

'And there's more,' I say. 'I've just been offered a job as a television presenter on the Creative World channel.'

'Seriously?'

'Deadly.'

'With that woman you have a girl-crush on?'

'The very same.'

'Woo bloody hoo! You're flying.'

It certainly feels like it. 'I've only just found out, but my feet haven't touched the ground since. I'm walking on air.'

'Good for you.' Robyn sounds sincere. 'We treated you really shittily, letting you go like that and I couldn't be more sorry. You make the best of this.'

'I plan to.'

'Say you'll come to the house. We'll have a barbecue one Sunday. Bring Finn.'

'I'd like that.'

'Ping me some dates,' Robyn says. 'I'd better go. Bat face is waving papers at me.'

'Play nicely with your new PA,' I tell her. 'She might grow on you.'

'Yeah, like fungus.' She tuts. 'I'd better go.' Then she's suddenly serious. 'I'm glad that it's working out for you, Christie.'

'Me too,' I say and, when I hang up, I'm still smiling.

Chapter Ninety-One

Two days later, my contract lands on the door-mat. I can tell from the thickness of the envelope and the fact that it has the Creative World logo on the envelope. You can't sneak much past me! I can't wait to open it.

Inside, along with the hefty legal document, is a note from Sheridan and four tickets.

Dearest Christie, we've got a couple of tables at the National Television Awards, her elegant handwriting informs me. *It would be great if you could come along. Bring Finn and his girlfriend. I'd love to meet them. I've put a 'plus one' in for you too. It's a gorgeous, glamorous, red carpet event, so put your glad rags on. It's also the perfect opportunity for you to get to know the team. I do hope that you can come. Best wishes. S xx*

Blimey. I haven't even put pen to paper yet and already I'm hobnobbing it. A red carpet event! Wait till I tell Mum and Finn about this.

They're all sitting at the kitchen table finishing off breakfast when I go through. I wave the envelope. 'My contract. And ... ta-dah! Four tickets to the National Television Awards.'

Mum's hand goes to her chest. 'Oh, my.'

'Oh, yeah,' I say. 'Christie Chapman superstar.'

'You haven't even been on telly yet,' Finn says. 'No one will know who you are.'

'Don't burst my bubble, Finlay,' I say, feigning

crossness. 'Besides, two of these tickets are for you and Ella.'

'Awesome!'

'You'd better keep on my good side, if you want them.'

'Can I text Ella now?'

'Yes. They're only a week away. She'll need to get shopping.' As will I. My wardrobe is currently all out of red carpet event dresses.

'Will I have to wear a suit?'

'Indeed. And wash behind your ears.'

'I don't think they'll check that, Mother,' Finn says.

'No. But I will.'

'Harsh,' Finn says and he busies himself texting his loved one.

'Who will you take, love?' Mum says.

And I know she's not fishing to be my 'plus one' as she'd hate it. Mum has trouble staying awake beyond *Midsomer Murders* these days; add to that a couple of glasses of fizz and she'd be snoring at the table. It's not Dad's thing either. The last time he wore a suit was at my wedding and he wasn't all that keen on doing that either. I think he'd lost the tie before he gave his speech. So who will I take?

'What about that nice man from the coach?' she suggests when she senses my hesitation.

'Henry?'

'You liked him, didn't you?'

'Yeah.' I give a shrug. Perhaps Henry would like to go. I currently can't think of anyone else who might be my boyfriend for the night. Well, I can, he just happens to be on a different continent.

Sadly. 'Good idea, Mum. I'll ring him.'

So I make up half a dozen cards in my summer-house while I think about what I'm going to say. Eventually, I feel brave enough to pick up my phone and call Henry. He answers straight away.

'Hi,' he says. 'I was just thinking about you.'

That has to be a good start.

'How have you been?'

'Busy,' I answer. 'Sorry, I haven't called.'

'I'm missing you in the mornings,' he tells me. 'My new travelling companion is called Jeff and I don't share my breakfast with him.'

That makes me smile. I sort of miss our shared breakfasts too.

'I hope your son's OK.'

'He's doing really well, thank you.'

'And the job hunting?'

'I'm already sorted.' I fiddle with the pile of buttons on my desk while I talk. Conversation isn't exactly stilted, but there's definitely a little awkwardness lurking. I wonder if it's because I told Henry we could only be friends. It makes me wonder about the wisdom of asking him to come to the awards evening with me. I plough on, nevertheless. 'In fact, that's partly why I'm ringing.'

'Oh.'

'I've got a job as television presenter,' I rush on before courage deserts me. 'On a craft channel.'

There's a slightly over-long silence at the other end of the phone before Henry says, 'That's amazing.'

'Thank you.'

'How? Why?'

414

'Well...' I'm not sure I want to go into this on the phone. 'It's a long story and I don't want to take up your time now. The thing is...' I take a deep breath, '...I've got tickets to the National Television Awards evening. Creative World have a table and they've asked me to be a guest. It's next week and I wondered whether you'd like to come with me?'

Again, there's another over-long hiatus.

'Er...' Henry says. 'Er...'

'It's no big deal.' I rush to fill the uneasy pause. 'I thought it would be fun.'

He sighs down the phone. 'The thing is, Christie. It's not my type of thing at all.'

Now it's my turn to say, 'Oh.'

'I hate all those media types and C-list celebrities. I didn't think it was your bag either.'

'I don't know if it is,' I confess. 'But I'm prepared to give it a go.'

'Count me out on this one,' he says.

'Right. I just thought...'

'I should tell you that I'm going back up north.'

'Oh.'

'I've got a job in Manchester and I'm currently working my notice. No more commuting.'

'I'm pleased for you.' And I genuinely am. He's a nice guy and deserves to be happy.

'I'm going to apply for custody of Kyra.'

'Well, I wish you every success with that. I hope it all works out for you.'

'Thanks. You too.' There's another awkward little space. 'Got to go.' Even down the phone, I can sense him looking at his watch. 'Let me know if you're ever in the market for a pub lunch up in

Manchester.' Henry gives a forced laugh.

'Yes. Will do.'

'I'll see you, Christie.'

We both know that he won't. Then Henry hangs up.

I can't help but feel disappointed. I put myself out there and have been smacked in the face. Serves me right. Perhaps that didn't sound 'ordinary' enough for him. Maybe he thinks I'm getting ideas above my station. Maybe he just hasn't moved on. Who knows?

But what I do know is that I want someone who's comfortable with me whoever I am. I realise that Henry would never be there for me. He has too many issues. Perhaps that's why it didn't work out with his wife. I want someone who's prepared to support me and not feel intimidated at the first sign of success.

I stare out of the window feeling flat. Then I get hit by a blinding idea. Of course I know who will come with me and I wonder why I didn't think of it before.

Chapter Ninety-Two

The week flies by and now the National Television Awards are tonight! Hurrah! Thankfully, my lovely Robyn has agreed to be my date, so I won't be a billy-no-mates. It would have been nice to arrive on the arm of a handsome, tuxedo-wearing man, but I know that I'll have a lot of fun with

Robyn and it will help to cement the little rift between us.

I'm in my bedroom now getting ready with Ella. Time is marching on and my hands are shaking as I put on my makeup. But at least they're shaking with excitement rather than terror. I hear the sound of someone humming happily and realise that it's me.

As I'm going to sashay into this place alongside Sheridan Singleton, I have seriously upped my game. Ella and I went to a dress hire place up the A5, not far from here: Star for the Night. With her expert guidance, I managed to bag myself the most stunning, full-length scarlet gown. It has a broad band which goes across one shoulder and then sweeps down to the waist, providing me with very welcome secret corseting. It's tightly fitted and fishtails out at the bottom, giving me a previously undiscovered va-va-voom. To top that, it's covered with a million Swarovski sparkles. Oh, my lordy-lordy. Even I think I'm hot!

'Fabulous,' Ella says. 'You look like a celebrity fit for *Hello!* magazine.'

I give another twirl. This has cost me an arm and a leg to rent but it makes me feel like a million dollars.

We also chose a dress for Ella. This one is equally amazing. It's made of reclaimed vintage lace — don't ask me, I have no idea. It's black, opaque but see-through too with long sleeves and a flowing skirt that's split to the thigh. It's embroidered with colourful dragons to give it a modern edge. She's wearing a plain black bra and boy shorts underneath it.

'Does this say brazen, not slut?' Ella asks as she poses in front of the mirror.

'You look incredible.' The dress is quite revealing but, frankly, if I had a body like that I'd get it out as often as I could. She looks so beautiful. 'Finn hasn't seen it yet?'

She shakes her head. 'I wanted to surprise him.'

I fear my son may propose on the spot if he sees her looking like this.

She teams it with some chunky jewellery and a long black pendant, then tops it with a funky black fedora. Her hair, purple today, is now cascading over her shoulders. Oh, the joy of extensions.

'They'll mistake you for a pop star,' I say. 'Move over Cheryl Whatever-you're-called-now.'

I've had a manicure and my hair done. I considered having a slimming wrap or something to lose a stone, but left it too late. Probably six months too late. I'll just not have to breathe and hope the dress makes me look sylph-like. Doesn't the camera add ten pounds or something? I could do without that.

'Come on, Mum,' Finn shouts from the hall. 'We need to be going.'

The taxi is booked for four o'clock as we have to be in the O2 arena by six and we don't want to be late. God forbid. Imagine going to all this trouble and spending most of the evening on the M1! Yikes. Maybe we should have booked it for earlier. Dad did offer to drive us, bless him, but I know that he and Mum want to be sitting on the sofa watching the programme going out live on telly, trying to catch a glimpse of us.

Getting Finn into a tuxedo was easier than I imagined too. I looked at the ones for hire and they were all vile. I wanted him to look sharp, not like he's off to a wedding. So I splashed out and bought him one from a fancy men's shop in the city centre. It has an edgy cut and makes him look like a boy band member. It also reminds me that he has over the last year made the transition from child to man.

I'm horribly aware that I've already spent a good deal of my first month's wages on this one night out and I haven't even started at Creative World yet! Being a wannabe telly presenter is proving quite costly. But I want to look the part. I'm going to be on show for the first time in my life and I want to be brimming with confidence. Consider it an investment in my career. I just need to keep repeating that to myself.

'Are you ready?' I shout back to him.

'Yes. Ages ago!'

'Five minutes,' I assure him and add the finishing touches to my make-up. Mum's lent me the diamanté earrings that she wore on her wedding day and they set off my outfit perfectly. I turn to Ella. 'Are we good to go?'

'I'm cool,' she says. 'You look great.'

'Thanks.' Then my phone rings. Robyn. 'Hi, lovely.'

'I can't believe I'm going to do this to you,' Robyn says, 'but I can't make tonight.'

'You're kidding me.'

'Sorry, hun,' she snuffles. 'Full of a cold.' A few coughs.

She sounds, at the very least, as if she has

419

double pneumonia.

'Oh, no,' I wail. 'What timing.'

'I'm sorry.' Cough, cough, cough. 'I hate to miss your big moment. I'll make it up to you. I don't want to come along and sneeze all over everyone.'

'It's fine,' I say, heart sinking. 'You get better soon.'

'Speak in a few days,' she mumbles and hangs up.

'Everything OK?' Ella looks concerned.

'My date just dumped me.'

'Never mind,' she says. 'You've got us.'

I smile bravely. 'Of course I have. It'll be fine.'

'Taxi's here!' Finn shouts.

'Is it?' I didn't hear it pull up. Yet, when I glance out of the window, I see an enormous, black stretch limo parking outside my parents' house.

'Oh, my.' I tug Ella's arm, pulling her towards me. 'Look at this!' She grins at me. 'You knew?'

'Finn booked it as a surprise.'

'It's that all right.' I bet the bill still comes across my desk. 'Come on, we'd better hurry up.' I don't want the clock running on that thing. Mind you, it does look fab. Much grander than arriving by some beaten up old minicab. Nice work, Finn.

We go out into the hall. Finn, Mum and Dad are standing waiting. I don't know who looks the most shocked out of them.

'We've scrubbed well?' I ask.

'You both look beautiful,' Finn breathes, but I note that he can't tear his eyes away from his lovely Ella.

'And you look very handsome,' I tell my son.

And he does. I don't think I've ever seen him looking so debonair or so grown up. Where did the boy with the untidy hair and the beanie hat go? I'm sure that I'll never stop worrying about his well-being, but it's so good to see that Finn's looking stronger and healthier with every passing day. It was only a short while ago that I thought I might lose him for ever. If I had, I've no idea how I would have carried on. I hug him tightly.

'Get off, Mum,' he says, squirming from my embrace. 'Don't mess with the suit.' He brushes down his lapels as I release him which makes me smile. How times change.

Then it's my turn to get the full force of parental caring.

'Oh, love,' Mum says, a bit teary. Now she squashes me and I resist reacting the same way that Finn did. I let her clasp me to her bosom and squeeze the life out of me. 'You look stunning.'

'Thanks.' When she lets go, I give my skirt a little swish to show it off. 'However, my date just dumped me,' I tell them.

'That's a shame.' Mum looks as if she's not that bothered at all.

'Yeah, well. These things happen. Who knows, I might get lucky tonight and bag me a C-list actor from *Holby City*.' The doorbell rings.

Finn grins at me. 'I think we might be able to do better than that.' He opens the door and says, 'Good timing.'

I hear myself gasp and, I swear to you, my heart actually stops beating for a minute. I couldn't be more knocked for six if I tried.

When I regain the power of speech, I stammer, 'What ... what ... what on earth are you doing here?'

Chapter Ninety-Three

The very last person on earth that I expected to see standing at my parents' front door is Max Alexander. Yet here he very much is. He's booted and suited, looking very dashing in his tuxedo.

'Oh, my.' Tears spring to my eyes.

'You look beautiful, Christie.' He steps inside and proffers the bouquet of red roses that he's holding. 'They match your dress perfectly.'

'Am I imagining you?' I ask, as I take the roses. I'm as breathless as if I'd run up and down the road for ten minutes. And I know all about that, these days.

'I had a call from Finn, asking me to be here.' He grins, obviously delighted with their subter-fuge. 'How could I refuse?'

'You flew in all the way from America, just to be here?'

'Yes.'

I look at my boy. 'So the whole thing with Robyn was a set-up and she hasn't got a cold at all?'

'Right,' Finn says.

'And Sheridan knows you're here?'

'She does. She's looking forward to seeing us both.'

I turn to my parents. 'And you two knew as well?'

Mum and Dad nod enthusiastically. No wonder Mum wasn't bothered when I told her I'd been dumped.

'I'm surrounded by schemers,' I say. 'And I'm so glad of it.'

Like the gentleman he is, Max takes Mum's hand and kisses it. 'Lovely to meet you.' Now she's pink-faced and grinning, clearly under Max's spell as much as I am.

Dad claps him on the back. 'Nice to meet you, Max. Christie's told us a lot about you.'

'All good, I hope.'

In truth, I've said very little about Max, but my parents aren't stupid, they can probably tell by the way I've turned to jelly that I'm carrying a torch for this man.

'We should go,' Finn says. 'We don't want to get caught up in traffic.'

'I hope to see you again soon,' Max says to my mum and dad. Mum goes all silly and flustered.

He holds out a hand for me and I take it. Then he leads me to the limo and I feel like a Disney princess. Finn and Ella follow us. In the car, I settle down next to Max, unable to tear my eyes away from him.

'You're here,' I say again. I want to touch his face to make sure that he's real and I'm not dreaming all this.

'I wouldn't have missed it for the world.'

Then I throw caution to the wind and rest my hand tenderly on his cheek. 'Thank you.'

He turns and gently kisses my palm. 'The

pleasure's all mine.'

We wave as the limo pulls away from the kerb and I smile at Mum who's frantically dabbing at her eyes with a tissue. I swear to you, she'll be on wedding websites before we've turned the corner.

Chapter Ninety-Four

Max pours us champagne as we're whisked in true celebrity style towards London and we all raise our glasses. 'What shall we toast?' I ask.

'To new beginnings,' Finn says.

'To health and happiness,' I add.

'To Christie Chapman, superwoman,' Max chips in.

Then we chink our glasses together. Max's eyes catch mine. 'To us.'

'To us,' I echo, my heart picking up a beat.

While Finn and Ella cuddle up, giggling with excitement, I turn to Max. 'I still can't believe that you're actually here.'

'Me neither,' he admits. 'It was all a bit last minute.'

'I'm so glad that you are.' Then, with all this new-found confidence brimming inside me, I say, 'So what does this mean for us?'

'I don't know,' he admits. 'I just knew that I couldn't stay away. I had to be here.' He toys with my fingers in his palm. 'We've a lot to talk about, Christie. But not tonight. Tonight's all about you. We're going to celebrate your new career.'

'Now that Finn's working with me and we have the online business, I'm hoping that I'll have more free time.' I smile towards my son and his girlfriend. 'Plus Finn has other things on his mind now; I'm going to have to learn to let go.'

'They make a lovely couple,' Max agrees. 'It nice for me to be able to meet him.'

Then I tell him what's on my mind. Shit or bust. 'I still can't be a passing fancy, Max. I've too much to lose.'

'I know,' he says. 'I'm glad you were honest with me. It gave me a lot to think about. I've spent a lot of time wondering what I want from the future.'

'And?' My heart flutters uncontrollably. What if, after all this, Max still doesn't want any kind of commitment? Where does that leave me?

He gazes at me for a long time before he answers, 'I want you.'

You have no idea how happy and relieved I am to hear that. My heart's still all of a flutter, but with a different kind of emotion. This time it's joy, untrammelled joy. 'I'm glad that you came to that conclusion,' I tease.

'Me too.' Max's face lights up and we grin at each other in a ridiculously dreamy manner. 'I've talked at some length to Dean,' he tells me. 'I'm looking at him taking over the CEO role in the States with a view to me opening up our European operation here.'

'In the UK?'

'Yes,' he says. 'It would mean I'd be around a lot more. Permanently. If you'd like that.'

'Really?'

He laughs.

This day simply can't get any better. 'I'd absolutely love it. Of course, I would.'

'I'm staying for a few days,' Max says. 'A well-deserved vacation.'

'In London?'

'No. I have a hotel booked locally. At a place called … Milton Keynes.'

I laugh. 'I'll be happy to be your tour guide.'

'I'd kind of counted on that. I hoped that we could spend some time together seeing the sights and discussing our future.'

Our future. 'I like the sound of that.'

'I know that you're going to be busy with Creative World, but I wondered whether you'd take on a role with us too. If I set up here, I'm going to need someone to demonstrate the products, not simply around the UK, but in Europe too. Does that sound like something you'd be prepared to take on?'

I think of how Finn is now and that I would be happy to leave him to travel. Mum and Dad wouldn't mind looking after him for a few days and it's less of a problem now that we're living there. 'Yes,' I say. 'In principle.'

'Great.' Max takes my hand and tucks it into the crook of his arm. 'We'll work something out so that we can be together. If that's what you'd like.'

I smile at him, love in my heart. 'I'd like that very much.'

'It looks as if we have a lot to talk about in the next few days, Ms Chapman.'

'It certainly does, Mr Alexander.' Then I settle

back, sip my champagne. All of my wildest dreams are coming true and wonder how I could be any happier than I am right now.

Chapter Ninety-Five

We join the waiting queue of limousines and, a few minutes later, pull up outside the O2 Arena amid a flurry of flashing press cameras. Even though I'm here very much in the capacity of newbie, I feel like a star for the night.

'Ready?' Max says and helps me out of the limo.

We step onto the red carpet, Finn and Ella hand in hand, close behind. The buzz is incredible, the excitement infectious. Spotlights sweep the crowd who are pressed up against the barriers, pointing iPads and phones, snapping photos, cheering anyone and everyone. The noise is deafening. I marvel, again, at how I came to be on this side of the ropes.

Ahead of us I can see Mary Berry and Paul Hollywood. David Tennant's here too and some of the stars of daytime television – Phil and Holly, Lorraine. I recognise Michael McIntyre, Piers Morgan, Dermot O'Leary and Peter Andre. The cameras flash again, in case we're anyone important. There are pop stars galore: One Direction, Pixie Lott, Little Mix. The cast of *Downton Abbey* are here and I think my mum would faint at that alone. But then Aidan Turner from *Poldark* rocks up and I know that would have her out cold. Ant and Dec are here too – I think they've won the award for the Best Entertainment Presenters or something for the last umpteen years or so and probably will do again. What a star-studded night.

'Do you know who any of these people are?' I ask Max.

'No,' he admits, looking blank.

That makes me giggle. No one has a clue who I am either, but I don't care. This does, indeed, feel like a new beginning for us all and the future is looking very bright and starry.

'Wow, Mum,' Finn whispers, 'this is amazing.'

And it is. I pause on the red carpet and look around me. This is so overwhelming that it's making my head spin.

'OK?' Max asks, concerned.

'Yes,' I say. 'I'm trying to drink it all in. This might never happen again.'

He smiles at me. 'I'm absolutely sure that it will. I'd like to bet that one day you'll be here picking up an award.'

'I think I'd like that,' I say. 'It will give me something to aim for.'

The crowd cheer and wave. We all wave back. I feel like a film star. This is the most fun I've had in years. It's going to be a great night and I'm going to enjoy every minute.

At the entrance there's an area set up for photographs, backed with billboards for the National Television Awards.

'This way,' the photographers shout to us, even though they have no idea who we are. We might be important one day, so they snap away just in

428

case. 'Look this way!'

Obligingly, we all stand together and pose. Ella and Finn work the cameras like pros. I hope Mum and Dad, at home in their armchairs, are seeing this. I cuddle up to my darling son and give him a surreptitious squeeze. I've never felt more proud of him. My heart could burst. Max slips his arm round my shoulders and pulls me close. I'd be happy to stay right here for ever. I feel as sparkling as the champagne we've been drinking.

When the photographers shout out again, asking me to smile, I beam broadly and it really isn't any effort at all. In a moment of giddy madness, I throw caution to the wind and wrap my arms around Max's neck and kiss him deeply. I'm in love and I'm loved. And I feel as if I'm floating on clouds as the crowd roar their approval and the cameras capture every moment.

The publishers hope that this book has given you enjoyable reading. Large Print Books are especially designed to be as easy to see and hold as possible. If you wish a complete list of our books please ask at your local library or write directly to:

Magna Large Print Books
Magna House, Long Preston,
Skipton, North Yorkshire.
BD23 4ND